LONG
WAY
DOWN

ALSO BY MICHAEL SEARS

Mortal Bonds

Black Fridays

MICHAEL SEARS

LONG WAY DOWN

G. P. PUTNAM'S SONS | NEW YORK

PUTNAM

G. P. PUTNAM'S SONS
Publishers Since 1838
Published by the Penguin Group
Penguin Group (USA) LLC
375 Hudson Street
New York, New York 10014

USA · Canada · UK · Ireland · Australia
New Zealand · India · South Africa · China

penguin.com
A Penguin Random House Company

Library of Congress Cataloging-in-Publication Data

Sears, Michael, date.
Long way down / Michael Sears.
p. cm.—(A Jason Stafford novel ; 3)
ISBN 978-0-399-16671-6
1. Finance—Corrupt practices—Fiction. 2. Wall Street (New York, N.Y.)—Fiction. I. Title.
PS3619.E2565L66 2014 2014008970
813'.6—dc23

Printed in the United States of America
10 9 8 7 6 5 4 3 2 1

Book design by Meighan Cavanaugh

For MLW

LONG
WAY
DOWN

1

The banker was not so much a traditionalist as he was simply a man who, somewhat lacking in creativity or imagination, greatly enjoyed the comforts of consistency in his habits. When he drank scotch, he took no water, soda, or ice, never pouring more than two fingers into a wide-mouthed, heavy-bottomed glass tumbler. When he snorted cocaine, he always rolled a crisp one-hundred-dollar bill into a tube and used the same pearl-handled miniature pocketknife to form the unvarying inch-long lines of the drug.

That night he had many crisp one-hundred-dollar bills to choose from. Five hundred of them. Five packets of a hundred each. Though they would easily have fit in a large envelope, or even the pockets of his suit jacket, they had been delivered in a small plastic attaché case. He removed them and stacked them on the glass coffee table. The briefcase went by the door so that he would remember to put it out with the garbage when he left for the office in the morning.

The Glenlivet 18 was running low. He thought he would finish the bottle that night. He wrote a note to remind himself to have a case delivered the next day. He was not an alcoholic—he rarely had more than two or three drinks in an evening—but he had a dread of running out and not being able to sleep. It was difficult to fall asleep alone. Ever since Agathe had taken the children and escaped back to his mother's house in Cornwall, he had begun to have problems sleeping. The big apartment, taking up the top two floors of the building, with views of Hamilton Harbour, the islands, and Great Sound beyond, felt both much too large and uncomfortably small. The humming of the electric clock in the kitchen could be heard in every room on the first floor. The electronic click of the American refrigerator—the one thing that Agathe probably regretted leaving behind—when the circulating motor turned on, could be deafening in the vast lonely emptiness of three a.m.

The suspicion that fifty thousand dollars was too much—too big a bribe for the favor he had performed—nagged at him again. He sipped the whiskey, surprised as he always was by the strength of the peat in the long finish. There was so little in the nose, on the lip, but so much remained long after the swallow.

He had facilitated opening an account without checking the man's identification. The man's name was unknown to him, though the name on the account was not. He had seen that name on the pages of the *Financial Times* often enough. Questions as to why such a man would want to open an account at such a small private bank had been quashed by the first utterance of the man with the cold gray eyes across the desk. He was being paid not to ask.

Tomorrow he would write down all of the particulars—everything he remembered about the man, the words he spoke, the details of the transaction—and send the document to his uncle, a London barrister, to hold "in the event of my early demise." Then he would forget about it all and enjoy the thought of fifty thousand dollars—invisible to the tax authority, to Agathe and her solicitor, and even to his grabbing bitch of a mother, whom he had been supporting ever since his father's death a decade ago and who repaid his kindness, generosity, and filial duty by siding with Agathe in this latest episode of the guerrilla warfare that passed for their marriage, now halfway through its second decade of insult, degradation, and remorse.

He took the little polythene baggie from his pocket and shook it, admiring the mound of white powder. The American had offered a gram or two along with the cash, but the banker had insisted upon a full ounce. His business was negotiation; he never took the first offer. An almost iridescent light reflected off the rocks and shards of the coke. It appeared to be quite pure. Even at his current rate of consumption, an ounce of uncut cocaine would last him a month or more. Weeks of not having to speak to the acned social misfit in client accounting, who regularly supplied the banker and his colleagues with the crystalline spice that made life in the stultifying environment of Bermuda banking bearable.

The little knife made a grating sound as he chopped the larger crystals into a fine powder. The consistency of the cocaine was slightly different than he was used to—flakier, he thought—a factor that he attributed to the described purity of the drug.

The banker broke the wrapper on a packet of hundreds, removed the top bill, and rolled it into a short tube. He preferred using American currency; it seemed appropriate, as the price of cocaine was, like petroleum or gold, universally quoted in U.S. dollars. The conversion factor for British pounds was something he knew much about, as the most updated number flashed on his Bloomberg Terminal all day long. Every transaction he engaged in for his clients—from purchasing German stocks priced in euros to South African real estate trusts offered in rands—he thought of in terms of pounds, making the conversion automatically and effortlessly. It was what his clients wanted. But whenever he thought of cocaine, and he thought of it often, he thought in terms of dollars. And with only a modest bit of self-discipline, he now had enough dollars to keep himself supplied for years.

He snorted the first line. The freeze hit immediately and he felt the left side of his face begin to numb. The cocaine was very good, possibly the best he had ever had. The big American with the odd request had outdone himself. The second line went up his right nostril, producing a similar glow and restoring his symmetry. He moistened the tip of his index finger and wiped up the remaining dust where the two lines had lain. He gently rubbed it across his gums and felt the cold numbness penetrate. Very good cocaine.

He put his head back and waited for the rush. A moment later, his eyes closed. He sat up abruptly. That was the strangest reaction he had ever had to the drug. He felt good, warm and safe, languid, and at the same time sexually aroused. His whole body had become a single erogenous zone. A momentary flash of paranoia tripped through his numbed consciousness. This was very unusual. But the thought was gone before it had fully taken shape. The soaring euphoria erased all fears. He may have been a very small god, even a lonely one, the ruler of a small bit of couch in an empty apartment, but he was still a god. He took a breath. He was suddenly very aware of his breathing, not that it took effort exactly, because he was all-powerful on this couch and effort had become a meaningless concept, as though the very air had become irrelevant.

The cocaine dripped from his sinuses down to the back of his throat, coating, soothing, numbing. He lost all sense of taste; his sense of smell was already gone. His fingers seemed to be a long distance away. They were clumsy and thick and wooden. He forced them to pick up the paper tube and they answered slowly and reluctantly. He leaned over and snorted up the two remaining lines and felt the top of his head lift off. His eyes bulged, and he exhaled in a hoarse rasp, unable anymore to control even his vocal cords.

The hundred-dollar bill dropped from his fingers and slowly

unraveled on the glass table. He stared at it, trying to think of why such a small piece of paper had any importance in his life, but his eyes closed and he forgot about it. He kept sinking. It was a long way down. Already half-dreaming, he took one last gasping breath. His heart continued to beat for a short while before it too gave up and surrendered.

2

We hadn't walked to school since Angie, my ex-wife and the mother of my unusual child, had been murdered on Amsterdam Avenue, shot by members of a Central American drug cartel. She had been protecting the boy, throwing her own body between a hail of bullets and her son. I should have been the target, not the Kid, not my ex-wife. Angie and I had our history and our baggage, and her death had not released me from all the anger, resentment, hurt, and betrayal. I carried all of those, plus the guilt that if I had done things differently, or been a different man, she would still be alive.

My second career—the first as a Wall Street trader and manager having ended with a two-year stint in a federal prison—often put me in dangerous spots. I investigated fraud, sometimes acting as a fixer or a finder in situations where street smarts met up with prison yard ethics. I straddled both worlds, in ways that often surprised me. The work had changed me—was still changing me. I had become both more tolerant and more skeptical, stronger and less fearful, yet more thoughtful and forgiving. What was legal was sometimes just not right, and those who broke the law were more often merely weak rather than evil.

The Kid had changed me, too. My son. Now six years and eight months. I had barely known him when I was sent away. I certainly had not known of his autism. Seeing life through his eyes had opened mine. If you graphed the spectrum with Asperger's on the far left, the Kid was definitely right of center, but he was verbal and a bright and curious learner. He was also a handful. And though I would not have wanted my ex back in my life in any capacity, my son deserved a mother.

The school was just a mile up Amsterdam and a half block over. The Kid used to run ahead each block, dancing impatiently at the cross streets, waiting for me to catch up and burning off a small percentage of his post-breakfast energy spurt. Not *spurt*. Explosion.

I had changed our route these past six months.

When we left early enough, we would take the bus, the M104, up Broadway and get off at Ninety-sixth Street. The Kid liked the bus. It was rarely crowded at that hour, as we were heading in the opposite direction of the morning commute. The Kid would take one of the handicapped seats up front—though he was not physically challenged, his autism gave him squatter's rights to those seats—and I would stand over him. The Kid watched the driver, and I watched him.

Most mornings, though, we were in a hurry and took the subway. The Kid was not an easy, nor an early, riser, but there were other issues that slowed us down. Getting his shoes on was near the top of the list. I had bought him more shoes than worn by the whole cast of *Sex and the City*, in a futile attempt to find ones that did not "hurt." It took the two of us a year to accept the fact that, though shoes are generally less comfortable than going barefoot, you can't go barefoot in New York City—especially in December. That morning we took the subway.

We were a few minutes behind schedule as we came out of the subway at Ninety-sixth Street and quick-walked toward Amsterdam. The Kid ran. I watched him as he bobbed, weaved, ducked, and sprinted, avoiding the many obstructions in his path—some of which were imaginary. I loved watching him run. When he walked, he tended to lock up his knees and hips, as though in constant fear of falling, so that he looked like a mechanical man, made up of nonmatching spare parts. But when he ran, he looked like a child. If not happy, at least untroubled. Free.

A blast of chill wind blew dust in my eye and I put my head down, taking the irritating assault on my nascent bald spot. For that one moment I was not watching my son.

The sidewalk was narrow just there, and broken, a nondescript and barren tree having driven its roots laterally in an attempt to seek nutriments in a concrete wasteland. On the other side was a short, spiked, black iron fence guarding the basement entrance, and empty garbage cans, of a six-story apartment building.

I looked up and my eyes watered and blurred in the wind, but I could tell that the Kid was not ahead, waiting at the corner. A momentary flare of anxiety caught in my chest and I whirled around in a panic. The Kid was a half block behind me, squatting at the curb and trying to engage the attention of a piebald pigeon.

Almost shaking with relief, I walked back to him, not trusting my voice to call, nor trusting him to come without an argument—and cursing myself for my inattention. I squatted down next to him. The pigeon ignored both of us.

"Come on, Kid. Time for school. Ms. Wegant will be worried about us if we're late." I had never seen his teacher worried, nor flustered, nor impatient, nor happy, for that matter. Mr. Spock had a wider range of emotion. "Come on," I tried again. "Mrs. Carter will be mad at me." This was much closer to the truth. Mrs. Carter held the desk in the entryway at the school, checking in all students and keeping out anyone who did not have a well-documented reason for being on school grounds. She was a large woman, but with both the strength and agility to carry it off. I was sure that I could take her in a fair fight, and I was just as sure that she wouldn't fight fair.

I took his hand. I was impatient. I knew better. He screamed.

I let go and stood up. The screaming stopped. A childish and unworthy thought of just walking away flashed through my head. I forgave myself. If I beat myself up every time I succumbed to despair, I would have been permanently covered with black-and-blue marks. I thought about just kicking the pigeon, but held back. I would wait. Patience was the best medicine I could offer my son. It also did wonders for me.

A sudden flash of déjà vu hit me. Not really déjà vu, more a distorted memory. When my ex-wife was killed, one of the assassins had escaped by running down a side street. Could it have been that block? Or was it a few blocks farther uptown? The Kid and I would have had to move out of Manhattan altogether to avoid any reminders of his mother, or her death. I had a touch of dizziness. Possibly, I had stood up too quickly. I was disoriented, the wind blew and my eyes blurred again.

Two men turned the corner, coming down from Amsterdam. They were short, squat, and brown-skinned. Latinos. One had a black brush of a mustache; the other, slightly taller, had a badly broken nose. Despite the cold, they both wore nothing warmer than dark hooded sweatshirts, their hands tucked into the pouches in front. They looked just like the men who had killed my ex-wife—who had attempted to kill my son, and who had threatened to kill me. And I had wondered ever since if they were going to come back and finish the job. Or when. And here they were. Moving quickly.

Stone-faced. Not angry, but determined. I imagined their hands coming out, holding small guns that grew in size every time I blinked.

The white van jumped the red light, accelerated across three lanes, and suddenly slowed. The sliding panel door opened and a long-barreled weapon emerged and began spitting red flashes. Phwat. Phwat. Phwat. *Like the sound of slapping a rolled-up newspaper against your thigh. Only, it wasn't a rolled-up newspaper, and people were falling.*

"Kid, get up. We go. Now." I took his hand and walked back toward Broadway. The Kid must have heard the fear in my voice because for once he did not scream or fight. He stumbled along with me, his feet barely touching the ground.

Just as we approached the entrance to the next building, a woman emerged with a small dog on a leash. I rushed forward and grabbed the door before it closed, pushed the Kid inside and followed him. The lock clicked as the door shut. We were inside and the two Latinos were outside. For the moment, we were safe. But only for the moment.

The Kid stood behind me, whimpering. He had caught my fear and absorbed it. His teeth were chattering and he was shaking. There was a mail alcove to our right. I pushed him toward it and backed him against the wall. I could see the street, but it would be very difficult for anyone to see in at that angle.

"It's all right, Kid. We're safe. Those men won't find us here." I didn't believe it and neither did he. He was crying and beginning to gasp. The gasping sometimes prefaced one of his seizures.

"I pick you up," he whispered. He never wanted to be held or picked up. Never except for the few times when that was all he wanted. I took him in my arms and held him tight. Squeezing helped. It helped both of us.

The two men stopped at the front door and stared in the window. The window was plastic—Lexan probably—with a wire mesh running through it. An older building, a holdover from a less safe era. The one with the mustache pressed a button on the intercom and spoke briefly. He looked familiar. Had I seen him before or did he look like a thousand other Latino men I had passed on the streets of New York City?

No one buzzed them in.

We were trapped. We couldn't move without them seeing us, but they knew we had entered the building and it would not take much heavy-duty guesswork for them to realize we must still be hiding in the lobby. They would figure out a way to get in soon.

The mustache put his face up against the window and yelled. The blood was pounding in my ears and the Kid was crying—I couldn't hear a thing. The man grabbed the door handle and shook it. The door suddenly looked a lot less formidable a barrier than it had a moment earlier.

I pulled out my cell phone. Who could I call? How fast could a squad car get there? Five minutes? It seemed much too long. There was no one else. I punched in the numbers.

"911. State the nature of your emergency."

"I'm being followed. By two men."

"Are you in immediate danger?"

Define the word *immediate*. "I think so."

"Name and location."

"Jason Stafford. I'm in the lobby of a building just east of Broadway."

A short, thin Latino man in overalls and a red plaid shirt walked through the lobby toward the door.

"What's the address, sir?" the voice on the phone asked.

"Please hurry." I stopped and called to the man. "Hey. Hey. Don't open that door!"

If he heard me, he gave no sign.

"Can you give me the address, sir?"

"I don't know. We just ducked in here." We were on the north side of the street, so it was an odd-numbered building. Broadway divided the block in two. "It's 249 West Ninety-fifth," I yelled into the phone. I thought it was Ninety-fifth. Could it be Ninety-fourth?

The man in the lobby stopped and looked at us suspiciously. "Can I help you?" he said, sounding like he had meant to say, "Who the 'f' are you and what the 'f' are you doing here?"

"Don't let those men in here. They followed us."

"Those men? I don't think so," he said with a sarcastic cough that could have been a laugh.

"No, really. I've got police on the way. Please wait."

"Hey! No cops. Shit! Look, I'm the super here. These guys work for me. They're my painters." He opened the door and spoke to the two men in rapid Spanish. The man with the mustache laughed. The other guy looked worried. Below their sweatshirts, both men wore paint-spattered baggy blue jeans and canvas sneakers. They no longer looked like hit men, they looked like painters. Mustache didn't even look familiar.

"Sir? Are you there? Can I use this number as a callback in case we're disconnected?"

"What? No. Sorry. Please cancel the call. I'm fine. It was a mistake." The three men walked past. The one with the mustache was grinning. The other painter didn't think it was quite so funny.

"Are you all right, sir? Are you under duress?"

"No, really. I'm very embarrassed. Everything is okay here." I wanted to melt into a pool of slime and seep out under the door and into the gutter. "Thanks anyway." I hung up.

The super was leading the other two through a door down to the basement. I called after them. "Sorry about that. Really." The mustached man turned and gave a wave and a last grin.

The Kid began hitting me in the chest with the heel of his fist. "Down. Down. Down."

I put him down. He shook like a wet dog and gave me a look of deep distrust. His beautiful strawberry-blond hair shimmered.

Angie lay on the pavement, partially hidden from view by two parked cars. I stepped up and saw the blood. She looked so small. The breeze from a passing car blew her hair off her face. She looked surprised. Death was something for which she should have planned ahead.

Nice work, I thought. I had panicked, managing to racially profile two innocent men, possibly causing them a hurricane of troubles if the police had arrived. And I had terrified my son. I was supposed to be his anchor, helping and supporting him against all of his usual terrors; instead I had created a new one. His father was nuts.

"Sorry, bud. I don't know what happened." Yes I did. I didn't like it but I knew what had happened. "Are you all right? Shall we get you to school now?"

He walked to the door and waited for me to open it. I followed, feeling stupid and useless—and drained. My hand shook as I pushed the door open. It wasn't the first time something similar had happened to me. I'd experienced those flashes of paranoia before. I needed to shake it off, get the Kid to school, do my morning run, and go to work. I didn't need to spend a lot of time thinking about it, analyzing it, or explaining it to a child who would not understand anyway. Hell, I wasn't sure that I understood it.

3

Roger, the Kid, and I went out to my father's bar that night for the closing party. The new owners, two retired New York City firemen, sat with us in a back booth, while Pop served free booze to all of his old regulars. He said it would make the inventory process go faster the next morning. At the rate the crowd was downing shots, there wouldn't be anything left to inventory.

"You gonna keep the name?" Roger asked. Roger was a semi-retired clown, and a full-time kibitzer. He was also my friend. We had met at our neighborhood bar when I was still single, and despite our differences in age, background, careers, education, and almost every other aspect of life, something had clicked and we had become friends. When I got out of prison, I discovered that I had far fewer friends than before. Roger was one of the ones who had stayed by me.

"For now," the older of the two said. "It doesn't matter what the sign says out front, everybody calls it Sweeney's, anyhow."

My father had bought the bar, and the building, from Mrs. Sweeney after her husband drank himself under the table one last time. Sweeney had tried a couple of different names in the early years, finally sticking with Broadway Bistro, though it wasn't on Broadway and served nothing that could be remotely called French, except the fries. But the fireman was right, everyone in College Point, Queens, called it Sweeney's.

The Kid dipped one of those French fries in a lake of ketchup, placed it in his mouth, and sucked off all the ketchup. I let him. It was a gross habit, but just one of the many compromises I made for him. With autism, you learn quickly to pick your fights or you lose.

"You two going to take turns working the stick?" I asked the firemen.

They gave each other a quick look. "Nah. Tim here is a good cook, but he's not the most entertaining guy you'd ever want to meet. He'll cover the kitchen, I handle up front."

"Where'd you learn to cook, Tim?"

"On-the-job training. When you go into a burning building, you know that your team is watching out for you. You make a mistake, one of those guys is going to bail you out. But if you're the guy who makes dinner every night, you've got the whole company making sure you get out in one piece."

I laughed. "I'd say he's pretty entertaining."

The older fireman gave a small smile. "That's his one good line. Ask him to tell a joke."

Tim shook his head. "I don't do jokes. I remember all the punch lines, but never the setup."

"Come on," Roger said, waving in the challenge. "You give me the punch line and I'll do the setup."

"I don't know . . ."

"Yeah, yeah. We can do this. Come on, give me one."

Tim thought for a minute. "Okay. How about, 'Don't sell that cow'?"

Roger laughed. "That's a good one. The dying what . . . ? Somebody's mother? The priest? Which version?"

Tim was laughing with him. "The priest."

"Ready? Here wc go. The old priest, Father McCluskey—the leader of his flock, the head of the parish—is dying, ya see. And the whole village is lined up outside the rectory, waiting to get in to pay last respects. And Mrs. Donahue comes in with a glass of milk—fresh, still warm from the cow. 'Oh, here ya are, Father, this'll set ya right up.' Well, the old guy takes one sip and starts coughing. Just about croaks right there. Everybody in the room freezes. Except for Mr. Donahue, who don't like to see his wife disappointed, ya know. He takes the cup, and while everybody is staring at the old guy still rasping and spitting, Donahue pours two fingers' worth of Irish whiskey out of his flask into the cup. He pushes forward and holds up the priest and gets him to take another sip. 'Come on, Father, this'll do ya good,' he says. Well, Father McCluskey swallows that first sip, sits right up in bed, grabs the cup and downs it in one go. Then he lies back down on the pillow, smiling like he already sees the gates of Heaven opening and the angels singing him in. He whispers something. 'What'd he say?' all the people yell out. Well, Donahue leans over and puts his ear by the old man's lips and listens for a minute. The old one whispers again and Donahue bursts out laughing. 'He said . . .'" Roger gestured to Tim.

"Don't sell that cow!" Tim yelled out.

Roger and I laughed. Even the other fireman laughed. The Kid held his ears and scowled. Abrupt loud noises were painful for him, but he was coping. Just one of the many ugly tricks that autism played on him every day.

"See?" Roger said. "You can tell a joke. Don't let 'em tell ya any different."

My father, looking rushed, harried, and happy, stopped by our booth. "Liam, you want to join me behind the bar? Lend a hand? Meet the regulars?"

Liam, the older fireman, stood up. "I've known half of them since grade school, but yeah, I'm with you."

"How's my boys?" Pop asked, looking at me but asking about the Kid.

"About the same," I said.

The Kid had a line of five toy cars in front of him. Occasionally he would reach over and move one a fraction of a millimeter. Mostly he just stared at them.

A momentary flash of pain dulled my father's eyes and he blinked, returning his concern for his grandson to its proper nook. He would keep it hidden there until, later that night, it could be unwrapped and shared with his sole confidant, Estrella Ramirez, a widow he had been dating for the past nine months. Estrella, in turn, would eventually pass on his troubling thoughts to me, in what served as deep communication between father and son.

"Come, Liam. Let's see if you're up to this crowd."

Tim slid out of the booth and joined them. "I think I'll see how he holds up."

Roger and I were left surrounding the Kid's long silence.

Roger sipped his cognac. I swallowed another long pull of Ketel One. I didn't think I liked drinking vodka, but it was an efficient drink. The second one always took the edge off, rounded the corners, softened the focus. For the next hour or so, I could put aside my frustrations and disappointments and smile at my life in liquid contentment.

"We should get the Kid home to bed," Roger said.

Roger's sense of self-discipline involved the better part of a fifth of cognac a day, but he still managed to keep a watchful eye on the comfort and well-being of my son. And me.

I nodded. "Yup." Never a third drink until the Kid was fast asleep, and then only when I really couldn't sleep. A nightcap. My sleeping draught. Harmless.

"You want to take another walk around upstairs?" Roger asked.

The apartment over the bar had been my home when growing up. Now it was a bare space waiting for a tenant. I had helped my father empty the rooms, quietly amazed at how few keepsakes there were from our lives there together. He had given me the framed photos of my mother, enshrined forever in the bloom of her twenties, dead before she turned thirty. Pop and Estrella had bought a nice two-bedroom condo on Bay Park Drive, with a view of the park, the river, the airport, and the jail on Rikers Island. Pictures of my mother weren't going to fit with the décor.

"Nope. There's nothing there, Roger. Pop and I watched Goodwill haul the last of it out on Tuesday. Time to turn the page."

Roger knocked back the dregs in his glass, I did the same.

"So, we're outta here," he said. "You riding with us, Kid? Grab your cars and come say good-bye to your Pop."

The Kid swept up the cars and stuffed them in the pocket of his hoodie. I reflected, with no jealousy or animosity, that what Roger had accomplished with a brief, almost brusque, command would have taken me ten minutes of one-sided negotiation, wheedling, empty threats, and pitiful begging.

I went first, pushing gently through the crowd of half-drunken well-wishers. There was a boisterous, yet gentle, preholiday air. I murmured hellos to those whose faces I recognized, some of whom I had not seen in twenty years or more. There was Jimmy "Ferrari" Ferrante, two years ahead of me in school, and still two inches shorter, though that had never stopped him from beating me up once or twice a year from about the fourth grade through middle school. He was sharing a bottle of Malbec with his mother and polishing off a double order of fried mozzarella sticks. Danny Griffin—"Griff"—whom I'd heard lost a string of oceanfront rental properties to Hurricane Sandy down in the Rockaways and Long Beach. He was still trying to collect from the insurance companies, and was now back living with his folks on 118th Street and working at Staples. Betty Polanski, from high school, now many dress sizes wider, who had informed me at our ten-year class reunion—the first and last one I attended—that she had always thought I was gay.

We tried pushing up to the bar, but it was packed three deep. Pop and Liam were swamped, but laughing together and loving it. I waited until I caught Pop's eye, gave him a wave and a smile. He blew big exaggerated kisses at me and the Kid and we headed out.

The Kid shuffled along next to me, with Roger close behind. Just as we reached the door, it swung open and Estrella entered. She was younger than my father, but by less than a decade. They both looked ten years younger than their ages. She wore her salt-and-pepper hair proudly, in an elegant sweep. My father had referred to her as a "class act," and he was right.

"Jason, you're not *leaving*? Just as I get here? You must stay for just one more." She kissed me on both cheeks and gave a quick hug.

I stepped to the side so she could say hello to the Kid. "I'd love to, but the Kid needs to get some shut-eye and I've got an early meeting."

"Hello, Jay," she trilled at the Kid. Another woman might have sounded phony speaking to the Kid in that high, musical voice. Forced. Unpleasant. Estrella sounded like she meant to entertain, and it usually worked.

The Kid did not look at her, but he raised his head and gave two short nods of recognition, then dropped his gaze back to the floor again. He didn't like to be called Jason. I was Jason. There couldn't be two. He chose his handle and insisted that everyone call him the Kid. Everyone but Estrella for some reason. She was allowed to call him Jay. I liked it and hoped it would stick, but he hadn't yet given me permission to use it.

"Well, I won't keep you," she said, throwing a brief and thoroughly insincere smile in Roger's direction. Most women had a similar reaction to my friend. He was neither lovable nor imposing. Or as Roger himself had once offered, "What I lack in charm, I make up for in ugly." She looked back to me. "I hope you are working on something interesting."

"The meeting? Not really. Kind of sad, actually. No matter how it works out, someone will be out of a job. I feel like the angel of death. I should show up in a black robe carrying a chess set."

She tipped her head in a sympathetic gesture. "You are strong. Like your father. Remember that tomorrow." Then she smiled and continued. "I want you to come to dinner just as soon as we get everything unpacked. Will you? And bring Wanda and Jay, of course."

"Wanda's a tough ticket these days. They're aiming to open the clinic the first week of the new year."

Wanda Tyler—the woman whom I called Skeli, a nickname bestowed upon her by an avuncular Greek restaurateur; the woman who made my toes curl in sheer delight; and the woman who had given me her trust at a time when I was not sure I deserved it—was currently in the frenzied rush of opening her own health clinic in SoHo, centering on non-medicinal pain management, using a combination of physical therapy, Reiki, and acupuncture. I was one of her main investors.

"Oh, no. It's the holidays. And who do any of us have but each other? I will call her." She smiled—beamed—at the Kid as we passed.

The cold air hit like a third shot of vodka. Only a week after Thanksgiving and it felt like mid-January.

"Jeeesus." Roger's teeth were already chattering. "Another month of this crap. I keep telling myself that I can do it, but it doesn't get any easier." Roger was almost due for his annual trip to Florida, where he would, for two months, sleep on his ex-wife's couch and visit with other retired circus performers. As much as he liked the sun and warm weather, two months was all he could take down there. The ex wouldn't let him drink while he stayed with her.

The Kid had no more reaction to the cold than an Eskimo sled dog. He hated bulky coats, refused to wear mittens, and screamed as though wounded if I tried to put a hat on him.

"Hold on. Let me zip you up," I said, and for a moment we wrestled in the doorway. That time I won. I got the coat zipped.

The Town Car was waiting at the corner, motor running, a wisp of exhaust in the air behind it. The Kid broke into a run like a greyhound out of the gate. I tried to keep up, but the two vodkas and too much inactivity of late slowed me down.

"Wait for Jason," I called in a forlorn hope that he might choose this erratic moment to listen to me. He didn't. He ran to the car and pounded on the rear passenger door until the driver came around and opened it. Roger and I caught up just as he wriggled inside and took the center seat. I strapped him in—feeling my usual stab of guilt at not using a car seat—and went around and got in on the far side.

While the Kid hated to be touched, hugged, or caressed, he did like to be squeezed. Roger from one side and I from the other made a Kid sandwich in the backseat. He wriggled against us, seeming to fight the feeling, but actually just trying to find his comfort zone. The moment he had it, he put his head back and passed out.

"Back to the Ansonia, Mr. Stafford?"

"Thanks, but we'll take Roger home first."

"Nah. I'll just jump out at Seventy-second Street. I'm not ready to call it a night yet."

4

Virgil Becker—he had dropped the *Von* to differentiate himself and his investment bank from his father's criminal past—was looking twenty years older than his age. It made me wonder if he was sick. Probably not, I thought, just mightily stressed.

The new offices were nothing like the old shop. The bankruptcy trustee had forced the sale of all the artwork by a range of twentieth-century American regionalists, from Benton and Wood to Wyeth and Rockwell; the collection of nineteenth-century American West memorabilia; the one-hundred-year-old Sultanabad carpets; and the flame mahogany open-horseshoe-shaped conference table with built-in videoconferencing, data support terminals, and rosewood inlay cup holders. Virgil's office, the only one at the firm with four walls, wasn't much bigger than my old prison cell up at Ray Brook. And like my cell, the walls were painted a flat gray, the only window looked out on an air shaft, and the shelving was metal with an industrial look. The sole remaining piece of Wild West flotsam was a framed hunk of fraying rope with a small brass plaque that read THE NOOSE USED TO HANG THE OUTLAW JESSE JAMES, JUNE 6, 1886.

Virgil caught me squinting at the inscription. "Notice anything odd about that? The courts let me keep it."

"I'm no expert on the Wild West, I never even watched *Deadwood*, but didn't Jesse James get killed by somebody he knew? He got shot, right?"

"Shot in the back," Virgil said. "And he was already four years in the ground when that hanging supposedly took place."

"Is this a weird joke?"

"Nope. My father paid almost twenty grand for that. Bought it from a dealer in Oklahoma. I keep it to remind myself that anyone can get conned—even my father."

Virgil's father had run a multibillion-dollar bank that was revealed, after decades of operation, to be a multibillion-dollar Ponzi scheme. Investors were still haggling over the remains, but the old man had chosen to avoid all the controversy. He had hanged himself in his cell while awaiting trial. Maybe that old noose had given him ideas.

I was there as a consultant, having been originally hired by the family to help clean up the father's mess. After tracking down some of the missing funds, and cleaning the stables, I had been rewarded with a near seven-figure job for life, helping to keep the troops honest and upstanding. I didn't answer to Compliance or Legal, I dealt directly with Virgil. I liked it that way. I had a hard time getting along with compliance officers and Wall Street lawyers. I worked when I was needed, otherwise I was free to take other consulting work, read books while in a recumbent position, or take my son to watch the dogs play in the park.

"So, what did you think? What am I supposed to do?" Virgil asked.

We had just interviewed two of Virgil's employees, a mid-level trader in the bond department and his manager, a man who had worked for Virgil and his father for almost ten years. One of them was lying.

"I know what you want to hear, Virgil. But I can't say the words. The trader came clean. He admitted he was mismarking his book. He's done it almost every year in December. I don't blame him. I'm not saying that it's right, but the deck is stacked against him."

Traders get paid based on their annual profits, but decisions about their bonuses are usually made the week after Thanksgiving. Therefore traders have zero incentive to post any excess profits in the final month of the year. But if a trader posts a big loss that month, he knows his bonus will get cut back. So traders sometimes fudge the books. Managers are supposed to know about this and keep it from getting out of hand. Zero tolerance is a nice goal, but it's not always the best option.

I knew more than a little bit about traders' tricks, having been one for years, and having managed others, until I had done some tricks of my own. The fraud that took me down was entirely of my own devising, and I had spent two years in federal prison regretting it.

Virgil got stuffy when he thought I wasn't seeing the big picture, as he called it. "I can't afford even the hint of impropriety. Half my life is dealing with regulators and auditors these days."

The trader had hidden almost a million dollars in profit by mismarking one of his more illiquid securities. I had found it fairly easily on a firm-wide scan—he hadn't made much of an effort to keep it hidden.

"So you want to fire the trader. The guy who has been making twenty mil or so for you every year for the last five years. That's a hundred million dollars, Virgil, and you're going to can him for putting one percent of that aside for a rainy day—or January, whichever comes first."

"It's not the money. He's mismarking a position. The SEC will have us restating earnings going back to the firm's inception."

I saw the big picture; I just thought there was a better way of keeping the crowd of pirates, hustlers, gunslingers, and cowboys that comprised the workforce at a Wall Street firm from degenerating into a gang of thieves.

"The SEC won't care if you don't tell them. They don't want to know about it. This is penny-ante stuff. You want to send a signal? You want to stop this kind of thing? Fire the manager. He sat here, looked you straight in the face, and lied his ass off, Virgil, and you know it. And he knew you knew it, and he didn't care."

"It's a matter of 'he said, he said.' I can't fire a senior manager over some finger-pointing mess. I'd cut the legs out from under every other manager I've got."

"You hired me to find the cheaters, Virgil, not to tell you how to run the firm. I found this guy. Give me another week and I'll find ten more. What they're doing is not that unusual. If you fire the trader, you will have a late-year boost to earnings as every other trader marks his book correctly. And next December everyone will have forgotten the lesson and it will be the same crap all over again. But if you can the manager and bring in the head guy on every other trading desk and tell them *why* you are canning him, you'll have a much better chance of never having to deal with this little problem ever again. And," I said, smiling for the first time, "you'll still get the pop in earnings, just as soon as they get back to their desks and lay down the law."

He saw the logic, but it didn't make him happy. "He stood by the firm when we were badly on the ropes."

I gave him a look of open skepticism. "He had no choice. Where was he going to go? The guy swears he had no idea his trader was mismarking the book. So he is either a liar or a total incompetent. Either way, he's a loser. Give him the boot."

"And the trader?"

"Tell him he's on probation. But pay him a bonus based on what he legitimately earned. My bet? You will never have to have another conversation with him about this. Case closed."

"I may lose some of my top managers this way."

"And you'll be left with guys who aren't afraid to tell you the truth."

He was sold, but it might take him a day or two to admit it. The manager was toast. If the guy had any brains at all, he was already sending out résumés.

"Anything else we need to discuss?" Virgil sounded more than tired.

"No," I said. "Just that if you upgrade your oversight systems, as I recommended, you won't have to bug me with this nonsense."

My whining amused him. "You are not being sufficiently entertained?"

"Challenged," I countered. My contract with Virgil was unbreakable. He owed me, and the paperwork confirmed it. This gave me a certain latitude when discussing my assignments.

"The new systems will be in place and ready for testing by mid-January."

"And by next year this time, your traders will all have figured out how to circumvent them—if their managers let them."

He shrugged, dismissing the subject. "Maybe you're right. Meanwhile, I may have something that will stretch your mental muscles a bit more. What do you know about insider trading?"

"It's illegal."

"True. But I may need you to develop a more nuanced view. Read up on the subject and watch the news over the weekend. One of the firm's clients may need us to bail him out by Monday morning."

Philip Haley, the CEO of Arinna Labs and an early wunderkind in the field of bioengineering, was being investigated, and might soon be charged with a single count of insider trading. It appeared that Haley had sold short the company stock, using an offshore bank, just before the board voted to announce the damaging news that the strain of algae the company was working on had been wiped out in a laboratory crash die-off. While this had happened before, and was a constant risk in this area of research, the board members were concerned that regulators might view silence as akin to fraud this close to a final-product rollout. Haley had repurchased the shares after the expected sell-off, and, in fact, the stock price had since recovered to its earlier level.

"Virgil, this sounds pretty open-and-shut to me. Can they tie him to the trade?"

"Mr. Haley claims that he did not do it."

ACCUSED SUSPECT CLAIMS INNOCENCE!

It was a headline ready-made for the *Onion*.

"Why does the firm care? Or is Haley a special friend of yours?"

Virgil made a steeple of his hands and tapped his index fingers together. I knew him well enough to know that was how he expressed great agitation. "The firm owns a substantial position of special nonvoting shares. A scandal could prove to be dangerously expensive for us. And, yes, Philip is a valued client. We have worked together through his first IPO, the subsequent sale of that company, and the creation of Arinna. And he has stood by me through the disaster my father brought down and the subsequent restructuring of the firm. I would like to see him cleared."

"I'll make some calls."

5

The Kid and I were finishing dinner. I had given his shadow, Heather, the evening off. Heather was a PhD candidate in psychology at Columbia, specializing in young children on the autism spectrum. The Kid and I trusted her implicitly. Someday she was going to finish her dissertation and venture out and get a more rewarding job, a thought that left me gasping in terror whenever I let myself dwell on the subject.

Skeli had a late meeting with the contractor and the designer, and I was enjoying having my son to myself for a bit. The Kid had his current favorite five cars lined up in front of him and his pencil and drawing pad near at hand. He wasn't supposed to draw until he finished eating, but I wasn't a tyrant about it. I had my laptop, which I wasn't allowed to touch until we had both finished eating. But the Kid wasn't a tyrant, either.

"How's the grilled cheese?" I said.

He looked down at his plate. Half the sandwich was gone, eaten all the way to the crusts, so that an uneven strip of toasted bread remained like a ribbon with crumbs.

He nodded once. Good.

"Eat some zucchini, too. Temple Grandin got where she is today by eating zucchini."

He squinted and wrinkled his forehead. He did not get it.

"That was a joke," I said. According to her memoir, she never ate anything but yogurt and Jell-O.

He took a tiny morsel of zucchini, chewed thoroughly, and swallowed it.

"Knock, knock," he said in his usual flat tone. His voice had lost much of the rasp it once had. He spoke more often and he no longer sounded as though it hurt when he talked.

"Who's there?"

They had been working on humor at school. They approached the subject as with most things—logic and necessity. Humans—NTs (neurotypicals)—engaged in this activity, therefore the students should learn about it. The Kid now knew three jokes. He could tell them over and over, never laughing himself. If I didn't laugh, he would become frustrated and angry. If I laughed too loud, he slapped his hands over his ears. I had negotiated a deal. No more than one joke at a time and no more than three repeats. And a chuckle counted as a laugh. So far it was working. Sort of.

"Mary."

"Mary who?" I said.

"Mary Christmas." Most budding comedians would have highlighted the punch line. Given it a little extra emphasis. Not my guy. It came out in the same monotone he almost always used.

I laughed.

"That was a joke," he said quite seriously.

I laughed again and he frowned. Could he have been mocking me? Teasing? It would have been a first. It was too much to hope for.

"Knock, knock," I said.

He ate another molecule of zucchini before answering.

"Who's there?"

"Olive."

"Olive who?"

"I love you!" I said, with a smile and a vocal flourish.

He took a large bite out of the sandwich and chewed ten times. Heather had explained to him that it was possible to choke and die on food that was not sufficiently chewed. He had decided that ten chews was the exact number required for grilled cheese and stuck to it. I thought ten chews was a tad overkill for a grilled cheese, but I kept that opinion to myself.

I had finished my grilled chicken Caesar salad with the lite dressing and no croutons. I would much rather have had the spaghetti carbonara from Piccolo, but Skeli had, rather gently, I thought, pointed out that my prison-honed physique was losing some of its edge. Curves were developing in places that had been planes. *Maybe I should join a gym,* I thought. I hated gyms.

The Kid was drawing. I checked his plate. He had eaten almost all of the zukes. A miracle. A very small miracle, but we take 'em any way they come. I stacked the dishwasher and stood for a moment, peeking over his shoulder.

It was a picture of a Camaro. No surprise. He had been drawing Camaros for two weeks. Cars were his passion. All cars, from Kias to Ferraris and everything in between. His pictures weren't great art; he was no savant. But they were recognizable, which I thought was outstanding for a six-year-old. They were better than I could have done.

"You sure you don't want to take lessons?"

He didn't look up, he just shook his head once. Negative.

"I think you've got talent."

He blew air out and covered his ears. I was distracting him. Annoying him.

"Heather says there's a great art class for kids your age at the

JCC. You guys could go there together after school. Like one day a week. Want to try it?"

My son growled at me.

I sat down and opened my laptop and began to learn about the new client. Rather than begin the search by Haley's name alone, I started with Arinna Labs. It was a mistake. I got the official biography. The sanitized version that had been told countless times in the *Wall Street Journal, Forbes, Fortune,* and dozens of other media outlets. Farther down the page there were links to articles in *People, Us Weekly, Slate,* and even the *Onion*. I ignored them and concentrated on the business magazines. It would be another week before someone directed me to the rest of the story. If I had read those stories first, the case would have taken a very different turn.

Philip Haley—born to Christina Haley, a waitress, just outside Georgetown, South Carolina, forty-six years ago. Exactly my age. Father unknown. Brown's Ferry Elementary School. J. B. Beck Middle School. Phillips Exeter Academy.

That was a jump. Exeter was among the toniest of New England boarding schools. Not many kids from that kind of background made it that far. Philip may have been unique.

I backed up and approached the issue sideways. A moment later, I found it. Football. Halfback. His middle school stressed both athletics and academics. An Exeter alumnus saw him play at state level playoffs and paid his tuition for the next four years.

Football carried him through undergrad, too. Princeton. Again a full scholarship, though he only played two years. His knee blew out during summer training before his junior year. It gave him more time for his studies. He finished a biotechnology degree—with a minor in economics—in four years.

Then there were two years at Prentiss Labs in Lincoln, Nebraska, working on various grains, where he must have saved every cent he made, because his next move was back to the East Coast and Harvard for his doctorate. His thesis had something to do with optimization of natural gene mutation in single-cell plants, which put it on the growing list of books that I would never get around to reading.

He stayed on in Cambridge, founding a tiny lab whose business model seemed to be that they generated ideas, which they then licensed to bigger companies. The model must have worked. The little lab got big, went public, and two years later was absorbed by one of the giant pharmaceutical firms for the kind of earnings multiple usually reserved for social media Internet tycoons; Haley did more than all right in the transaction. The year before he turned thirty, Haley totaled his sports car coming back from his summerhouse on Cape Cod. The car was a McLaren F1, a super-high-end street legal rocket that the Kid had once told me retailed for approximately one million dollars.

While recuperating, Haley must have gotten bored waiting for his two hundred stitches to stop itching, and his two broken arms and a skull fracture to heal, so he went back to school. Harvard again. For an MBA this time.

Which is where our boy wonder met the woman of his dreams. Selena Pratt, sole heir to a coal mining fortune, and beautiful. Glen Head Academy. Yale. Harvard MBA. Straight through. Despite the pedigree and education, she must have been a bit of a rebel. She skipped her debut, turning up three days later at a Phish concert in Florida.

Her mother died while Selena was still at Yale—probably from shame that her daughter would never be accepted in society—and her father soon after. The grandfather was her guardian until she turned twenty-one and inherited three hundred and fifty million dollars. Selena sold off the balance of the coal business and began investing in alternative energy start-ups. She was also a philanthropist, I found, supporting various causes around the world—most of them having to do with the environment, poverty, and health care. In the last few years, she had also contributed heavily to a charitable foundation that supported infertility research.

She and Philip had no children.

6

Two hours later, the Kid was asleep and I should have been. There was more I could have read, but I was standing in the kitchen, debating whether to go ahead and have that third drink or try to go to sleep without it. I upended the empty glass and put it in the sink.

There was a light knock at the front door, followed by the sound of a key in the lock. My father had a key. The building management had a key. And Skeli had a key.

"You're up," she said, as she glided through the doorway. Skeli was tall, right at the upper limit for a Rockette, a job she had held before she traded in her dance classes for graduate school and a doctorate in physical therapy. She had the kind of face that responded well to artfully applied makeup—she could be stunning when she worked at it. But I liked looking at her best when she looked as she did right then. Strong, intelligent, with laughing green eyes. And she still had great legs.

"This is a nice surprise," I said, greeting her with a hug and a cheek kiss.

She shrugged off her long overcoat and draped it over a chair.

"The cab pulled up in front of my building and I couldn't get out. I thought about climbing those stairs to that empty apartment and I just told the driver to take me here. Is it all right?"

"More than all right. Anytime. I'm happy to see you."

She noticed the music. "What are we listening to?"

The Grateful Dead. *Dick's Picks Volume 9*. Madison Square Garden. September 1990. They were still breaking in Vince Welnick on keyboards, but Bruce Hornsby was there pushing Garcia into jazzier realms, and Jerry was pushing right back. They had just finished a haunting version of Dylan's "Queen Jane" and were sliding into "Tennessee Jed."

"The Dead. Want me to change it?" We agreed on so many things, music just didn't happen to be one of them.

"No. How about we turn it down a touch?" She put her head to one side and smiled. "How's the Kid?" Her voice was thin. Tired-sounding.

"Good," I said, adjusting the volume. "A minor meltdown at bedtime, but he kept it together."

"What set him off?"

I shook my head. "Aliens."

She plopped down on the couch. "Is there any wine open?"

"That kind of day?" I went to the kitchen and opened the new wine cabinet, designed to keep expensive wines at exactly the proper temperature for all eternity. I was already feeling silly about it, as most of the wine we bought would have been just as happy in the door of the refrigerator. "Nothing open, but I'd be happy to uncork whatever you like."

"Is there any of the Cloudy Bay left?" A New Zealand sauvignon blanc that had recently become her favorite white wine.

I opened a bottle and poured her a glass. Then I poured myself a tall glass of tap water and joined her on the couch.

"None for you?" she said.

"I'm already two drinks ahead of you."

Her eyes gave a flicker of concern, but she said nothing. She sipped her wine. "Aaahh."

"Want to talk about it?" I said.

She sipped some more, staring out the window at a cold and wet Broadway. "Not just yet."

I put my glass down, knelt on the floor, and removed her high-heel boots. Then I massaged her feet, working her toes and the ball of each foot.

"How did you know?"

"Women's shoes are nothing more than cleverly camouflaged torture devices."

"I can't always wear sensible shoes. I need to convey an image. Women clients come to me to get healthy so they can go back to wearing the kinds of shoes that caused their problems in the first place. It's part of the business model."

"You don't have any clients yet."

"I am visualizing my future success."

"Don't you have a chiropractor on staff? What does she say?"

"She recommends finding a nice man to rub my feet. Come here, sit with me."

I did.

"With your arm around me," she said.

I put my arm around her. She leaned into me and we kissed.

"Mmm."

"Mmm-hmm," I replied. I tasted the wine on her lips. "Nice wine."

She sipped some more. "I'm beat. I've been going full-out six and seven days a week for months, switching hats every time I turn around. And today the contractor stopped avoiding my calls and I sat him down. We're not going to be ready for January second. The carpenter is running a day or two behind, but that sets the electrician back and he's booked somewhere else the following week, and then blah blah blah, the plasterers, the painters, and we're looking at the fifteenth."

"Two full weeks?"

"It seems that the painters I have contracted don't work Christmas week. They all go home to El Salvador and don't come back until after the first."

"Well, it's only two weeks."

"The ad copy reads January second. The flyers will all read January second."

"They're not printed yet. Change them."

"Stop trying to fix it," she said with the slightest touch of impatience. "I'm just upset. You don't have to fix me."

I sipped my water. "Sorry. I couldn't fix you, anyway. You're already perfect."

She snorted a laugh. "You're right. I forgot for a minute. I must be tired."

I gave her shoulder a squeeze. A half hug.

"How was your day?" she asked after a pause.

"Virgil has something interesting for me to do. I'll know more on Monday. Maybe earlier."

"Nothing scary?"

"I don't see how. It's something to do with insider trading."

We both drank and watched the flicker of lights down Broadway, distorted by the rain into metallic streaks of red and yellow and white.

"You know," I said, "there could be a positive side to this delay. We could go away. Someplace warm. With sun."

She gave a soft chuckle. "And rum drinks."

"Painkillers."

"Can we bring Heather? So you get a break?"

"I'll talk to her on Monday."

"And Jane?" Heather's partner and soul mate. Jane taught women's studies at City College and sometimes did stand-up at one of the downtown clubs. I found her a little intimidating but very funny.

"Do they share a room?" I asked.

Skeli laughed lightly. "Of course. And so do we."

"So, you agree? It's decided? I can find some place and make plans? You're in?"

She buried her face in my chest. "I don't know. I can't talk about this now. You can't go away, anyway."

A technicality. I needed permission to go away—from my latest overworked, underpaid, and much distracted parole officer, who would look at my record over the last year and a half, and the FBI letters in my file regarding my frequent invaluable assistance to them, and rubber-stamp just about any request for travel. But I didn't push it. I could make the arrangements and present them to Skeli when all she would have to do is pack a bag.

"Not to worry," I said. "Another glass?"

She shook her head and frowned in thought.

"Looks serious," I said. "You sure you don't want to let some of those bad thoughts out? They might do some damage, you keep them locked up like that."

I earned a rueful smile. "I'm exactly where I've dreamed of being for the past four years. My own clinic, run the way I want. And I'm grateful, really, to you and your friends for making it possible."

Virgil Becker and an old friend named Paddy Gallagher had joined with me to provide Skeli her start-up funds.

"Investors. We plan on sitting back and spending all our time counting the money you'll be making for us."

"Somehow, I don't see any of you three just sitting back."

"I spent two years sitting back as a guest of the federal prison system. That was enough sitting back for the next forty years."

"But now that all this is coming together, I'm looking at everything else in my life and thinking I want more. Or something else. It's like the closer I get to what I want, the more I want."

"Just a bad day?"

"I am woman. I am strong. I eat bad days for breakfast and spit out the seeds."

"Nerves? Opening-night jitters?"

She shook her hair down over her face and forced a small shudder. "Suddenly, I hate my apartment. The only nice thing anyone could say about it is that it's big. I could fit a family of eight in there and we'd hardly ever run into each other, but it smells like onions, and half the outlets don't work, and when it rains, the light fixture in the kitchen fills up with water and I have to get the stepladder out of the closet and . . . God, I sound like such a whiner. What is the matter with me?"

"You can't get the landlord to take care of any of those things?"

"My landlord, as you well know, is my ex-husband and a shit. I think he only pays for heating the building because he's afraid of Mrs. Berliner down on two."

"She is a force to be reckoned with."

"And I know only crazy people give up three-bedroom apartments on One-hundred-tenth Street, even if it is the only unrenovated building on the block."

"This is New York. Real estate is our religion."

"But I need something else. Something more."

"Move in here," I said for possibly the thirty or fortieth time.

She sighed. "You are sweet." She kissed me. "This is your apartment. It is becoming, slowly, also the Kid's apartment. But to me, this is where I live out of a leather tote bag."

My one-bedroom with alcove was over a thousand square feet, huge by New York standards, and more than adequate for the Kid and me. We both had privacy when we needed it, and plenty of room for my music and the Kid's toy cars. But a third person—a female person, with makeup in the bathroom, shoes on the closet floor, and, in Skeli's case, having lived in a sprawling three-bedroom on Cathedral Parkway for the past ten years, an expectation of a certain level of privacy that would be unmatched in our apartment—was a fond impossibility.

"So we'll move," I said.

"You love your apartment," she said with a one-armed hug.

"I do."

"And you can't make the Kid move. He'd hate it."

Life is change. The Kid was learning that, but at a glacial pace. And until I was sure he was ready, she was right. "So, maybe not right away. But we can think about it, can't we? We can look. Maybe there's something opening up here in the building."

She was quiet again for so long that I checked to see that she hadn't fallen asleep. "I know what it is," she said.

"You're tired. You're disappointed about delaying your opening. Your feet hurt."

"All that *and* . . ." She paused briefly. "I want to have a baby."

I forced my arm to stay around her shoulders. It wanted to retract, or wither and fall off. I managed to keep my mouth shut.

She waited just long enough to realize that I wasn't going to say anything. "You just shut down on me. I know I'm scaring you, but I can't have you shutting down on me."

I hugged her again. "Sorry. I'm with you. You were saying . . ."

"I'm thirty-nine. Too old already. I never thought I'd be saying this, but this is really what I want."

I didn't say anything to Skeli for a long time. I was already questioning my abilities as a father. The Kid was more than a handful—he was three or four handfuls. And I knew the figures. One child in fifty was diagnosed as on the spectrum by the time they reached high school. One in eighty-eight diagnosed by elementary level.

That left a lot of children misdiagnosed, or ignored, or merely undiagnosed and unhappy for years. And I knew that the incidence increased with the age of the parents at conception. Especially for fathers over forty-five. I was forty-six. And I also knew that the incidence increased exponentially for second and third children when there was an older sibling on the spectrum.

"You sure you want me to be a part of this?" I said.

She hugged me again. She'd read the same articles I had. She knew what she was asking.

"You're the trader. Would you take a bet like that? I can't do the math, you can. What if the odds were one in ten? Or one in two? What would you do?"

The day that Angie brought our child home from the hospital, I was up to my eyeballs in a mountain of trades all designed to hide a series of other fake trades. I built a monumental tower of false profits that finally toppled, sending me to jail. In all that time, I failed my son miserably. I failed Angie, too, but for that I take no blame. She paved her own road to hell—and it was a four-lane superhighway.

But now I was making myself into the Kid's father. I thought of the way he wriggled and twisted when he wanted to be squeezed, the way we said our hellos and good-byes by sniffing each other's hands, and the way he had once given Skeli a full lecture on the subject of the old Volkswagen Karmann Ghia, punctuating his delivery with a cry for ketchup, which moments later ended up in her hair.

I had never regretted taking the Kid into my life after Angie abandoned him to an attic room in Beauville, Louisiana. But it had not been easy. On one level, I knew that he was as responsible for my salvation as I was for his rescue, but each day was a trial. Not *each* day. Most days. But I wouldn't change a thing.

"We're going to need a bigger apartment," I said.

7

Virgil called Sunday morning. My father and Estrella had just picked up the Kid for a trip to the Museum of Natural History—my father was convinced that my son could become fascinated with dinosaurs. I had my doubts. They didn't have wheels. I was enjoying a second cup of tea and working my way through the *Times*.

"I just got off the phone with the *Journal*. They wanted to know if I had any comment on the story. They're running it front page tomorrow."

"On Haley?"

"He's being called to testify before a grand jury next week."

"Moving the timeline up quite a bit. They must be ready to roll on him."

"If he's arrested, there's no going back. We need to head this off immediately."

"What did you tell the *Journal*?"

"'No comment.' I'll give an exclusive to the *News of the World* before I talk to those bloodsuckers."

The *Journal* still took every opportunity offered to remind the world of Virgil's father's crimes.

"What have you been able to come up with so far?" he continued.

"Aside from basic research on Haley, I'm having dinner tonight with someone who's an expert on insider trading. That ought to give me everything I need on the subject, then I'll be ready for Haley himself."

"Check in with me tomorrow morning. I'll contact the board and ask them to give you all the assistance they can. I've already spoken with Haley. You can meet with him out on the Island, late morning." He rattled off the name and number of Haley's secretary. "She'll give you directions."

"I'm on it," I said.

8

"I'm guilty. I broke the law. I knew exactly what I was doing and I knew it was illegal and I did it anyway. You want to know why I did it? Same reason every other money manager does it. I didn't think I'd get caught."

Sunday night. I was having dinner at Sparks with Matthew Tuttle, recently convicted in federal court of insider trading and currently awaiting sentencing. It was a tad ghoulish, but if there was anyone who could give me a crash course on the subject, Matt was the man. Matthew and I had been at Wharton together, but had gone our separate ways as soon as we finished the training program at Case Securities. I had started on the foreign exchange desk, Matt on the block equity trading desk. Against the odds, there was already a trader in the equity department named Matt Tuttle, so Matt had been renamed Rufus. It had stuck and followed him from firm to firm. Every night, he left his desk, got on the commuter train, and somewhere between Grand Central and Darien, Rufus morphed back into Matt. His wife, Alice, whom I had met a few times over the years, had a habit of correcting people when they called him Rufus. "It's Matt, or Matthew." I had known him before he'd become Rufus, so I never developed the habit.

"But you went through a trial. Why not take a plea?"

"Because the only offer the U.S. Attorney made was to wear a wire and go to work for the Feds. No jail time. Community service and a fine."

I stabbed another chunk of the cold lobster cocktail. "So why not take it?"

Matt looked at me like I hadn't been listening. "Kevin McNab. Remember him?"

Kevin McNab had placed the muzzle of a ten-thousand-dollar Italian side-by-side double-barreled shotgun in his mouth and pulled the trigger. Only one barrel fired, but that was all he needed. The story made the *Post* and the *News*, but the nationals ignored it.

"The Feds had him on a leash for four years. They caught him red-handed. He'd been paying a clerk at Goldman to get him draft copies of research reports the day before they were released. He'd put in an order overseas and unwind it a day or so later. Like me, he didn't think he'd get caught."

He paused while the waiter cleared the plates and divvied up the Caesar salad.

"Another round, gentlemen?"

I was experimenting with potato vodkas and had discovered one distilled on Long Island, of all places. LiV. It was very smooth and went down like water. My glass was empty. Matt's glass of Macallan was still half-full.

"Same again?" I said.

He picked up the glass and drained it. "Might as well. I don't think they serve this where I'm going. Did you know McNab?" he continued after the waiter had left.

"Never met him."

"He wasn't a nice guy. His rep on the Street was pretty shady and he drove two nice women to divorce him. They both had to sue to get him to pay his child support. Maybe his mother liked him, but nobody else did. What I'm saying is, he wasn't someone who would normally warrant my sympathy. But once the Feds got their hooks in him, they made his life hell. They had him wired and turning in everybody he ever worked with. Anybody with so much as a speeding ticket. They pushed and pushed on him, sending him after bigger and bigger fish, until finally he broke. Even he developed a conscience."

"You could argue he was helping put away some bad guys."

"Do you believe that?"

"You don't?"

"First of all, insider trading is a misnomer and it's not always illegal. An insider is someone with a fiduciary responsibility to a company—a director, an officer, an employee, or maybe a vendor. For one of those people to trade on nonpublic information, to make a profit, or avoid a loss, that is insider trading. It is illegal in most countries. But if the same people trade on public information, or on a whim, or because they need to pay for the kid's tuition, it is still insider trading—only it's not illegal. You with me?"

"So the question comes down to whether the information is publicly available or not."

"That, and intent. So, if you *think* you're breaking the law, you *are* breaking the law. It's a little like being Catholic. And Milton Friedman argued that trading on nonpublic information actually forces the information to become public, and therefore the trade is beneficial to the markets."

"That's not just some philosophical rationalization?"

He laughed. "Yeah, well, maybe in my case. But people write papers on this. Smart people. Professors." Now he had *me* laughing. "I'm serious!"

Our entrées arrived. Steak fromage for Matt. Crabmeat and bay scallops for me. Sparks was the unusual steak house where the fish was as excellent as the meat. And I was still working on remaking myself into Skeli's idealized version of me. We both dug in. My meal was great. His looked better.

"How hard are they going to be on you? It's only the single count, right?"

He nodded. "Oh, I'm fucked. No doubt. My lawyer won't even handicap it. Twenty years is the max, but the prosecuting attorney isn't pushing for it. What he really wants is the five-million-dollar fine, but I'll do time also."

Times were harder. Sentences were longer. I wanted to help but there wasn't much I could do, and sympathy wasn't part of our culture. You take your chances and take your lumps. That's what the market taught us. "I can recommend someone to prep you on prison life. How to get through it."

"My lawyer has me set up with a consultant outfit in Baltimore. They help with pre-sentencing, how to survive, and reentry. I've been meeting with them for a while."

"I don't think there is any way to prepare for reentry. No matter what, you're never getting your old life back. But you'll figure something out. It just won't be anything like what it once was. It might be better."

He looked unconvinced. "What was the worst?"

I thought about my first night, listening to the psychos and the sobbers threatening and crying in the dark, an auditory outer ring of hell. I remembered my first fight, the only one that was more than a scuffle but that had earned me the right to be left alone; the constant lack of trust, knowing that no one is your friend, but you can't afford to have a single enemy; the way your brain shrinks, so that thoughts of life outside become limited to food, sex, and fresh air.

"The boredom."

He was surprised. "Not the violence. Rape?"

"You're too old. Sorry."

He laughed. Embarrassed. Relieved. "All the TV shows, you know?"

I nodded. "Yup. It's there, but you're not going to a maximum security facility. You might even end up at a camp, which is no garden party, but it is better. And, by the way, you really are on the old side. Guys in their teens and twenties are the main targets. They either fight or get punked—or both."

We both sat thinking about that for a few seconds.

"Jesus Christ," Matt said.

"Yup. According to the stats, five to ten times as likely."

"Some kid gets popped with a little too much weed in the trunk of his car, and . . ."

"Yup. More than half the prison pop in the U.S. is there for nonviolent crimes."

"Jesus Christ," he said again.

"Amen."

He waved his fork as though dispelling all such ugly thoughts. "You know, a hundred years ago, what I did wasn't just legal. It was how you played the game. That was the job. You maintained your network, traded favors and rumors. If you heard your buddy made a pile of dough and you weren't in on it, you had every right to be pissed off."

"So why not do it all the time?"

"Because it's illegal! I was managing close to a billion dollars—three ETFs—all leveraged equity funds. I was making a nice buck. Why would I want to screw that up? It's one thing to write research papers or op-ed pieces on the subject, but it's another whole bucket of worms to get caught doing it."

"And yet you did."

"Yeah, so I screwed up. It's not like this was my business model, like some of these guys. This is all public information now, so it doesn't hurt if I tell you the story. I bought a lousy fifty thousand shares of Myo-Life Labs at forty-two on a Tuesday afternoon. I thought it was oversold—it was down over ten percent in three days. As soon as I did the trade, I hated it. You ever get that feeling? Like you're buying something you think is so cheap you're practically stealing it, and then you sit back and say, 'Uh-uh, that was *too* easy.'"

I knew that feeling. Every trader has had it.

"That night, I'm having drinks with two other fund managers. We never talk our positions. Ever. Not only is it against the rules, but we are all way too competitive. And these days, too paranoid. You never know who's gonna be wired. But we got together once a month or so, just to shoot the shit. Those nights got very liquid, but there were some things we never talked about."

I saw that my glass was empty, but I thought it might be a good time to start slowing down.

"Anyway," he continued, "at some point I come back from the bathroom and there's a group of guys standing around our table. Everybody is laughing over some story one of them is telling. I don't know these people but it's obvious my buddies do. I sit down and smile and try to catch up, but at this point in the night, I'm already getting hazy."

I was feeling a bit hazy myself at that point. I drank a glass of water and tried to convince myself that it would help clear my head.

"It turns out that I know the guy doing the talking—he's a banker over at Pierce and one of his accounts is Myo-Life. I know this and right then I should have said something or walked away. But instead, I listen. Myo-Life is toast. They're going to announce in the morning. Eight years of research, and instead of coming up with a new antiviral, they've got a few thousand petri dishes of brown scum. Everybody's laughing because the CEO checked himself into New York Hospital so he wouldn't have to face the press in the morning. The punch line to the story is 'Chest pains!' and they all keep repeating it and cracking up some more."

"And you?"

"I'm ready to barf. How could I have been so stupid? I bought into a 'way back' trade without doing my homework. A rookie mistake. I focused solely on the price action and now I'm in the shit. I panicked. I excused myself from the table, went out on the sidewalk, and called the Coast. I figured that no one back at the table knew I had the position, and no one anywhere else in the world would know I had the information. I unloaded the whole position at better than forty. The next morning, they delayed the opening until the firm made the announcement. The stock opened up at twenty-four, traded as low as eight, before it bounced a bit and closed just under ten. I took a two-point hit and saved my investors a buck and a half."

"But you weren't an insider. You traded on hearsay. Rumor."

"No. I traded on nonpublic information. I had every reason to believe that the banker had the goods and I was privy to something solid. According to the law, I should have waited until the information became public."

Privileged information rarely affects the foreign exchange markets, unless it's who's buying or selling or how much. Governments release economic stats and the markets move or they don't. Occasionally there might be a leak and everyone would get in an uproar for a day or two, but this kind of parsing of what was legal information and what was not was well beyond my experience.

"How did they catch you?"

"Routine review. The SEC is all-seeing. They ran all the trades in the week leading up to the announcement. They do that kind of thing as a matter of course. But if I had been the only one front-running the announcement, they still wouldn't have been able to make a case. I trade too frequently. They'd have had a hard time showing intent. It turned out that the banker had told a few other people that week. On paper, it looked like a major conspiracy. They rolled all of us up."

I had no appetite left. The man across from me had made a mistake—I had made a flood of them. But it doesn't take much to destroy a career—a life. Just one misstep.

"And now?" I asked.

Matt grinned sadly. "Now I'm enjoying a great steak, and living in the moment. So get us another round. And pass the spinach."

9

Stone walls in varying stages of disrepair lined both sides of the road as I looked for the turnoff to Westwood, the Haleys' compound/estate out on the North Shore of Long Island. I passed a golf course, a vineyard, a discreet conference center, and a development of luxury homes for people who insisted upon living in mansions the size of hospitals on deforested lots close enough to their neighbors on either side to absorb every detail of marital or familial discord—all of which had been, at one time, portions of the vast robber baron estates of the nineteenth century. But a very few of those estates still survived, as evidenced by the occasional gated drive that led back into the heavily wooded acreage. I tapped the brakes and slowed as a fox burst out of the brush on my side of the road and ran across, disappearing instantly in the tall grasses on the far side.

Few of these gated drives exhibited numbers or names—either of the owners or the homes. It was apparent that if a visitor did not know exactly where he was going, he was simply not welcome. Haley's secretary had emailed me directions, and now that the rain had let up, I could see well enough to follow them.

I took the first left after the second golf course and slowed for a series of speed bumps. The posted speed limit was five mph, and it appeared that they took this seriously. Hitting one of those obstructions at anything over ten would have destroyed the suspension on the rental car and bounced my head off the roof. Thirty yards or so past the third bump, I came to the gate. I stopped the car and, as instructed, rolled down the window.

"May I help you?" The voice, a no-nonsense, testosterone-laden male with no discernible accent, seemed to come from right outside the car, though there was no one around. It was creepy, but not impressive. My Bose stereo system was just as capable of distributing sounds to specific parts of the room.

"Jason Stafford. Mr. Haley is expecting me."

There was a pause.

"Would you please look to your left?"

I looked to my left and tried smiling for the camera, though I couldn't see it.

"Thank you." The metal gate swung back almost silently on rubber wheels. "Take your second right turn into the employee parking lot and have a nice day."

Another first experience in life; I had just been wished a good day by a clump of brown spikes of hydrangea.

The drive was barely wide enough for one car to safely pass a bicyclist or pedestrian; they must have had some way of holding traffic at either end. It would have been impossible to back up or turn around. I passed the first turnoff. It led to a stone house and tower complete with crenellated battlements that must have been the gatehouse—or guardhouse. It looked highly efficient either way.

The woods cleared slightly as I took the turn at the second break and I got my first view of the property: tennis courts, a long greenhouse, a riding ring, stables with a long, low building attached that may have been an indoor ring, and the vista of Long Island Sound from atop a thirty-foot cliff. Nice digs.

The money was not all Mrs. Haley's—just most of it. A few minutes' research that morning informed me that she was the sole surviving fourth-generation heir to the estate and remaining fortune of a coal mining tycoon by the name of Wilford Potts, who had assured his place in history by being the first to direct the use of a machine gun on striking workers. He fathered three daughters and lived long enough to see them all married, one to a Vanderbilt, one to an Italian count, and the third to a Pratt. His great-grand daughter, Selena Pratt, had met Philip Haley at Harvard Business School. He was already a bioengineer with several patents and a mid-eight-figure multimillionaire. By all accounts, it was a love marriage, though a cynic would have pointed out that Mr. Haley had simply found the most direct route to three hundred fifty million dollars in capital to expand his already successful business.

Their house, which I caught a brief glimpse of as I rounded the last turn of the driveway before pulling into the parking lot, was a magnificent example of the opulence and excess of Long Island's historic Gold Coast. Built by Selena's great-grandfather as the family's summer retreat, it was half medieval castle, half neo-Georgian–mid-Victorian–Turkish revival, wrought in dark brownstone with granite highlights. An industrious real estate broker would have said it had character.

The laboratory, a five-minute walk from the house through a century-old forest of rhododendron, was housed in a modern brick and glass eyesore, which some kindhearted landscaper was trying to hide, or at least obscure, with a series of groves of birch trees. It almost worked. The vertical, somewhat slanted, white trunks diffused the appearance of the squat red walls, but the vast expanses of gray glass reflected only the winter sky. The place had the appeal of a nearly vacant office park in some rust belt suburb. Beige drapes in every window hid whatever operations Haley was using to turn the energy industry on its ass.

A khaki uniform–clad man with a gun on his hip passed me driving an electric golf cart. He was wearing mirrored aviator sunglasses. On a cloudy day in December. If the look was meant to intimidate, it would have worked better with another vehicle. It's tough to look badass on a golf cart.

Haley's secretary, a tall, sleek brunette wearing black-rimmed glasses that failed to hide the ice in her eyes, was waiting for me in the bare lobby. She looked out of place; perhaps she ought to have been serving the world's elite in some Park Avenue glass tower with teak paneling, thick carpeting, and recessed lighting. Instead, she was out here in the mad scientist's laboratory, with bare concrete floors, asbestos drapes, and metal fireproof doors.

"This way" was the sum total of her greeting to me.

I am not a fan of ice people. I was one at one time—traders are rarely rewarded for being warm and huggable—but I had it all burned out of me in prison. The hot metal savagery of a tattooed, three-hundred-pound, muscle-bound berserker at large in the anything-goes confines of a prison yard can turn ice into a lukewarm liquid running down onc's lcg in a flash.

"Look at the screen and try not to blink," she said, pointing to a small monitor set in the wall.

A flash went off so quickly I could not have blinked if I'd tried.

"A retinal scan?" I asked.

She nodded. "You now have limited access. This way."

I followed her up a narrow stairway, our footsteps clanging and echoing on the rust-stained metal treads. The second floor was a mostly open space surrounded by glass-walled offices. A long conference table, littered with old newspapers and used paper coffee cups, ran down the center of the room. The carpet was worn and the walls had not been painted in much too long. It wasn't the kind of environment to inspire fiscal confidence.

Philip Haley's office was as utilitarian as the rest of the floor, with a long metal lab table for a desk and a minimum of chairs. It was a workspace, not a room for high-level meetings, or investor schmooze sessions.

"Phil will be with you in just a minute. He's getting changed," my guide said in a whisper, as though we were standing in a chapel. "Can I get you anything? Water? Coffee?"

She didn't want to get me anything, I could tell. But then, I didn't really want anything, either. "Thanks, I'm fine."

Philip Haley walked into the room. The secretary looked like she wanted to genuflect. Haley was a remarkably handsome man in a very masculine way and he gave off the kind of charismatic glow that you see in some actors or politicians. He had large blue eyes, like that kid in *A Christmas Story*, and at some point he had spent a lot of money on dentistry.

"You're Virgil's man," he said, extending a well-manicured hand. We shook. His grip was strong, but he didn't push it. He wasn't trying to prove a thing. "Thank you, Kirsten. Let them know downstairs we'll have a visitor in . . ." He checked his watch—a no-nonsense Tag Heuer. ". . . fifteen minutes." He turned back to me. "I'm late. I know. Forgive me. I will explain later, if there's time."

There was nothing of South Carolina low country in his voice. He must have worked hard at that at some point in his life.

"Actually, I had just arrived."

"Good. Good."

"Pretty Spartan surroundings," I said once we had settled into two straight-backed chairs that practically screamed, *Don't get comfortable!*

"I spend money on security and research. Everything else is a waste. If I have the product, and can keep the Chinese from stealing it, it will sell and we'll make money."

He wasn't bragging. He was supremely confident, but without a hint of arrogance. I thought of mentioning the upkeep on the riding stables, but accepted that his wife's lifestyle and his business standards might be viewed as entirely apart.

I thought he might respond to the most direct approach. He did not like to waste time any more than money. Neither did I.

"Virgil was afraid they might have charged you by now."

"I will testify early next week. If it becomes necessary. I expect all of this to go away."

"You think they'll let you walk?"

He scowled. "I'm being set up."

"You're saying that you did not trade shares of your own firm based on nonpublic information using a secret offshore banking account."

"Exactly."

"And you expect me to take that on faith."

"Take it any way you want. It's the truth. My lawyer arranged a lie detector test and I passed. I am innocent."

All it takes to pass a lie detector test is a total disregard for the truth or the consequences of one's actions. Sociopaths passed them all the time and innocent people failed almost as often.

"Then let me hear you say it," I said. "Say the words."

He scowled again. "I had Kirsten look into your history. Why does Virgil have your confidence?"

"I fix things. I find things. If you violated securities laws, broke trust with your investors, and pocketed a few bucks in the process, there's only so much I can do to help you. My advice? Cut a deal."

"But I didn't do it!"

"Even if that's true, it might still be worth your while to cut a deal. These people don't believe in the concept of innocence. And fairy tales just piss them off."

"This is what my lawyer has been saying all along. Is this Virgil's response, too? I ask him for help and he sends you to deliver his message?"

"Nope. I'm a bit of a loose cannon. I speak for myself. And I'm still waiting for you to say the magic words."

"I said I didn't do it."

"Repeat after me. I did not trade shares . . ."

"Why don't I have you tossed out of here?"

"Because if you really didn't do it, if you really are innocent, then I'm your guy. I'm good at what I do and I don't quit. But if I think you're too dumb to tell me the truth, I will be wasting my time, and I'd rather be taking my son to the playground."

He took his time thinking it through. "Come on," he said, standing up. "I'll give you the backstage tour."

I stood with him, but I made no move to follow. "I really do want to hear you say it."

He cleared his throat, looked me in the eye, and said, "I did not trade shares of this company—or any other—based on privileged, nonpublic information. I do not have a secret offshore bank account."

I believed him. "Well, all right, then. From here on, I've got your back. Let's see your operation."

There was another scanner inside the elevator. Haley went first.

"Just look into the viewer and try not to blink. The doors won't open until we've both been scanned."

I looked in and blinked. I blinked a few times. The doors opened anyway. I thought they would.

There was a brief hiss of moving air and I felt my eardrums pop.

"We keep a slight negative pressure in the immediate environs outside the lab," Haley said. "Sorry. I should have mentioned it. Some people find it painful."

"Negative pressure? Won't that help your experiments escape to the outside world where they will destroy all life as we know it?"

He smiled indulgently, but without humor. "Our algae are rather fragile. They were all designed in a lab environment. Contaminants could easily undo months of research." He punched buttons on a security pad in the door and it slid back with a *whoosh*. We stepped into the lab.

Not quite *into* the lab. We were in a glass-enclosed corridor that ran down the center of the building. On either side of us, figures in white protective suits briefly looked up from their work, then ignored us. Green slime had them all enthralled. There were vats of it and small dishes of it. Green was the only color in the room, otherwise everything was white.

"Is this what they mean by green technology?" I asked.

"Very funny," he said, though it was obvious he didn't think so at all. "What do you know about Arinna? Our work?"

"I did do some homework," I said, which was true as far as it went. "You grow algae and turn it into biofuel. How am I doing?"

"I came to algae late. There are people in Europe and out west who were working on it long before I got involved. But most of my competitors come from chemical engineering backgrounds. They see energy produced from algae as an alternative to solar panels. The problems they see are ones of increasing efficiency through better use of structural materials."

"I'm a math guy. I never took an engineering course in my life."

"Not important. Engineering is important, but it's not the answer. It's limited. Eventually, inertia wins. Let me ask you this. What do these three things have in common? A simple battery, a can of gasoline, and a lump of coal."

"It's easier to talk about what makes them all different," I said.

"Yes, yes. But the point is that they are all ways of storing energy. When you need some energy, you can plug in your battery to run an electric motor, or burn some coal to boil water for a steam engine, or explode some gasoline in the engine of your car. All energy systems are similar in that energy needs to be both stored and released again when needed. And every system is limited by its own parameters. Efficiency, as we view it in the twenty-first century, must also address refuse, be it dross, residue, or effluvia."

"Batteries? Aren't batteries clean?"

He wrinkled his nose in disgust. "Filth. Poisonous semiprecious metals that cannot be intelligently recycled. Acids leaking into groundwater. Batteries are forever. You're better off with nuclear waste. At least that has a half-life."

"I see."

"And the damn things are heavy. You can't change that. You may be able to make them marginally more efficient, but don't expect to fly to Tokyo in a battery-driven commercial airplane. You would need to rewrite all the physics books first."

Haley led me back down the corridor and out to the elevator. "Will it be green?" I asked. "I mean, sustainable? Clean?"

He spread his fingers and waved his hands. "Buzzwords. Pop media. Listen. I will make it simple. What are the two main problems with solar energy?"

"I don't know. It still costs too much to be competitive?"

He shook his head. "One. Once you have collected the energy, you still need to store it. You need to turn lights on when it's dark outside. You still need to run your microwave on rainy days. We've already covered batteries. They are not the answer."

"I can see that."

We didn't have to go through the same security measures on the way out. Haley pushed a button and the elevator door slid open.

"Two," he continued. "Solar energy is limited. Only so much of it reaches the earth's surface. Much of it is reflected off our atmosphere, which is a good thing. Otherwise we would all have been baked into ashes before we evolved beyond seaborne amoebae. But the amount of energy that actually reaches the ground is a limited figure—quantifiable, but definitely limited. The closer to the poles you are, the less solar energy hits the surface. Smog deflects it and absorbs it. So does dust. The Sahara gets an average of more than twice what we get here in New York. So efficiency matters, but only up to a point. Chemical or mechanical systems will only be able to reach a certain level of productivity. After that, modifications to improve efficiency will, almost by definition, become too expensive to pursue."

"Are we back to nuclear?"

He ignored me. "And much of the energy comes in a form that we can't use. It comes in wavelengths—colors—that do us no good. It is not readily transferable. The usable band is less than half the total."

"Infrared?"

He nodded excitedly—his pupil had said something intelligent.

"This is why algae makes so much sense. You agree?"

I didn't see, but I kept it to myself. "I'm still listening."

"Algae grow with sunlight, water, and carbon dioxide. One of your 'greenhouse gases' according to the popular press, though carbon dioxide is quite natural and very necessary to life on this planet."

Someone had made an attempt to make the office rooms a bit more presentable, clearing the conference table of litter and straightening some of the chairs. My bet: It wasn't the ice lady.

"There you go," I said. "Water. Another limited resource."

"Yes, but algae actually love dirty water. Briny is best. Clean water is a limited resource. Salt water constitutes over seventy percent of the surface area of the planet. Not a problem."

I was starting to see it. "And carbon dioxide is fairly abundant."

"Well, yes. Not always in optimal concentrations, but, yes. Algae remove carbon dioxide from the atmosphere, takes briny, undrinkable water, and mixes them together to form an oil that is combustible and that requires little processing to turn it into biodiesel. The algae also create proteins that can be used for animal feed, and excrete carbohydrates—sugars—which can be processed into ethanol."

We settled into the chairs in Haley's office. There was only one picture in the room—a framed photo of his wife that sat next to his computer monitor. Haley saw me looking and turned it, possibly unconsciously, so that it faced him alone.

"What's the catch?" I said. "There's got to be some reason we're not all doing this already. Where does oil have to be trading before this becomes competitive?"

"As I mentioned, sunlight is limited—finite. You cannot improve your per-acre energy capture by increasing sunlight. So where do you get increased efficiency? Most of the industry is taking an engineering approach, improving their technology. Most of them are using a very commonly found algae. It is much more efficient than corn or sugar beets, and it is easily replaced in case of catastrophic die-offs—algal crashes—due to drought, or predators, or too little sunlight for extended periods. However, the theoretical best, the ultimate, that current systems could hope for would be a return of approximately eight thousand barrels of diesel and four or five thousand barrels of ethanol. That's per acre."

I ran some numbers in my head and whistled. "Not too shabby."

"Indeed," he said. "But suppose you could quadruple your production per acre?"

"But you can't. You said it, sunlight is finite."

"Sunlight is finite, yes. But remember, the algae only capture a percentage of it. And can only process up to a certain percentage of what is captured."

"And that's where you come in. 'You' being Arinna."

"Arinna bioengineers more efficient algae. Producers who use our algae will have fewer pool crashes, capture a wider range of available light, and process a much higher percentage of that light energy into fuel. And our product actually captures more carbon dioxide than the burning of the fuel releases. The holy grail of biofuels."

"How close are you?"

"We have a product that performs flawlessly in the laboratory. It has done quite well in our research farm in Arizona."

"Where do you get water in Arizona?"

"There's plenty of water. It's just not fit for consumption—filled with salts and minerals. But it's perfect for our needs. The air is cleaner than we would like, but every site is a trade-off to some degree. But location is not really our concern. I'm not a farmer. I just want to sell my superior product to farmers."

"So, you don't need my help there."

He did finally smile at one of my feeble jokes. "I am at a loss as to why I need your help at all, Mr. Stafford. I have explained to my lawyer that I am innocent. Eventually, investigators will discover who is promoting this scheme."

I was stunned. The man was certainly intelligent—a genius—and experienced. "Didn't you go to Virgil Becker for help?"

"Virgil is our banker. His firm took us public. Of course I spoke with him about the situation. But I made it clear to him that there is no cause for concern. I am innocent and that will be demonstrated."

I am often amazed at how remarkably stupid some smart people can be. In most of those cases, I could see the underlying cause—usually arrogance or inflated sense of privilege. But Haley should have known better. For the first time, I began to doubt him.

"Mr. Haley. You say you know my history. You know part of it. I went to prison. But I've been out for a while and I've managed to help some people out of serious jams. I helped Virgil after the mess his father left him. I can help you. But if you're only telling me part of the story, you are tying my hands. Understood?"

He didn't like it. He did the scowling thing again.

"I've been set up," he said finally.

"So be it. Who would do this? Do you have any enemies?"

He gave a short, unamused laugh. "Hosts. I am decidedly from the wrong background. Despite that, I am successful and I married a beautiful, wealthy woman."

"All right. So you have lots of enemies because you married the only remaining heir to a Gold Coast fortune and you live in a castle. But somehow, I don't see some jealous polo-playing twit running this kind of scam just to put you in your place. Sorry."

He almost blew up at me. I could see it coming and he pulled back. He thought for another moment.

"The Chinese. They'll do anything to stop me. To keep my product off the market. If they can't steal it. They've sunk trillions into battery power; they can't afford to have me beat them."

That struck me as possible. It was also paranoid, delusional, and racist. But as the Chinese had already hacked into the *New York Times*, the *Wall Street Journal*, and the Pentagon, I supposed that I would have to treat it seriously.

"What do your IT security people say?"

He glowered. "I will not use firm assets or personnel in what is essentially a personal matter."

"Okay, but they must have given an opinion."

"I have not asked." He was past the slow-rolling boil, but not quite to the point of screaming with released steam.

"All right," I said. He was stonewalling, but I wasn't going to let it get in my way. "I know people who can look into it. Or at least steer me in the right direction." I had remained in touch with a young computer whiz, now attempting to better himself by studying law at Yale. If he couldn't help, he would know someone. "I was thinking someone closer. A family member. Senior staff. A board member. Someone with clout and connections—and money."

He cleared his throat a few times as he fought for control. He was again very much in control when he finally answered. "Arinna has a small board. My wife and me; Chuck Penn and Harve Deeter are the moneymen; Helen Ward, from Teachers' Retirement—our corporate conscience; and Don Kavanagh, our general counsel. Virgil usually sits in with us—the firm owns a large block of nonvoting shares. I get along well with all of them. I respect these people and would want you to treat them as they deserve."

Charles Penn was a big fish—a whale. A multibillionaire with interests in everything from start-up tech companies to minerals mining. Harvey Deeter was an oilman and even wealthier. Helen Ward had referred to me in the press as "just another small-time crook" when I had been convicted. I didn't think she would take my call this time around.

"I can finesse when need be. I'm multitalented that way." I would have Virgil make the call to Ward and the lawyer. "Anyone else? Competitors? Jealous family members? Jilted ex-lovers?"

"I'm quite serious about the Chinese. You should look into that connection."

"Okay, but I might start with your wife."

He opened his mouth as though to object, then closed it and sat staring at me blankly.

"Can I reach her here?" I asked.

He snapped out of whatever reveries had caught him. "At the house? No. She'll be at our place in the city." He gave me the number. "Let me walk you out," he said, standing.

His mood had changed when I mentioned the wife. He was no longer as confident. He had gone from the assured CEO to the beleaguered husband.

We were shaking hands in the parking lot when he suddenly shook off the change in mood. "Do you have a minute? Let me show you something. May I?"

I had plenty of work to do and not much time to do it, but a minute or ten wouldn't make a difference.

"Lead on."

We walked up through the rhododendrons, the curled brown leaves rattling in the wind and sounding like a wooden waterfall. I was cold already, but Haley didn't seem to notice it, though he was wearing no more than his suit.

"I was late getting back this morning. Checking my lobster pots and trolling for whatever fish are still around this time of year."

Nothing on the Internet had hinted that he had a hobby of any kind.

"I'm surprised. I didn't see you as a fisherman."

"I grew up dirt-poor in Georgetown, South Carolina. You either fished or worked at the paper mill. Or went hungry."

The stables were just to our right. From this perspective I could see they were empty and needed work. The white paint was flaking badly in spots and the outdoor riding ring was partially covered with bare brown weeds. We kept walking.

The house was both arrogant and pitiful. Arrogant in size and with all the Gold Coast love of over-ornamentation, but pitiful in that it failed so abysmally at conveying any sense of beauty or grandeur. The path we were on would lead us directly to the front door. I wasn't interested in a house tour.

Haley must have sensed my reluctance. "Almost there. We'll take a right up here around the hedge."

I followed him and found myself in a low-walled garden in back of the house. The flower beds were all piled with mulch and only the brown stumps of rosebushes along the stone wall gave any indication of what this area would look like in early summer. At the end of the garden was all of Long Island Sound.

Water views and wealth are inextricably bound and will be so even after the oceans rise twenty-five feet and turn Manhattan into a twenty-first-century version of Venice. Virgil's mother lived in a castle with a view of Newport Harbor. Every multimillionaire on Wall Street had to have a water view, if only at the summerhouse, and every lowly intern and trading assistant dreamed of getting there one day. But few had dreamed this big.

Beyond the wall was a steep cliff of clay and rock, pushed here by the Wisconsin glacier of the last ice age that had scraped away everything in its path down to bedrock before being defeated by warming weather, gravity, or friction. The glacier melted and left the Sound.

And from that garden, I felt like I could see all of it. Far to the west was Manhattan, the towers looking like sparkling crystals in the afternoon sun. A lighthouse, which must have been miles away, looked like a toy replica. Across the water I could see the hedge fund mansions in Greenwich, the soaring bastions of banking in Stamford, and in the distance, the towers of the power plant at Bridgeport. To the east, water stretched to the horizon, giving the illusion of infinity. It was impossible that such a view belonged to one family alone.

"Is this the highest point on Long Island?"

"No. Not even close. It's not even the tallest point on the North Shore."

"Why isn't this a national park?"

"It may yet get there. But come over here. I want to show you my farm."

It was too odd to question. I followed him to a set of steps that led down to a rocky beach in a set of switchbacks along the cliff. Far below us, a rock jetty stuck out from the beach for sixty or seventy feet into the Sound. I made the mistake of looking straight down and felt my equilibrium shift. The ground was very far away and there was very little between me and it.

"Right out there," Haley said, pointing at the water a quarter mile or so offshore.

I looked, but I didn't know what I was looking for.

"See that row of white dots on the water? There and there and there."

Then I did see them. "Okay. Sure." I had no idea what they meant or why I was supposed to be impressed, but Haley was certainly excited by them.

"Those are my pots. My lobster pots. That's where I was this morning."

He went on about conch and black sea bass and winter flounder with as much enthusiasm as the Kid talking about muscle cars. I tried to maintain a pretense of interest. The wind coming across that cold water was going right through my camel's hair overcoat. I was cold.

"You go out on a boat in this weather and haul up lobster traps? For fun?" I gave up on all pretense.

He laughed like a little kid. "It *is* fun."

"Do you catch anything?"

He laughed again, this time ruefully. "Not much. I'm probably not very good at this. But when I'm on the boat, I'm not thinking about balance sheets, or failed algae batches, or Chinese saboteurs, or . . ."

"I hear you." Or a wife who prefers to live twenty miles away, or an SEC investigation, or who might be stabbing you in the back. "I don't know how you do it, out here in just a jacket, but I'm dying."

"Of course. Of course. We'll head back and I'll let you go."

Haley pushed the pace back to the parking lot, and by the time we got there I was beginning to think that I would live.

"I'll be in touch," I said. "Anything else that comes to mind, please let me know right away. I'll report back to Virgil, but with your permission, I can also keep your lawyer in the loop."

"Right. Give him a call," he said airily. He was back in his denial phase.

"By the way," I said, "where do you keep the boat? I didn't see it down there."

"Oh, no. There's no real dockage here. I keep it in the cove just down the coast. Come back in warmer weather and I'll take you out. We'll head out east for bonito. Good fighting fish on light tackle."

The wind was making the birches next to the lab groan and complain as they swayed. I hustled into the car and put the heater on high. It blasted cold air for a minute, then neutral, and, finally, blessed heat. I turned the fan down and started the long drive home.

10

There was an accident in the left lane just before the Cross Island Parkway, and the Long Island Expressway had become a parking lot. I was close enough to see the flashing lights up ahead, which was also close enough to see that the only lane where traffic was moving was the exit lane to the Parkway. I pulled out my phone, fitted in my earbuds, and made a call—almost hands-free.

Straight to voicemail. "Hi. This is Fred Krebs. I'm not available right now, but if you leave your name, number, and a brief message, I will be sure to get back to you."

"Hello, Spud. Sorry. Fred." Spud had been a junior trader who had helped me out in the past, but now that he was in law school—at Yale—he was trying to lose the old nickname. "So by now you've guessed who this is. I thought you might need to make a few bucks to buy Christmas presents. Give me a call."

I tried Skeli.

"Hi. What's up?" She sounded busy.

"Are you busy?" I asked.

She let out a breath. "I'm always busy these days, aren't I? I didn't use to be, you know. Or at least it felt less busy. I miss it, sometimes. What are you doing?"

"I'm stuck in traffic on the LIE."

She laughed a great whoop. "Your worst nightmare. And you called *me*. What a romantic you are." She gave a soft chuckle. "Poor baby."

"Thanks. I didn't know I needed that until you said it."

"Call when you get back into the city. I need a break from all this. A long relaxing session with you."

"I'll try and fit you in," I said.

"I love it when you talk dirty to me." She disconnected.

A Chrysler 300 in the middle lane suddenly put on its blinker and attempted to force its way into the left-hand lane. As no cars were moving, he didn't get very far, though he now managed to block two lanes rather than one.

My phone rang. Spud.

"Hey! Thanks for getting back to me so quick."

"I only called to say I can't help. I'm buried."

"I don't need much. I think."

"It's finals. Law school finals. People regularly take their own lives in all kinds of dramatic and mundane ways to avoid what I am going through."

"Come on. By this time you either know it or you don't."

"I want to make law review."

"Five minutes? Less, if you stop trying to put me off."

"You always try to cheese me with that 'five minutes.' It is never five minutes."

"I will wire you the money the minute I hang up," I said.

"Banking by phone?" He laughed. "Are you finally embracing technology? Leaping blindly into the second decade of the twenty-first century?"

"Are you in or out?"

"Shoot," he said.

"The client is accused of shorting stock in his own company just before the release of some troubling news. The news wasn't really all that awful, but the stock dipped almost ten percent that day and didn't recover for almost a month. He bought back at the lows and made himself a couple hundred grand."

"That's it? He risks losing everything over two hundred grand?"

"I have considered that. Let's say he didn't think he would get caught," I said.

"The SEC combs through every trade looking for just that kind of thing."

"The trades were done through an offshore account."

"That makes it slightly harder," he said. "They'll go after the bank. They'll get the records."

"They did. His name is on the account."

"Then tell him to cut a deal."

I gave a sigh. "I did. He says he didn't do it. He says he was set up. My question to you is this. Could he be telling the truth? Is it possible?"

"Sure, it's possible." He sounded as though he would need a lot of convincing.

"But unlikely."

"Yeah. Kinda."

"How would *you* do it?"

"That's way beyond my skill set. You'd either need to bribe someone, or hack directly into the bank's system. Or both. Either way, I wouldn't know who or how."

I could see a tow truck pull away with a wreck on the bed. The flashing red and blue lights began to break up. The middle lane began to move. Now a Prius tried to muscle its way into that lane. Traffic stopped again. Horns started blaring around me.

"Really, Jason. Save your money on this one. I know someone

you might try, but it's not me. He's more than a little odd, but he's a genius. Guaranteed. He was a TA when I was an undergrad. He left before he finished his thesis. I'll text you his contact info."

"Thanks, Fred. 'Luck on your finals."

I clicked off and focused on the milling traffic. Once again they were all jockeying for position that might possibly shave tenths of a second off their commute. The last accident had just been cleared—in front of our eyes—and the madness began again immediately.

11

I hated going to the gym. I hated gyms. And I held a deep suspicion of those who claimed to like them. Their priorities were askew. In my trading days, Case Securities had offered executives a heavily discounted membership package to a gym in the basement of the building. I paid every month and never went. Later, when the fraud that I was running was taking up all of my waking time, I would go downstairs in the evening for a steam, a shower, and a nap on one of the massage tables before coming back up to watch the markets open in Tokyo. I never once lifted a weight. I never ran on a treadmill or biked in place. I hated gyms.

However, as a defense against boredom more than anything else, I had picked up the habit while in prison. The weight room was a no-combat zone. None of the prisoners wanted to lose gym privileges. My shoulders and chest filled out, my waist shrank. I was no bodybuilder, but I progressed and benefited.

I had not lifted a weight in the sixteen months since I came home. I ran, though I would never be competitive, but that did nothing to maintain the upper body muscles I had developed.

Skeli was right. It was time.

Tuesday morning. Roger told me there was an old Yiddish saying about luck coming with new ventures begun on a Tuesday. I had no idea if there really was such a saying or how Roger would know, but after dropping the Kid at school, I had nowhere else I had to be until early afternoon. I walked down to the West Side Y. There were plenty of gyms in the city, but the Y was an easy choice. No one I knew would be there.

I went on a tour of the facilities, signed forms, submitted my credit card, and engaged the services of a personal trainer for ten sessions. Having done all that, I thought I could reward myself by skipping a workout, but I knew I wouldn't be able to look Skeli in the eye.

I did a quick two miles on the track that ran around the second-floor balcony in the main gym, the sound of barbells clanging occasionally breaking through my usual running trance. Then, still pouring sweat, I went downstairs and began lifting.

The rhythms came back. I was not lifting the same weight as I had in prison; I wasn't even trying to. But I found that I wasn't quite as soft as I had imagined. I focused on my routine, free weights only. The machines all looked complicated. I'd let the trainer break me in when we finally met. I concentrated on not hurting myself.

There was a mirror I was trying to avoid looking at on the far side of the room, but every time I came up from a barbell squat I caught sight of a scowling man. I knew that scowl. It had been my normal face for years while I traded currencies. But I thought I had begun to lose it in the months after my release from prison. It was back.

I added ten pounds to each end of the bar and did a dozen dead lifts. I didn't have to focus as hard on my balance and could afford to look away from the mirror. I finished the dead lifts and paused. Was I still scowling? Did I scowl only while lifting? I looked at the mirror. I was scowling.

The Kid didn't like my scowl. He didn't like my smile much, either. He responded best when I assumed a relaxed implacability. Skeli didn't seem to mind. Or maybe I just scowled a lot less when she was around.

I did six clean and press before I realized I still had the extra weight on the barbell. I was lifting far too much over my head. I should have had a spotter. This was only twenty pounds less than I'd been pressing at my peak. It was nuts. And exhilarating.

The seventh was a strain. Eight caused me to burst out with sweat again. I could feel it running in rivers down my back. At nine, my arms began to shake. I pushed through. I looked in the mirror. I was still scowling ferociously.

Ten. I could quit there. Pretend that I did reps of ten rather than twelve. But I couldn't. The old lifer who ran the weight room in prison had told me that only wusses and punks did reps of ten. My body almost stalled on eleven. My right arm extended, but my left remained bent. My left had always been weaker. I tried to breathe, but I was already straining too hard, too tight across the chest. I made another push and my arm finally went straight. I released and almost lost control as the bar came back down. It occurred to me that Skeli would be really pissed if I strained my back my first day in the gym.

I blew air out and gasped it back in. Three times. Forcing oxygen back into my blood. Grab. Clean. Up and slow press. Hold. Three count and down. Done. A full dozen.

I was no longer scowling. I was smiling. If that's what it took to get a smile on my face, I thought, we were all going to have to settle for a rare small grin.

Then I saw her. She was standing behind me and off to one side. If I had turned my head even slightly, I would have seen her earlier. She was watching me, but from her angle she wouldn't be able to see that I could see her in the mirror. She was worth watching.

I guessed her to be in her early twenties, half my age. Much too young. Young enough that any sexual thoughts on my part would be self-censored on the basis of general creepiness. But I was looking. Admiring. A few inches shy of six feet. She wore a white leotard, gym shorts, and pink sneakers with flaming red laces. Her bosom was just shy of startling. Hips an inch too small for perfection. Her face was, of course, beautiful, but not the kind of beauty that anyone with a big enough checkbook can get these days. She had character. There was intelligence there. Honey-blond hair pulled back in a ponytail. I don't particularly like the ponytail look, but she was at the gym. Working out. I could make allowances. She was still looking at me.

I checked my smile in the mirror. Still there. She was approaching. I sucked in my gut.

"You're Jason Stafford, aren't you?" she said. If the smile had had any effect on her, it didn't show.

"I know we haven't met before," I said. "Believe me, I would remember."

"Savannah. Savannah Lake. Roger pointed you out the other day. Roger? 'Jacques'?"

"I know Roger," I said. Jacques-Emo was his stage name.

"I'm his assistant. In his act. He's a clown."

"I know. I've known Roger for years. He has phenomenal taste in assistants." Skeli had been his assistant when we first met. Roger had introduced us.

A brief frown flickered across her face. She thought I was flirting. I wasn't.

"My girlfriend used to have that job."

"Wanda?" She looked both relieved and a bit excited.

"Wanda the Wandaful." I had begun calling her Skeli on our first date. The rest of the world still knew her as Wanda.

She laughed. "I'm Stormy Savannah."

"You've met her?" I asked.

"She's great. Roger introduced us."

"Nice to meet you," I said, and we shook hands. I managed to maintain eye contact. I thought that in fairness to the rest of us who used the gym, someone should introduce her to the concept of sports bras. Maybe Skeli could do it. I could not imagine how I might broach the subject.

"You were really pushing it," she said, indicating the barbell. "You look good. Great form."

I had felt very sloppy. Almost dangerously sloppy. "Do you lift?"

"No. I work the machines. I'm not looking to add bulk."

"Neither am I. Just trying to stay fit."

"Oh, you are. You're in great shape."

I was eight pounds heavier than when I came home from prison. I tried to think of a way of telling Skeli that Sultry Savannah thought I looked "great." *Stormy*, not Sultry! Dope.

"I mean for your age. You're what? Fifty? You could model. You should think about it."

Maybe I wouldn't tell Skeli that Savannah thought I looked great.

"I'm probably too busy to really make a go of it," I said.

"Well, nice meeting you. Say hi to Wanda for me."

"Will do," I said. I watched her walk away. The hips were definitely too thin. Not exactly scrawny, just boyish. Not my type at all.

I looked back at the mirror. I was scowling again.

I rarely go to Westwood anymore, Mr. Stafford. It was not a happy place to grow up, I'm afraid. Too many ghosts."

Selena Haley had the somewhat forced vivacity of a woman just past her prime and all too aware of it. She was still a beautiful woman but she did not glow. I knew she had just turned forty, but forty had been less kind to her than to other women. And she was tired. Tired enough that I could only assume that some malady—either physical or mental—was the cause.

"It's a beautiful property," I said.

She gave a soft laugh. "And a hideous house."

"With a great view. The whole Sound laid out like that—from Stamford over in Connecticut to that lighthouse back toward the city. Impressive."

Her apartment was impressive also. Two floors on Fifth Avenue, views of the park and the Met, lots of mid-twentieth-century American art on the walls, including an Edward Hopper that I had once seen in a retrospective in Paris. We sat in an alcove off the living room. Mrs. Haley served coffee from a silver set that probably retailed for the same price as a year of school for my son.

"Impressive, I will grant you. Do you know the story of the lighthouse? Execution Rocks, they call it."

"I've heard of it. I grew up not far from there." In working-class College Point—five miles and three or four zeros from the kind of wealth you needed for entry level to the Gold Coast.

"During the Revolution," she said, "the British chained prisoners to the rocks and left them there at low tide. The tides there are eight to ten feet. More than one hundred years later, the Coast Guard had trouble keeping the lighthouse manned. The men said they could hear screams whenever the tide came in." She delivered this macabre story with the air of a debutante discussing a flower show at the Armory that she had heard about.

"We didn't cover that in seventh-grade history," I said.

"And later, in the early 1920s, there was a serial killer, Carl Panzram, who dumped the bodies of his victims in the deep water just off the reef. My grandfather claimed to have met him one time."

"And lived to tell about it."

"My grandfather drank, Mr. Stafford. Copiously. Frequently. I learned early to take his stories more as fable than as fact. His cousins ran Standard Oil and he was always frustrated that he did not rise to their prominence. He had the name and the pedigree, but not the knack—nor the initiative. Desire without drive. You're left with envy. Have you known anyone like that?"

I had met more than a couple of them, in and out of prison. Wall Street drew them like flies to garbage. Connections got them in the door but did not guarantee their success. They became complainers, hangers-on, or crooks. "Too many."

"He enjoyed frightening me," she said in a musing tone.

"Your parents allowed him to?"

"My parents were lovely people, incapable of seeing the bad side of anyone. And they were in love and therefore blind. They spent their time traveling the world together. They passed within a year of each other."

I didn't know what to say. "My condolences." But they'd been dead for some twenty years. Skeli would have had just the right words, I was sure of it.

"Oh, no. This was all a long time ago. While I am sure there is never a good time for one's parents to die, it was an awkward time for me. I was still acting out. It must have been quite annoying for them. I like to think they would have approved of the way I've turned out. But I will never know, and now it is no longer that important." She seemed to run out of air saying all that in a bit of a rush.

"You were left with your grandfather."

"Who tried to break the terms of the trust. Six months before my twenty-first birthday, still mourning my parents, in my senior year at school, and trying to figure out what I wanted to do with my life. I fought back. And won."

"I'm starting to see why you don't like Westwood."

"He wasn't done, either. He sued again after Philip and I were married. And very nearly won."

"I didn't see any of this when I Googled the family."

"We are discreet."

"Obviously you won again in court."

"No. My grandfather died. He was drunk—as he was most days from lunch, until he went to bed or passed out in his chair, whichever came first—and must have wanted to go for a walk on the beach. He fell down the staircase and broke his neck."

I had seen that staircase when her husband walked me out to the cliff the day before. It rose a full four stories from the beach. A tumble down that would have been as lethal as a bullet.

"And what moral should I take from that? Don't drink and walk on the beach? What goes around, comes around? Karma's a bitch?"

All this talk of death on her part had been delivered in the same bemused but unemotional voice, as though she were floating on a sea of liquid Xanax. As though all these tragedies had been someone else's life story.

She smiled at me. "Am I being morbid? Forgive me. But let me answer your question anyway." She put her head back and closed her eyes. "Evil people, I mean truly evil people, look just like everybody else." She opened her eyes again. "What do you think?"

I thought for a moment. "I'm an optimist, I guess. Or a romantic. I think anyone can be redeemed, if they want it. But I'm also a skeptic. I don't believe most people want to be redeemed. They just want to win."

"Or to take revenge for not winning."

"Is that your take on this? Your husband is being set up out of revenge?"

"Certainly not."

"Do you believe your husband is innocent?"

"Do you mean to be insulting?"

"I'm just looking for answers, and so far the only stories I'm getting are about jealous ex-beaux and Chinese masterminds."

"Preposterous."

"I agree. But that doesn't get us any closer." We had reached an impasse. I would have to change direction or admit defeat. "Are any of the board capable of doing something like this?"

"Capable? An interesting word choice. Two of our board members are both wealthy and powerful enough. And arrogant enough."

"But would they? Does either have any reason to hurt your husband? Or the company? Without your husband, would there be an Arinna?"

"Point taken. There would not. Therefore it makes no sense."

It was still early days, but not much about this was making any sense.

"I am sure of one thing. Whether he did it or not, my husband will be cleared. He never fails, and he never fails to survive. He is very dependable that way."

Faith, fact, or pharmacy, or good old-fashioned denial. Whatever she had going, it was working for her.

13

"You've got a vacation coming up soon," I said.

The Kid did not respond. I had not asked a question nor had I given any of the other signals that he understood to mean I expected a response. I knew better.

We were having a reading party after dinner. The Kid was looking at one of his car books, a Dover paperback with full-page photos of antique autos. I was reading one of my new books, *Daily Crises on the Spectrum*. I had just read this paragraph:

> *For some children, holidays and vacations can be stressful, rather than relaxing. Engage your child in the process early. Empower them by letting them know that their feelings matter.*

"I want to take you and Wanda and Heather and Heather's friend on a nice vacation. Someplace with sand and sun and warm water. What do you think? Is that something you would like to do?"

He was staring at a picture of something that looked like an insect on wheels. I couldn't see the description. I waited. Eventually, he turned the page. I was preparing to make my approach a third time, when he answered.

"No." For about three heartbeats, he looked at me with arched eyebrows and bulging eyes. The cartoon image of a sincere wish to communicate honestly. Heather had been attempting to get him to look at people when he talked. The results were more troubling than encouraging.

I waited to see if he wanted to elaborate. He didn't. He went back to the book.

"What do you think you would like?"

He flipped a page. I thought I knew what he was looking at. "That's an old Buick roadster, isn't it? With the jump seat in back."

He flipped the page angrily. "No."

I went back to my book.

Remember, the child on the spectrum sees change as a threat. Your first attempts may be unsuccessful.

"Do you like the ocean?"

He looked up and his brow furrowed in concentration. "I don't know."

"Maybe we should try it out and see. Maybe you'll really like it."

He went back to his book. He slowly flipped a few pages.

"No."

Sometimes you will find that the stresses of planning a trip are themselves the cause of your child's anxiety. In this case, you may want to offer the idea as a "last-minute surprise treat."

Brilliant. Don't surprise him unless that doesn't work, in which case try surprise. But don't be surprised if that doesn't work. I closed the book and placed it in the "not worth reading anymore" pile. It was the largest pile. "To be read" was the second largest pile. "Really worth keeping" was the smallest.

"Hey," I said. "Get your shoes and coat. I want to buy you an ice cream."

"'Nilla," he said, leaping up.

"You got it."

Getting in to see a pair of multimillionaires had required a minimal bit of planning and arranging. Getting in to see a pair of billionaires was proving to be much more frustrating. Getting to talk with a college professor was in a world of its own. But if he was as good as young Mr. Krebs had indicated, I could put up with a bit of frustration.

"Is this Mr. Stafford calling again? I can recognize your voice."

I could recognize her voice, too. Ms. Sharp. Department secretary. The gatekeeper for the great man. Benjamin McKenna.

I might have to get one of those scramblers to disguise my voice. There was probably an app for it. I could use my tablet. If I remembered to keep it charged.

"Yes, it is. I'm hoping to avoid a drive all the way out there."

"Dr. McKenna has office hours Tuesdays, Wednesdays, and Thursdays from eleven to twelve. I remember telling you that yesterday."

"Doesn't he ever talk on the phone?"

"You may leave a message."

"I left a message yesterday."

"I gave it to him."

"But he didn't call me."

"Then the obvious conclusion is that he doesn't want to speak with you."

You can't fight that kind of logic.

Wednesday morning at quarter to eleven I arrived at the Department of Information Studies at the university in New Jersey. I liked driving through northern New Jersey even less than driving on Long Island, but there were more roads per square mile than anywhere else on earth. This allowed free roam to my inherited obsession with maps. My father and I had near photographic memories where maps were concerned, and any time either of us set out on a journey greater than crossing Broadway, we were compelled to calculate every possible route to our destination. New Jersey was like a kaleidoscopic carnival ride.

There were four women at work in the office on the main floor when I walked in. None of them looked up or offered to help. No matter my age or accomplishments, I always felt like a student when visiting a school—powerless.

I walked up to the long, tall partition that separated the students from those who actually did something there. "Excuse me," I said. "I'm looking for Dr. McKenna's office."

No one looked up, but the woman closest to me—a thin woman with a haircut that looked like it had been modeled on a rag mop—swung around in her chair and called out to one of the two women in the back of the room.

"We don't have a McKenna. Am I right?"

A face like Winston Churchill's appeared around the edge of a computer monitor. "McKinley?"

"No," I said. "It's McKenna, not McKinley."

"He says it's McKenna, Lydia," the thin woman called out, though the room was no bigger than my living room and everyone there could hear every syllable of the conversation.

"No," Churchill said.

"There's a McKenna in Engineering," a disembodied voice said from behind another large monitor.

"Benjamin McKenna?" I asked.

"No," the voice answered.

"Well, then, could I speak with the department secretary, Ms. Sharp?"

"I'm Lydia Sharp," the woman in the back said. She stood up and walked with a sailor's rolling gait up to the partition. "What do you need?" She said this last as though everyone she ever spoke to had some sad, desperate need and it was her lot in life to deny them all. She sounded nothing like Ms. Sharp.

"Did we speak on the phone? Monday? Yesterday?"

"No."

"I didn't think so. Is it possible that there is a Dr. Benjamin McKenna in this department and you four wouldn't know about him?"

"No."

"A visiting professor, maybe?"

"Is he a student?"

I didn't think so, but I was ready to try anything. "I thought he was a teacher."

"Try Room 108. Downstairs. TAs use it for tutoring sessions. There's a list on the door. Maybe you'll see McKenna's name there."

"Thank you." I backed out of the room, not comfortable turning my back on the four guardians of knowledge.

There was a list on the door of Room 108. There were eight names on the list, each with schedules for student assistance. McKenna was not on the list. There was no one signed up for the eleven a.m. slot on Tuesdays, Wednesdays, and Thursdays.

"You being helped?" a deep masculine voice said just over my shoulder.

I turned to find a black-bearded, ponytailed man in his late twenties wearing the uniform of his generation—checked flannel shirt and knitted watch cap. His eyes flicked briefly across my face and he looked away.

"I'm looking for a professor, but no one seems to know him."

"Who's that?" he said, looking over my shoulder.

"Dr. Benjamin McKenna," I said.

"That's funny."

"Why is that funny?"

"*The Man Who Knew Too Much*. Hitchcock. 1956. James Stewart and Doris Day."

"Sorry. Don't know the flick," I said.

He seemed disappointed. "No biggie."

"So you don't know him," I said.

"Somebody told you to look for Ben McKenna?"

He would not make eye contact. Was it Asperger's? Or did I detect fear? Or both? It felt different from the Kid's fear—and I was glad he didn't spring the bulging-eye look on me.

"I guess I made a mistake," I said.

"What's your name?"

Definitely not Asperger's. His fear was bordering on aggression. "Jason Stafford. A mutual friend said to look him up."

He nodded, his head bobbing many more times than was warranted.

"Are you a TA here?" I asked.

He was still nodding. "This mutual friend? What do his friends call him?"

We were playing an odd game. "Spud."

He handed me a scrap of paper and quickly walked away. The note was brief and neatly typed.

GO TO STARBUCKS. GET A COFFEE.
DON'T LOOK AT ME.

The instructions were clear, even if nothing else was. I went back up to the admin office and got directions to the nearest Starbucks. There was one in the Student Union, just past Dodge Hall, the Humanities building.

"Just a small black," I said.

"One short," the girl called out. "Anything with it?"

Everything in the showcase looked good. The blueberry scone looked particularly good. It had blueberries. It was practically a health food. It was also about forty-five minutes of laps around the track at the Y.

"Just the coffee," I said, feeling almost saintly. I took a small table away from the window, with a view of the front door. I only had to wait a few minutes.

The bearded man came in and went directly to the bar, where he ordered a grande something-or-other. He took his time with the sugar and half-and-half before taking a seat on the far side of the room. I tried to look like I was not looking at him and found that it was easier just to not look at him. A moment later, my cell phone rang.

UNKNOWN CALLER. "Stafford," I answered.

"Mr. Stafford? This is Ms. Sharp calling. Can you hold one minute for Dr. McKenna?"

It was not the voice of the Lydia Sharp in the admin office. It was the same voice that I had heard twice before when trying to reach McKenna. I risked a look across the room.

"Mr. Stafford? Are you there?"

The man was speaking into the microphone on his plugged-in earbuds, which were connected to a laptop, and through it, to a cell phone.

"Holy hell, that's you," I said. "How do you do that?"

"It's an app," he said in his own deep baritone.

"Impressive," I said. "But why all the spy stuff?" I thought it was more Maxwell Smart than James Bond. "Can't we just have a conversation?"

"I checked. You weren't followed."

"That's comforting." I would have been quite surprised to find out anything but.

"Spud says that I can talk to you. What do you want?"

"How about we start with names? You know mine. Is McKenna your real name?"

"I have no name."

"Well, what would you like me to call you? 'Spud's friend'?"

"Joy is my name."

I was beginning to wonder if Spud was taking revenge on me for some unknown slight on my part.

"Fine. I will call you Joy."

"You may call me Dr. McKenna."

I counted to ten. "How about Ben?" I said, just to get one shot back at him.

He paused. "No. Dr. McKenna."

"Okay, Dr. McKenna. Now, will you tell me why all this secrecy?"

"I have enemies."

"Obviously."

"Have you heard of a company called NEQUISS?"

"Never."

"I created NEQUISS. North Eastern Quadrant Internet Security Systems. White hats. We helped keep the black hats out of your systems."

"What's the product? Anti-malware? Antivirus?"

"High-level security. IDS Plus."

"Is there an IDS Negative?"

"Intrusion detection systems. Most packages are defensive-only. Passive, reactive, or preventive. They are all defensive. They let you know that someone is trying to hack in, or where they've been. Preventive systems actually work to keep them out."

"So how is NEQUISS different?"

"Active. It's like hiring armed mercenaries with big dogs to patrol your perimeter and take out anyone who tries to break in."

"Take out? Like terminate?"

"We didn't kill people, but we'd send them home limping—or infected."

"So you made some enemies."

"Last spring we were called in by a defense contractor in northern Virginia. You'd know the name. They had very good systems in place, but someone was getting in anyway. We identified the baddies as a team of Iranians—military. They'd managed to come in the front end and bypassed all the first-line systems, but they had set off an alarm. They hadn't gotten through to any sensitive areas but they were getting close. Our team isolated them and guided them down a rabbit hole into a honeypot."

"You're losing me."

"We let them see files that were worthless. Manufactured. They looked real, so the hackers kept going deeper."

"But really it was a dead end?"

"They copied a full set of plans for a fictitious surface-to-air missile designed to target drones. What they didn't realize was that they were also getting a worm we had embedded in the plans."

"What did it do? Crash their computers?" I said.

"No. The worm was a sleeper. It did nothing but migrate until it found its target. This one was designed to attack the power grid. It took a week to travel to the right network and then there were rolling blackouts in Tehran for the next three days."

"Cyber warfare."

"That's just one example. This goes on every day. All the time. Ten years ago, it was kids. Geeks like me. Getting kicks, which is what teenagers do, right? Woo-hoo, I hacked the *New York Times*! I rule! Only now it is serious shit. Al-Qaeda. The Russian mob. The Albanians stole one hundred twenty million credit card numbers—full identity, name, address, social, everything including where you go to church—and they made it look like the Russians did it. The Chinese? They've got an army regiment that does nothing but hack."

"My client thinks that's who is causing him all of his problems."

"Could be. They're good. But the U.S. is way out in front. They've got the edge."

"What's the edge?" I said.

"English. All computer languages parallel the language of the originators. Most were written by people whose first language is English. So, the code follows similar logic, sentence structure, and syntax. I'm not saying you can't understand it if your first language is Mandarin or Farsi. But if you grew up speaking English, you've got an edge."

"And most of the educated classes around the globe now speak English."

"God help us if the Indians ever start hacking," he said.

"Sounds like a good business. It's like being an oncologist in Florida. If you're any good, clients find you. If you suck, you're probably still making a fortune."

"We were very good. But fortune is the devil's servant. It seems we pissed off more than a few people. There were death threats, which we ignored for the most part until they started coming to our homes."

"You'd been hacked," I said.

"Maybe, but the more likely scenario is that we were sold out. We reported everything to the police. The next thing we knew, the FBI shut us down. They seized all of our assets, threatened the employees with prosecution, and arrested my partner and our CFO."

"What about you?"

"I got a text message warning me. I walked out my front door, and before I got two blocks there were about a dozen government vehicles converging on my house. I've been off the grid ever since," he said.

"I don't get it. Why is the FBI after you? I thought you worked for the good guys."

"We've talked long enough. I have to switch phones." He hung up.

I watched him close up the flip phone and dig into a battered backpack. He pulled out another phone, identical to the first, connected it to his laptop, and redialed. My phone rang again.

"I have to keep switching phones or they'll find me."

"You didn't answer my question." If I was going to do business with this scary young man, I wanted to know what enemies I might be taking on.

"Someone who was very good hacked into SOCOM. Special Ops Command. The black helicopter guys. Ninjas. The hackers didn't really get anything juicy. Certainly nothing we haven't seen before on cable news. Not secret, just sensitive. It was a feint, nothing more. But they left footprints. Footprints that made it look like we were the ones breaking in. And they left a door open, which led to a site used for coded Taliban communiqués."

"Was it your work?"

"Of course not. We would never have been so sloppy."

"So you're in hiding, your buddy's in jail—"

"In the system. I don't know that he is in jail, actually."

"Okay. 'In the system.' What happens next?"

"His wife and kids are with her parents. They've hired a lawyer. I get messages from her. When it first happened, I asked for help online, but in the hacker community we've always been unpopular. But there's a few good guys I've emailed with. Eventually, we'll get through it. Straighten things out."

"That's optimistic."

"Yeah. Or not. Did you get the blueberry scone? It's good."

"No. No offense, but you've got some heavy baggage. I don't know what Fred thought we could do for each other."

"He said you had a client who'd been hacked."

"Not exactly. Look, I don't doubt that you know your way around the Internet or whatever, but I think you're too busy running to do me any good, and I really don't know what I can do to help you. I think we're stuck."

"I need cash. I've been couch surfing, moving on every couple of days, but eventually I'm going to get tripped up somehow. I need money—cash money—to stay hidden."

"I can do that. But I still don't see what you can do for me."

He began tapping at his laptop. "Give me a minute."

It took him a bit more than a minute. Four minutes.

"I'm going to put more cream in my coffee. When I stand up, come over here and look at the screen."

I waited until he was at the counter. No one was paying any attention to him—or me. I picked up my things and made myself walk slowly across the shop. As I passed his table, I looked down and froze.

My bank account was open on McKenna's laptop. Cash balance, $3,480.11. My check for estimated federal tax must have cleared already. Money market account, $157,323.44. Mortgage balance, $0.00. Paid off before I went to prison. Home equity LOC showed a balance of $34.82, which I kept forgetting to pay off.

I knew I was staring and that someone would soon notice, but I was transfixed. The knowledge that a bit of magic is possible, and that the technology behind the trick is not even that difficult, takes very little away from the actual performance. I wanted to punch the screen with my index finger and close the page. Instead, I willed myself to look away and take another seat facing the window.

My phone rang a minute later.

"How did you do that?" I said.

"Your ID is your email account. You should change that. Your bank should have caught it. I found that in less than a minute. Maybe you should change your bank. Then I ran a password-busting program I designed. It's essentially a pattern-checking iterative cracker with various dictionaries to back it up. Much faster than Cain and Abel or John the Ripper. Your password is only thirteen characters. My program can break anything up to thirty in less than five minutes."

"It took you just over four."

"If it can't find a pattern, it reverts to brute force. Sometimes that takes longer. What is it, by the way?"

"You don't know?"

"The program does it all. I don't ever need to see it."

"It's the site of one of maybe three Shakespeare quotes I know. HVIPt2A4S2l84. Henry VI, Part 2, Act 4, Scene 2, line 84. It's where somebody says, 'Let's kill all the lawyers.' It's easy to remember."

"It's not bad. It would keep most lowlifes out. Add a space break somewhere in there and it will up your bit strength a thousand percent. Most people just use their name and a couple of numbers. Or their dog's name. I don't have to know their dog to find it out. The program will run dog names."

"King?"

"King123. You wouldn't believe. Then you get the math or techno geeks who think they're being smart. They use the decimal value of pi, or a series of prime numbers, or a Markov chain. Pattern checkers pick those out in nanoseconds."

I had used prime numbers for my password when I was back at Case. One of the IT security guys had cracked it after only five attempts.

"But if I screw up typing it in, the website will stop me out after three tries."

"It will stop most hackers because they won't want to spend the time, but if you have enough monkeys typing . . ."

"What about those systems that use a randomizer program to generate passwords?"

"They're good, but truly random is not easy to attain. For example, it takes seven shuffles of a deck of cards to remove the patterns from the previous game. Show me a history of randomly generated passwords, and I can predict with a fair degree of accuracy what the next password will be."

"I'm impressed. No, I am awed."

"Well, it's not me. The program does it. Unless you've got a Department of Defense–sized computer generating your passwords, there will be holes. In theory you can create an unbreakable code, but the reality is somewhat less than."

"You're hired."

"Thank you."

We worked out details. The money request was surprisingly modest, and McKenna said the work would take him less than a week. I gave him as many details of Haley's story as I could think of, and we agreed to meet again in Manhattan in a few days.

If he managed to stay a step or two in front of the Feds.

16

I had owned a house in Montauk.

There was no water view unless you count the backyard pool—although out there, Long Island is so flat and narrow that all you really need for a water view is a third story. Montauk, unlike the Hollywood Hamptons to the west, tends to look down upon ostentatious wealth and twenty-thousand-square-foot stone mansions built on shifting sandbars. My house had no third story, or second. It was a Santa Fe–style ranch on two acres and surrounded by deer-tick heaven—scrub oak, pitch pine, and poison ivy—but it had a faux coyote fence that enclosed a terrace of slate and river stones, and an L-shaped pool long enough to make swimming laps possible if not exactly comfortable. And it was very private.

Angie had never liked the house. She had used it, entertained friends there constantly—all summer and every summer until the Kid turned three, when keeping an eye on him around a pool all day had become more an ordeal than a vacation. But she did not love the house. It was small—though three bedrooms and two and a half baths, plus the full apartment in the pool house, seemed adequate to me for a family of three. It was only small if a necessary piece of the weekend curriculum was throwing a lawn party for a couple hundred gin-guzzling hangers-on. And for Angie that was the single unforgivable inadequacy—the house was too far from the party circuit of the Hamptons.

But I loved that house even before I knew Angie. I bought it from a woman who had just survived a messy divorce, and I bought it furnished. The furniture was all Mission, with plenty of quarter-sawn oak, both masculine and feminine in feel. The fabrics were all in vaguely Southwestern colors and design, but a bit muted to give a more sedate, East Coast atmosphere. The touches that I added on my own were few, but each had a meaning or memory for me: the powder room mirror with the hummingbird motif in pressed tin that I bought in Cabo; the framed photo of my father behind the bar, beaming into the camera with love and pride, that stood on the fireplace mantel; and the set of handmade fireplace tools in the shapes of various dragons that I had found in Hong Kong.

When my legal bills began moving up into the seven-figure range, I was forced to sell. The people who bought the house from me wanted it gutted. The salt air had pitted the silvering on the mirror so badly it went straight into the trash. The picture of Pop had survived our downsizing and the trek back into the city, but disappeared somewhere when Angie moved out of our Tribeca apartment. While I doubted that she had been heartless enough to toss it on purpose, she may have been simply too inebriated to notice. I don't know what happened to the fireplace set.

Charles Penn's secretary had granted me twenty minutes with the great man, but I would have to haul my tail out to Montauk first thing in the morning to meet with him. When a billionaire gives an audience, no matter how brief, the wise man shows up early. That was not one of my father's pithy aphorisms; it was one of my own.

I entertained myself with computing various routes as I drove uptown and east to the Triborough Bridge. The Grand Central to the LIE was the only way to get started, the other bridges and the tunnel being impossible unless you were traveling in the middle of the night. I took the Sagtikos to Southern State to Sunrise Highway rather than stay on the Expressway. The LIE depressed me. And on Sunrise, once past Patchogue, it's a clear run all the way to Southampton. The Pine Barrens is Long Island's only remaining wilderness and it's almost soothing to drive through.

In the old days, I never drove it. After work on a Friday night, I would catch the Hampton Jitney a block from the office, and after putting on my Bose headphones, I was fast asleep before we left Manhattan. I usually woke up as the bus swayed through the dips and rises of Hither Hills, minutes before arriving in Montauk. I once hitchhiked a ride with Burt Terwilliger in his seaplane—he ran the firm's M&A group, and though he made enough money to have bought a place in Southampton, he spent his weekends deep-sea fishing, and Montauk is where you go for that. I arrived out east in such a jangled, exhausted state that I politely declined the invitation to join him every weekend. In my worldview, airplanes are big things that, one hopes, never land on water.

Midweek, in the gray days of off-season, it was not a bad drive. Two hours from the bridge, I took the left at the Tower and drove up toward Gosman's Dock. I was an hour early. Dangerously early. It meant that I had plenty of time to drive by the house and dig around in all the old wounds. I could have had a leisurely breakfast at one of the two dueling pancake purveyors, or I could have sat and watched the seagulls fight over the barnacles on the jetty. Instead, I took the right and headed over toward Lake Montauk.

My house was at the end of a twisting lane that threatened at times to turn into a tunnel with the kudzu and out-of-control wisteria arcing overhead. It was dead of winter and the tendrils of vine looked as wispy and fragile as the last strands of hair on an old man's head. The town would send a crew through in the spring and they would chop it all back, allowing in the light and making room for the cycle to begin again.

The house was dark, with plywood shutters hung on the outsides of the south-facing windows. I pulled into the short driveway, almost bottoming out on the same old spot. When I lived there, I had filled it with fresh sand every winter, and by the Fourth of July, the geologic forces would have hollowed out a hole again. It was comforting that the new owners had not been able to come up with a more permanent solution.

There were sparse weeds poking up through the gaps in the slate around the pool, two and three feet tall with feathered tops. The pool cover was weighted in the center with a small swamp of dead leaves, tannic rainwater, and a patina of green algae stubbornly resisting the onset of winter. The patio furniture—chairs, tables, and four chaise longues—were all piled together and wrapped with motorcycle chain. A carved sandstone ashtray sat, almost hidden, in a nook of the river-stone wall, black scorch marks ground into the rock, waiting for the first cigar of another season.

I imagined my current family gathered there. My father grilling steaks, wearing long black pants and black oxfords in July because that is what he always wore. Heather and possibly her partner, lounging in dashikis and baseball caps and drinking from quart-sized containers of iced green tea with honey and ginger. Where was Wanda in my daydream? My Skeli? Working, no doubt. Back in the city, because weekends would be prime time for her services. Maybe not. We would have to see how many of her clientele would actually be in Manhattan on summer weekends. Maybe she could get Sundays off. I imagined her there on a Sunday. Multiple copies of the *Times* spread over the glass-topped tables, the scent of fresh-brewed Zabar's coffee, and a bag of jelly-filled croissants from the Montauk Bake Shoppe.

A far cry from the days when Angie was there.

Despite Angie's disdain for the house—or the neighborhood, at any rate—she entertained there all summer long, bringing out limos full of old friends from her modeling days. Few of these friends were men, and as both body hair and tan lines were verboten in the industry, my backyard on a Saturday afternoon in July was guaranteed to be filled with traders and securities salesmen who found, or manufactured, a good excuse to drop in, even though the twenty-mile drive from East Hampton or Water Mill could take a good two hours in summer traffic. I cannot claim to have become entirely inured to the sight of three or four stunningly beautiful women wearing nothing but straw hats and sunglasses, but I did learn to stop staring. And they did draw a crowd.

Greg was part of my team back at Case. He traded a basket of Asian currencies. He was also a frequent visitor out in Montauk before he got married. He was at the house so often one summer that I thought we would have to name one of the bedrooms in his honor. Greg had a share in a big house a block off the beach in Amagansett, but every other Saturday he would load his Chevy Tahoe with surfboards, three or four other weekend surfers, and a cooler filled with iced Bud Light and head east. They typically spent the morning surfing at Ditch Plains, arriving at my house in time for a late lunch—just as the girls began waking up and venturing out to the pool. Greg was the perfect gentleman—he filled glasses, kept the conversation going, and was always ready to volunteer to apply sunscreen. To the best of my knowledge, Greg never once got lucky at my house, nor did any of his pals, but that didn't stop them from returning. Late Saturday night, as Angie and posse were on their way out to another round of parties and personal appearances at the restaurants and clubs down the road, Greg's friends would pour him into the backseat of the Tahoe, sunburned, exhausted, and awash with a case or two of St. Louis' finest, and carry him back to Amagansett.

There are few secrets on a trading floor—there are no walls, no partitions, and every conversation is public, no matter the subject matter. Early on, Greg realized that I was using very creative accounting and hadn't said anything about it. We drifted apart, neither of us quite able to meet the other's eyes. He stopped coming by the house.

Somehow, while I'd been focused on the stumbles of my own life, Greg had acquired a wife and three kids and become a deacon in his church. He was still trading, still at Case. I had given him a call when I first got out of prison. He was polite, but distant. We hadn't spoken since.

I checked my watch. It was time. I had a billionaire to talk to.

I left my memories in the yard and retreated to the car.

Gosman's, like most of the businesses east of Main Street, East Hampton, was closed for the season and wouldn't open again until well into the spring, but that's where Charles "Chuck" Penn had asked me to meet him. And when the eighth wealthiest man in the world (according to *Forbes* and a cover article in *Fortune*) gives a harmless and idiosyncratic reply to a request for an interview, it is only politic to accede.

Penn had made his money in metals, first as a wildcatter in South America, later as a pure speculator, buying and selling mines, stocks, and commodities, using as much leverage as the world was willing to grant him with futures contracts, options, and promises of future deliveries. He was now on the boards of a major U.S. bank and another in Mexico, the world's preeminent copper mining and distribution firm, an Australian newspaper and radio conglomerate, a Brazilian lumber company with licensing rights to three-quarters of the privately owned forests on the continent, a fair-trade Colombian coffee company dedicated to sustainability, and a Southeast Asian motor scooter company called Whoosh that had leading market shares in Cambodia, Vietnam, Myanmar, Laos, and Bangladesh, and soon expected to expand into Bhutan and Nepal. Penn was a British subject, though he had lived in the U.S. for the last twenty years. He had turned down an Order of the British Empire because of his Welsh ancestry, announcing that he would not accept it until Wales was declared a separate nation. Penn was also listed on the mastheads of the Boy Scouts, Outward Bound, and the NRA.

Along the way, he had managed to pick up a wide range of enemies. South American far-left guerrillas, Russian Bratva gang leaders, Afghani warlords, and Chinese bureaucrats all had major grudges against the man. At times, his word had been called into question. At other times—at least three discovered by MI5 and revealed by the *Guardian*—there had been assassination attempts. There could have been more; Penn refused to discuss it.

He arrived exactly on time. A Town Car and a black stretch limo glided into the parking lot. A man wearing a black overcoat and dark sunglasses—despite the gray sky—got out of the first car and came to meet me.

"Mr. Stafford?" He looked at my face and compared it to an image on his cell phone.

"I look better in profile," I said.

He stepped forward and waved a wand over my arms, legs, and torso. I passed.

"This way, sir." He held open the rear door of the limo and I slid inside. A blast of warm air hit me—the temperature must have been in the high seventies. Charles Penn was tapping on an iPad, dressed in an open-neck button-down white shirt and dark blue pinstripe pants. He put away the iPad while I got settled.

"Jason." He put out a hand. "Call me Chuck. Nice to meet you."

He was a big man, big-gutted, thick-necked, but he gave the impression of power rather than obesity. His thick black hair looked like someone may have done some minor color touch-ups, but otherwise there was no sign of physical vanity about him. He wore no rings or watch. The reading glasses he tucked into his breast pocket looked like the ones you can buy next to the checkout counter at Duane Reade.

"I know it's a bother that I dragged you all the way out here," he said. His voice reverberated around his forehead and came out sounding like a church organ. A Welsh church organ. "Accept my apologies. There is a method to my madness. I want you to see something."

"No bother, Chuck," I lied politely. "I used to have a house out here. It's nice coming back."

He gave me a smile that said he didn't believe me but appreciated my gesture. "They'll be along any minute."

I wanted to ask the question *Who?* but there was no point if I was going to find out any minute. Instead, I pushed ahead with my agenda. "Then do you mind if we get started while we wait?" I said. "Your secretary told me I had twenty minutes, no more, and I can feel the clock running."

He held up a single index finger and stared fixedly out at the harbor. I withheld a sigh of frustration.

When he indicated that something was to happen "any minute," he had neglected to say *which* minute, and I was very aware of how many of my precious twenty minutes were ticking away, but eventually he relaxed, smiled, and pointed at the harbor. Coming up from the Star Island Marina, chugging along at a sedate pace, was a big powerboat of some kind. It looked like a luxury version of a working boat, without the sleek lines of the cruisers or deep-sea fishing boats I was used to seeing in that harbor.

"Come on," he said. "We'll salute them as they go." He opened the door, and still dressed only in his shirtsleeves, stepped out into the cold mist.

I followed reluctantly.

"That's what I wanted you to see." He began waving his hand wildly. A young man stepped out of the cabin door on the bridge and waved back—a bit more controlled in his enthusiasm. "My son. You see? Family. That's who I am, what I am about. It's all about family or it's worth nothing."

I knew from my research that Penn was thrice divorced, but I didn't think that was the time to point this out.

"He's going out to sea in December? Is that wise?" The boat looked to be eighty feet long or more and was very solid-looking—if you had to be on the water in winter, I supposed that was the way to do it, but I could not imagine what emergency would cause me to make the attempt.

Penn was still waving, his face alive with almost tearful pride. "He and three buddies are taking the boat to Belize. They were all in his marine biology program at university, and they'll be doing research down there on the coral reefs." He gave a short bark of a laugh that might have been scornful or not. "Saving the world."

Two other young men came out on deck and waved to us. This time I joined in waving back.

"Four kids fresh out of college are taking that boat all the way down the East Coast and across the Caribbean in winter?" I thought I was allowed some incredulity.

"There's a full crew on board. And they can do big chunks of the trip inside—the Intracoastal Waterway. They're not babies. At their age I was running a copper mine in the mountains of Peru and fighting off Shining Path terrorists."

I had read the accounts. If they were not exaggerated by time and publicists, he had been a very brave young man, and very handy with an M16. At that age I had been starting grad school and my biggest fear was being called on in Professor Dietch's Advanced Accounting Seminar.

"So, is this scientific expedition connected with school?"

He gave me a look that held just a flash of anger. "No. You're missing the point. It's my gift to my son. The boat, the trip, the whole thing. The boat alone cost me eight mil. It'll cruise at nine knots and has a range of about two thousand miles. Of course, it burns twenty gallons of fuel an hour. Marine diesel. It's like burning a twenty-dollar bill every quarter of an hour. But it doesn't matter. It's family. I take care of my family. Do you have family, Jason?"

"I have a six-year-old son." And he had enough challenges in his life to face every day—he wouldn't need an eight-million-dollar boat.

"Then you understand. You can read all the stories about me and my wealth and how I got it and what I do with it, but if you don't see that I'm all about family, you don't know me. Clear?"

The boat continued past us and out between the jetties. Another young man joined the others and they all gave one final wave. There was a shift in the breeze, and the boat disappeared into the mist. Gray upon gray upon gray.

What was clear to me was that Charles Penn had enough money to buy his boy anything he wanted. I wasn't jealous or appalled. Or impressed. It was also clear to me that other messages had been delivered. That though this man was powerful enough to move metals markets around the world with not much more than a raised eyebrow, he had to prove to me that he could make me waste five hours driving the length of Long Island twice for an all-too-brief opportunity for him to flash his wealth at me.

"You have two other sons, don't you? What are they up to? Backpacking in Antarctica? Biking across the Sahara?"

Penn gave me a hard stare, giving nothing away, and then broke into a big grin. "I like you, Jason. We see life much the same way. We've both been on top and had to fight our way back up there after getting knocked down. We're going to get along." With that little speech he turned and walked quickly back to the car. He called back over his shoulder. "Set something up with my secretary for dinner sometime soon." He paused before closing the door. "We'll make it a long night. You ask me anything you want. We'll talk." He slammed the door and was gone, into the fog.

Wet snow mixed with rain—a wintry mix—was falling. The Kid had no hat, no gloves, and his black puffy jacket was open.

"Cold," he said.

"So can I zip you up?"

"No."

He took my hand and we crossed Broadway. He ran to the subway entrance. I thought about white sandy beaches and being so hot that I sweated while lying down.

We walked up to the head of the platform—I walked, he skipped—so that we could get the first car. The Kid liked riding in the first car with his face pressed up against the window of the door at the end, next to the engineer. He loved the exhilaration of watching the stations fly toward us and the sudden glimpses of the inside of the tunnels as we passed worklights. Sometimes we saw people down there. Track inspectors in their fluorescent vests or repair crews working under brilliant white lights.

"Still cold?"

He thought about it. "Yes."

"Express or local?"

"'Spress!"

The express got up to higher speeds, bypassing the Seventy-ninth and Eighty-sixth Street stations.

"So if you're cold, why don't we go someplace warm?"

He sensed a trap. "Why?"

"I'm thinking of nice warm sand under our feet, a blue cloudless sky overhead, the sun shining on our backs as we look out over turquoise waters."

A local train came out of the tunnel at the far end of the platform. The Kid covered his ears and opened his mouth in a silent scream. The train came to a stop and a young couple—German or Eastern European tourists, I judged by their bad haircuts—came out onto the platform. The Kid scurried over to my side. He did not trust having strangers close on the subway platform.

The young woman approached me, her companion hanging back with an expression of disdain on his face.

"Excuse me. We want to go to museum." Her accent was very pronounced.

The Kid kept behind my leg while gripping my pants in an iron grasp.

"Which museum do you want?"

She spoke rapidly to the young man, who answered in a mumbled whisper before handing her a small colorful brochure. She opened it and pointed.

I recognized the picture. The Museum of the American Indian. They were Germans.

"Ah," I said. "You are heading uptown. You need to go downtown." All the way downtown. As this information was met with blank stares, I tried demonstrating with big gestures accompanied by overly loud simple words. "Over. There. Down. Town."

The man was clueless. The woman got the gist of it, but pointed at the intervening sets of express tracks between the two platforms.

"Yes," I said. I felt like I was playing charades—and losing. I pointed up the stairs and then walked my two fingers across the space between us.

There was a map upstairs by the turnstiles. I could show them the stairs to the downtown tracks.

"Oh shit," I said, waving. "Follow me. Come on, Kid."

The Kid did not want to leave. "'Spress!" he shouted at me.

"Yes, I know. We'll be right back. Let's go."

"'Spress!" he wailed.

He was right. I could hear it. If we went upstairs and showed the tourists how to get down to Bowling Green, we would miss our uptown train.

The woman caught on. "Is okay. Is okay. Thank you, mister." She turned to leave.

The young man was staring down the tracks, watching the flickering light of the approaching train reflect off the station walls. The Kid peeked out around him and for a moment they were less than two feet apart. I was two steps away.

The man turned to follow his partner, and as he did he reached over and patted the Kid on the head. It was the kind of thoughtless but well-meant gesture that makes any parent's blood boil. It turned the Kid into a demon. He swung around and leaped forward—teeth-first.

Luck kept the man from a trip to the hospital. He was still turning when the Kid struck, and the Kid missed his target—the offending hand. I covered the two steps between us and lifted him up by the waist. He hated it. He kicked at me and scratched the back of my hand.

The young man turned and ran to the stairs where his companion was already mounting to the station above. She had missed the incident entirely.

I put the Kid back down as our train pulled in. He forgot his anger with me immediately and covered his ears.

"Let's go, my little tiger cub." I would not reprimand my son for attempting to bite someone who had no business touching him in the first place. Let them sue.

I got on the train and held the door. The Kid looked at the two-inch gap between train and platform, sucked in a deep breath, and leaped over it.

"That's my brave boy," I said.

18

Harvey Deeter called me from his private plane, en route to Dallas from Marathon, Ontario.

"And colder than my in-laws' hearts, son. Kee-rist, 'bout froze my pecker off. What is it you want to know? My secretary tells me you are a very dogged individual. She didn't say it quite so nicely, though."

"I work for Virgil Becker. I handle certain things for him or for his clients. You're on the board of one of those companies."

"Son, I'm on the board of more companies than my daddy's dogs' got fleas. Virgil, now. He's a bright young man. Not as smart as his daddy, but he's a lot more honest, and that counts for something fierce with me. He did mention you'd be calling, now I think about it."

Deeter impressed me as one of those men who need to be a bit slippery, no matter how inconsequential the subject. It kept them in practice for when it did matter. I decided to be as direct as possible. "What can you tell me about Arinna? Phil Haley?"

"Another bright boy, but he worries me time to time."

"Does he?"

"I put forty-two million dollars into his company. You better believe I keep an eye on what goes on where. You ever try to raise a raccoon kit? I mean as a pet?"

I was nineteen when I saw my first raccoon taking apart a trash can in back of the dorm at Cornell. "No."

"They're cuddly and they're smart. You put one in a cage and it will work at the latch until it figures out how to open it. You got two of them? One will teach the other. Put it back in the same cage a year later, and it will remember. It'll have that door open in seconds. That's no lie."

Report from Animal Planet. "I didn't know that."

"But then one day it'll turn on you. Biting, scratching. Don't you leave one in a room with a baby in it. They can't be trusted."

"I see. This is an allegory. You believe that Phil Haley can't be trusted. Is that what you're saying?"

"I'm just saying, you try to domesticate a wild animal and you'll get bit. He's a southern boy, though you'd never know it. Lowcountry white trash, of course, but just like the Apostle Peter, he'll deny it 'til the cock crows. Never trust a man who's not comfortable with his roots, Mr. Stafford. You're a New Yorker, aren't you?"

"Born in Queens," I said.

"Mets fan?"

"No. Yankees. Like my father."

"Ho! I bet you got your share of ass-whuppin's growing up."

I ran, but I didn't feel any need to share that information with him. "Do you invest in other alternative energy projects? Is this diversification for you?"

"Not many. There's too many tree huggers out there looking to do something good for the world. If I want to do something for the family of man, I put a little extra in the collection box at church."

"So why go with Arinna? If he wins, he means to put you out of business, doesn't he?"

"Let me tell you something. There's more awl under the ice in Antarctica than all the awl we've ever taken out of the ground. So why don't we just go after it?"

"Isn't there some international treaty about not exploiting the continent?"

"Oh, piss on that. You ask my great-great-granddaddy about treaties, son. He was a full-blood Choctaw. Treaties get *mah-dified*." He stretched the word out to extract every drop of irony. "No. The reason is engineering. No engineer living has figured out a way to extract crude from underneath a mile-high pile of ice. Engineering. That's what I invest in. Not awl. Engineering. That's my business. This fella Haley is one smart engineer and he's got a lot of other smart folks working with him. That's where I put my money."

"Do you think he shorted the company stock?"

"I do not. I think that what that's about is someone taking him down a notch. The man is not tame, but neither is he stupid. He knows which way to run when the rabbit breaks."

"Any thoughts on who would set him up that way?"

"I had a dog one time—a mutt. Part hound, maybe. He didn't hunt, he didn't fetch, he barely answered to his name. My older brother called him 'Stupid.' But no matter what room he was in, that dog would always find the warmest spot in winter, or the one spot with a nice draft in summer."

If this was another allegory, it was well beyond my abilities to discern its meaning. He went on. "It's a sneaky way of getting at Haley, isn't it? He told me it was the Chinese government did it. Could be. Spies and secret codes and all that. Hackers. But, no. I'm not worried, though. Something'll come along and make this all go away. I'd bet my last dollar on it."

19

Saturday night. It had been a long day. The Kid had been offsides from the moment he woke up. Breakfast was a disaster because the last two eggs in the refrigerator had tiny dark dots in the yoke and were, therefore, inedible as far as the Kid was concerned. I took him across the street to the Greek coffee shop we frequented on Sunday mornings, and he had a meltdown. It took me ten minutes to persuade him that it was all right, we could have scrambled eggs there on Saturday, and still come back for French toast on Sunday. So we were late for his yoga class. Not by much, but just enough. Rather than simply join in with the rest of the class, the Kid had to start exactly the way he always did, progressing through the usual regimen. It was a little like watching a movie on a broken DVD player. He sped through some exercises and faltered through others, always a move or two behind the class. His anxiety crescendoed as they approached the newer movements—the ones he did not know as well. And though the teaching assistants did their best to help him relax, he did not trust them, so by the time the class reached the final point of total relaxation, the Kid was fidgeting angrily and kicking his heels against the floor. He refused to get up off his mat when they were done and I had to rescue him.

"Let's go, son. There'll be other days."

He whimpered, whispered something.

"Sorry, Kid. Say again?"

"Bed."

"You want to go to bed?"

He nodded, rolled away, and hugged his knees to his chest.

"If that's what you want, it's okay by me. But one step at a time, okay? First we get up and get ready to leave. Let's go. Roll up your mat."

He got up, but he showed his defiance by not rolling up the mat. He walked toward the double gym doors with his head down, his shoulders hunched, and his feet dragging, looking just like A-Rod after getting picked off trying to steal second with one out and Gardner at the plate. I grabbed the mat and followed him out.

I let him get a few steps ahead of me as we negotiated the crowd in front of Fairway—when did double-wide strollers become the norm in my neighborhood?—and I was still catching up when he stepped off the curb onto Seventy-fourth Street.

"No!" I leaped across the intervening space, grabbed his hand, and jerked him back to the sidewalk.

He reacted predictably. He dug his fingernails into the back of my hand and clawed at me with the ferocity of a trapped wolverine. Though he failed to draw blood—Heather and I kept his fingernails well-trimmed for just such exigencies—his actions did draw the attention of a heavyset, white-haired man with a cane who told me, "If that were my boy, I'd put him right over my knee."

I added this bit of advice to the mental file STUPID THINGS PEOPLE SAY THAT I SIMPLY NEED TO IGNORE, and focused on the Kid. If I were ever foolish enough to resort to corporal punishment, I would lose his trust forever. And I was afraid that if I ever tried "putting him over my knee," he would bite a hole in my thigh.

"That was bad, Kid. You know that. No walking in the street alone. You need to take my hand." He had not made that mistake in a very long time. Months. It scared me. He had come so far in such a short time. Could he slip back into his unresponsive, undisciplined shell of indifference just as easily?

He pulled his hand free of my grip. "'Kay," he yelled at me.

I let him have his moment of defiant defeat. Behind him a woman pushed her stroller—a single—a bit too close to him. The passenger—a bundled-up toddler wearing ankle-high Timberland boots—was swinging his well-shod feet in a bored manner and managed to connect with the back of my son's leg.

The Kid was a New Yorker. He was used to being jostled on the street at times. He hated it, as we all do, and a lot more than most of us. But he had learned to take it in stride. He attended a school where almost every student dealt with issues of physical coordination. He no longer blindly reacted when something like that happened.

But it was not a typical day. The Kid whirled around, his jaw snapping, teeth bared, growling like a much larger wild animal. The woman, an overdressed and over-accessorized young mother—and when did women under thirty in my neighborhood begin wearing full makeup to go grocery shopping on Saturday morning?—screamed and fell backward, tripping over her own three-inch-heeled boots. The toddler continued to kick desultorily, apparently unfazed by my son's threats of attack. I grabbed the Kid by the collar of his jacket, lifted him off the ground, and swung him away.

"Home. Now!" I marched him into the street, simultaneously checking for traffic and calling "Sorry" over my shoulder, while the Kid tried unsuccessfully to twist his head around far enough to bite me.

The rest of the day was quiet. An uneasy truce kept the two of us from communicating in more than grunts and monosyllables. I was stretched just far enough that I had no wish for any further confrontation, and no energy to repair the rifts of the morning. Lunch came and went. The Kid didn't eat. He decided that he didn't want to take a nap, so he commandeered my seat—the sprung, torn leather easy chair facing the window and Broadway—where he looked at car books until he fell asleep just before Skeli was due for dinner. But Skeli called at the last minute to say that she was still downtown and would it be terrible if she canceled on me?

I bit back my disappointment, made sufficient soothing noises, and poured myself a tall vodka on the rocks. If I'd added a few olives, I could've called it dinner. An hour later I considered making another, and almost did so, stopping myself at the last minute and pouring a glass of water instead.

My laptop was sitting on the dining room table, humming contentedly, the Firefox main page open and empty. I stood over it, sipping the water, until I found myself typing *Deeter* into the search box.

Despite the down-home, aw-shucks accents and colloquialisms, Harvey Deeter was a Rhodes scholar who had graduated second in his class from UPenn with a degree in geological engineering. He spent his two years at Oxford studying chemistry, returning home to take a field management trainee position with his father's wildcatting company. Eight years later, his father nearly died of a stroke and passed the reins to his son. The firm's leases, holdings, and operations were then estimated to be worth somewhere in the high eight figures. He had grown the company and taken it public while maintaining a majority interest. His shares were now worth enough to keep him in the top twenty on *Forbes'* list of billionaires. The public persona of having raised himself up from West Texan hardscrabble was a carefully crafted fiction. His success in building one of the world's most profitable energy development companies was still impressive, you merely had to take into account that he'd had a ninety-million-dollar head start.

Beyond that, there were few surprises. He contributed to political campaigns on both sides of the aisle, as long as those public servants voted with Big Oil, but otherwise kept his political opinions to himself. He was also a very large donor to a high-profile, nonprofit research facility, whose sole purpose seemed to be to argue loudly whenever and wherever possible that global warming was unproven, and even if it did exist, it was not caused by man but by regular cycles in the planet's climate. As the think tank's list of donors included every major oil company in the world, I did not fault Deeter for this bit of scientific dishonesty. It was just part of the job.

I poured myself another glass of water and considered putting the Kid to bed. I wasn't ready for another face-off, but it wasn't going to get any better if I waited. On the other hand, it wasn't going to be any worse. I went back to the computer.

NEQUISS <enter>

The screen went to black.

This had happened before. The power cord sometimes needed a hard push, or else the jack wouldn't set in place correctly. I could run the machine until the battery gave out, but then it would shut down without warning.

I removed the jack and replaced it. Nothing happened. Again, this was not a surprise. If the battery was too depleted, I needed to charge it for a few minutes—or as much as ten minutes—before it reached liftoff. I took the battery out and put it back in. Sometimes that worked. It didn't that time, but I felt good about following the ritual.

The Kid gave a long dreamy sigh. I set the laptop on the table and went over to him. He was still sound asleep, but his beautiful face was twisting into various cartoonish expressions of unhappiness. I dreaded interfering with whatever demons had him at that moment—he was as likely to side with the demons as with me—but I knew that I could help. I got a spare sheet out of the linen closet and carefully wrapped it around him. With each wrap, I pulled it tighter. The pressure helped him for some reason. I didn't understand it, I simply accepted that sometimes it worked. The grimaces went away and his face muscles went slack. I lifted him gently and put him in bed.

His features were all his mother's, but I only saw the relationship when he was asleep. When he was awake, I was always fully aware that he was himself and entirely unique. Only in the middle of the night, sometimes after a drink or two, did I see her face in his. And the guilt and pain came back.

I poured another glass of vodka. It was late enough, it no longer mattered if I was in fighting trim. My computer was up again, the screen lit. Beneath the search window there was one line of script.

(0) results for NEQUISS

I tried a search on Bing. Same result. Google. The same. McKenna seemed to have created the greatest stealth company the world had ever known—or he was lying. I didn't think he was lying. A third possibility occurred to me—that NEQUISS had ceased to exist. How difficult would it be for a government body to purge any mention of a company from the Internet? The fourth possibility only came to me later that night.

The alcohol started to hit, taking the rough edges off my world. I would worry about NEQUISS, Haley, Virgil, and all the rest of it another time. I typed in the words *Vacation Rentals Beachfront Costa Rica*. I spent the next hour fantasizing about Skeli, the Kid, and me staying in one rain-forest, treetop, ocean-view, extravagant mansion after another. Vacation porn. It brought me no closer to actually booking somewhere for us to escape to over the next few weeks, but for an hour I indulged myself with harmless waking dreams. I never finished the glass of vodka. I fell asleep in my chair, the last website still open, showing a place in Hawaii where children on the spectrum could swim with dolphins. Dolphin therapy. I heard myself chuckle as I drifted off. What the hell, even if it had no therapeutic value whatsoever, the Kid would have a ball.

There was someone in the room with me. An intruder. Had I dreamt it? I opened my eyes. The computer was still lit, so I hadn't slept long. The energy saver was set for fifteen minutes and the screen would have shut off. I got up and checked the Kid's room. He was fast asleep, the sheet I had wrapped him in was partially kicked away. He looked like an angelic version of a mummy. There was no one else there.

I cased the rest of the apartment. I checked the lock on the front door. I opened closet doors and made sure that the windows were closed. Nothing was amiss. But still I could not shake the feeling.

The kitchen clock read 3:18. No wonder my back ached; I'd been asleep in that chair for almost five hours. I went into the bathroom and brushed my teeth. I turned off lights and went to bed. I had just placed one bare foot back on the floor and was about to remove the sock from the other when it hit me. My computer screen was still on. And it was active. After five hours.

I got up and went to the table. Images were flickering across the screen. Sites I had visited. Pictures and files from my documents folder. The cursor was jumping back and forth, clicking on buttons and opening new sites and private folders. The machine was possessed.

I was being hacked. Someone was inside my computer and examining every aspect of my life.

Scared. Vulnerable. Mad. Naked. Violated. Mad. Panicking. Mad. Mad. Mad.

I fought for control. The hacker was opening my bank account. I hit the power button. No response. I tried typing. Nothing. The drive was not responding to the board. I pushed my panic back down and tried to think.

The modem. I rushed across the living room to the space on the shelves where once there had been a television set. The cable wire was there with the modem and router. I pulled the power cord out, then detached all the wires, just for completeness, knowing that it was unnecessary, but unable to stop myself. I wanted to kill whatever it was that had entered my space. My digital space.

The computer screen was still. I moved the mouse. The cursor answered. I closed the Firefox window and a pop-up informed me that I was no longer accessing the Internet. I shut the whole thing down. A moment later, the screen went to black accompanied by the sound of someone popping their cheek with a finger.

The computer was no longer an evil entity, it was simply dirty, defiled. I'd buy a new one in the morning and begin the annoying and arduous business of re-creating the more organized aspects of my life. I made a mental list of calls I would need to make—to the bank, credit card companies, everyone in my address book.

McKenna. I needed to warn him. The number Spud had given me to contact him was compromised. He had to get rid of it.

"You have reached the offices of Information Studies outside of normal business hours. Please call back between ten and four, Monday through Friday. If you wish to leave a message for Lydia Sharp, please press one at the prompt."

I pressed one.

"Ms. Sharp. This is Jason. This number is no longer safe. Please contact me when you can."

McKenna would understand. So would anyone pursuing either of us. All I had really gained with being circumspect was a juvenile level of deniability. I tossed the phone across the room.

I sat and stared at the laptop, wishing it gone and out of my house. I could spend the day getting drive-wiping software, saving all my sensitive files to a CD, cleaning the computer, and reloading the entire operating system and still have a computer I would not be able to trust. Or, I could take a sturdy screwdriver and bust the thing up into component parts and feed them to the incinerator. There was a good screwdriver in one of the kitchen drawers.

20

Skeli and I were sharing a precious hour together. Such hours were available to us less often, as I struggled with the Kid, and Skeli's Total Wellness clinic took as much time from her life as she permitted—and then some. We had taken to meeting at an anonymous little bar in the neighborhood—the Emerald Inn, recently relocated to the space that had once been the All-State Café—and what it lacked in romantic milieu it made up for in privacy. It was habituated by solitary drinkers, their eyes on the TV or the *Post,* and some neighborhood regulars who came for the hamburger special. It was close to, but just far enough from, our regular haunt that we had a low probability of running into anyone we knew.

"You're back to drinking beer," she said. "Does that mean this case you're working is going well?"

"Not necessarily?" It was my first beer all week, since I had started working out. I would greatly have preferred that Skeli notice the awesome improvement of my physique than which poison I was pouring into the temple of my body.

"I have noticed that when you need to shed stress, you drink vodka. Otherwise you barely drink at all."

A fair assessment—and the last few months I had been "going clear" more often than not.

"I'm beginning to believe that the rich are different than us. They're more nuts. Maybe money chips away at their inhibitions. They can afford not to have them."

"Virgil's not like that."

"No. Virgil is so sane he's scary. But Virgil's not in the same league as these people. He works for a living. Mrs. Haley's idea of work is showing up for a board meeting. She seems totally indifferent to the fact that her husband may go to prison and their business could go right down the tube."

"Maybe she thinks she can buy him out of trouble."

"Not a long-term winning strategy. And these others? One likes pretending he's sitting around the cracker barrel sipping moonshine and the other made me kill half a day just to demonstrate that he's some kind of family man. Hell, you could say Saddam Hussein was a family guy—both his sons worked in the business. One was in charge of murder, the other ran torture."

"You're not in danger, are you?"

"Me? No. That was a bad comparison. Sorry. I'm just feeling frustrated. The sanest one I've talked to so far is Haley, and he believes he's going to walk away from this for the simple reason that he's innocent. And as soon as he gets his chance to tell people that, it will all be settled."

I looked up. The bartender was doing his best to pretend he wasn't eavesdropping. His best wasn't good enough.

"Do you have any peanuts?" Skeli seemed to burn calories at the same rate as a platoon of marines. She was always hungry, and always in perfect shape.

The denizens all gave her a look of mild surprise, as though the idea of actually consuming a salted nut while sipping a beer had never occurred to any of them.

The bartender pried the plastic lid off a gallon-sized metal can and poured a few grams of peanuts into a rocks glass. He placed it in front of us. "You ready for another?" he said, squinting at me in what might or might not have been a disagreeable manner.

I had finished half of my lite beer. Skeli had taken two sips of her white wine. I wondered if we were not maintaining the correct pace for drinking at his bar.

"Not just yet," I said, sliding a twenty across to pay for the first round. He took it, smoothed it over the rounded edge of the rail on his side, and retreated to the register.

"You know," I began as soon as our privacy was restored, "if we are going to have a child, we need to spend more time actually making one." I found that the thought of making love without any form of birth control was joyously erotic.

"I know. But we're both incredibly busy."

"True. But—"

"Somehow I get the feeling that this conversation has more to do with libido than with babies."

"Unfair!" I cried. "I want time to recite poetry in your ear, while massaging warm, scented oil into your aching feet and feeding you chocolate-covered strawberries."

"All at the same time? You're a wonder. But how will the baby benefit?"

"We're talking chocolate here. How can you even ask?"

"Well, don't get the massage oil on the strawberries. I hate that."

"I'm afraid that you are not taking the problem seriously."

Skeli choked on her wine while stifling a laugh. "All right. I'll give you a choice. You can take me back to your place"—she checked her watch—"for twenty minutes of naked, or near-naked, intimacy, or you can take me to that Chinese-Latino place where the Kid doused me with a plate full of ketchup last year, and buy me an order of that crackling chicken salad."

"Can we get the chicken to go?"

"I don't think I've got that much self-control."

"Twenty minutes?" If she agreed to forty, we had a chance to accomplish both dinner and—

"I'm meeting Debra, the lighting designer, at seven. She's giving up a cooking demonstration to meet me. 'Mushrooms Make Romance—Light His Fire with Shiitakes.' She made a point of telling me all about it."

There was a sudden blast of cold air as the door opened. Everyone at the bar turned and gave the intruders an unwelcoming hard stare.

Roger and Savannah came in, shedding warm coats and knit hats, and bringing with them a hint of the freezing weather outside.

"How ya doin'?" Roger greeted us.

"This can't be coincidence. How did you find us?" Two minutes later and we would have been out the door.

"And nice to see you, too. I hear you already met Savannah. My new assistant."

"At the gym," I said, still hoping that someone would comment on my one-week results. "Hello, Savannah."

"Hey."

Skeli and Savannah touched cheeks.

"My god, you are cold," Skeli said. "Let's get something to warm you up. How about an Irish coffee?"

Savannah shook her head. "Diet Coke. With a lemon."

Roger gave a *What can you do with these kids today* shrug. "She's branching out. Usually she only drinks Tab."

The bartender placed a Rémy in a mini snifter on the bar and Roger took a deep draught.

"How did you know we'd be here?" I asked. The moment where

I got to say *We're just leaving* had never arrived, or if it had, I had missed it.

"PaJohn told me."

PaJohn was another member of the regular crowd at our usual watering hole. I thought of asking how he knew where Skeli and I were meeting in private, but gave up. New York is a very small town sometimes.

"What's wrong with Tab?" Skeli asked.

"Who drinks Tab?" Roger scoffed.

"Me, for one. Well, not anymore, but back when I was dancing. I didn't just count calories, I parsed them out like they were gold bars."

"Where do you buy Tab?" I said.

The three of them looked at me like I had just started speaking in tongues.

Roger answered. "Whaddya talking? This is New York."

"They still sell it? In stores? I haven't seen a can of Tab in twenty years. Thirty. More."

"'In stores'? Of course in stores. Whaddya think? They sell it off the back of a truck out on Highway Nine?"

"Don't tell me you drink it?"

"*Pff.* Stuff is poison, you ask me." He swallowed another half ounce of cognac.

Roger was short enough, or Savannah was tall enough, that when they stood too near each other, her magnificent breasts were just above his eye level, which caused his eyebrows to twitch furiously. I'm sure it worked well in the act, but in private it was a constant distraction.

"Roger, pull up a barstool and sit. Your eyebrows are going to fly off your face in a minute."

He gave a final leer and sat next to Skeli. Savannah sat down next to me.

I did not leer. "As I've often said. He's my friend, but he is an acquired taste." I had not run into her at the gym again all week. My schedule could be best described as erratic.

"I don't mind him. I thought this was just a job, you know? It's easy money and it'll pay for my acting classes. But I'm learning so much. The guy has incredible timing. Brilliant. And great delivery. He gets a laugh and immediately tops himself. I've seen him lay out four toppers in a row, keeping the single laugh going until people are almost hurting. He's a pro."

Savannah was something of a surprise. Her blond good looks combined with her physique made one assume she was a total air-head. I had not made all the connections in her past until Skeli had pointed out the fact that "interning in the theater program at A.R.T. in Cambridge, Massachusetts," meant that she had been attending Harvard University at the time.

"You're working your way into the act?"

She shrugged, already all talked out on the subject. "Roger said you were on Wall Street."

"Yup."

"So was my father."

"He's not there now?"

"He walked away. He says he escaped."

"It's not for everybody," I said.

"Roger said you went to prison."

Roger had a big mouth. "Yup. What does your father do now?"

"Plays a round of golf and then drinks expensive scotch until he falls asleep."

"Hmm. The sleeping part sounds good," I said.

"You don't golf?"

"I have enough bad habits."

She laughed. It was more polite than amused, but I gave her points for diplomacy. "Roger says you're a 'fixer.'"

"Sometimes I find things. Other times I uncover things. I like to think I help people."

"On Wall Street?"

"It's the world I know."

"What have you found lately?" she said.

A missing billion dollars. "Right now I'm trying to save the planet."

"So you're a superhero."

"I'm trying to keep somebody out of jail so he can finish creating the next green revolution—in energy."

She nodded. "Solar something?"

"Solar, yes, I guess. It's all about algae."

"Algae? Nope. It doesn't work. Biofuels from algae release more carbon dioxide than the algae takes out of the air. You get fuel, but you don't get sustainability."

She was so sure of herself. Did Harvard instill that or did you need it to get there? "Sustainability," I said, letting the word roll out syllable by syllable.

"Sustainability," she repeated. "I took a course in it. It was a soft science credit. All the English majors and drama majors took it."

I was glad to hear that one of America's finest universities still provided a rounded educational experience, even to drama majors. "Then you're way ahead of me. Say what you said again. Or different."

"Algae needs water, sunlight, and carbon dioxide to grow. That's good. It takes carbon dioxide out of the atmosphere. Like a baby rain forest."

"But?"

"But when you turn it into fuel and burn it, it puts more CO2 back into the atmosphere than it took out in the first place. Lots more."

"How does that work?"

"How does what work?"

"How can it be negatively efficient? Doesn't that violate some law of conservation of matter or something?"

"How do I know? It was science for theater majors, for the love of Pete. I took it pass-fail."

"Suppose you could turn that around? Create a fuel that really was efficient that way."

"It would be like turning carbon into gold."

"The client claims to have done it."

"Really? Who's this?"

I saw no harm in telling her. If it was already on the front page of the *Journal*, it wasn't exactly private. "A company called Arinna."

She shrugged again and shook her head.

"Philip Haley is the CEO."

She laughed. "Philip Haley? Are you kidding?"

"You've heard of him?"

"If it's the same guy, everybody has." She took an iPad out of a leather shoulder bag the size of a pillowcase and tapped at the screen for a minute. "Same guy?" she said, turning the screen so that I could see it.

It was the same guy. But the guy that I'd met had been wearing his tie around his neck rather than around his forehead and he had not been guzzling from a bottle of Dom Pérignon. The picture was at least two years old. Philip Haley, a married man, a successful businessman, and something of a genius in the field of genetics according to the caption, had been the paparazzi's Man of the Month.

She tapped again and swiped her finger a couple of times. "Here you go."

It was embarrassing to look at. Haley out and about, getting his picture taken while leaving various New York and L.A. clubs, always with a different, and much younger, woman on his arm. I scrolled through shots from all the scandal sheets and celebrity magazines. It was a midlife crisis acted out on an operatic scale. All the pictures were from the same period.

"Where did you find this stuff?" I said.

"This is all real old—like two years ago. He was all over the tabloids."

Of course. I had searched the financial press and the mainstream media. Savannah had gone straight for the dirt.

"I'm an idiot," I said. "I missed all of this."

"Keep going," she said.

Phil the Party Boy came to an abrupt end on the next few pages.

Philip Haley was named as the "mystery man" in the breakup of Hollywood's sweetheart couple, LeJo—LeMar Tilles and Jolene Harris. As kids, they had played next-door neighbors with a mutual kiddie crush on the Disney Channel's most popular show. Twenty years and two perfect children later, they could still guarantee two hundred fifty million dollars in worldwide first-run ticket sales on a remake of *Beach Blanket Bingo*. There were pics of Jo and Haley kissing on a beach in Eleuthera, holding hands across a table in South Beach, Haley helping her out of a limo in Paris. And no sooner did Jolene serve papers on LeMar and move out of the mansion two doors down from Oprah, than the "baby bump" pictures began showing up. They went on for a month or so until the player announced that he was returning to his wife in New York. Much farther down in one of the articles, it was mentioned that the wife was the single largest shareholder in Arinna.

Jolene went into seclusion and "lost" the baby.

"He's a creep!" I said.

"Who's that?" Skeli asked, turning from her conversation with Roger.

"Haley. He's every bit as nuts as the rest of them."

"You don't remember any of this?" Savannah asked.

Two years before, I had been in prison. The reading matter had been strictly limited. What was truly frustrating was that, in all my Internet research on Haley, I had ignored the scandal sheets and thereby missed the more revealing story.

"No. And how come you remember it so well?" I asked.

"I was a junior in college. I ate this stuff up."

"Thank god for the free press." I scrolled through more of the noxious headlines. "And what the hell was this Jolene thinking?"

"I'd say that thinking had very little to do with it."

21

I woke from a recurring dream—the one where I have to go back to prison—and knowing that I wasn't going to get back to sleep until the adrenaline rush subsided, I got up for a glass of water. New York may be the city that never sleeps, but Broadway at three in the morning, midweek, looks at least a bit drowsy.

Philip Haley was not a nice man. But that didn't make him a criminal. And what did I care if another man was unfaithful to his wife. It wasn't jealousy. It wasn't anger or regret over my first wife's infidelity. No, it just indicated that the man was not entirely reliable. That what you see might not be exactly what you get. Deeter was right. Haley may have been brilliant, but it was best not to be blinded by the glare of his self-assurance.

I rinsed the glass and put it in the dishwasher. Carolina, our invaluable undocumented housecleaner from Central America, emptied the dishwasher whenever she came—that was once a week. Who emptied the damn thing the rest of the week? I couldn't remember the last time that I had done it. If ever. Or did the Kid and I use only one load's worth of dishes in a week? I doubted that Heather, the Kid's justifiably expensive shadow, would have done it, but maybe I wasn't giving her enough credit. I was too much a coward ever to ask her, however. Suppose she had been doing it and stopped when I asked?

The soft glow of reflected light from the Kid's bedroom ceiling gave his pale face and hair an elfin glow. I was struck again, for the hundredth or thousandth time, how much he resembled his mother. He was beautiful. He might transition into handsome at some point, but I thought a bit of androgyny would always be retained in his features. Middle-school girls would go nuts for him. In high school, there was a good chance he would be picked on. In college, he would be dangerous—killer. He'd have coeds, grad students, MILFs, and cougars all lined up to stare into those perfect blue eyes.

Of course, first he would have to learn that it was okay to be touched. One step at a time.

It was all right to dream for a bit. Dreams weren't all bad. I lived with the reality all day, every day.

I thought of Mrs. Stewart from the eleventh floor who, whenever we got on the elevator with her, stood as far from us as possible, as though the Kid were contagious, and always managed to say something so back-assed rude, in the kindest way, that I congratulated myself each time for not murdering her.

"But he's *sooo* cute, you would never know."

My son was not cute. Beautiful, yes. Cute was like that round-faced kid on the Oscar Mayer wiener commercial. Cute was approachable. It was not the monster who, in the time it took me to go to the bathroom, managed to climb up the front of the bookcase and bring the whole thing down on top of himself, transforming an antique sake set of near museum quality into porcelain gravel. By some miracle the Kid had not earned as much as a scratch in the process. Cute does not bite when told to eat some green vegetable. Cute does not wet himself in a diner rather than use the facilities, because the bathroom is "icky," the state of which he somehow knows even though he's never been in one. I wasn't complaining. I applauded my son's growing ability to engage the world and make decisions about his wants and needs. His life was going to be hard, much harder than mine, and he would need to be strong. But some days I did wish that it was all just a bit easier.

I went to the bathroom, relieved myself, and as I was washing my hands I noticed that all of the toothbrushes had been removed from the plastic cup that always sat just to the right of the cold water faucet. Someone had laid them carefully on a hand towel on the side of the low cabinet that held spare toilet paper, cleaning supplies, and other necessaries. The Kid's four brushes, variously colored to match his specific outfits for that day; my two brushes, because I could never throw away an old one until I had well-broken in a new one; and Skeli's single bright red toothbrush that could never be mistaken for anyone else's.

My first instinct was to check to see if the brushes were wet, as if they had possibly fallen into the toilet and been rescued. Only the Kid's black one and my new one were even slightly damp. So at some point, after I had brushed my teeth and gone to bed, some person had come into the bathroom and taken the brushes out of the cup and laid them out very carefully.

Where was the cup? The mystery of who had done this might be revealed if I had the cup. I looked around. No sign of it at eye level—at adult level. I looked around as though at a diminutive six-year-old's level. Success. The cup was on the floor between the toilet and the tub, tucked back and hidden by the curve of the bowl.

I reached down and realized that it was almost full of liquid. I picked it up and sniffed. Urine. It appeared that my son was now saving his piss. My little Howard Hughes. I imagined a closet full of mason jars, each holding a quart of this golden liquid.

That was the moment when the television sitcom dad would smile ruefully at the outraged sitcom mom and say, "I'm sure there's a perfectly logical explanation for this." Not in my world.

I poured the urine into the toilet and flushed. There might be recriminations for this in the morning, or it might all be forgotten. Who knew? Each day was different. I rinsed the cup and placed it in the dishwasher.

I went back to bed.

22

The first sneeze took me by surprise. I turned my head to the side and exploded. I had a cold.

One of the odd advantages of being the parent of a germophobic, asocial child is that one misses many of the colds and viruses that plague nursery and elementary schools, traveling through whole families with the speed and chaos, if not the full destructive power, of a hail of bullets. This can lead to a myopic sense of invulnerability. As other parents coughed into elbows or rubbed at chapped red noses, I maintained a smug aloofness. My son and I did not get colds. Usually.

I had no time for a cold.

An hour later, my cell phone rang.

"Hello," I croaked. I was wrapped in a down comforter, lying on the living room couch with a cooling cup of jasmine tea on the end table. I wished that I had a television. The Kid and I had now survived sixteen months without one and I was long rid of any withdrawal symptoms, but there is something about being home alone and sick that demands a *Law & Order: SVU* marathon.

"Jason Stafford?"

"Hello, Ms. Sharp. I recognize your voice."

"I barely recognize yours. Are you all right?"

"It's a cold."

"Can you meet with Dr. McKenna?"

"Today?" I tried to keep the reluctance out of my voice. Penn had agreed to meet me for dinner in Florida if I could make it. I had a miserable cold and a three o'clock flight to catch.

"If you can."

"Where and when?"

"Noon. The Starbucks at Astor Place."

I didn't like the Starbucks at Astor Place. Usually, I don't develop strong likes or dislikes for something as inconsequential as a coffee bar, but both the staff and the clientele there were too tribal, too insular for my tastes. The customers were all either overprivileged NYU students with serious entitlement issues busy cutting class, or wannabe authors nursing a single coffee all day long and ultra-protective of their usual stool and place along the window. The real authors were always over at the Second Avenue store, and the less idle NYU students grabbed their mocha lattes at Washington Square, where it was possible to place an order and get it within a reasonable amount of time. Astor Place got all the losers.

I took the express down to Forty-second and switched to the R train. Door-to-door, I was at Astor Place in just over twelve minutes. How could I ever live anywhere other than New York?

A tall, thin bald man in a long black puffy nylon parka was coming down the wrong side of the street on one of those blue bikes the city provided, yelling at the pedestrians in the crosswalk to "Clear aside! Clear aside! Coming through!" Sometimes I just hated New York City.

"I'd like a tall green tea."

"Latte?" She made it sound like a requirement.

"No, just a tall green tea."

"Small? You'll have to speak up."

"Tall." I raised my voice as much as I was able and tried to pack as much displeasure into the single word as I could.

"Two-seventy."

I gave her three singles. She handed me my change. A quarter and a nickel. I put the nickel in the tip jar. My phone rang before my drink arrived.

"A change in plans. I need to see if you're being followed. Go outside and walk down Waverly to the park. I'll follow you to check for tails. When we get to the park, take a seat and wait. I'll go on and you check for anyone following me."

He was gone before I had time to respond.

I did not want to play *I Spy* in Washington Square. I did not want to change plans. I wanted to be back home, sipping my own green tea, wrapped in a blanket, saving up my energy for the flight to Florida that afternoon.

The baristas were backed up—or just slow. My tea wasn't ready yet. I abandoned it and walked back out into the cold. Across the street were a drugstore and a gym. There used to be a bookstore there. My city was dying. Watching for wrong-way riders on blue bikes, I crossed over and walked west, down to the corner of Broadway. I managed not to look over my shoulder.

The first bench in the park was empty. Most of the benches were empty. Those that weren't were occupied by homeless men and women all dressed in shades of gray. It wasn't the kind of day to hang out in the park. I was wearing a full-length camel's hair overcoat from Burberry, a little tight in the shoulders and more than comfortably loose around my middle, a relic from my pre-prison days. It had the hidden buttons and the shallow V profile, and with it I wore a paisley silk-wool blend scarf that Skeli had picked out for me. I couldn't have been any less conspicuous if I had set myself on fire.

I almost greeted McKenna as he walked past, head down, hands jammed into coat pockets, the wind whipping his ponytail. I didn't think I was suited for this kind of work. I let McKenna get to the middle of the park before I stood up. Then I sat back down.

A man in his early forties, dressed in layers of sweatshirts, a down vest, jeans, and workboots walked by speaking into his sleeve. A pale beige wire ran from a small device in his ear down inside his collar. His jeans were worn but not stained. The workboots were new. I let him pass and waited. Seconds later, a second man, outfitted by the same tailor, ran across the intersection and down University.

I couldn't see McKenna anymore. I pulled up Recent Calls and rang him.

"Where are you?" he hissed.

"Still here on the bench. You have two men following you." My mouth was suddenly very dry.

"Where?"

"One is coming through the park. The other was hustling down University to take the long way 'round."

"The construction workers?"

"You've seen them before?"

"Yeah. Not a problem. Cross the park and meet me at the library in ten minutes. Wait inside the main doors."

It didn't seem to be the time to tell him that I had a plane to catch. I checked my watch. As long as I was in a cab to the airport in less than forty-five minutes, I was fine. I walked to the library. I went inside, blew my nose, and watched the park across the street.

Five minutes later, McKenna ran out onto the sidewalk facing Fourth Street, screaming and waving his arms. He looked like a raving lunatic in the midst of a mental seizure, a picture not that unusual in Washington Square Park. He looked around wildly and ran toward University Place, plowing into and knocking down the faux construction worker waiting for him on the corner. McKenna was up first and darted through traffic across the street. For a big man, he could move. He sprinted down the sidewalk next to the library and disappeared.

The tail picked himself up and yelled something into his sleeve. A split second later, the second man ran down the path from the Garibaldi statue. I watched a dumb show of recriminations, denials of responsibility, and the exchange of very little information—the first man pointed in the direction in which McKenna had run. They were still exchanging last-gasp accusations when a black car pulled to the curb beside them. A black Crown Victoria with no decorative trim and a nonmetallic paint job. Standard government issue. It couldn't have been more identifiable if it had "FBI" on the side in white eighteen-inch block letters. Then a second came up behind it, swerving to the right to block traffic. Two men in suits jumped out of the back and began running after McKenna, though he was already out of sight. He had a team of eight FBI agents tailing him. The two construction workers hopped into the back of the second Crown Vic and the two cars raced toward Mercer Street—the first place to make a right.

McKenna walked in the door of the library a minute later, coming up West Fourth Street from the other direction. He wasn't even winded.

"Here, take this," he said, handing me a thin plastic card.

It was a student ID for one Amanda Blair. Amanda was round-faced, sad-looking, and had long black hair parted in the middle.

"What do I do with this?"

"It gets you past security."

"Where did you get this?" I said.

"Guys sell them in the park. They steal purses, or find them. Let's go."

"Do you realize that you have a full team of FBI agents following you? I just saw eight with two cars."

"Yeah."

"This doesn't terrify you?"

"It did at first. But they're watching me, not arresting me. They found me at a flophouse over on East Third Street, so I don't stay there anymore, but I still pay for the room. When I want to take them out for some exercise, I walk around First Avenue or Alphabet City until I pick up a tail. That way they think I'm still downtown all the time."

McKenna walked in front of me, gave a salute to the two security guards behind the desk, and swiped his card. He went right through and turned to me. "Make your own rules."

What could they do to me if it didn't work? Suspend me from school? I followed close behind.

One of the guards frowned at me as I went through, and for a moment my heart stopped. I forced a smile and nodded. He nodded back. I was in.

"It's not exactly CIA headquarters, is it?" I whispered as we moved away from the lobby.

"Come on. I know you've got a plane to catch." He walked to the elevators and hit the call button.

"How the hell do you know that? Are you hacking into my private files again?"

"I act with benevolence and virtue. Besides, I had to check that your new computer was clean. It is. You're welcome. Okay?"

The elevator doors opened.

"Whatever," I said, recalling some bit of an adage about how people who made deals with the devil had best not object to the smell of sulfur on their hands.

"We need a study room with a mainframe portal. There's usually one free."

There was. There were a few free. The semester was over and the only people around were older grad students who saw us and scowled us away, protecting their lonely turf. We took a room with four desks and settled in.

McKenna opened his backpack and took out a laptop and a rat's nest of wires. "I'll show you what I've got and where I'm headed. You'll make your plane."

"Why are we here?"

"Because I can use the university computers to do things that would take too long otherwise. I've got the programs set up on my laptop, but I'll let the mainframe do the searches. You follow?"

I followed in that I understood all the words he used. The verbs seemed a little vague.

"All right. Show me."

"The first thing I looked at," he said, typing quickly, "was the bank. Harken and Cromarty is an unusual choice for someone who wants to hide their activity."

"Why's that?"

"Bermuda is relatively transparent. Much more so than Switzerland, and as you probably know, there are even better places—the Caymans, Panama, and so on. Bermuda will cooperate with U.S. courts without much trouble. Also Harken and Cromarty is a very old firm. Very conservative. Few clients. I looked back through their files. For the last five years, two-thirds of their new accounts were for offspring of current account holders."

"I see. So why would someone pick them?"

He grinned at me in triumph. "Because their security systems are so old and simple, a room full of chimps could break in." He typed again and a fresh screen popped up. "You see? I'm in."

I felt like I was watching Roger make hard-boiled eggs appear out of his ear.

"Why would Haley pick a bank with such a feeble security system?" I said.

"I thought our operating premise was that Haley didn't do it."

Roger would pull out three of the eggs before his assistant—Skeli, when I saw the act—would give the audience a big wink and start aping the trick. Only, she would turn sideways so that everyone could see how it was done. Roger's reaction—anger, frustration, amazement, and chagrin all rolled into one—always brought down the house. "But this is how it was done, wasn't it?"

"Yup. From here I can change profiles on accounts, buy and sell securities, authorize wire transfers. Wanna try it?"

"No, I'm content to watch and be amazed," I said, remembering an afternoon some years ago when a friend, newly licensed as a pilot, took me up from Teterboro in New Jersey for a trip around New York Harbor. While I thoroughly enjoyed the view, his persistence in offering me the opportunity to take the controls dampened my exuberance considerably. He topped it off with a laugh and, crossing his arms, put both hands under his armpits, expecting that I would grab the wheel and save us. I did not. Nor did I laugh about it anywhere near as much as he did. "Can you tell if someone has tried this before?"

"Here? Yes, but I'll get caught. Do we care? Is that important?"

"How do we get caught?"

"Not *caught*, but they'll know I've been there. They have a second-level security system, an IDS, that tags anyone who gets in. I ran an SQL injection to see all the bank files, but if I try to search the security system itself, I'm going to leave a trace."

"SQL?" I said.

He looked at the ceiling for divine assistance. "Do you want me to explain?"

I didn't have to think about it very hard. "No. But haven't you already left a trail? Just by going in?"

"No. I tread lightly."

"Even so, this is all highly illegal, am I right?"

"It's only illegal if I leave a trace."

"How much will they know about you?" I said.

"Nothing. But they'll know some entity from the university was in there. They can probably trace it to the library, maybe even this portal, but they can't read my laptop."

I thought about it. We may have been burning our single bridge into and out of the system, but it would be worth it to see what clues the other intruders had left behind.

"Go ahead. If we have to, we'll switch to Columbia. There's plenty of college libraries to choose from."

"They're not all this easy, but okay." He tapped for a moment, then pulled a big flash drive out of his backpack. "My password cracker. I wrote the code when I was fifteen. It still beats Brutus or any of the other programs available out there." He sat back. "This may take a minute or two."

It took four.

"Oh, that's not right. Look at this. The only reason these guys aren't being robbed blind is that no one knows who they are." A list scrolled down the page. "These are all break-ins."

"This month?"

He laughed. "No, they're not that bad. Since the system went live." He peered at the screen. "In '04. They've done all the updates, but somebody should tell them there's better systems out there. A VPN is only as good as the wall around it."

"Leave them a message," I said.

He laughed again. "Most excellent!" He typed something. "There. I left the names of two much better security programs."

"Go back to the list."

We read through the list of intruders. Much of it was coded information, but McKenna was able to translate instantly. I gave him the trade dates and he pinpointed the applicable lines. The account holder information appeared and my heart sank.

"Oh shit."

"Sorry," he said.

The break-ins that had directed the trade in question had been authorized by an IP address at Arinna Labs. I had just discovered the evidence that would guarantee Philip Haley an all-expenses-paid one-to-five-year stay at one of our federal government's gated communities.

I sat back in the hard plastic study chair, closed my eyes, and exhaled a load of pent-up frustration. Virgil now had a problem, too. The firm's investment in Arinna was going to be worth less than the price of a ham sandwich in Smithfield, Virginia. Maybe I could just tell him to dump the stock. If I didn't tell him why, would it still be considered insider trading?

"Hey, Virgil. I think you should sell Arinna."

"Really, Jason? Why is that?"

"I can't tell you. But I really, really, really think you should."

Nope. It smelled just like insider trading. That would be compounding the problem.

"That's weird," McKenna said.

I opened my eyes and tried to focus on the page in front of us. "What's weird?"

"Well, look."

I didn't see what he was talking about.

"The account that he used? It was set up three weeks before the trade."

Okay, I thought. *Haley planned ahead.* "So?"

"Arinna didn't set it up. The IPs don't match. Haley couldn't have done it."

"Are you positive?"

"I will be—once I get into Arinna's system. I'm working on it, but it may take me more time. Arinna is a hardwired private network with full Internet access available only through a group of well-guarded ports. I left a sniffer there and eventually one of the employees will log in unsecured. Then I'll have their password and I'm in. But for now I'm fairly confident that it was not Haley. He wouldn't have the skills. Whoever it was, hacked in and created the account using the Chinese government as a front."

"What do you mean? Why couldn't it be the Chinese themselves?"

"Because I've seen their work."

"Haley thinks that's who's setting him up."

"No. No. No. The signature is all wrong."

"Then who?"

"I don't know who. But that's where the trail dead-ends. Someone must have piggybacked, the same way we're doing."

"Through the Chinese government's computer system?"

"Not impossible."

"Who could do this? Could you?"

He thought about it. "I don't know. Theoretically? With the right resources, yeah. I'd want to assemble a team."

"Could Philip Haley have done it?"

"Not a chance. You'd need a dozen or so top people working on this for weeks. A government could do it. The U.S., Israel, Russia. But why would they bother? A major corporation could put the right people in place, but you run into the same question. Why?"

"What about amateurs? Anonymous, for example."

"This wasn't some mass attack on a system. This was a surgical procedure. I suppose some billionaire with a grudge could assemble the right people to do it."

"That's interesting. I'm on my way to see a billionaire this afternoon. I'll try and find out if he has a big enough grudge."

23

The Palm Beach Yacht Club is not in Palm Beach. It is in West Palm Beach. That is a world of difference. You can see Palm Beach across the Intracoastal Waterway, but Palm Beach real estate is much too valuable to waste on yacht clubs. Banking, wealth management, high-end shopping, and golf take up all of the space not devoted to luxury homes.

There were three Bentleys lined up at the entrance to the club, waiting for the uniformed valet attendants to help two septuagenarians out of a Ferrari. I paid off the cab and bypassed the rescue attempt before they resorted to the Jaws of Life.

The club was halfway out on a floating dock, and all the boats I passed must have cost more than my Manhattan apartment. Those were the small boats. The big boats out at the end of the dock were more in the apartment building range.

New money was welcome at the club as long as it behaved like old money.

I shared the elevator ride to the second floor with a well-dressed couple in their fifties—well, he was certainly in his fifties. I couldn't tell with her. The blond ponytail said late teens, as did the minidress and the gravity-defying lift of her breasts, but she'd obviously had so much work done on her face and neck, she might have been the guy's mother for all I could tell.

I was overdressed. The only other men wearing ties were working there.

My ears were still crackling and popping from the plane ride and all the mucus clogging my sinuses and it took me a moment to translate the words that the maître d' was saying.

"Mr. Penn is not expected until six-thirty. Would you care to wait at the bar?"

I had taken two cabs and a two-and-a-half-hour flight to get there at six p.m. and Penn was coming from less than a mile away across Flagler Bridge. And he was going to be late.

The bar was lined with women. There was one man—short, balding, and looking every one of his seventy-something years. The rest of the space was filled with women sipping martinis, cosmopolitans, or glasses of white wine. The age range was almost impossible to determine, but I gave a guess at mid-forties to late sixties. Or more. Not one wore a wedding band, though there were plenty of diamonds adorning the rest of their fingers, as well as their wrists, necks, and earlobes. The whole room sparkled and flashed.

I ordered a tonic with lime. I was afraid that if I had a real drink while waiting, the alcohol would gang up with the cold medicine and I would be comatose by the time Penn arrived.

The appraising looks from the women were not coy and flirtatious, nor were they cold and disdainful. They were merely calculating, and in the first two minutes I was there I felt that every woman in the room knew everything about me—suit size, boxers or briefs, left or right, and marital status—and they had determined my bank balance and credit score to within a percentage point or two. Then they all lost interest.

My suit, a three-season, silk-wool blend, custom-made at Saint

Laurie, was too heavy for Florida—even in December. My complexion was pale, ergo I was a snowbird and not part of the "season." I was both too old and too young, neither to be kept nor a keeper, too well-off but nowhere near wealthy enough. Mr. In-Between. There on business. A hint of history, or mystery, but not enough to be intriguing. Harmless.

"The lobster bisque is just too rich. I can't eat it," I overheard. "It's not worth the time on the StairMaster the next day."

"Mmmmm," answered another woman. "It's worth every minute."

I took my tonic and lime and retreated to the window. A spectacular sunset was bleeding purples, pinks, and deep reds all over the low West Palm Beach skyline, reflected in the windows of the hotel across the water. There was a CD playing—Chris Botti. More refined and restrained than I usually liked, but his lush tones fit the mood. Skeli would have liked it there, though she might have preferred hearing Lyle Lovett. The women at the bar would not have seemed sad to her, and they would have welcomed her, recognizing a fellow survivor and one with a great laugh. I missed her.

A blue-black sky crept westward, dousing the reds and pinks. In minutes, the last rays were extinguished and replaced with a display of more sparkling diamonds splashed across a velvet sky.

"Mr. Stafford?" The maître d' was back.

"Yes?"

"I am so sorry, but Mr. Penn sends his regrets. He will not be able to join you for dinner this evening. He asks that you call his office in the morning if you wish to reschedule."

I found that I was speechless. Blame it on my cold, or the medicine, or blame it on the environment, but I did not explode in exasperation. I mumbled something about everything being "just fine."

"Certainly, sir. Mr. Penn did say that you might still want to take his table and that anything you order for you or any guests would, of course, be on him."

My head cleared. "Really?" I was still calculating—the value of my lost time, and time away from my son and Skeli. I looked down the bar and did a quick count. "Will Mr. Penn's table hold a party of eight?" I said.

The maître d' allowed a frisson of stress to show in one eyebrow before answering. "I am sure that is not a problem, sir. Can you give me ten minutes?"

"What's your name?" I said.

He hadn't expected the question and almost stalled before answering. "Uh, Brian, sir."

"Well, Brian, ten minutes will be just about perfect. As Captain Picard would say, 'Make it so.'" The last time, Penn had given me five minutes of familial piety before brushing me off. This time, he hadn't even bothered with the burlesque. Figuring in all my travel time at my usual rate, he owed me large. I turned back to the bar. "Ladies! Could I have a moment of your time? Ladies?" I spoke just loud enough to get their attention and yet not alarm anyone. "It seems that I am fated to dine here alone. I have been stood up by a business acquaintance. Unless, of course, you all agree to join me. I hear the lobster bisque is to die for."

Not everyone at the bar agreed to join me for dinner, but I did manage to persuade four of the women to accept Mr. Penn's unknowing largesse. Marc Devereau, the seventy-something man at the bar, agreed to anchor the other end of the table.

"Would you be willing to help me with the wine list?" I asked him.

His chest puffed out and he smiled his acquiescence.

I passed the book to Melissa, who handed it on down the table, the movement setting off a shower of brilliant flashes and rainbows from her wrist. "May I admire your bracelet? Or watchband. What do you call it?"

"A reward for bad behavior." She briefly lowered both eyelids in a blatant parody of bashfulness. And she put a hefty dose of heat behind it. I was sure it had worked for her more than once before.

The articulated metal band was more than an inch wide and covered in diamonds, easily complementing the oversized watch face, itself sporting a dozen eye-catching jewels.

"More like a going-away present," the fourth woman said. Lani.

A comradely giggle erupted from Barbara and went around the table. Marc smiled. He had, I was sure, heard the line himself more than once before.

"Are you here long, Mr. Stafford? I would love to show you something of our town," Carol said, leaning forward just enough to reveal the depth of her décolletage.

"I was brought up to never disappoint a lady, but in this case I'm afraid I must. I'm on the last flight back to New York tonight."

"You won't even stay the night? Winter sunrises are so beautiful."

"Then I'll have to come back," I lied. It was a white lie.

"You'll be welcome anytime," she cooed.

Mentioning that I was already spoken for would have been boorish. Instead, I let her squeeze my hand while giving me the kind of smile that should be reserved for just before the lights get turned out.

"If we're all starting with the bisque," I said to the table, removing my hand while I still could, "then I think we should have a hearty champagne." To Marc: "Did I see a Veuve Clicquot Ponsardin Rosé? It will stand up to the soup." It was also the second most expensive champagne on the list.

Marc looked over his Armani bifocals. "An excellent choice."

"And pick a red, would you? I'm having the rack of lamb."

Because I was missing Skeli and knew that's what she would have ordered.

"Well, if you don't mind a touch of infanticide, there's a '99 Château Margaux that would go nicely."

Marc was already well into the spirit of the occasion.

When the champagne arrived, I proposed a toast to "the absent Chuck Penn," but when I saw the measured response I quickly added the words "to his absence." This won me a laugh from Lani and polite smiles from all the rest. But everyone raised his or her glass, and Marc soon called for a second bottle.

"*Two* more bottles," I said. At that moment, I was feeling the old recklessness that came from trading unimaginable sums of money and partying on expense accounts. "And can we get some appetizers for the table? Hot *and* cold."

Out of politeness or indifference, no one asked me about my relationship with Charles Penn. They asked me questions about my business ("financial security consultant," which could have meant just about anything) and they asked me where I lived.

"The Ansonia? Yes, I love it. I had a cousin who moved to the West Side."

And who probably hadn't been heard from since.

I let the topic turn from me to a discussion of the "season," parties to be attended or avoided, and pointed but harmless gossip about people I did not know. Lani made a point to fill me in with CliffsNotes descriptions of these people, mixing politeness toward me with a catty appreciation of her neighbors.

"The Ellisons. Saint Louis. Old money, but you know what they say about old money. The way you get it is by never spending a cent of it if you don't have to."

"Joan Price. A bore, but a really nice bore, if you know what I mean."

"Tom Ketchum. A bully at heart. He was something in finance.

Not hedge funds. He married two doormats before meeting Sybil. As you can hear, we're all rooting for her. She is *such* a bitch."

I ordered two bottles of Corton-Charlemagne to accompany the salads and appetizers that came next. I ate some of the buffalo mozzarella and tomato salad. I can always persuade myself that I'm eating healthy if it's buffalo mozzarella.

"Lani, you all seemed to have a similar reaction when I mentioned Chuck Penn. Is he not entirely welcome here?"

I could hear Marc entertaining the rest of the table with a story about Emperor Charlemagne's wife—his fourth—who was the first to insist that white grapes be planted in the Corton vineyards. She had objected to the red wine stains on her husband's white beard.

"Oh, I think you want Carol to tell you about that."

Carol turned from listening to Marc. "About what?"

"Our host was just asking about that arrogant prick, Penn."

Carol was a still-very-attractive fifty-something. I had no doubt that she'd had "work done"—I was the only one at the table who hadn't, I was sure—but it was well done and minimal. A flash of anger went across her face before she spoke.

"Pour me another glass of that white wine—a big glass. I love telling this story, but it also takes something out of me." She took a fortifying sip that lowered the level in the glass by a good half inch. "There was a woman here in Palm, married to a man who owned a chain of local newspapers. You know, the ones with two pages of things the mayor wants you to know, and which no-neck wonder is this year's scholar athlete, and when the library will reopen after the hurricane, and then ten pages of classifieds and public auction notices from all the people who won't ever use Craigslist. It was a good business. The man wasn't a particularly good man, but he treated the woman well, took good care of his kids, and never let his mistress call the house."

She broke off as the entrées arrived. I was pleased to see that no one had ordered anything inexpensive.

"I'm all ears," I said after letting her get a first bite of her lobster fra diavolo.

"Mmmm. One moment. This is delicious."

So was my lamb.

"Well, along came Mr. Penn. He wanted to buy the newspapers. The man wouldn't sell. Penn waited six months and offered him twenty percent less than the first time, acting like he was the only bidder in the world. But the man didn't want to sell, told him so, and thought that would be the end of it."

"What did a billionaire want with a few million dollars' worth of newspapers?"

"Oh, they were worth a good bit more than that. The man owned hundreds of them all through the South. So here's where Penn got crafty." Her jaw was set a bit firmer, her eyes a bit steely. "He made a play for the woman. Convinced her that what was good for the goose and all that rubbish. As many times as I have heard that said, I can't tell you how many times it has proven to be *so* not the case. Anyway. He seduced her. It wasn't really that hard. She was lonely and he's a good-looking man, if you like that big bull look. She thought she was having some fun."

I was beginning to anticipate the ending to this story—and it was ugly.

"But the husband found out," I ventured.

"Someone sent him pictures."

"I see."

"So there was a lot of yelling and finger-pointing and many awful things were said before they finally agreed on a divorce. Only, splitting the assets became a problem. She didn't want to own half of a chain of newspapers. He didn't have the cash to buy her out. The lawyers fought over that like two pit bulls."

"And Charles Penn comes back into the picture."

"Oh, yes. He made a lowball offer to 'help them out.' All cash. The lawyers wanted the man to take it. The judge ordered him to."

"And Penn got the newspapers for pennies on the dollar."

"No. The woman finally had her eyes opened and saw what that snake had been up to all along. She agreed to a thirty-year note and a trust. Saved the man's ass. Her ex-husband married the mistress—who all agree is a bitch on wheels—and kept the papers. He has never missed a payment. If he does, he forfeits everything, so the ex-wife is well taken care of. The kids all sided with her. She's happy."

I looked at Carol in the evening candlelight. She may have been easily ten years my senior, but she was a good-looking woman. Assured. Comfortable with herself.

"She's content," she said.

But, I thought, *sometimes she invites men to see the sunrise from her bedroom window.*

"Though if she ever gets the opportunity to put a stake through Chuck Penn's heart, believe you me, she will do it." She drained her glass and I poured her another.

The combination of the wine, cold medicine, and exhaustion caught up with me on the way to the airport. The slog through security felt like a marathon that I was running in ankle-deep sand. I was fast asleep before we left the gate.

I woke up when the wheels hit the New York runway a little on the hard side. Still, the plane didn't bounce, so the pilot earned a short burst of ironic applause. There was drool on my chin, and from the looks I was getting from the other passengers in first class, I had been snoring. Probably pretty loud. Business travelers in particular frown upon snoring.

And, I realized as I walked zombie-like through the nearly empty airport, I had run afoul of another business traveler's axiom—when you get on a plane with the beginnings of a cold, you will get off with the rest of it. My eyes itched, my throat burned, and my sinuses felt as though they were packed with cotton. Cotton and cement.

The line for cabs was mercifully short and the cold rain barely registered through my misery.

"The Ansonia," I croaked.

"What's that?" the young Latino said, in an accent that I could use to almost pinpoint which block on Northern Boulevard in Woodside the kid had grown up on.

"Into the city. Broadway and Seventy-third."

"Not a problem."

I was glad that it was not a problem. What would we have done if it was a problem? My head fell back and I felt the exhaustion washing over me again, but a mote of attention to duty pulled me back. I'd had my phone turned off for three hours. Too long in case Heather needed me for an issue with the Kid. Of course, there was no Kid problem that Heather couldn't handle a lot better than I, but a general sense of responsibility, or guilt for having been away, dictated that I at least check for messages.

I had three text messages.

5:48 Virgil Call me.

8:39 Skeli What time do u get in? Love u. Give a call.

9:13 Virgil Chk ur vcemail

I checked voicemail. One message.

"Call me whenever you get this. The prosecuting attorney leaked Haley's grand jury testimony. We have major damage control issues."

Virgil's phone went straight to voicemail.

"Got your message. I'll call you at ten." My voice sounded like someone stripping gears on a dump truck.

Heather was asleep on top of the covers on the Kid's bed, squeezing him up against the wall. He must have loved it. I didn't wake her.

I made myself tea, swallowed a glass of raspberry-flavored

Emergen-C, put on some music, and swaddled myself in a blanket before plunking down in my chair by the window facing down Broadway.

I called Skeli.

"Are you up?"

"Well, I'm not in bed yet. Actually, I fell asleep watching the Grand Prix of Figure Skating and now Jimmy Fallon is on. So that's what? Two hours? Three?"

"It's late." I was too hot. I sat forward, slipped off my jacket, and sank back into the chair again.

"How was your trip? You don't sound good."

"Just a cold. Penn blew me off. But I learned something. I have to see how it fits in." My jacket slipped off the arm of the chair and fell to the floor. I leaned over and picked it up. Four white or cream-colored business cards fell out of the side pocket and onto my lap.

"What are you listening to?"

"10,000 Maniacs," I said. "Unplugged. Old stuff." I flipped through the cards. Carol. Melissa. Lani. Barbara. They were all sleight-of-hand magicians; I hadn't noticed any of them slipping their cards into my pocket.

"I think I like it."

High praise from someone who once told me she didn't like Emmylou Harris because she was too "rocky."

"I'll get you a CD." I tossed the cards onto the end table and couldn't suppress a chuckle.

"What's funny?" Skeli asked.

"I missed you," I said, choosing to hold off on describing my dinner party until sometime in the distant future. Or never.

"How about this weekend? Do you have any time to look at apartments?"

"There's a happy thought. I'll let you know tomorrow. Can you make time for that vacation? I think the Kid is coming 'round."

"Yes. Emphatically so. What was his objection?"

"I think his biggest problem is that I suggested it. If it came from you, or Heather, or even my father, he'd be on board already."

"He's worried about you," she said.

"Yeah, well, I'm worried about him. We're made for each other."

"I'm not worried about either of you. You'll both figure it out."

We rang off with the usual expressions of mutual affection and I went and gently roused Heather.

"It's late. Take twenty for a cab," I said, proffering the bill.

"I live less than a block from the subway. Besides, I'll never get a cab in the rain."

"Anything I should know?"

"He did the thing with his pee again. I don't know what it's about either, but I think it's harmless. Ignore it. For now."

I nodded. I trusted her judgment more than my own.

"You okay?"

"Just a cold."

"Get some rest."

I did.

25

An email from Lydia Sharp suggested that we meet for coffee up by City College. I didn't know the Hamilton Heights–Sugar Hill section, but McKenna hadn't offered an alternative. If I thought about it at all, it was northern Harlem. I knew that the area had been the home to the elite of black culture, politics, and business—from Cab Calloway and Count Basie to W. E. B. DuBois and Thurgood Marshall—but all that had been a long time ago. By the time the Giants left the Polo Grounds and moved to San Francisco, the neighborhood had deteriorated badly

I was surprised, therefore, at how far it had come back. I walked over to Amsterdam from the 137th Street subway station, after riding up on the Number 1 train, getting off twice, and waiting for another train, to be sure that I wasn't being followed. I wasn't.

There was still a neighborhood feel to the street-level businesses, which had nearly evaporated over the years around the Ansonia. The low-rise apartment buildings showed the effects of ten years of gentrification, but the people on the street reflected a mix of ethnic and economic backgrounds. There were still plenty of gated first-floor apartment windows, but the hustle on the street was good.

I found myself fantasizing about finding an apartment up there big enough to raise a growing family.

A block uptown from the campus was a basement-level coffee shop, two steps down from the street. I was early, but I was sure McKenna was already somewhere nearby, watching to see if I had been followed. I went in and ordered an Earl Grey with lemon and a tall water. There was an empty corner table where we would be able to watch the door and the whole café. The place was half-full with an assortment of students, Internet entrepreneurs, bloggers, and freelancers, and a couple of retirees reading the *Times* online. I swallowed a handful of vitamin C, aspirin, echinacea, and a caplet of elderberry extract and ginseng, and sucked on a zinc lozenge. I didn't know if I was doing any good or slowly poisoning myself, but I was making Skeli happy. If it worked, all the better.

Virgil rarely took my phone calls before all the markets were open and it was still forty-five minutes before the NYSE bell, but I tried him anyway. He answered with a growl.

"Where the fuck are you?"

Virgil was not given to cursing as a rule. I was sure it was the first time I had heard him use an f-bomb.

"Working. Uptown. What's up?"

"Haley, that frigging idiot, sank his own battleship."

"He failed the grand jury test?" I said.

"He told them off."

"What's the call?"

"Order imbalance. They're hoping to get an opening price by late morning."

That was bad.

"What's the buzz?"

"The floor trader thinks it bottoms down by thirty percent. Give or take."

A disaster. The firm was going to take a bath. Should I have tipped Virgil off to what McKenna and I had found? I still thought I had made the right decision. But as Virgil might have a different view on the matter, I kept it to myself.

"What the hell did he say?" I said.

"Aw, hell. What didn't he say? He answered every question with a speech. The prosecuting attorney let him deny, deny, deny for an hour, and then sprung his trap. They had the bank records. The trade authorizations were generated from Arinna Labs. Probably from his computer."

"Did Haley have a comeback?"

"At that point, he took the fifth."

"Oh shit. Making himself look like a total liar."

"Yeah. He may as well have put the noose around his neck and stepped off the scaffold. The grand jury took about a minute and a half to come up with a true bill."

"Did you ever talk to the other board members? Ward and the lawyer?"

"Yes. Helen Ward has already resigned in protest. Kavanagh's a straight arrow. Neither one profits in any way over this. You don't seriously think either of them is involved, do you?"

"No. I'm just tying up loose ends. I'm getting close." I took a breath and plunged on. "I need to talk to Haley's lawyer," I said.

"I'll see what I can do. But why?"

I wasn't ready to say what I believed; I wanted a few more bits of confirmation. "It's complicated."

"Did you find something and you are not sharing it with me? Who the hell pays your fat salary? If you have any pertinent information, you owe me!"

I had never heard him so near to losing control. I still didn't want to get into particulars, but I gave him the conclusion. "It looks bad, but Haley didn't do it."

"And when the fuck were you going to get around to telling me?"

"You didn't need to know," I said. "And you don't pay me a salary—you are paying me money I already earned."

"Do you know how much you've cost the firm today?"

"I couldn't let you trade on that information. It was nonpublic. The SEC would have shut you down—and put my sorry ass back in jail."

"Well, now they won't have to shut us down. The market is taking care of that, no thanks to you."

"I was protecting you," I said.

"That wasn't your decision," he yelled.

"Since when is my not going back to prison *not* my goddamn decision?" As soon as I said it, I realized that I already had the attention of everyone in the coffee bar. "Shit!"

"You're fired," he said.

I didn't believe him. Besides, he couldn't fire me. "I have a contract. Buy me out."

"Sue me."

"And I'll win." And I would. But I was speaking to a dead phone. Virgil had hung up.

I looked around at the faces, some openly staring, some ostentatiously not looking. "Sorry," I said. "I just got fired. It's not my day."

There was a round of nodding commiseration from the crowd and an understanding, motherly smile from one of the white-haired retirees.

You know that your life is much too complicated when you have to stop and think which of your lawyers you need to call to handle a given circumstance.

I had just started dialing when a young, bearded Hasidic man dressed in a black suit and broad-brimmed hat came down the steps and walked in. He had a pronounced limp and was carrying a thick black briefcase. He got a cup of coffee and came over to join me. I shut down my phone and shook his hand.

"What'd you do to your foot?" I asked.

"I put a pebble in my shoe to remind me to limp," McKenna said. "It changes my physical profile. Recognition software won't be looking for someone with a limp."

"You're worried about recognition software in west Harlem? Aren't you taking this just a bit far?" I said.

"You never know what is enough."

"Where's your FBI guys?"

"Thirtieth Street and First Avenue. Intake for the men's shelter system," he said.

"They won't suspect?"

"Processing can take all day there."

"What do you have for me?" I may have been fired, but that didn't mean I had to stop working. Virgil would be back.

"Arinna Labs. I think I have a way in, but we may eventually have to go on-site. I'll let you know."

"On-site? Out to the lab itself?"

"Is that a problem?"

Add breaking and entering to my list of LinkedIn talents. "It's a last resort."

"Okay. I've also worked on the bank again. The trade instructions definitely came from Arinna."

"We knew that."

"But the account creation definitely did not. It would have taken a good-sized team with some powerful systems to make that happen. And though I won't be able to tell you who they were, I can say that they were very good. Among the best."

"Can we show it to Haley's lawyer?"

"*You* show it. I'm not quite ready to surface."

"What do I need to tell him?"

"There's another wrinkle to it. The account had to have been approved. Meaning a bank officer had to go into the system, put in his own password, and make the account go live. Without that, it's just bits of electronic data."

"They had to get to a banker," I said.

"Not impossible," McKenna said. "But you'd need someone to do some research and find out who was approachable. You can't just wait outside the bank waving hundred-dollar bills and expect to successfully bribe a banker." He laughed. "Well, maybe you can, but I think you'd want to be a little more discreet."

"Do you have a name?"

He shook his head. "Only a password. But they're unique. The good guys will find him."

"I'll get it to the lawyer."

"Can you get his email? I'll forward all of the materials to you."

"I'll see. I was fired just before you arrived."

"Does that mean I'm fired, too?"

"Nope." I took a thick envelope from my inside pocket and handed it to him. "You still work for me. But for right now, we're both living off my money market account. When we go through that, we can start on my line of credit. We'll both be okay for a while."

He pushed his chair back. "Is that it for now? I'll get you the email."

"No. I need help with something else. Surveillance equipment. Who can I talk to? I may want to pick up a few things, but what I really need is advice."

"Not a problem. We have to go back downtown. There's a guy in the West Village who I can trust."

"And one other thing. I need to start shaking things up a bit. I have an idea for setting up a sting, but I need you to hack into someone's private computer. Maybe a couple of people's."

He hunched back over the table and took his laptop out of the briefcase. "Who do you want me to start with?"

"Mrs. Selena Haley," I said.

26

Barneys on Madison sells clothes, but the restaurant in the basement is the main draw for the ladies who lunch. The sign says FRED'S AT BARNEYS NEW YORK, but I never heard anyone call it Fred's. It was "Barneys." I was not the only man in the dining room—most of the staff was male and there were two men eating at a table on the far side of the room.

Selena Haley was checking her watch as I approached. Her lunch date was already five minutes late.

"Mrs. Haley?" I said. "May I join you?" My voice sounded strained, nasal, and flat. I promised myself a nap just as soon as this was done.

She looked up and for a moment she was beyond speechless. Guilt, anger, and fear fought for top billing. But she was good. Breeding and training. She recovered almost immediately.

"Mr. Stafford? I'm so sorry, but I'm waiting for someone. She should be here any minute. But thank you for asking." I was dismissed.

"Dolores Cutler? I'm afraid she's been held up." I pulled out the chair and sat.

At that moment, Dolores Cutler was most likely still desperately trying to convince the painting crew that I had sent to her apartment that she had not hired them, did not want her apartment painted that day, and that she had no time to discuss colors with the short, pushy man with the sad face. Roger would be sure to buy me at least half an hour.

This time it took Selena a bit longer to recuperate. Her mouth opened, closed, opened again, and closed once more. She reached for her purse and pulled out her cell phone. I waited until she had finished dialing before hitting the button on the jammer in my jacket pocket. McKenna's friend had assured me that it was efficient, well-charged, and illegal. She scowled at the phone, tried again, and finally dropped it back into her purse.

I forced my scratchy voice to sound as calm and forceful as possible. "If you try to leave, I will stand up and make a scene. I will make loud entreaties that you not abandon me, and think back on all we have meant to each other. There will be references to specific sexual acts that you enjoy."

Her face lost all color. "How dare you? Lies! Who would believe it? Or even listen?"

I looked around at a hundred or more well-dressed, Botoxed, and surgically enhanced women shoppers. "I'd bet most of them. You'll be on Page Six tomorrow." I smiled politely. "I'm having the crab and shrimp salad. What about you?"

"You're insane."

"But only north-northeast, and today the wind is southerly. Bear with me. I only need your attention for a few minutes. Then I will go and you may never have to see me again."

"I'm leaving." She pushed her chair back.

I stood up and leaned over the table. "Selena!" I cried. "You can't! Please. I left my wife and child for you."

Her head rocked back. I had the attention of everyone within three tables of us. If I turned up the volume just a bit, I would have the whole room hanging on every word. Some women were already smiling in anticipation of a coming scene. No one was even bothering with being too polite to listen.

Selena spoke through clenched teeth. "Please sit down, Mr. Stafford."

The headwaiter was approaching. I winked broadly at the women at the next table. They giggled like seventh graders. I grinned and sat down.

"Thank you for agreeing to see me," I said.

"May I be of some assistance?" The headwaiter hovered, now unsure if he was intervening or interrupting.

"Thanks," I said. "I'm having the lump crab and shrimp salad. Mrs. Haley will have her usual."

He took it in stride. "Mark's salad, no dressing. And to drink?"

"Water for me." I turned to her. "A glass of Sancerre?" Amazing, the depth of information that Internet search engines maintain.

She stared the waiter down for a moment. "No. I will have a vodka martini. Up. No fruit."

"Certainly, Mrs. Haley."

We waited for him to get out of range. There were still a few surreptitious glances from the crowd around us, hoping for a bit more of a show, but the background murmur began to grow again, the sounds of silverware on plates, the small laugh suddenly overwhelmed by the catty crow.

"What in hell do you want?"

What I wanted right then was a fresh pack of tissues so I could blast a clear path to my sinuses and stop feeling like I was drowning on land.

"Yesterday, your husband came close to torching his whole career and earning himself an extended stay with the BOP. And look at you. Out celebrating?"

"That's vile."

"Did I get too close? To the truth, I mean."

"I have nothing to say."

"Then I'll just keep the conversation going on my own, shall I?" I felt a sneeze coming. I twitched my nose to divert it. It didn't help.

The drinks arrived. I sipped my water. She took a long slug of the martini.

"I hired a hacker. He got into your home computer—your address book, calendar, email. That's how I was able to find you here and arrange for Mrs. Cutler's apartment to be painted."

"Why are you telling me this?"

I ignored the question. She knew the answer. "My guy is not quite as slick as the crew you used, but he found their footprints. They're good. You got your money's worth." I gave a small cough in the hopes of persuading my nose that a sneeze really wasn't necessary.

She took another slug. Two-thirds of the cocktail was gone. "There's no connection."

"Legal connection? No. I'm sure of that. Still, they're hackers. Hackers don't bribe bank officers and that's what someone would have had to do to set up the account in the first place. You had help there."

The salads arrived.

"Mrs. Haley would like another martini," I said. She didn't object.

"But that was a minor hurdle," I continued. "It's sad. The banker is probably going to be the only one to take a dive on this. Once I show your husband's lawyer the evidence of hacking, he'll be in the clear. Unless the banker has someone to roll over on, he's going down."

She gave me a long appraising look. "What do you think you know?"

The urge to sneeze was becoming unbearable. "Excuse me," I said, grabbing the white linen napkin just in time. I squeezed my nose as hard as I could and let the spasm rock me. I refused to sneeze into the napkin. The back draft sent pinwheels spinning across my eyes. For a moment, I was deaf, blind, and stupid.

"Sorry," I said. "It's a cold."

"Take your time," she said, smiling happily at my discomfort.

"I know the story. I know how your friend works. I know who helped you on this." I wasn't lying. I did know. The story about Penn had given me everything I needed to know about him—about the way he worked. Proving it was another story. It wouldn't hurt to exaggerate just a bit. "I have the proof, and when I'm ready, I will sink his boat and let the news-reporter sharks pick over his remains."

I thought I had her. I could see her waver. She finished the drink and looked around for its replacement. The prospect of a second martini must have restored something in her. The steel in her voice came back. "You can't touch him. And don't waste your sympathy on the banker. He was a cipher."

So much the better, I thought. Once we found him, he would be that much easier to flip and give evidence.

I took a bite of the crab, amazed that I could taste it. Taste anything. It was good. She ignored her salad.

"Were you involved in the negotiations?"

"No. I just picked up the tab."

The shrimp was good, too. I finished the crab first. *Feed* a cold? I thought that was right.

"Then you waited until the special board meeting. Who called it? You? Or did someone else front it? Your special friend? Or someone else. It wouldn't have been difficult for you to talk one of the others into calling for it. Your husband didn't want to go public with the test results, but you forced his hand. You must have enjoyed watching him gloat two weeks later when the news had been absorbed, forgotten about, and the stock was back where it was in the first place. Of course, by that time, you had already set him up quite nicely."

The second martini arrived.

"Keep your voice down."

"Sorry," I whispered. "But I'll only be more conspicuous if I start whispering."

"How much do you want?"

"To bury the story? To let your husband go down for something he didn't do? I don't think even you can afford that." I could feel another sneeze coming on. If I held that one in, too, I might possibly blow my eardrums out or burst a blood vessel.

"Then what *do* you want?" She still hadn't taken a bite of her salad, but was already well on her way to finishing the second drink.

"Tell him. Or I'll tell him myself. I'll give you twenty-four hours. Tomorrow at noon I start dialing the newspapers." I stood up, took some bills from my pocket, and dropped them on the table. "Lunch is on me." I took the napkin—I was going to need it.

27

Virgil called while I was trying to flag a cab on Madison. I decided to walk while I talked.

"What do you mean, 'He didn't do it'? What else do you know?"

I blew my nose again before answering. I tucked the despoiled napkin into my back pocket. "So I'm still working for you?"

"Goddamn you!"

"Is that a yes?"

He took a minute before answering. "I'm sorry," he said. "I was wrong. If you had given me that information earlier, I might have sold our shares and opened the firm up to insider trading charges. Thank you."

It was a nice speech. I tried to match it. "And I'm sorry I didn't trust you with the information, but it's not all bad. In fact, it's very good. Someone had to bribe a bank officer to open that account. And they had to have hacking skills way beyond anything Haley might have come across."

"You can prove this?"

"Get me the lawyer's email and I will make sure he has all he needs by tomorrow afternoon."

"So who's behind it? Is Haley right? The Chinese?"

"I think the answer is a lot closer to home. I've learned a few things in the last twenty-four hours. I've guessed at a few more. And I just had lunch with one of the major co-conspirators."

I filled him in on my lunch. He didn't interrupt.

"Penn and Selena working together?" he said at the end. "They're an unlikely couple."

"This is how Penn works," I said. "He seems to have a knack for finding unhappy women and using them to get where he wants to be."

"What do you think she'll do?"

"I leaned hard. Not everything I said is, how shall I put it, verifiable. But I think she bought it. I gave her a deadline of tomorrow. Though I doubt it will take her that long to make up her mind. I give it eighty-twenty she confesses the whole thing to him tonight."

"How much can I tell the lawyer?"

"Right now? I gave her twenty-four hours, Virgil."

"And the stock is off twenty-four percent."

"The goddamn markets can wait a day," I heard myself say.

"Hah! I never, *never*, would have expected you to come out with that statement."

"I'm serious. You tell the lawyer, and ten minutes later the stock will be trading up like a rocket."

"What about the banker? Can we start trying to identify him?"

I couldn't see the harm in getting that process moving. I gave Virgil the name of the bank and the banker's authorization code. "They'll probably put up roadblocks if you go straight at them. And to get a court order in Bermuda could take an eternity."

"I'll use my contacts in London. I'm sure I can get someone to finesse this our way."

I checked my watch. "London's closed. They'll all be gone from their offices by this hour."

Virgil chuckled. "Then I'll call them at home."

"Once Selena talks to Haley," I said, "I see this whole thing splitting wide open."

He gave a sad sigh. "She may end up doing time."

"Come on, Virgil. She'll write a check and take a plea. Rich women don't go to jail."

"Martha Stewart. Leona Helmsley," he said.

"All right. Point taken. Will the wife be our next client, then?"

"She is the single largest shareholder. We can get along without her for a while if we have to, but I think we owe her our support."

"And you do run a full-service firm," I said.

"Left to its own devices, money makes enemies. If you want to be around for the long haul, you need to work hard at making friends."

28

I rarely turned on my phone before the Kid was at school. Mornings were just for us.

Besides, the cold had traveled into my throat while I was sleeping. I felt better, but I sounded like I'd been singing death metal all night.

The Kid finished his cereal—Cheerios with a few slices of banana—and left the table as soon as he could. My cold scared him, and the sound of my voice made him doubly uncomfortable. Luckily, he was on remote that morning and went about getting ready without much fuss.

My iPad beeped at me while I was reading the *Journal*. Haley and Arinna Labs were still a big story. They were about to get bigger.

I opened my email. Virgil. *Your phone is turned off.*

I wrote back. *I know.*

CALL ME.

I was sure that Virgil would know that the use of all capitals indicated that he was yelling. It was very early in the morning for him to be yelling. I thought about ignoring the message, but that would only put off the inevitable, and had a good chance of making it much worse.

"Virgil here." He sounded more defeated than angry.

"What's up?" I said, trying not to sound like an escapee from *World War Z*.

"Haley's been arrested."

"Damn. That was fast."

"Not for insider trading. For murder. His wife was found late last night. Dead on the beach by their house on Long Island. At the bottom of the steps on the cliff."

A cold, strong hand was squeezing my heart and there was a deafening rush in my ears. I had set that woman on the path that got her killed.

"Any chance it was an accident?" I was a coward.

"Not unless she accidentally shot herself on the way down."

I felt no grief—I barely knew her—but a mountain of guilt was bearing down on my chest. Angie had been killed because of my actions, and now this stranger. If Haley had pulled the trigger, I vowed that I would see him pay. And if he hadn't, I was going to find out who did.

"What can I do?"

"The lawyer is going in to see him in an hour. Go with him. Carry a briefcase and no one will question you."

"Should I bring the evidence I found?"

"I don't think it makes a difference at this point, but why not?"

"And the lawyer's okay with this?"

"He doesn't like it, but he's not in charge. Haley wants you there."

That was interesting. Did Haley think he could con me? Or did he think he needed me? "Where is he?"

"NYPD found him coming out of some downtown club at four

this morning. They're giving him the VIP treatment. He's at One Police Plaza until they take him out to Nassau County."

"I'll be there." I went to hang up and another thought came to mind. "Wait! Virgil. Are you still there?"

"What is it?"

"The banker. Any luck from your London people?"

"They say they'll have an answer this morning."

An hour later, I met Haley's lawyer in front of One Police Plaza. Though he had been up since Haley's call soon after the arrest, he still looked ready to argue an appeal in front of the Supreme Court. His starched white shirt whispered when he moved.

I gave him a CD with McKenna's and my work on the insider trading case. "I know there are bigger issues right now, but this might come in handy down the road."

He didn't look at it or ask any questions. The CD went into his briefcase. "If anyone asks, I will tell them that you are my investigator. Do not try to pass yourself off as a lawyer." He scanned my suit, overcoat, and briefcase. "Though you do look the part. Maybe no one will bother to ask." He looked the part, too. Tall, hawk-nosed, pale-eyed, and expensively dressed.

No one did bother to ask me anything. A grim-faced, overweight uniformed cop ushered us into a cramped conference room.

The room was so small that the mild claustrophobia that I had developed while in prison advanced to a state of aches, itches, tics, and an ocular migraine that threatened to transform into a headache capable of putting me in bed for a week. Haley wasn't looking much better. He was red-eyed, hungover, and his sweat and breath smelled of alcohol.

"I didn't do this thing." He was speaking to me—desperation and grief mixed with the all-night partying made his voice more hoarse and strained than mine. The last time he had proclaimed his innocence, I had been much too skeptical. It had blinded me. I was afraid to make the same mistake again.

The lawyer made one more play for getting me out of the room, but Haley shut him down. "This is the man who has been working to prove to the prosecuting attorney that I am innocent of insider trading. If I remember correctly, your advice was to plead guilty to a lesser charge. You're here because you have to be. He's here because I want him to be."

The lawyer took defeat gracefully. He gave me a brief smile and turned back to Haley. "This is not my usual type of case. I'll have someone else from the firm at your arraignment in Hempstead. At this point, my only advice is to say nothing. To anyone."

I didn't bother with the niceties of the law or the advice of a specialist in corporate law. "Just tell me what happened."

Haley had spent the day in his office out at the lab, and trying not to watch what the market was doing to the price of his stock. He stayed there late—the rest of the staff had all left—when security told him that Selena had just driven onto the grounds. This was a rare event. He left the lab, watched her drive up to the main house, and followed.

He found her in the sitting room at the back of the house. Her territory. The room had a broad view of the Sound and the steps leading down the cliff. On the rare times she visited the house, that was where she would stay for hours at a time, drinking glass after glass of white wine.

Haley confronted her. He was going through this gauntlet of reporters and prosecutors and he expected her support. She had already opened a bottle and was defensive and prepared for an argument, rather than a reconciliation.

"Did she tell you that you were set up? That she did it?"

"How did you know?"

"Because I saw her yesterday afternoon and told her that she had to tell you or I would."

He nodded sadly. "I asked her straight up why she did it. She told me that I knew why."

"Did you?" I found that if I focused entirely on Haley's face, the room dimensions remained stable and I was able to function.

He looked down at his hands and after a moment twisted his wedding ring. "Selena was complicated. Her grandfather was a monster. The longer we were together, the more those issues came between us."

The lawyer cleared his throat and spoke. "One thing that I know about murder inquiries is, they tend to uncover layers of secrets. If there are issues that you think may be relevant, this is the time to air them. Before the prosecution finds them."

I gave the guy credit for loosening up enough to see that I really was trying to help and that Haley's full cooperation might be key.

Haley stared at him as though trying to read his mind. Then he seemed to make a decision. "Our marriage was in trouble for a very long time." He stumbled over the last couple of words and stopped. When he began again, he spoke very quietly. "Early on, she was very into me. I mean, she was very into sex with me." His temples flushed a deep red. He was blushing. It was both funny and touching and it made me believe that I was hearing the truth. "Anyway, it was great. I'd always had an easy time with women, but this was something else. We were living in Cambridge after grad school. Things began to go wrong, though, as soon as we moved back here. I didn't put it together for a long time. I blamed her drinking, but that was just another symptom, not a cause."

I had been married to a drunk also. It's an ugly word, an ugly way to describe someone you love, but if you've lived through it, you know just how accurate it is.

"Meanwhile, you're trying to start a business together."

"We never had any problem working together. I set up the lab, Selena worked her contacts, put together a board, began exploring future distribution avenues."

"But?" I stifled a sneeze. Someone had once told me that you can't sneeze with your mouth closed. They were wrong, you can. But you can just about give yourself a concussion. My eyes were already seeing strange patterns in the air from the migraine; now I had added butterflies and spinning stars.

"Eventually, she moved back to Park Avenue. There were just too many ghosts at that house."

I concentrated and forced my brain back on track. "We're back to the grandfather?"

He nodded.

"Was it abuse?" I asked.

He looked up in surprise.

"A guess," I said.

He looked down again and spoke to his hands. "It was rape."

"When did you find out?"

He shook his head to dispel a cloud of ugly images that all of us could see. "Last night. She told me last night." A single tear ran down his cheek.

"Jesus Christ!" the lawyer said, blowing up his patrician reserve in one explosive breath. "You were married to her for fifteen years and she never told you?"

"I was a bastard to her. When she stopped sleeping with me, I blamed the booze and gave myself permission to sleep with anyone I chose."

"But eventually you came back," I said.

"She promised to stop drinking."

"How many times?" I'd heard the same line from Angie, but never when she was drinking. Only when she was hungover or sick with remorse about the fight the night before.

"It worked for a while."

"This was after the affair with what's-her-name, the actress?"

He sat straighter and pulled his shoulders back. "Jo Harris. I take full blame on that, and I earned it, but I did not break up a marriage. There never was one. It was all image. The two of them hardly ever slept together. Their marriage was cooked up by publicists and agents. Give it another year or two and the Hollywood machine will start working and they'll be reconciled and remarried and *People* will pay them a few million for exclusive pics of the wedding."

"The pregnancy?"

"That was real."

"And that's what your wife couldn't forgive."

"Selena couldn't have children."

"Finish the story. What happened last night?" I said. "Did she tell you how the setup worked? Who helped her?"

He shook his head. "She was barely intelligible. We screamed at each other for a while and I left."

I was sure that I knew who her accomplice was, but until I had proof I wasn't prepared to say anything.

"What time did you leave?" I asked.

"Ten, maybe."

"And she was alive?"

"Yes."

"Go on."

"We had run out of ugly things to say—the fight was getting repetitive. I got in the car and left."

"Who found her?"

"I don't know."

The lawyer answered. "Security. The housekeeper heard two people—a man and a woman—arguing on the rear porch."

"No one heard a shot?" I said.

"The gun could have had a suppressor."

"What's the timeline? When was this?"

"Just before midnight," he said.

"So where were you at midnight?" Turning back to Haley.

"Sitting on my boat—at the dock—trying to decide whether to go back home or go get drunk."

"Anyone see you? A watchman, maybe?"

"I doubt it. And it was coming down sleet, snow, and rain. I stayed down below."

"Below? The boat has a downstairs?" The boat that Penn bought for his son had at least three levels.

"A cabin," he said.

"How long were you there?"

"I don't know. Until twelve-thirty or so. One, maybe?"

My throat was on the verge of giving out. The rasp was getting noticeably worse, and I could feel another giant sneeze building. "That's a long time to be just thinking about it."

"I had a lot to think about."

"Okay." I stopped and did a preventative nose blow. The nose still tingled, but I had deferred the explosion. "Tell me about the security at the house. The camera at the front gate. It must show you leaving three hours earlier."

"It also shows another car coming in and leaving again later on," the lawyer said.

That was the first bit of good news for our client.

"Have you seen the tape?" I asked the lawyer.

"No. I called out there and spoke to Carl Jenkins. He's head of security."

"How would anyone get in? Don't you have to be buzzed in by security?"

"Not if you have the code. It changes daily," Haley said. "But there are only four people on the distribution list. Selena, me, my secretary, and Jenkins. Anyone else needs to be cleared every time."

"All the staff?"

"Jenkins keeps security tight."

Not tight enough. But that wasn't the time or the place to start explaining how my friend, Dr. Benjamin McKenna, was exploring all the loopholes in the system. "How is the code delivered?" I said.

"Email."

"So any one of you could have been hacked." I turned to the lawyer. "I hope you're taking notes. I can see alternative versions of the crime heading in at least eight different directions."

"I will pass all of this on. Any one of them could have added someone else to the distribution list," the lawyer said.

"Your wife could have let her killer in," I said.

Haley broke. He gave out a single strangled sob and then began to cry again. The lawyer and I sat back and took turns staring at the ceiling until Haley pulled himself together.

"Can you get a call to this Jenkins?" I said. "I'll want to go out and talk to him and he won't see me without your say-so."

Haley looked to the lawyer.

"Here," he said, reaching into his briefcase, "use my phone."

I left them there, dialing the security guy. A deep, phlegm-filled, angry cough caught up with me halfway down the hall. I wanted to be back in bed.

29

For once, the traffic behaved. I pushed the little rental until it was on the verge of lifting off, bouncing over every seam on the highway.

"Virgil, I'm on my way out to talk to security at Haley's house." I had my iPhone plugs in with the little microphone built into the wire.

"Who is this?"

Sometimes the mic worked better than others. I pulled the wire around in front of my mouth, wondering if this still counted as "hands-free."

"It's Jason Stafford. I need you to do something for me."

"You sound terrible."

"It's just a cold."

"How's Haley?"

"A bit of a shipwreck. He answered some questions, some of them a bit vaguely, but he was adamant he didn't do it."

"*Did* he do it? What do you think?"

"I'll know more after I talk to security out at the house. But I think he's got a chance at pointing the finger elsewhere. While I'm out here, have one of your people check on Charles Penn. Where was he last night between, say, nine and midnight?"

"I can't just call up Chuck Penn and ask him where he was when Selena Haley was getting murdered."

"No. I was hoping you could be a touch more subtle than that. Give it some thought."

I clicked off before he thought of any more reasons why he couldn't do it. I stopped at a drugstore on the way and loaded up on cough drops and tissues, pretty much guaranteeing that I would start getting better immediately and not need any of it. I sucked on a mentholated Ricola and put a few more in my pocket.

There was a mashed mound of gray and black fur at the side of the road, a quarter mile or so before the turn to Haley's house. Raccoon. We'd have them occasionally in Montauk. They would find a way to scramble over the fence, defecate in the pool and all over the slate walk, and screech horribly at each other—whether in anger or in lust, I had no idea. They always made me wish I owned a shotgun and had the heart to use it.

"Jenkins!" I yelled at the disembodied voice at the gate. "It's Stafford. Let me in."

"Who do you wish to see?" the implacable voice said.

"Is this Carl Jenkins?"

"You wish to speak with Mr. Jenkins?"

"Listen up, sport. I'm a bit rushed. Tell Jenkins that Jason Stafford is here, then let me in. I'll give you three minutes before I drive through the gate. It's a rental, so I'm not afraid to try."

"One minute."

He was as good as his word. The gate started moving and an older, tougher voice came from the invisible speakers. "Take the first right. I'm down at the guardhouse."

The guardhouse was obviously what would have been called the gatekeeper's cottage in times long gone by. It was a whimsical concoction of deeply slanted slate roofs, a crenellated square tower, lead-paned windows, and a heavy wooden door that I half expected to lower down on chains, rather than swing open on wrought iron hinges.

A heavyset man in a khaki uniform and a Sam Browne belt, with a holstered black Glock on one side and a handheld radio on the other, greeted me at the door. It was the man I had seen riding the golf cart on my first visit. Without the mirrored sunglasses, his eyes looked watery and a little sad.

"I'm Jenkins. Mr. Haley called. No need to push your way in, you were expected."

"It's an old habit." That would have to do for an apology. Impatience is not always a bad trait for a trader. A bit of push is often needed to get something done—and expected. But it doesn't always travel well to the outside world.

Inside, the cottage had been reduced to an architectural style more akin to functional minimalism. There was nothing quaint about it. The walls and ceiling were a neutral gray—the gray you would expect to find on an aircraft carrier. Two metal desks faced a wall of television monitors. The images changed every ten seconds, showing different views of the property and the lab from varying heights and perspectives both indoors and out. Computer keyboards—one on each desk—were there to override the automatic changes.

A younger man, almost painfully overmuscled, wearing a similar khaki uniform with the same accoutrements, sat at the far desk. He looked away from the monitors and gave me a quick nod of acknowledgment. Not exactly hostile, but not far from it, either.

"I was in the can," Jenkins said, sounding only slightly aggrieved.

TMI. "Show me your system and tell me anything you can about last night."

Two hundred forty cameras located at various points around the property and in the buildings gave a continuous feed to a bank of computers. The system was wireless, which occasionally caused problems due to severe weather, electronic interference, or even sunspot activity. The images were reviewed by a filter program. All images with no movement were immediately sent to a trash file that was automatically dumped. All images that showed movement of any kind went through a second filter to remove leaves falling, rain or snow, wind blowing treetops, and animate objects too small or too slow to be deemed a threat, like squirrels or birds. Everything else was reviewed by a human eye.

"That's the biggest part of the day. Going over the tapes. There are deer on the property. We pick them up all the time. But the only time we hit save is when there is something unusual."

"Show me."

He opened a file. "Here's Mrs. Haley arriving yesterday. That's unusual in itself. She doesn't get out here very often."

I watched as a light-colored Porsche convertible stopped at the gate and paused. It was almost dark and a light mist was falling. A moment later, the gate swung back and the car proceeded.

"How did she open the gate? Did anyone speak to her?"

"We don't need to. There's a code for Mr. and Mrs. Haley. Fay, the housekeeper, gets one, too. And me. Oh, and Mr. Haley's secretary. My staff. A couple of the senior technicians at the lab, in case they're working early or late. Each one is different, so we can keep track of who's on the grounds."

And any one of whom could have shared their code with another party. No matter how good the technology, it still required humans to operate it—and make exceptions to each and every rule.

And Haley's belief that only four people had a code each day was a fond delusion.

Jenkins was still talking. "The codes change every day. It's set up as an app. You plug in the eight digits on a smartphone and the gate opens."

The lock was about as effective at keeping out the unwanted as a doorknob.

"So that could have been anyone in her car. You never saw her face."

"That's the way she wanted it."

"Did she ever give the code out? I mean to friends or delivery people."

He looked uncomfortable. "When we first installed the system. Mr. Haley spoke to her about it."

I took that as a yes. "Finish about last night."

He raced through the file, stopping again a minute later. "Here's Mr. Haley leaving." The bottom of the screen had the time and date. A few minutes after ten, a black sedan exited the gate. Though it was lit from a spotlight above, it was hard to make out the make or model. It was raining harder, and the car splashed through a small puddle as it turned out onto the main road.

"And how do you know that's him?"

"That's his car."

It was most likely his car, but you couldn't have proved it by the images that I was looking at.

"All right. Keep going."

"An hour later." Headlights flickered in the darkness and a large automobile turned into the drive. The overhead spotlight went on, revealing the distinctive front grille of a Rolls-Royce. There was a vague shape behind the wheel, but whether man, woman, or chimpanzee, it was impossible to see. The gate opened.

"Whose code did he use?"

"Mr. Haley's."

"Now, that's very interesting."

"The police thought so."

"They would. Can you get the license plate?"

"Not from this angle. The camera can get it, but the light's too high."

"Why not lower the light?"

"It would blind the driver."

"Really?"

"According to Mrs. Haley."

"What do you say?"

"I say it's her house. The camera picks up all the license plates during the day. There's not much traffic at night. Mostly Mr. Haley. Sometimes one of the lab techs stays late, but not many people coming in."

"They don't have guests? Parties? No one stops by to say hello?"

"Mrs. Haley is hardly ever here. Mr. Haley is either working or out on his boat."

"Back to the files. Who else have you got coming in?"

"No one. We've got the Rolls leaving an hour or so later and that's it, until the police arrived."

"When was that?"

"First car arrived at eleven forty-two. The shift supervisor called them at eleven thirty-five."

"Nice fast response time."

"They don't skimp on police in this part of the world."

"Who found the body?"

"The shift supervisor. He was going through the evening's files before end of shift and found a glitch."

"What was that?"

"The cameras along the cliff were all in and out of service for a couple of hours. It could have just been the weather, but he went out to check."

"He climbed down those stairs in that weather?"

"He had to. There's three cameras right along there. All three were on and seemed to be working, but we were getting no signal."

"Sounds a bit convenient that those cameras were all out while this was going on."

"Maybe," he said, unconvinced. "The wireless reacts to weather. Any weather. Rain, snow, lightning, even big winds. Also sunspots and solar flares. I'm waiting for it to start reacting to the phases of the moon."

"Are there any lights down there?"

"He had his flashlight."

"Still, I'd say he's lucky to have found her. Rain. Pitch-black out."

"An hour later and the body would have been washed out on the tide."

"And no one heard anything? The shot, I mean."

"Fay told the police she heard a man and woman arguing, but then thought it could have been the television. Her apartment is at the far end of the house. Unless the Gruccis were setting off a major fireworks show, she wouldn't have heard a thing."

"Let's go back for a bit. The car that came in after Haley left. The Rolls. You must have other film of it."

"Not film. It's all digital."

"Files, then." I bit off a more exasperated reply. "Show me."

Most of the images were nothing more than an indistinct blur of a black shape moving over a black landscape. The car bypassed the turnoff for the lab and went straight to the house. The front entrance was well lit by an overhead lamp, suspended from a chain and a wrought iron fixture, and two wall sconces that bracketed the front door. But the car pulled past the doorway and stopped in the graveled turnaround just beyond. The rear door opened.

"So, someone drove him here," I said.

"The police asked about that. I don't know who it could be. The Haleys don't have a chauffeur. Or a Rolls, for that matter."

The man was tall and broad-shouldered—it *could* have been Haley. He was wearing a floppy broad-brimmed hat and had a waterproof poncho wrapped around him. He began walking toward the house.

"Can you zoom in on him? Is there a shot of his face?"

"Nope." He demonstrated. "You see? He knows he's on camera. He keeps his head at an angle. Now watch."

The man veered away from the front entrance and the light and walked around to the side of the house.

"See? He either knows where the cameras are located or . . ." He trailed off.

"Or?"

He shook his head. "I've got no 'or.' He knows."

"Is there more?"

"One sec." He switched to another viewpoint. "I'll show you."

This time the camera was in back of the man as he walked along a stone pathway. A light came on over another door as he approached. Someone had been waiting for him. Expecting him. The door opened.

"That's Mrs. Haley. You'll see her in just a moment."

I did. She stepped into the light. She was holding a stemmed wineglass and looked as though she had emptied it more than a couple of times already. She waved toward the man in that *Hurry up* way that you do when the other party seems to be taking his time and the heavens are pouring down on you both. The man entered the house and the door closed behind him.

"Do you have more? Can we see him inside?"

"Cameras in the big house? No. That's definitely out-of-bounds. We can monitor all the entrances, but Mrs. Haley wouldn't let us do anything more than update the alarm system. She did not want cameras watching her in her own home."

I thought of the cameras at the Ansonia. Discreet. Camouflaged in the molding in the lobby, or hidden behind the mirrored ceiling in the elevator. I had no problem with them. Then I imagined them inside my apartment.

"I can see her point of view," was all I said. "Is there more?"

"Nothing until this."

The tall figure reappeared, emerging from the black night behind the house, head inclined against the rain. He passed under the camera and Jenkins switched viewpoints again. The man got back into the Rolls and it drove out of the picture.

"Where did he come from? Not the same door?"

"No. That path leads around to the rear of the house overlooking the cliff. The cameras were on and off all night. I'd guess he came out onto the porch and down."

"Could he have been coming from the steps to the beach?"

Jenkins nodded sadly. "If the police can show that that's Haley, it puts him at the murder scene at the right time."

It could have been Haley. It could also have been Penn. Or any other tall man with broad shoulders.

"Is it the right time? When did the housekeeper say she heard the argument?"

"Well, she said it was a bit later, but she's not a hundred percent."

He typed again. Black on black appeared. Again the flicker of approaching headlights, this time from behind the camera. It was the front gate again. It swung open and the spotlight went on. The Rolls rolled through and out of the picture.

"Can you freeze it?"

He did. The license plate was visible, but blurred and unreadable. Jenkins zoomed in until the plate filled the screen. It didn't help. The rain or the motion of the car or wireless interference had turned the image into a vaguely whitish-gray smear.

"It could be a New York State plate."

"It could be anything," I said. And what murderer leaves the scene in a chauffeured Rolls-Royce?

The Number 2 train got to Park Place and sat. The doors opened, closed, and opened again. I checked my watch. I was still all right for my ten o'clock with Virgil. I pulled out my phone and checked messages. None. None was becoming the standard. None as in zilch. Nobody. The doors closed again and the train lurched and stopped. The doors opened again.

"This train is being taken out of service. Please exit the train immediately. There is another Number Two train at Fourteenth Street that will be here momentarily."

Unless it gets routed onto the local track, I thought. Or held up at Chambers. Or turns around and goes back uptown, for all I know. I checked my watch again as I stepped out onto the platform. Still okay. A conductor slammed his way through the door at the end of the car, striding purposefully, checking to see that the train was empty. He exited at the far end and continued on down.

A short, broad-shouldered woman in a dark overcoat and helmet-shaped wool hat pushed by me into the empty subway car and took a seat. I thought about telling her that they were taking the train out of service, but then decided not to.

"Hey! Lady!" A young-looking black man dressed like a typical white suburban teenage male, in baggy jeans, a Jets hoodie, and a flat-brimmed Yankees cap with the size sticker still prominently displayed, gave a hoot and called to her. "Yo! That train is going to the yards. You s'posed to get off."

She glared at him and stayed put. The doors closed and the train sped off.

The young man looked over at me and shrugged. I nodded back.

Minutes ticked by; the second train did not arrive. I checked my watch again. If I left the station and walked quickly, I could cut down Ann Street and get to Virgil's offices with four minutes to spare. The foot traffic on Ann was always less than Fulton or Broadway. I decided to split the difference and give the New York subway system—the most efficient method of transportation in the industrialized world—another two minutes to make good. The seconds ticked off. It was a bad bet, but I pushed it another thirty seconds. No luck. No train.

I ran upstairs, caught the light at Broadway, crossed over and quick-walked around the corner to Ann Street. My watch told me I was doing just fine, but I pushed up the pace. Two blocks later, I rounded the corner onto William and saw my goal just past Fulton Street.

The blast of December-morning sunlight, streaming over the old fish market and up the hill toward Broadway, left me momentarily blinded as I entered the dark canyon on the far side. A crowd of straphangers emerged from the Fulton Street station as I reached the stairway; the young black man in the Jets hoodie jostled me slightly and mumbled a quick apology, sweeping past me in nonrecognition. I stumbled for a step, and as I recovered, I saw the car.

It was a 7 Series, black, idling and hugging the curb just past the subway entrance. There was nothing unusual about a large luxury car idling on a downtown street, nor in midtown, nor even in much of my uptown neighborhood. But the license plate caught my eye; someone had obscured it with strips of gray duct tape. Too precise to be accidental, it stuck out. It was unusual.

The driver saw me and registered both surprise and recognition. He knew my face, had expected me, but not from that angle, not out of the blinding sun. He had been watching for me to come up out of the subway. I don't know how I knew this, but it was as clear to me as the front page of the *Journal*. Just as clear was the menace I saw in him. There was nowhere to turn, no way to avoid it. I walked faster. I saw a flicker of panic in his eyes; we were already way off script. He said something over his shoulder to someone in the backseat. I kept coming.

The rear door opened and a man's head appeared. He wore a knitted watch cap pulled low, covering his eyebrows, and a pea jacket buttoned to his neck with the collar up. I registered a dark, full Turkish mustache that could as easily have been Iranian or Argentinian, or Nebraskan for that matter. His dark, almost black, eyes focused on me and his arm came up, still partially blocked by the car door.

I may have seen the gun first, or just reacted to an imagined view. But I recognized the intent. I spun on my right foot, lifted my left leg, and kicked the door—hard. The man was jolted back and I rushed forward, grabbed the side of the door and swung it into him again and again. The gun, a long-barreled handgun with a silencer attached, fell to the ground between us and I kicked at it frantically. It skittered out into the street. I took the door in both hands and slammed it into him, catching the side of his head as he tried to duck back into the car. Blood splattered over the glass and I heard him groan in pain.

I felt, rather than saw, the front door opening, and realized that the driver was a large man and that he was about to pull himself out and come for me. I turned and ran. The big guy almost caught me.

His hand swiped my shoulder; it felt like I'd been hit with a line drive. I started to fall, and for a moment I scrambled on two feet and one hand, running like a three-legged dog. I tripped over the step at the head of the subway stairs and tumbled down the next three steps. At least I tumbled faster than he could run. People were screaming, some in fear, some in anger. As big as he was, he wasn't prepared to face a crowd. I hit the bottom of the stairs and looked back up. He was gone.

I gulped air and reviewed the damage. I was all in one piece, no gaping wounds, no broken bones, though I thought my shoulder might be sore for the next few days and my right shin was scraped. The camel's hair overcoat was a total loss; I had split the shoulders on both sides, rolling down the stairs. The coat was a throwback, custom-fit to a younger version of myself—with narrower shoulders and a bit too much room through the middle. I wouldn't miss it as long as I stayed out of the wind. I left it draped over the top of the nearest trash can.

My pulse was returning to normal and I discovered that, despite the December chill, I was covered in sweat. I felt jumpy and fragile, like I needed some tea and a nap—or a shot of vodka. None of that was going to happen.

Someone wanted me dead. It wasn't the first time, but that didn't make it any easier to swallow. I was pain-averse and death-averse. In high school, I was a math club geek, not a tough guy, not even an athlete. Now, just months after some monster with a gun had killed my ex-wife—a bullet that should have been for me but that was pointed at my son—the monsters were back.

I was no hero. The little almond-shaped section of the brain that governs those kinds of emotions—the amygdala, I think it's called—functioned quite well in me. If someone wanted to kill me, I was terrified. But I had learned something in the last few years. There are worse things than pain, worse than death. In prison, I fought back and I found that others would bend when I did. I hadn't really known that before. And when I became a parent, an event that, because I was stupidly preoccupied, only occurred years after the birth of my son, I learned another lesson: I will fight to protect him. I will kill to protect him, if necessary. And, I believe, I would die for him—if only because the thought of living without him would kill me anyway.

I walked up the stairs, pausing for a moment as my eyes reached ground level. The car was gone. The pistol in the street was gone. The two men were gone. I continued up and crossed the street. I had a meeting with Virgil Becker, and I was late.

31

Virgil poured me two fingers of Jameson 12 Year Old and sat me down.

"Thank you. I'm not hallucinating or making this up. Someone did just try to kill me. They screwed up, but they were professionals. No doubt."

"Are you hurt?"

I'd have some aches and pains; I didn't roll down subway stairs often enough to do it without getting a few bruises. "I'm all right." The whiskey went down well. "I'm not a whiskey drinker. Is this good stuff? I should sip it, right?"

"It is very good stuff, but at this moment, it is medicinal. Pour it down if that's what you need."

I sipped it. "I could get used to this."

"We need to report this."

I shook my head. "I had a fight with two men on the street. They got in their car and drove away. Oh, and by the way, I started it."

"You saw a gun."

"No one else did. Those two were waiting for me to come up out of the subway. Who knew I was coming here? You, me, your secretary." I held up one finger for each of us.

"Are you suggesting that I had something to do with this?"

"No, no, no. I don't know who's behind this, but they have very good information. How often am I here? Two, three times a week on average? They didn't look like they'd been sitting there for two days hoping I'd just pop up. They knew I was due here and at what time. And if the trains weren't screwed up, I would be dead right now."

Virgil looked thoughtful—and frightened.

"What is it?" I said.

"The banker. London got back to me just before you arrived."

"Did they come up with a name?"

"Yes. Dillman. But the man is dead."

I took that in.

"Murdered?" I said.

"No. Or not obviously so. He died of an overdose of cocaine mixed with a powerful painkiller. Something called fentanyl. Very dangerous stuff, I'm told."

It could quite easily have been murder. "Last night?" Was he dead because of me? Because of the threat I had made to Selena?

"No. Weeks ago. Before all this started."

And right after he signed off on the account authorization, I thought.

"His housekeeper found him. He'd been dead for hours. The drugs were right there."

These people didn't like to leave loose ends. Virgil was right. I needed help.

"Who's your friend at the FBI?" he said. "Call him. If you won't report it to the police, at least talk to him."

"Put him on speakerphone."

I gave him the number, and a few rings later Special Agent Marcus Brady answered. We had a history together. We would never be friends exactly, but I trusted him. And, just as important, I believed he trusted me.

"It's Jason Stafford. I'm calling from Virgil Becker's office. You're on speakerphone."

"And I imagine you need my help. When else do I hear from you?"

"When's your birthday? I'll send a card."

"I saw a draft of a letter about you the other day," he said. "The U.S. Attorney is petitioning the judge to rescind your fine after what you pulled off last summer."

I still owed more than half a billion dollars in fines and reparations from the fraud that had landed me in prison. I had no intention of ever paying it, but getting it off my back would still be a relief.

"That'll be great, if I live to enjoy it."

"What's that?"

I told him the story of the attack.

"What does the NYPD say?" he asked.

"I'm not telling them. I'm telling you." The NYPD and I had a complicated relationship. At various times they had treated me like a hero, like a patsy, or like a perp.

"And I understand why, but you should make a report anyway."

"Come on, don't be a cop," I said.

"Then what did you call me for?"

"I want you to tell me who's trying to kill me."

"You think this is something out of your past coming back at you? I doubt it. You piss off a lot of people, but very few of them would bother hiring guns to get you back."

"The Latin Americans?" I said.

"We've had this conversation before. We covered your tracks on that pretty well."

"Would you know if they were after me?"

"If you are asking if the multiagency task force that I work with is operating wiretaps and other surveillance on specific Latin American cocaine caballeros, I would have to say, 'No comment.' But if in the course of my normal workday I ever found anything that I thought might constitute a legitimate threat to a valued source, I would take immediate steps to ensure his safety."

"All right. So it's not the guys from Honduras."

"Who have you pissed off lately?" he said.

Selena Haley. She was dead. Chuck Penn, if and when he got the bill from the yacht club dinner. But hiring assassins seemed like an over-the-top response to my prank.

I hated giving him information without getting some back. "I may have stepped on some toes."

"You're not giving me much to go on, pardner. Make a report."

"The NYPD can't keep me safe. Or my family."

"Neither can I, if I don't know what's going on."

I wasn't getting what I wanted. Maybe I could get something else.

"Just give me a ride uptown. In return for past favors."

"Oh-ho. The FBI now runs a car service?"

I gave up. "On the way, I'll tell you a story." Or at least part of one.

Virgil raised his eyebrows. I made reassuring motions and continued.

"The Haley case has a big hole in it," I said.

"It's not my case."

"It's a good story."

"It had better be."

32

So what are you going to do now? I mean, right now?"

Brady and I were sitting in the back of an FBI motor pool Crown Victoria—I half expected the windows to have roll-down handles.

"Make my family safe. I have some ideas, but you'll forgive me if I don't share them. I seem to be having a hard time keeping important information confidential. No offense."

"None taken, but be careful. These people seem to have the kind of resources usually reserved for governments or multinational corporations."

The fact that there were two more armed agents sitting in the front seat gave me a rare feeling of invulnerability, but my concern was primarily for those who might be used as targets in place of me.

"There's not much I can do, you know. I'll pass your information along, but Haley is not my case—either for insider trading or for murder. I have zero pull with the SEC and the white-collar-crime guys in our office."

Brady had once been one of the white-collar-crime investigators in the FBI New York office. Moving over to the interagency drug task force had been a major career boost. He had gone from a third-tier forensic accountant to a rising star with an impressive arrest record.

"And the Nassau County DA's office might as well be on foreign soil. They'll listen to Haley's defense attorney before they'll take my call."

"As soon as they identify that Rolls-Royce, they'll release Haley. How many can there be in the New York area?"

"That's a joke, right? I'd guess tens of thousands for a start and those are just the ones with local license plates. Now add in all the tax dodgers who keep an address in Florida. Without the plate number, they have no chance of finding this guy."

"What about following up on the connection with the banker?"

"The dead guy?" he asked by way of answering my question.

"It's too convenient that he just happened to OD right after signing off on that bogus account."

"Oh, it was murder all right. Fentanyl is not your garden-variety recreational drug. It's much too dangerous."

"So is heroin," I said, more to elicit information than to argue the issue with an expert.

"Fentanyl is a synthetic opioid and about one hundred times more powerful than heroin. They give it to terminal cancer patients. Every once in a while we get cases of junkies OD'ing on it. Some low-level dealer who's trying to hawk heroin that's been stepped on one too many times might add a small taste of fentanyl to boost the high on his product. But killing your customer is generally considered to be bad for business, even in the street-level drug trade. If some idiot made a speedball of coke plus that stuff, it was manslaughter. If he had a brain, it was murder. There is no way to reverse the effects of an overdose. The respiratory system shuts down first. The guy would have suffocated within minutes."

"Is it hard to get hold of?"

He raised his eyebrows. "We live in a capitalist society. Supply will always meet demand. The only variable is price."

Economic lessons from the FBI. "I should go," I said. "There're things I need to get started on. If you don't hear from me in a few days, start looking."

"Where shall I start?"

"Don't worry. I'll leave a trail."

The feeling of invulnerability disappeared the moment I stepped out onto the sidewalk. I felt cold, tired, bruised, and much too visible. I walked quickly toward the doors to the Ansonia.

I saw the man coming out of the corner of my eye. Raoul, the doorman, saw him, too, and came out to head him off.

"Hold up, Jason," the man called in a hoarse whine.

I didn't stop, but I turned my head to look him over. He knew me—or my name, at least. When I examined him, he looked a lot less frightening. Unpleasant, but not threatening. He was a bone-thin, gray-bearded man in an ancient trench coat and filthy sheepskin bedroom slippers. Though he looked like he had survived on the streets for years, a well-aimed gust of wind would have sent him flying like a page from yesterday's newspaper.

"Fuck off, pal." Raoul stood between us.

"I got a message," the old man said, holding out a small envelope. "The man said you'd give me five bucks for it."

"Not fucking likely," Raoul said. "Now move off."

"Just a sec." I dug in my pocket and pulled out a bill. "Give me the letter."

"You can't encourage these guys, Mr. Stafford."

"That's okay, Raoul. You can help most by getting me inside as quickly as possible."

The old man and I exchanged our bits of paper. He turned and immediately began shuffling toward Broadway.

"Is this from Dr. McKenna?" I called after him.

"Don't know the man. Said his name was Kimble."

I knew that game. "Richard Kimble?" *The Fugitive.*

He was still moving away. "Dunno. Said he was a doctor."

Raoul had the door open. I rushed inside before opening the message.

RUN

Followed by a ten-digit number beginning with 917. A cell phone.

33

I tipped Raoul a twenty and borrowed his cell phone. McKenna was frightened, but in control.

"Get rid of your phone. Destroy it. Same with your computer."

"I just bought that laptop."

"Have you signed on to any Internet sites as yourself?"

Not more than a few dozen. "I'll toss it." I told him about my two would-be assassins.

"And my FBI tail disappeared this morning," he replied. "They've been replaced. The new guys aren't watchers—they're hunters."

We talked for almost an hour. He didn't frighten me—the two men that morning had already accomplished that—but he did give me the tools and knowledge I needed, starting with his ten basic rules for vanishing. I told him to keep working on the Arinna computer system and asked him how we would keep in contact.

"When you're ready to come look for me, I will find you," he said before the line went dead.

Dr. Benjamin McKenna's Ten Basic Rules for Vanishing

1) Tell no one.
2) Change your habits. All of them.
3) All cash, all the time.
4) Create false trails.
5) Take nothing but cash. Nothing.
6) Unplug.
7) Use disposable prepaid cell phones—lots of them.
8) Change your physical profile.
9) Wear hats.
10) Avoid eye contact.

I followed my father's Olds out the LIE to Veterans Highway, hanging back a few hundred yards and watching to see if anyone else was tailing him. Pop changed lanes, slowed ridiculously in the center lane, and played with his blinkers almost constantly. He was having fun. By the time we reached the turnoff for the Islip airport, I was comfortable that the only drivers who might have wanted to kill any member of my family were the poor souls directly behind him.

It had been a long weekend, calling in favors, making arrangements to keep my family safe. They needed to disappear, too, only not in the same direction as me. Skeli had put up the most resistance, until she convinced herself that keeping the Kid safe had to be her responsibility, at which point she turned into my greatest advocate. Virgil arranged for the plane. Matt Tuttle lent us the house, saying only, "I won't be using it for a while." I had violated McKenna's first rule of vanishing, but I believed that my family would be safe. None of us went out all weekend. We ordered in food, clothes—including a new Burberry overcoat for me—and spent any downtime trying not to fret. Sometimes we succeeded.

Pop dropped Skeli, Estrella, and the Kid off at the private-jet offices, a few hundred yards from the main terminal, then he took the car to long-term parking and left it all the way in the back. I pulled up next to him as he waited for the shuttle bus.

"Going my way?" I called.

"Jeeesus! Hell on rye, son. You scared the piss outta me."

"Come on, hop in. There was no one following you."

"I didn't think so. If there had been, I would have driven 'im stark raving."

He slid into the front passenger seat and I pulled back out onto the main drive.

"How's everyone holding up?" I said.

"Good. Good. Wanda's been telling backstage Broadway stories and keeping us in stitches. Speaking of which, did you know Hugh Jackman's married? I mean to a woman. He's not gay."

"How's my boy?"

"Good. He's going to be fine. Wanda's great with him. He trusts her. We're going to be fine."

"Just don't let her cook, okay? Not even cold cereal."

"You always say she's perfect."

"She is perfect. She just can't cook. And my standards in that area are pretty low."

"We'll be fine."

I dropped him at the corner, leaving him a short walk to the small gray building. "Here, take these." I handed him a plastic shopping bag with six of the prepaid cellular phones. "Use one to call me when you get to the house. Then smash it and throw it in the ocean. Deep ocean. Save the others for emergencies."

"What do you do now?"

"Stop asking me, Pop. I've got a plan."

He leaned in the window and kissed me on both cheeks. "Take care." He turned and hurried off.

Ten minutes later, I heard the whine of the Lear's engines start up and a few minutes after that I watched the jet take off. I stayed there until I lost sight of the plane, carrying almost everyone in my world, until it disappeared in the wintry southern sky.

My next stop was in a sleepy village on the North Shore and the tiny First Bank and Trust of Long Island. The first step in my own disappearance.

"May I help you?" The speaker was a pleasant-looking gray-haired woman who appeared to be in her early sixties. She was wearing a heavy brown cardigan sweater over a ruffled silk blouse and a plum-colored woolen skirt. A pair of reading glasses on a gold chain around her neck was her only accessory. She might have been running the thrift shop at an upscale church.

"I'm interested in opening an account."

"Oh!" she said. This was obviously an unusual request. "Are you new to the village?" she asked, trying to regain control of the situation.

"I'm thinking of relocating," I said. This was true. I was thinking of moving to another apartment if I was still alive in the new year, and in the meantime, I was thinking of going into hiding.

She helped me fill out paperwork for a checking account and a charge card. I could have saved a fair amount of time by filling out the paperwork without her help, but then what would she have done for the rest of the day?

"We're quite proud of our clearing system. If you deposit a check today for up to one thousand dollars, we can have funds available in just two days. How much were you planning to deposit?"

"I want to wire in fifty thousand. And I'm going to need almost immediate access."

"Oh!" she said again, flushing a bright red across her cheeks and forehead. "I may need to make a phone call for that."

Thirty minutes and a half dozen phone calls later, I walked out of the little storefront bank with five thousand in cash, a book of blank checks, and a temporary debit card. The credit card and my account documents would all be sent to my father's old address in College Point. By the time the post returned them, I would have corrected my "mistake" or I would be dead.

I gave my tic free rein and plotted three separate routes to get myself to LaGuardia Airport, weighing and rejecting, until I decided upon Northern Boulevard to the Cross Island to the Whitestone Expressway to Grand Central, instead of either the LIE or Northern State. There were lights and traffic on Northern Boulevard, but I would avoid the possibility of getting stuck in a major tie-up. I had a plane to catch.

The shuttle bus driver at the rental-car park wanted to wait until he had a few more passengers. I offered him a twenty to leave immediately. He took it.

When whoever it was who was after me tracked me out to the bank and back, they'd see it as a simple dodge and not look into my further trip out to Islip. The private-jet crew had filed a flight plan to Miami, and wouldn't request the change to Puerto Rico until they were less than an hour out. Even if someone saw through the whole thing and set up an ambush in Miami, they'd have no time to rearrange and beat the plane to Puerto Rico. My family would be safe in Saint Thomas by dinnertime, and then leave for the British Virgin Islands first thing in the morning.

Next I had to provide a reasonably believable alternative for the killers to pursue. My false trail.

The departures board at LaGuardia Airport showed the usual number of delayed flights, another two that were currently boarding, and six flights that were leaving within the hour. Minneapolis, Boston, and Chicago—too cold. Not Miami—I was trying to misdirect, not target. Dallas. I could fly to almost anywhere from Dallas. On the other hand, the carrier was Spirit Airlines and no one would believe that I had flown on Spirit Airlines if there had been any other alternative. I chose Santa Fe. I had never been there. The name sounded warm.

I bought the last seat on the flight, inadvertently cheating some frequent flyer out of the upgrade to first class. I paid with my new debit card and made it to the gate with minutes to spare, despite being profiled and pulled out of line by security. No checked baggage and a last-minute purchase. Who else but international terrorists would travel in such a manner?

The flight to Santa Fe was risky but necessary. Though I had to look like I was setting up a real getaway for the Kid and me, if they were already monitoring flights, I was giving them seven whole hours to set up a trap for me when I arrived. *They* and *them* had already entered my mental vocabulary and sounded frighteningly normal. The trip was a calculated risk, but I had made a career out of calculated risks. I thought the odds were with me.

The setting sun outpaced us, and as the plane dropped down toward the Santa Fe airport, we fell through dusk, then evening, and landed at night. I was up front—seat 3B, on the aisle—and felt the dry cold reach in and wrap itself around my ankles the minute the flight attendant opened the door. Why had I expected Santa Fe to be warm in winter? The pilot informed us that we were still seven thousand feet above sea level and that the thermometer was reading in the low twenties and still falling. I sneezed.

I was second in line at the car rental counter and missed their only remaining full-sized sedan.

"I can put you in an SUV for the same price," the young man with the eyebrow stud said in an encouraging voice.

"I was hoping for something a bit more inconspicuous," I said. "A white Malibu maybe?"

"This is Santa Fe. If you want inconspicuous, you want an SUV." He checked his computer monitor. "I've got a Ford Escape in black or a Chevy Traverse in white. Your pick."

"Anything with a bit more pep?"

"For another eight dollars a day, I can put you in a BMW X3."

"What color?"

He raised both eyebrows. "Dark blue."

"GPS?"

He checked the computer. "No. But I can rent you a handheld," he said, his eyes brightening.

"Keep the GPS. I'll take the BMW." I reminded myself to take a picture of it for the Kid.

He then tried to sell me three different kinds of insurance.

"Sorry," I said. "I'm allergic to it. Just the car, please."

"You want the fuel option?"

"Doesn't it have fuel in it already?"

He brought out a chart, sealed in plastic, to demonstrate the fuel option. I stopped him before he got started.

"I think I'll take my chances on being able to find gas for sale somewhere here in town. Thanks."

The cold hit me again as soon as I stepped outside. The skin on my bare face and hands felt tight and dry and my eyes watered. For a moment, I couldn't see. I brushed a hand across my face. On the far side of the parking lot, just past the halo of the overhead lights, was a white Jeep Wrangler. Exhaust was coming from its muffler. I couldn't see past the reflected glare of the windshield, but I was sure that someone was sitting behind the wheel—watching me.

The rental cars were all lined up along a chain-link fence. I had no trouble finding mine. I jumped in and started it up. Despite the cold, the powerful engine started immediately, and the fan began pushing out lukewarm air. In less than a minute, it was hot. I sat watching the Jeep. Other cars, trucks, and SUVs moved around the lot, taking away the other passengers. I didn't want to be left there alone with the man in the Jeep. I pulled out and joined the queue for the exit lane. I checked the mirror. The Jeep pulled into line three cars back.

I had been followed before and I had driven with the FBI when following someone else. Losing a tail is not an impossible task. All it takes is a bit of creativity, and an utter disregard for safety and sense.

I gunned the engine and pulled into the oncoming lane. There was no oncoming traffic on the short road into the airport. I raced up to the corner, passing four surprised drivers on the way. A big pickup was sitting at the intersection, waiting for a slow-moving minivan to get by. I barely touched the brakes as I made the turn in front of the pickup, cutting off the mini and earning a blast of the horn from both drivers. I raced down Airport Road, taking only a brief look in the mirror—the Jeep was still back in line. He had made no move to follow me.

At the next light, most of the traffic was lined up to make the left, the rest continued straight on Airport Road. I took the right and pushed the pedal to the floor. The big Beemer roared forward.

There is a vast difference between being paranoid and being hunted. I was confident that I was being hunted, and if the Jeep was not part of the hunt, I had only made a minor mistake. Not to have taken it as a serious threat could have been a major mistake. Luck is not a substitute for action.

The speedometer continued to rise up over a hundred, but I didn't let up. I was surrounded by a black-on-black featureless desert. Ahead, and coming up quickly, was I-25, my route back into the city. I eased off the gas and aimed for the entrance ramp. German engineering pushed hard against the laws of physics. The SUV swayed and I felt the left tires begin to lift, but it held the road. I gunned it again as I rose up to the top of the ramp and took a look back toward the airport. A single set of headlights was coming down the road I had just left. It was hard to tell at that distance, but they looked high and close together—just like the headlights on a Jeep Wrangler.

Two miles and much less than two minutes later, I took the next exit and headed up Cerrillos Road. There were lights and stores and shopping malls with movies getting out and people moving in all directions in all manner of conveyance. There were hundreds of SUVs in all makes and colors. It is always easier to hide in a crowd than in the desert. I slowed and joined the flow.

The Comfort Inn and Motel 6 were too upscale for what I needed, their systems too efficient. I was looking for the kind of place that respected cash over credit, and more cash over the need to show ID. I wanted anonymity. I couldn't know for sure if that Jeep was really following me or not, but at some point those nameless, faceless men would pick up my trail, and I could only afford to have them find the clues I wanted them to find. I needed to keep them one step behind, and yet not lose them.

The Taos Trail Motel fit the bill. It was not on the old Taos Trail, that was a fragment of poetic license, but the flickering neon sign out front promised both air-conditioning and heat in every room. As the outside temperature on the dashboard readout was hovering just above single digits, I hoped the place lived up to at least some of its advertising. The final selling point was that the parking lot was in back, away from the main road.

The woman behind the counter had that four-season golden hue of the Southwest desert dweller, and a face so windburned and sunlined that she could have been forty or eighty. Either way, she looked tough enough to stand up to floods, droughts, windstorms, and desperadoes. I gave her two twenties and took my change. She gave me my room key and had me fill out a card with my name, home address, and the license plate of my car. I wrote that I was John Forbes Nash III of Princeton, New Jersey, and my vanity plate read MTH MJR. She didn't even look at it.

"Where can I get a bite to eat nearby?"

She checked a big clock over the door. "Not much this late. Kitchens tend to close earlier in winter. How far you willing to drive?"

"I don't need much. Anything in walking distance? I've been sitting all day."

"Taco Bell."

I was in a city justly famous for its blends of Native American, Mexican, and American cuisines, and for my one night there, I was not going to eat ersatz fast food. How could Santa Fe even support a Taco Bell? Who would eat there?

"Or pizza. Plenty of places that will deliver."

I thought of sitting in my room and waiting for a knock at the door.

"Where's the Taco Bell?"

34

I woke up early—before dawn—still on New York time. I pulled the curtain aside and checked the parking lot. There was no white Jeep out there stalking me. A light snow was falling, dusting the ground and the cars. It was too early to hear from my father or Skeli. They would just be waking up in Saint Thomas. The boat that was to take them across to Tortola wouldn't be there for hours. There was no chance that they would call before they got safely to Tuttle's house. That didn't stop me from wanting them to call.

I showered, shaved, and got dressed, not because I was in any hurry but because it gave me something to do. It was the solstice. The shortest day of the year and I had plenty to do, but I wasn't going to get anything done until the sun came up.

The snow stopped and the sky began to lighten. I turned on the television and watched the local weather. Sunny, high of thirty-eight. Zero precipitation over the next thirty-six hours. Possible light snow again tomorrow night. The only relief was the forecast for a thorough lack of humidity. My sinuses were already opening up, causing my ears to pop repeatedly as bubbles of pressurized air burst upon my eardrums. It was the first time in a week that I woke without having to clear my throat of a suffocating lump of mucus. Mountain air must have agreed with me.

The national weather map filled the screen. Eighty and sunny in San Juan. Nice day for a boat ride from Saint Thomas to Tortola.

The neighbors to my right were up and arguing in Spanish. She spoke loudly—but much too quickly for me to understand anything. He mumbled in a low growl, but I caught the word *chinga* every other beat. I turned off the television and checked the time. Still early, but I couldn't stay put. I was going to start pacing in a minute and the walls would start closing in. I took a deep brave breath and walked out.

The door to the room to the left of mine opened as I was crossing the parking lot. Two rough-looking men in jeans, down vests, and baseball caps came out, and I froze. They were either looking right at me, or right through me, I couldn't tell. I was trapped. The only way out of the lot was through them. The car was somewhere behind. I'd never get to it in time. I braced myself.

"Morning," said one as he walked by. The other just nodded.

They started to get into a big pickup. There was a logo for an Albuquerque construction firm on the door.

"Say, hey," I called.

The one who had spoken to me stopped and turned back. "Hey."

"Where can I go for a good breakfast around here?" I thought I should give some parameters to that request. "Local food. Someplace off the main drag."

He nodded. "Try Counter Culture over on Baca. It's not far."

I nodded thanks and got in my car. I was going to have to get control over my fear of pursuit or I'd be jumping out of my skin every time I saw someone looking at me.

The breakfast burrito with red and green chili was everything that Taco Bell wasn't. I sat over my coffee, studying local maps, reading the real estate ads in the local paper, and making calls until the café began to get noisy. I placed a five in the tip jar on my way out.

The snow was already gone, sucked up in that dry atmosphere as soon as the sun was fully up. Though I knew the temperature was still only in the thirties, I felt overdressed in my New York overcoat and suit jacket.

More cars were coming into the little parking lot in front of the restaurant and few were leaving. It took me a few minutes to edge my way out to the street. Coming out of a driveway directly across the road was a white Jeep Wrangler. This time I had no trouble seeing the driver. He was a tall man, made taller by a white cowboy hat. He was wearing a raw shearling coat unbuttoned, revealing a blue-and-white plaid shirt. His face was partially hidden by the brim of the hat.

I couldn't race my way out of this, there was too much traffic around me. I would have to think my way out.

There was certainly a chance that this Jeep was not the same one as the night before. I had never seen such a gathering of big four-wheel-drive vehicles. Did everyone in Santa Fe harbor some fear of being caught in a dry riverbed as a flash flood came hurtling down at them out of the mountains? Or being stuck in a snowed-in mountain pass where the only hope of survival was to scramble over the mountaintop, wheels spinning and sliding?

But the odds of this being a different Jeep were outweighed by the risks. I drove up Cerrillos toward the center of town. The Jeep hung back but followed. I caught a quick sight of the driver talking on a cell phone. Preventative action was called for.

There was a Whole Foods coming up on my right, and an idea occurred to me. I hit the brakes and swung into the parking lot. The Jeep, now two cars back, did the same.

I drove around to the back of the building, quickly parked, got out, and began to quick-walk back to the street. The guy in the cowboy hat watched me, trying to figure out the game. He could have parked and followed on foot, but instead he elected to keep the car and follow from a bit farther back. That's what I was counting on.

The map of downtown Santa Fe had shown a warren of one-way streets. Driving through the center of town while following someone on foot would be impossible. I crossed Paseo de Peralta and began weaving up and down, in and out, never traveling with the traffic but always against it.

It was early and cold. The streets were empty. Crowds were what I needed. I could melt into them. I wasn't going to get my wish.

I checked my watch—my first appointment with a realtor was not for another half hour. I needed to kill time and lose the cowboy in the Jeep.

The central plaza was surrounded by shops, many with rear doors that let out into smaller plazas that in turn led to other shops facing other streets. I dashed through stores selling silver and turquoise jewelry, pottery, woven baskets, glass sculptures, skulls and skeletons of various animals from longhorns to rattlesnakes, bundles of dried sage, red chili pepper decorations, calendars, recipe books, T-shirts, aprons, sauces, powders, mixes, and enough of the dried and fresh peppers to give heartburn to all of New York and New England combined. When I found myself back on a street, I immediately began walking quickly again—against traffic.

My winding perambulations finally led me onto a residential street with dusky red adobe fences broken by bright blue wooden doors, and cracked concrete driveways. I caught a faint whiff of woodsmoke on the air. It was so peaceful it terrorized me. I'd been in constant motion for thirty minutes.

The Jeep pulled into view at the end of the block.

The street was one-way—against him. But there wasn't another person or automobile in sight. The Jeep turned and began racing the wrong way, straight toward me.

I vaulted over the nearest four-foot-high adobe fence and ran toward the back of the house. I could hear the Jeep's engine racing out in the street behind me, then the squeal of brakes and the *thump-thump* of a car driving up onto the sidewalk. Another short fence slowed me down for just an instant, then I kept on running.

That next house had a longer yard with two scraggly fruit trees, not much taller than big shrubs, and a lattice frame supporting some nasty-looking thorny vines. On the far side was a taller chain-link fence. I jammed the toe of one of my five-hundred-dollar shoes into the fence and jumped up and over it and hit the ground running. I was halfway across the yard before I realized that I was not alone.

The dog had a head like a bowling ball with teeth, and four stubby legs with almost as much muscle mass as Conan the Barbarian. It didn't bark, growl, or even give me a dirty look. It just bared its fangs, jumped off the back porch, and ran straight at me. Two more long strides took me to the next fence. This time I didn't bother sticking my toe into the mesh. I twisted and threw my body into a high jump, the first I had attempted since Mr. Marciano, the track coach, made me try it back at Edward Bleeker Junior High School, sending me immediately after to the school nurse. I wasn't very good at it then, and though I wasn't much better this time, I was good enough.

I heard the snap of the dog's jaws in the air where my ankle had been an instant earlier and I imagined that I could feel its breath on my leg. But I sailed over the fence, one of the jagged tines catching and tearing the tail of my three-day-old overcoat and spinning me over so I landed ingloriously on hands and knees, bouncing off the winter cover of an outdoor hot tub. The dog didn't try to follow.

Behind me there was a clang and a clash as the man in the hat hit the first chain-link fence and jumped over. He saw me pulling myself erect over the next fence, and for a moment our eyes met. He meant to kill me. His right hand reached inside the shearling coat. If there was a gun there, he never got ahold of it.

The dog hit him mid-thigh, latched on, and shook, knocking the man to the ground. In the moment of falling, his face froze in terror with the knowledge that the predator had just become the prey. He landed badly, his right arm trapped under him. Encumbered by the coat, his face in the dirt, there wasn't much he could do to defend himself. The dog released its hold on his leg only to run up his back and bite again—this time into the nape of his neck. The man began to scream. Loud, terrified screams. The kind of screams that come when you think that you are being eaten.

I ran, brushing through a hanging forest of wind chimes, setting off an unmelodious harmonic din that did nothing to hide the man's ongoing screams. He wasn't calling for help, he was howling in primitive terror.

Another voice yelled out of a window, telling the dog to back down. I didn't wait around to see if the mutt obeyed.

Back on the street, I saw the Jeep, two wheels on the sidewalk, driver's-side door open, motor still running. I did not think twice. I jumped in, slammed the door closed, put it in gear, and hit the gas. I pulled into the first open driveway and made a quick three-point turn and raced back down the street—this time in the right direction. No one saw me, but at that point to have been stopped while driving the wrong way on a one-way street would simply have added the last touch of absurdist hysteria to the events and have sent me into screaming fits.

I made a left at the corner and tried to keep from racing through the streets on the way back to the Whole Foods. The parking lot was full of big SUVs, motors running, spewing hydrocarbon and nitrogen compounds into the atmosphere; spouses keeping the heaters going while their partners were inside shopping for organic, earth-friendly, naturally produced, sustainable, fair-trade food items that they would take home in hemp bags. The exhaust fumes created a gray haze outside the door. I slowed to a crawl and circled the building to the rear parking lot. The BMW was gone.

"Well, that answers that question," I said to myself. "You really can steal a BMW."

Whoever was after me had just delivered a very detailed message. First, the cowboy wasn't operating alone—there were more of them there in Santa Fe. Second, they were very good. I knew that in Europe, BMWs were sometimes hacked and stolen, but I had thought it was impossible in the U.S. Apparently, I was mistaken. Third, they wanted me to know. Therefore they believed strongly in their own power. And fourth, they were playing me. They wanted me frightened, but free, until they figured out why I had come running to this western town.

I wasn't ready to let them find out. Not quite yet.

These were not the Central Americans who had tried to have me killed six months earlier and ended up killing my ex-wife. Those men had been violent and impulsive. The men who were after me now had access and resources far beyond those of some pissed-off drug gangers. These guys had been able to hack into airline manifests and track me across the country. They were able to get men on the ground, waiting for me, thousands of miles away. Brady was right. If these guys didn't work for a government, they worked for an organization with equal power and assets. I'd been lucky with the cowboy and I would need a lot more luck before I was through.

I drove the Jeep the few blocks back into the center of town and parked it in an enclosed garage.

"How long you going to be, mister?" the slack-jawed youth at the gate asked me as I left.

"As long as it takes, son. You're not planning on closing anytime soon, are you?"

"I have to collect in advance, if you're staying overnight, that's all."

"Well, thanks. I'll be long gone by your dinnertime." I had many miles to go.

I had called and left messages for three different real estate brokers while I was sipping my coffee at Counter Culture that morning. The three with the most high-end ads in the newspaper. One had called me back. She was about to win first prize.

Her office was on the far side of the main plaza, between the library and a Vietnamese restaurant. I got there just as she was opening the door.

"Mrs. Montoya? I'm your nine o'clock. Jason Stafford."

Mrs. Montoya's jewelry must have weighed as much as she did. She was so thin she could have worn my old wedding ring as a bracelet. But the platinum would have clashed with all of her silver, turquoise, and coral bracelets, earrings, rings, pins, and necklace. She jangled when she moved, and she was in constant motion. Driving her car—a big Lincoln Navigator—her head, arms, shoulders, and hands were all gesticulating all the time, emphasizing the opportunities in Santa Fe real estate.

"There are three houses I can show you that all meet your specifications to one degree or another. But I really want you to consider something on the north side of town. I can do so much more for you there and the views are spectacular."

"My son has special needs. He'll be going to school in Albuquerque and I'll be driving him both ways every day. North of town adds thirty minutes to my drive—in each direction. Sixty extra minutes a day."

"Well, not really. And only if you go through town. There's a house in Tesuque three minutes from Route 84. If you take the highway, you can bypass all the traffic. At most it adds ten minutes to a commute like that."

"But if I'm down off Rodeo Road somewhere, can't I be on 25 South in minutes?" The map was as clear in my mind as the Pythagorean formula.

"What? Ragle Park? On a map, maybe, but you'd be stuck in traffic. And you won't get the kind of privacy you said you wanted. You'd have to be halfway to Pecos—an extra half hour! Well, twenty minutes. But you know what I mean."

"Do you just do that naturally?"

"What?"

"Compare various routes to get places."

She laughed. "My mother got me started. She was impossible that way."

I had found my long-lost twin. Separated at birth in some alternate universe.

"So's my Pop."

"You do it, too?"

"I look at a map once and it's like it's seared into my brain and if I don't figure out every possible combination of routes from one place to another, I find that I can't think about anything else."

"Yup. Listen, let me show you Tesuque. You'll see. Trust me. This place is so much better than anything I can show you south of the city."

I never did see the houses south of town. The place in Tesuque was perfect. So perfect I wished that I really was going to live there. Five acres on a cul-de-sac, the only house at the end of a winding road. There was an electric gate at the bottom of the drive and a tall coyote fence on three sides. The back of the property had only a short wall, to keep casual strollers from stepping off the steep cliff. It had privacy.

The house itself reminded me of the Montauk house without the pool. Instead, there was a partly covered porch that surrounded the house with views of the whole valley. Four bedrooms. The master suite with its gas-fired kiva fireplace and mountain views for Skeli and me, another small suite for the Kid so he could have his own bathroom and keep it as germ-free and spotless as he needed, a third bedroom that could easily be converted into a nursery, and a guest room for my father and Estrella. I couldn't believe that I was fantasizing about this house as though I might actually live in it. It was a ruse. An expensive, and I hoped convincing, blind alley for my pursuers.

"Twelve minutes to Whole Foods. Less if you shop at Albertsons," she said.

"Let's talk money, shall we?" I answered. We didn't talk long. I was easy.

The overhead light in the master bedroom's closet had two electrical outlets. I took out one of my cell phones and a charger and plugged it in. I was building my communications network.

The moment the seller's lawyer deposited my check into an escrow account there would be the beginning of a digital trail. A trail that I hoped would lead my pursuers to the inescapable conclusion that Jason Stafford was preparing to abandon New York—and possibly the now extremely dangerous investigation—and relocate to the relative remoteness of New Mexico. I made sure Mrs. Montoya had my instructions about where to send documents and any mail that would arrive. She would contact the bank and the title company and get the appraiser out there—all of which would cause a flurry of paper and digital code to appear.

My more immediate concerns began with the fact that my current ground transportation was liable to be listed soon as a stolen vehicle, making me a target for any police officer. I left Mrs. Montoya at her office and ducked into the Western boutique across the square. In fifteen minutes I emerged, transformed by cowboy couture. *Change your physical profile. Wear hats.* Boots and stiff blue jeans changed my stance, my pace, and my walk. The hat and long shearling coat changed my profile. I added sunglasses and a scarf. The saleswoman called it a bandana. I stuffed my suit into my bulging backpack, left the brand-new but already torn and muddied camel's hair overcoat in the changing room, and walked back to the garage, confident that I was virtually unrecognizable to any of my pursuers.

"You're back already?" the young man at the garage greeted me, looking up from his graphic novel. *Sexual Encounters of the Third Kind.* On the front cover, there was a werewolf attacking what appeared to be a big-busted Klingon. They were both snarling.

"Is that for a book report?" I asked. "What do I owe you?"

"Two dollars."

I peeled off two singles and a fifty. "This is for you. You will now forget you ever saw me. Agreed?"

He agreed.

I felt the slightest twinge of guilt as I switched license plates on the Jeep with a Toyota 4×4 from Texas, but I didn't let it slow me down. I would now be driving a stolen vehicle with stolen plates, doubling up on my personal crime wave, but I would quadruple my chances of staying clear of the police for the next few hours. I planned on being far away by then.

It was time to "resurface" and leave another false trail. I drove out of the parking lot and headed south. Albuquerque was an hour away.

35

The drive gave me time to think—always a devil's bargain. It was just over twenty-four hours since I had last seen the Kid or Skeli and I felt their absence like a cold stone in my chest. This wasn't how I wanted our life to be. My family in hiding, me being pursued by grim-faced men. I reviewed the steps, the minuscule, irrevocable decisions that had led me, cumulatively, to this point. There was nothing I could have done differently. Unless I changed everything. Maybe an escape to a house in Santa Fe was exactly what I needed. I was a father, not a secret agent or a bounty hunter. Soon I was going to be a father again. The process may have already begun. I could rationalize that I was doing what I did to provide for my family. That it was all for them. But I would be lying. I did it because I enjoyed the stimulation. I liked solving puzzles and I liked feeling amped. I had worked for years on an adrenaline high, and my body still craved it. I swore that I was different, that I had changed, but the bottom line was that, when I took on a challenge, I let nothing stand in my way. And I was beginning to like catching bad guys.

I took the exit for the Albuquerque airport and booked myself into a room at the airport's Hilton. I tipped the woman at the front desk, the concierge who helped me book my flight to JFK for the next morning, and the doorman just for being pleasant. I would be remembered. I declined the valet parking, making a point of saying that I would be going out soon to drop off my car at the rental lot. The truth was that I wanted to be able to leave quickly, and I did not want anyone looking too closely and possibly remembering that Jeep.

Once in the room, I worked quickly. I splashed water around in the bathroom, ran the shower, got a towel wet and left it on the floor. Returning to the bedroom, I took the cover off the bed and mussed up the sheets enough to make it look as though I had slept there. I took two of the bottles of Absolut Vodka from the minibar and poured them down the toilet. I left the two empties on the night table, making sure to leave as many fingerprints on as many surfaces as possible. I took one last look around. What was I forgetting? A tip for the maid! I took a page off the notepad by the phone and wrote *Thank you* and wrapped it around a twenty. She would remember me even if she never saw me.

Then I went back to the car and drove to Denver.

I had reservations on two different airlines from two different New Mexico airports to return to two different airports in New York the next afternoon. But if everything worked out, I would be back in town first thing in the morning.

Driving between cities out west is different than back east. My compulsion could lead me to plot half a dozen routes to go from New York to Boston, or Newark to Washington, all within an hour of each other in travel time. Albuquerque to Denver soothed me. Unless I was willing to add hundreds of miles to my trip, there was only one way to go. North on I-25, passing Santa Fe again, and taking the southernmost pass through the Rockies coming down onto the westernmost edge of the Great Plains. Five hundred miles. I made it in less than six hours.

I left the Jeep in a strip mall parking lot, blocking two spaces in front of a liquor store and a Chinese takeout shop. Directly overhead was a large sign that stated that any cars parked there for more than three hours would be towed at the owner's expense. I hoped it was true. I had a beer and a burger in a dive bar nearby and had the bartender call me a cab to the airport.

Again I had to take a calculated risk. To get on a flight out of Denver, I needed to show ID and pay with plastic. I would be traceable again. Whoever it was leading the pursuit, they had no problem tracking me through the system. I could only hope that the other two reservations would cloud my real plan.

The business-class lounge had no showers, so I changed in a cubicle in the bathroom. Getting rid of the stiff jeans—which had already chafed my thighs raw—and the boots—which one should remember were designed to be worn while riding a horse, not walking the length of an airport concourse—improved my life significantly. The fact that my suit was creased and rumpled would only serve to make me look like every other business traveler getting off the red-eye flight in Newark. I had stopped at a kiosk on the concourse and traded my two-hundred-dollar, barely worn cowboy hat for a garish black, orange, and silver ball cap advertising the Denver Outlaws. I was assured that they were a local sports team, and since they didn't play baseball, I felt my allegiance to the Yankees was not being challenged.

The little desks along the back wall had no access to electricity. Some of the more savvy and experienced travelers had already taken the few seats that were near outlets on the other side of the room. I noticed that they also had the foresight to bring three-way sockets. I took out my bag of cell phones and sat as far from the noisy bar as possible.

I dialed the number of one of the phones I had given my father. When he answered, I rattled off the telephone number of the phone I had hidden in the house in Santa Fe. Then I hung up and waited. A minute later, one of the other phones in my bag began to ring, the call automatically forwarded.

"Hello, son. How ya doing?"

"Staying one step ahead," I said. "How's everyone there? No surprises, right? No problems?"

"This place is lovely and no, no surprises. We got here this morning and we all feel very safe."

"How was the boat ride?"

He ignored the question. "We were just starting to worry," he said. "About you, I mean."

"I'm good," I said. "Tired. I've been going almost nonstop now for a day and a half. But, like I say, I'm good."

"You've sounded better."

The sound of his voice, quiet, strong, calm, was releasing waves of feeling. I wanted to be where he was.

"I got over my cold. How's my boy?"

"I'm giving him swimming lessons."

"You can't do that, Pop. He's not ready for the ocean."

"In the kiddie pool. All right?"

"All right. How's he doing?"

"Give me a break, will ya, it's only his first day."

"I mean, how's he doing otherwise?"

"Brilliant. That's what the little Aussie lifeguard says. 'Brilliant!' How's your day? 'Brilliant!' How's the food here? 'Brilliant!' How about that barracuda chomping on your leg? 'Brilliant!' It was cute the first time."

"He's eating?"

"Eating. Sleeping. Playing. He likes the water. He likes the sun. He likes the little lizards or whatever they are that run around here. He was pretending to be one this afternoon, lying on a rock and doing these funny half push-ups."

"Don't let him get too much sun. He's got his mother's coloring." Pale skin and blond hair.

"Junior, there are two strong-minded women here making sure he's covered with Number 45 or whatever, or wearing a hat or a shirt or both, or under the umbrella. Believe me, the Kid doesn't need me weighing in on the subject."

"Okay. Sorry. I'm being annoying. An idiot."

"It is very touching to hear you talking like a concerned parent, but you're right. It is annoying."

I laughed. "Is he asleep?"

"Long time. It's after midnight here."

I was losing track of time zones. "Christ, I'm sorry. Did I wake you?"

"Me? No. We're all still up. But he was so tired he had a hard time keeping his head out of his spaghetti."

"Spaghetti?" I felt a pang of jealousy that someone else had gotten him to try something new.

"Estrella's doing the cooking. She does a kind of Puerto Rican version. A little spicy. Like her."

Our conversation was so normal, so lacking in the paranoia I had been running from the past few days. I could have remained there, listening to voices of loved ones, who were safe and together.

"Can I talk to Skeli?"

"Estrella just took her for a walk down to the beach. She was beginning to get that faraway look. Can we set up a callback?"

She wasn't all right. My little fantasy of them all smiling and happy in the sun blew apart. I felt cold.

"I'm not boarding for another few hours, but in case I miss her, let's set a schedule. Call that number every day sometime between noon and two your time. If I can't answer, I'll try and leave a message. I'll call again when I can. Give her my love."

I clicked off before my voice began to break.

36

Even in first class, the red-eye from Denver to Newark is a brutal flight. Three and a half hours is not enough time to get any deep sleep, and I arrived feeling a bit like a visitor from another dimension. Newark Airport at six in the morning had a two-dimensional feel to it. Nothing seemed real.

My plan at that point depended, again, upon luck and odds. I had bet that if anyone was tracking me through the computer, he would have seen my booking on a flight that would not even leave Albuquerque for another four hours and another out of Santa Fe for later in the morning. Plenty of time to stake out the airports there, or, even easier, simply wait for me to arrive at JFK or LaGuardia late that afternoon. Additionally, I was betting that having found one or both of those bookings, he would stop looking, and therefore miss my arrival in New Jersey ten hours earlier. I hesitated to assign numerical probabilities to my calculations, but I thought I was safe.

I wasn't.

There were two of them. They were both sitting in the waiting area facing the gate as I came off the ramp. One was big, the other bigger. They weren't cowboys, they were dressed in puffy black jackets, baseball caps, and jeans, and both wore heavy workboots. Neither one looked like he was built for speed. They might be hard to stop, though, once they got going. Force equals mass times acceleration.

The first guy was easy to read. He hadn't expected to see me. The calf-length shearling coat, the Outlaws headgear, and the designer sunglasses didn't faze him. He recognized me right away, but I was a surprise. I hoped that meant they weren't there in force. Someone had merely sent two low-level thugs to check out the long shot on the flight from Denver. It'd paid off.

I thought since they were here inside the secured area of the airport, they wouldn't be armed, not even with knives. And they wouldn't try to take me there with a hundred witnesses coming through the gate behind me. I had a chance, I just didn't know what it was yet.

The bigger man dropped his eyes to watch my feet as I approached. It was effective. He didn't look like he was staring at me, but he could follow me easily. The other guy lacked any subtlety. His eyes flashed at me and I could tell he was holding himself back from rushing right at me.

I turned to the left and let a few more of the first-class passengers catch up with me so that we walked in a loose group toward baggage claim and the exits. I felt the two big thugs follow, hanging back ten feet or so.

There was nothing to stop them from taking me as soon as we got outside. For all I knew, they had help nearby. They could whisk me into the back of a car waiting out front and no one would ever hear from me again. The only thing that I had going for me was they were bound to underestimate my desperation. To them I was a white-collar pushover. I had the element of surprise, if I could find out how to use it.

The cleaning crews were out, pushing big yellow carts with

mops and cleaning supplies, toilet paper and towels. The men's room ahead and to my left had a yellow plastic A-frame sign in front. CLOSED FOR CLEANING. I broke away from the other passengers and headed right for it.

A short, slight man in the standard khaki uniform was about to start mopping the floor. He looked up in surprise. I didn't give him a chance to tell me to leave. I took the mop from his hand and yelled at him, "Not now! Out! Come back in five. Beat it!"

He tried to take back his mop, but I held it away and kept yelling. I was more than a full head taller and considerably broader. And I was acting nuts. "Five goddamn minutes, that's all I want. Now leave!"

"Okay, okay." He put up his hands in mock surrender and walked quickly out the short hallway.

I grabbed the gallon container of liquid soap and squeezed about a quart of it onto the floor. I could hear the cleaning guy telling his story to someone right outside. The thugs would be coming as soon as the entry was clear of witnesses. I unscrewed the mop handle and stood against the wall and waited.

The smaller of the two came first. He was impatient, aggressive, and probably a bit arrogant. He was also dumb. He saw me moving out of the corner of his eye and turned his head. By the time his brain told him to raise his hands it was too late. I caught him square on the bridge of his nose, swinging the long mop handle like a stickball bat. It broke with a loud crack, sending a jagged fragment bouncing off the tiled wall and skittering across the floor. Or possibly the loud crack was the guy's nose breaking. He hit the floor knees first, face second. His Mets cap rolled under the sinks.

His bigger friend came around the corner much more carefully. He rolled his shoulders like a boxer and moved easily around to my right, circling to force me back into the corner. There wasn't enough of my mop handle to do me much good, but I held on to it, raising it between us like a crucifix in front of a vampire. He smiled at me. He was going to enjoy tearing me apart.

I feinted once with the broken handle—a short, controlled swing, just to let him know that I could still be dangerous. He grabbed it, pulled it out of my hand, and threw it to the floor in back of him. Then he took off his cap—Baltimore Ravens—and ran a hand around the inside facing. He took out a long thin wire that had been coiled in there and stretched it between his two big hands. A garrote. He was armed. I wasn't. I imagined the wire squeezing around my neck, cutting into the skin while I choked to death in his arms. He smiled again. He knew what I was thinking.

I stepped back. He came on. I stepped back again. He came forward—and stepped right into the pool of liquid soap. His foot slid to one side and he lurched, almost fell. I took my one shot. I kicked him between his legs, hard enough that I would swear both of his feet were off the ground. He gasped, but he wasn't done. He was hurt, not crippled, and he pulled himself upright. But now both boots were coated with the soap and the moment he brought one foot up to come toward me, the other foot shot out from under him. His arms windmilled, the wire went flying, and he went down, one knee and one arm breaking his fall. I kicked his arm and pounced on his back, driving him down flat on the floor. I grabbed his ears and slammed his face into the tiles, grunting with exertion each time like one of the muscle-bound idiots at the gym. Then I stopped because I realized that he was no longer struggling. He was limp.

I got up and rolled him over. He was breathing. Bloody, but definitely alive. He looked familiar, but I couldn't be sure. His buddy groaned and tried to roll over. I went over and kicked him in the head. He stopped groaning.

I wanted to take one of these two and shake out of him who he was working for, but there was no time. I had to move.

The cleaning guy was standing outside the entrance, hands on hips and ready to lay into me.

"You see! Now I got to wait for two more of you guys to finish in there. This is not the only men's room, you know. I got work to do."

"Well, give them another few minutes," I said. "I think they're having an even worse day than you. By the way, I broke your mop." I pulled another fifty off my roll and tucked it into his shirt pocket. "That oughta cover it."

I walked as fast as I could. No one paid any attention to someone moving quickly in an airport, but they all would have stared at someone running. The cleaning guy might hold off for another few minutes before going back into the men's room, and then my clock would start. I headed straight for the taxi line.

37

The cabbie dropped me at the end of the Holland Tunnel where he could loop around and go right back to New Jersey. I walked up Hudson, past the Saatchi building and the main passport office, and over to Varick to catch the Number 1 train. The subway was already packed at that hour. My head was nodding and bobbing the whole way up to 181st Street. Barely two hours' sleep in the last twenty-four and I still had quite a ways to go. I walked up to the bus terminal at the George Washington Bridge and bought a ticket for the first bus to Fort Lee, where I got out and walked four blocks. It was time for Jason Stafford to resurface briefly and lay down another false trail. Hopefully, the final one.

I have often made the spurious claim that you can get anything in the world in New York at any time. Bored with your local Ethiopian restaurant? There's a restaurant in Harlem that serves Eritrean dishes. Want to find that sausage you had in Umbria last fall? Ninth Avenue. There's a place that makes it fresh. Clothes, books, art, tools for any art or craft, fine wines and dive bars, the choices add up to the greatest cornucopia on the planet. But there are limits.

When you want to buy a used camper truck, you have to go to New Jersey.

The smell of fresh-brewed coffee hit me like a slap in the face when the salesman unlocked the door and let me in. I told him that if he poured me a cup, I could guarantee he'd make a sale in the next half hour. He didn't quite lick his lips in anticipation, but he did manage to get me a restorative cup in record time before showing me what he had on the lot.

"I don't carry much inventory this time of year. This here is a Roadtrek. It's basically a Mercedes with a luxury camper on top. AC, microwave, convection oven, flat-screen TV, satellite, GPS with worldwide maps preloaded. Two years old, twelve thousand miles. It's not cheap, but I've got a lot of capital tied up in it, and I'd be willing to cut a very good deal."

GPS was a deal killer.

"What's the cheapest, oldest, most basic thing you have? What's that?" I asked, pointing to a two-tone pastel minibus.

"You've got an eye for class. That's a '71 VW bus. It's a classic. Needs some TLC on the interior, but it runs nice. New brakes. You familiar with the old VW?"

"I think I saw one in that movie about Woodstock."

"The engine is air-cooled, which means the heat works terrific in the cab."

"Does it have GPS?"

"GPS? You're kidding, right? It doesn't even have a radio."

"Will it get me to Santa Fe?"

"California?" he asked, exhibiting the typical East Coaster's grasp of geography. "No problem. But it's slow uphill. Not a lot of torque. They make smaller engines today with a lot more power, but, as I said, this is a classic."

An antique. Santa Fe was an uphill drive from the Mississippi River on. But I wasn't really going to need it.

We agreed on a price quickly. I knew I overpaid. I wanted to be remembered.

"I want to drive it away today. Can you make that happen?"

"You came to the right place. My cousin sells insurance. We'll rush the paperwork. You keep the tags. If you mail them back when you get settled out there, I'll put a ten-dollar credit on your charge card."

I was sure that I would also overpay for the insurance, the expedited paperwork, and the tags.

"That's great." I put everything on the debit card.

Less than an hour after arriving, I putt-putted out of the parking lot. The bus did run nice. Just not fast. But the brakes worked, and once I'd been driving it for a quarter of an hour, the heat began to warm up my toes.

My next stop was an ATM, where I took out as much cash as the bank would let me have—three thousand dollars. I stopped at a Target and bought two sleeping bags, long underwear, and pairs of thermal socks—one each in my size, one each in a size fit for a small six-year-old. Then I drove around until I found a McDonald's. I bought a Happy Meal, a cheeseburger, and two drinks and paid again with the debit card. I held on to the Diet Coke and threw everything else into the trash on the way out.

I had done my best to leave a digital trail making it appear that the Kid and I were in a camper van traveling west, headed for our new home in New Mexico. If not perfectly hidden, we were at least in hiding.

Every slight gust of wind threatened to push me out of the right-hand lane on I-80, and the engine shuddered if I tried to push the speed over fifty-five. There was a slight smell of exhaust, but I wasn't concerned about carbon monoxide vapors because the windows and doors all leaked and there was a constant whistle of wind passing through the van. The view from the driver's perch took some getting used to. It felt as though I were out in front of the van, which, with the engine in the rear, was just about the case. If I made too sudden a stop, there was a good chance that I would land in the backseat of the car in front of me.

It was still early in the day, and there were occasional traffic tie-ups, but all in the other direction. Westward traffic flowed easily, and in less than two hours I was traveling through the Delaware Water Gap, smiling for the surveillance cameras at the tollbooth. I took the first exit in Pennsylvania.

The bridge back over the Delaware up at Milford had no tollbooth heading back into New Jersey, no surveillance cameras on that side of the road. It was an hour drive from the Gap by the most direct route through the park, but I took the less scenic route and it was midafternoon and the shadows were already getting long when I finally drove back over the Delaware. I had not yet heard from Pop or Skeli, which had me a bit nervous, but I had been in and out of cell phone zones for hours. I took a break, pulled over, and checked my phone.

Two messages. Both calls had come through from the phone in Santa Fe.

"Hi. Your Pop says you're all right, but I want confirmation. I want to hear your voice caressing my ear. I want to hear you lie to me and tell me that you're in no danger. I want to tell you in person that I love you and miss you. I want to hear you call me Skeli."

The second message was no less touching, though there were considerably fewer words.

"Hello." A long silence followed. Then there was the sound of encouraging whispers in the background and the Kid spoke again. "I like the beach." More whispers. "Bye."

38

Create false trails. I had done my best. Standard surveillance cameras along the highways—usually set up underneath overpasses or on tollbooths, and good enough to read license plates and even identify faces in the front seat of a vehicle—had picked me up and logged my location all the way to Pennsylvania. There were considerably fewer of those cameras set up on the secondary and tertiary roads I took on the way back to Fort Lee.

Route 23 took me as far as Wayne—bypassing West Milford, which is east of Milford, Pennsylvania, north of Milford, New Jersey, south of Milford, New York, and west only of Milford, Connecticut—more than eighty miles away. After Wayne, I stayed on the back roads through Paterson and Hackensack, and pulled into the tall municipal parking lot well after dark. I was two blocks from where I had started that morning.

I fed cash into the machine, paying for a one-month pass, then drove up to the second-highest level and parked the RV in an empty corner spot. I took another cell phone out of my bag and plugged it into the cigarette lighter. A backup to the phone in Santa Fe might come in handy. The van was clocked on the lot's CCTVs—I could see the little clear domes on the ceiling on each floor—but I thought someone would have to know where to look to find it. Whoever, or whatever forces, were after me would be looking a lot farther west.

I took my backpack and the larger of the two sleeping bags—I might have to sleep rough before this was over—and left everything else in the van. I needed to travel light.

The Fort Lee diner makes a great zucchini and tomato omelet. That and three cups of coffee made me believe that I might yet survive the day. I caught the bus across the bridge to Manhattan and took the Number 1 train down to Seventy-ninth Street. I was cold, exhausted, and if I stopped and thought about it, still terrified. The shearling coat was distinctive and I would gladly have ditched it, but the temperature had plunged into the teens and I desperately needed it.

Roger lived in a rent-controlled one-bedroom apartment on the fourth floor of a walk-up brownstone. There were ten apartments and only four tenants remaining. The landlord had bought out or forced out the other tenants, planning on eventually renovating and converting an empty building to co-ops. The plan had foundered when it was discovered that the outer walls were slowly buckling. The building was being held up by inertia and the two neighboring brownstones. The renovation would have to include a new steel frame erected within the existing structure, and a complete gutting of the shell. It wasn't going to happen. So the four tenants lived with a creaking staircase, cracks in the walls, intermittent heat, a broken intercom, and a busted lock on the front door. Landlord and tenants spent an inordinate amount of time in court, but neither side could budge. The tenants, all on rent control, wouldn't be able to find affordable alternatives anywhere in the five boroughs; the landlord could barely afford to pay the property taxes with the rents he was receiving. His only economical solution would have been to have the building declared uninhabitable and tear it down, but the Upper West Side Landmarks Preservation Commission wouldn't let him. It was the kind of situation that once would have been taken care of with a few gifts to the right politicians, but Manhattan, unlike some of the outer boroughs, had been suffering too long with a relatively honest and community-responsive local government. Nothing was going to change until the landlord declared bankruptcy or the tenants all died.

"Roger!" I pounded on the apartment door. "Come on, open up."

"Whaddya want?"

"I'd like for you to invite me in."

The locks clicked and turned and the door opened. Roger was dressed in a blue plaid flannel bathrobe, which hung open revealing a white wifebeater and bright red boxers with a Hawaiian print. I looked him over. "You look like the American flag on acid."

He looked at the shearling coat. "Do I call you Tex?"

"It's a disguise. What are you doing?"

"I'm working. I didn't know I was going to have company."

"I'm not company. I'm your friend. Let me in."

He stood back and held the door. "Where did you disappear to? Nobody's seen you since last week. Everybody's asking. Wanda's voicemail is full. It's like you guys moved to the suburbs or something."

I sank onto his couch. "Close the door, would you? Who's been asking about me? Any strangers?"

"Two guys in tracksuits. They been coming into Hanrahan's two, three times a day. They order tap beer and don't drink it. They ask some questions and leave a twenty on a fourteen-dollar tab. They don't carry badges."

"Don't get in their sights."

"Oh, they know who I am. You want something? I'm drinking tea."

"Tea?"

"I told ya. I'm working." He gestured toward the thirty-six-inch round oak table that served as his dining table, desk, and, judging by the mounds of old newspapers, his recycling center. Almost hidden by the piles were a stack of yellow legal pads and a laptop.

"What are you working on?"

"New jokes, working Savannah in better. Wanda's tall, so I did a lot of short jokes. Savannah's tall, too, but not as much, and it's not her height that catches your eye, if you see what I'm saying." He turned the heat on under the kettle and put a tea bag in a mug.

"I thought all your jokes were old jokes."

"Anybody ever tell you, you were a rude son of a bitch?"

"Take a number," I said. "What I mean is, don't you have, like, card files of jokes?"

He held up his Apple laptop. "This is the twenty-first century, bozo-brain."

"Exactly," I said. "So you just go over your files and pull out some boob jokes and—"

"Stop! Please. The depth of your knowledge of my business is like the Black Sea."

"Explain that."

"Shrunken, shallow, and it stinks." The kettle whistled.

"Aral Sea," I said.

"*Whaaat?*" he asked in an incredulous whine.

"I think you mean the Aral Sea, not the Black."

He jumped up. "No, no, no! Black is funny. Aral is not funny." To him, these two statements were as clear, and as absolute, as night and day. He made the tea while he continued. "Look. You can't just do boob jokes anymore. I've got to make Savannah look like the one in charge, the brains of the team, while I act like the Cro-Magnon."

"I can see why this is such a challenge."

"Sarcasm is the second-lowest form of humor. Please. Leave the jokes to the professionals."

"What's the lowest?"

"Puns," he said, handing me the mug.

"I thought it was slapstick."

"Slapstick! Slapstick requires perfect timing, incredible agility, and gobs of creativity, and it's got to look real, or it's nothing. Slapstick is art. Only farce is greater. Puns! Please, change the subject before I decide you are too dumb to go on living."

I took a sip of the tea. It was strong and hot and went down like ambrosia. "I need to crash here for the night."

"Stay as long as you like."

The bathroom door opened and a voice I recognized called out. "Roger? Is there somebody here?" Savannah.

"No," he called back. "Just Jason."

Savannah came down the hall, wrapped in a white towel with a second turbaned around her hair. "Hi, Jason." She stopped and looked me over, cataloging my shearling coat, wrinkled suit, Outlaws ball cap, and no-longer-white dress shirt. "Well, look at you. Are you in costume?"

The towel covered her from collarbone to mid-thigh, leaving plenty of room for the imagination. Mine was traveling in so many directions at once that I was knocked speechless.

"Hi," I said.

She walked across the room and performed a perfect bunny dip, reaching down next to a battered easy chair and coming up with a large purse. "So, where have you been? You're, like, the big mystery at Hanrahan's these days."

"Savannah," Roger said in a hushing tone.

"Sorry," she said to him. "I'm not supposed to ask," she explained to me. She rummaged through the big bag and pulled out a plastic cosmetics container. "Excuse me," she said, and walked back to the bathroom. I made a point of not watching her leave the room.

Roger was staring hard at his laptop. I didn't know what to say. I was more than twenty years older than Savannah, and while I acknowledged that it was impossible to ignore her looks, the idea of any kind of sexual liaison with her made me feel like a pervert. And while a part of me was prepared to salute my friend for his apparent good fortune, another voice in my brain was screaming in outrage—he was more than twenty years older than *me*. I didn't know whether to shake his hand or have him arrested.

Roger tapped a few keys. "What were you saying?"

I thought back. It appeared that staying the night was going to be very awkward. Maybe I could find a bed in a flophouse somewhere uptown. I had no idea where to start looking.

Roger looked up and gave me a questioning look. "Oh yeah. You want to stay. Sure. Sure. Whatever. As long as you like. How's the tea?"

I cleared my throat and responded to the least problematic thing first. "The tea's fine. Thanks."

He repeated the questioning look. "You all right?"

"Maybe it would be better if I didn't stay," I said.

The questioning look morphed into confusion, then alarm, as my friend read my thoughts. "Oh, no. You have got to be shitting me." He put his head down and covered his face with one hand. It took me a moment to realize that he was laughing. He finally looked up, his eyes wet with tears of laughter. "I guess I oughta be flattered."

A really useful app would be one where you could dial back time and edit out the really stupid things you have just said.

"It looked . . ." I trailed off.

He continued to laugh, now at my embarrassment. "I told you. We were working."

"Yeah, but . . ." I did it again.

"Yeah, well, they're doing work in her building and they've got the water turned off."

"I see."

Savannah came back down the hall. She was dressed in an off-white turtleneck sweater, black jeans with a silver belt, and tall black boots. Her hair was still wet, but she had combed in a part and applied a minimal amount of makeup.

"What are you laughing about, you dirty old man?" She turned to me. "Was he making boob jokes again?"

Roger laughed harder.

"No," I said.

She turned back to Roger. "Well?"

Roger grinned. "The great detective here saw you in a towel and did some deducing. He basically added two and two and came up with sixty-nine."

Savannah looked at me. I did not deny, thereby giving her full confirmation. She looked back at Roger in his boxers, wifebeater, and threadbare robe.

"Eeeuuuw," she said.

"I'm sorry," I said.

They both laughed. Savannah turned back to Roger. "You've got some weird friends, Roger."

I thought of defending myself—then I thought better. "Please excuse me," I said. "It was a dumb mistake."

"It was gross, is what it was." Savannah tried to look deeply offended, which cracked up Roger again.

"Can I change the subject?" I said.

They both gave another laugh.

"Really. I came here for your help." Some bit of desperation in my voice must have gotten through.

Roger responded first. "What do you need? You know you can stay here as long as you want."

Savannah flopped into the big chair and threw one leg over an arm. "What can I do?"

"Thanks, Roger, but I've got to keep moving. I'll be gone in the morning. If I stay, those guys in the tracksuits will eventually find me."

Roger and Savannah shared a quick look. "Those guys are scary," she said.

"Someone has been tracking me—all over. They've tried to kill me. Three times."

"Where's the Kid?" Roger asked.

"The Kid and Wanda are safe. And more than comfortable. I've got them hiding out on a beach somewhere warm."

"I volunteer to watch over them," Roger said.

I smiled. "Not this time. I've gone to a good bit of trouble to make sure they're far away from any danger."

"What do you need?" he said.

"I need to leave a phone here—plugged in and charging. It won't ring, it will just forward calls to me."

"Fine. Leave it behind the couch."

"And me?" Savannah swung around and leaned forward.

"The two of you. Tomorrow morning. These guys may already be here and watching the building. They know Roger and I are close. I need a diversion so that I can get away. Can you come back here in the a.m.?"

They shared another look and both nodded. "We'll work out something," Roger said. "But where will you be going?"

"If you don't know, then you don't have to lie when those guys come around the bar asking."

I left Roger and Savannah to their planning and stretched out on the couch. I was asleep in seconds.

Roger shook me awake. Savannah was gone, the lights were low, and the television was on softly.

"Sorry, but I thought you might want to see this."

The ten o'clock local news. A perky Asian-American woman was telling the world that there was late-breaking news in the Selena Haley murder case. Defense team computer analysts had been able to reconstruct the image of the license plate from the "mystery Rolls-Royce" seen leaving the Haley estate the night of the murder.

I sat up, fully awake.

"Philip Haley has maintained his innocence ever since his arrest last week outside of a New York City nightclub. He was released on bail Monday, after paying a five-million-dollar appearance bond and surrendering his passport. He has been in seclusion at his wife's estate on the North Shore of Long Island for the past two days. Haley's lawyer spoke to Channel Eight tonight as this new evidence has come to light."

They cut to the lawyer and another talking head, who took their time repeating the information the woman had relayed much more succinctly. The lawyer refused to speculate on the owner of the vehicle in question. He used the words "digitally enhanced" like he knew what they meant. Then they cut to a clip showing the Rolls leaving the driveway—the same footage that I had watched with Jenkins almost a week ago—only this time the camera zoomed in on an easily readable plate.

"I expect to hear from the Nassau County DA's office first thing tomorrow morning. They will, no doubt, be dropping all charges against my client." The lawyer finished strong.

"What do you think?" Roger asked.

"I saw that picture last week, Roger." The news continued with a story about Lotto winners who had gone broke within a year or two of winning. "Turn it off, okay? There's no way somebody reconstructed anything from what I saw. 'Digitally enhanced,' my ass. This is some very fresh bullshit."

"Really? I thought they could do all kinds of things with digital pictures these days. I saw it on *24*."

"Maybe," I said, though I didn't think so at all. They could make them fool the eye—that was easy—but a good technician would know the image had been altered. "But I know a guy."

"Call him up," Roger said.

"Not so easy," I said. "But tomorrow I'm going to set about finding him."

39

Roger and I were huddled inside the security door to his building, watching the street and waiting for Savannah's call.

"You think it's just the two of them?"

"Has to be," I said. "If they're covering all of the possible places I could be holed up in around the city, they've already got a small army at work."

There were two men, white and early forties, dressed in shabby suits, white shirts, and no ties, sitting in the front seat of a dented and dusty Chevy Impala across the street. A steady stream of gray smoke came from the muffler—they were running the engine to keep warm. The car was blocking a fire hydrant. Maybe I'd get lucky and a police car would come by and force them to leave.

"Who are they?"

"No idea. Private detectives? Off-duty cops? Russian gangsters? Mercenaries? I'd bet someone like Chuck Penn can hire hundreds of guys like that with one phone call."

Roger's cell phone rang, causing us both to start, even though we'd been waiting for the signal for ten minutes.

Roger put the phone to his ear and listened. He nodded once and clicked off. "Magic time," he said.

"Break a leg," I said.

"Call me sometime when you just want to catch a beer or something, will ya?" He pushed open the door and walked out. He climbed the three steps to the sidewalk and hurried across the street.

The two guys in the car saw him, followed him for just a moment with their eyes, and dismissed him almost at the same moment. They weren't there looking for a short, older man with a slightly bowlegged walk. Roger slipped between two parked cars and stopped in front of the awning of the apartment building across the street. He leaned against the wall and waited.

A yellow cab came down the block and pulled to the curb. A tall, leggy redhead got out wearing a long winter coat and carrying a big leather purse hooked over one arm. The coat hung open, revealing a magnificent body, barely contained within a black minidress with a hemline that stopped one stitch this side of indecent exposure. Savannah managed to look both elegant and slutty. She strode toward the door of the building in tall heels, the coat swinging wide.

I checked on the two watchers. The guy on the passenger side had definitely noticed the woman only twenty feet away. He tapped the driver on the arm and his head swung around also.

Roger came off the wall and spoke to Savannah as she passed him. She stopped, turned, and put both hands on hips and jutted out her chin before saying something back. It appeared that the two of them were having a particularly rude conversation. It escalated quickly. A second later, she began screeching.

"You bass-tid. You little bass-tid," she shrieked in a tone-perfect impersonation of a girl from Ozone Park. She swung the big leather bag. Roger put his arms up in defense and backed away, Savannah coming on strong. She staggered wildly on the towering heels and the red wig came off, sending her into even greater screams as she pounded on my friend. Savannah was a good actress.

It was such a great show that I almost stayed watching too long. The two guys in the Impala were smiling, pointing, and laughing. I pushed open the front door and slipped out. I kept my head down and walked in the opposite direction, toward Amsterdam. I looked back quickly as I turned the corner. The doorman had come out of the building and was trying to calm the lady down. Roger took his opportunity and ran, making his escape.

I lengthened my stride and made mine as well.

It used to be called Hell's Kitchen, but that was when the Westies ran the West Side. They'd been gone for a while. What the police, the Mafia, and Rudy Giuliani had separately or collectively failed to do had been accomplished by Yuppies and gentrification. The tenements had been converted into condos or torn down and replaced with luxury high-rises. But there were still some relics of the past.

St. Patrick's Thrift Shop catered to a mixed crowd. There were two well-dressed twenty-somethings going through the racks of silk blouses, designer camis, and once-worn party dresses, and there was a sable coat–wearing matron haggling over a Liberty scarf. And there was me.

I had missed more than a few hours of sleep in the past few days, and I hadn't shaved since waking up in Santa Fe; I looked the part of a once prosperous executive on the verge of becoming homeless. I just needed to fill out my costume.

"I want to swap this," I said, indicating the long sheepskin coat, "for a woolen overcoat. A warm hat. Gloves would be good, too."

The clerk—a watery-eyed woman in her seventies, wearing a quilted cardigan and the kind of soft-soled sensible shoes that I had thought did not exist this side of the Hudson River—looked me over. My wrinkled suit, my graying white shirt, the sleeping bag under my arm. I confused her.

"Navy? Black? Gray? Camel's hair? I have some in blond, and one or two in brown. What size do you need?"

"Something very large and very long. Something I can sleep in if I need to."

Twenty minutes later, I was outfitted in a voluminous charcoal-colored woolen coat that hung two inches wider than my shoulders and almost reached my ankles, a blue woolen scarf with a Giants logo, and a pair of stained ski mittens. I looked myself over. The coat was far too clean, but a day or two on the street would fix that. Shoes! My Allen Edmonds looked like new.

"Do you have men's shoes?" I asked.

"There's not much of a selection," she said.

"I'll swap you these for anything that fits."

She looked and then raised her eyebrows. "I think you ought to keep those. I always think a man looks so put together when he's wearing wingtips."

Skeli liked wingtips. Angie had always tried to get me to buy Italian slip-ons. I never liked them. They made me feel like I was always about to float up off the ground.

The clerk and I compromised. She sold me a beat-up pair of Eccos, with a sole that appeared to be made of tractor tire, and a canvas backpack into which I placed my wingtips and the gear I was carrying. The backpack helped to complete the picture. The essential accessory for the well-fitted-out urban homeless man.

I didn't haggle. I paid in cash. Her eyebrows shot up again when I pulled out the roll of fifty-dollar bills, still thick enough to choke a python. I made a mental note to carry some smaller bills in another pocket, so that I wouldn't be flashing the kind of money that might get me killed on the street.

Then I went looking for Benjamin McKenna. Or Richard Kimble. Just as long as I didn't have to play Jason Bourne.

40

At least it was sunny. It was also very cold.

I skirted the edge of Foley Square and took a seat on a bench opposite the park. One more homeless man on a bench across from the courthouse would not draw anyone's attention. There were four other men who looked much the same as I did within fifty feet. Nevertheless, I tucked the cell phone into my sleeve and hunched over. A homeless man talking on a cell phone might stand out just enough to get me caught.

Special Agent Marcus Brady answered his phone on the first ring, as though he had been waiting for the call.

"Brady."

"Hello. Just an old friend calling."

He gave a long, low whistle. "Hello, old friend. You've become almost famous. Did you know?"

"I kind of figured."

"That little dustup at Newark Airport put you on the map."

"It's amazing what you can do when you're terrified."

"Self-defense? That's good. Be sure and use that argument when the janitor tells the court how you bloodied both of those men and walked away without a scratch."

"Who were those guys? Do you know?"

"One left before security got on the scene. Cameras caught him getting into a cab. The driver says he dropped him in Newark. He's gone. Where are you?"

"Across the street," I said.

"Uh-huh. I didn't really think you'd give me a straight answer."

"And the other one?"

"The one you popped with the mop handle? He told the Jersey troopers that he didn't want to press charges. They didn't give him the satisfaction. When they asked for ID, he handed them a phony passport. Then they called us. He's being held by ICE until we sort things out."

"I was worried I might have killed him."

"So now you have the FBI looking for you, along with everybody else."

"Any idea who they were working for?" I said.

"You are not my case. All I know is what people are talking about on the elevator."

"But did you hear anything?"

"The guy with the broken nose has since forgotten how to speak English," he said.

"Could he be Honduran?"

"Do they speak Russian there?"

"Russian?" I said.

"He's hired muscle."

"I think the other one—the one who got away—was driving the car last week when they tried to shoot me."

"An incident that never officially happened because you failed to make a report—despite my advice."

"It happened."

"If you get pulled over for anything—a broken taillight—keep your hands in sight. From your description, you are a very dangerous person."

"The police won't find me. That's not who has me worried."

"You should come in. They know about the VW van. They tracked you as far as Pennsylvania. They know you've been using secondary roads since, staying off the highway. All you need is for some local deputy who's seen too many Clint Eastwood movies to get all heroic and your son gets to watch his father bleed out on a back road somewhere in Pennsyltucky."

"They know the Kid's with me?" The sleeping bag, the clothes I bought. The Happy Meal.

"I know that you have a generally negative view of the abilities of people in my profession, but don't get comfortable with it. These guys are very good."

"That's great."

I caught him offsides. "Really? And why is it good?"

"Because if you guys think he's with me, then the bad guys think so, too. And if they're looking for him with me, they're not looking somewhere else."

"Come in, Jason. You're not safe out there. The Kid's not safe."

"I can't. Someone is trying to kill me and he's got access. You put me in some nice safe jail and he'll find me in no time. Believe me, I'm much safer under the radar."

"Next time you call, I will be tracking your phone."

"Hah! Come on. You're already tracking me. Next time I call, you can tell me where I was and I'll tell you how well you did. Later."

I clicked off.

Was it safe to assume that if the FBI thought I was still on my way west, that anyone else who was chasing me would think the same? One of the first rules of trading—assume nothing.

41

McKenna had stopped staying at SROs when he got spooked. Someone had discovered that Selena Haley's computer had been hacked the day that she had been murdered. They traced it back to McKenna's laptop. He was pretty sure it wasn't the police or the FBI, because they don't normally leave death threats. He ditched the computer and dropped through the cracks. I knew where not to look for him. He would avoid the city homeless shelters—they were run like prisons and could be just as dangerous. The soup kitchens, rehab centers, and methadone clinics all had their regular communities where a new guy on the street would stand out all too easily. McKenna would want total anonymity. And so did I.

The city had closed—consolidated—many of its libraries, but I still had plenty of stops to make. I checked every public library on the west side of Manhattan, walking from Bryant Park to 179th Street. I walked because I didn't want to show up on any of the surveillance cameras in the subway, and because waiting for a bus would have slowed me down.

Somewhere, McKenna was holing up, but he had to have Internet access. The carrels in the public libraries were as close to anonymous as one could get—and they had wireless Internet connections. Homeless people rarely get rousted from a library unless they create a nuisance, like letting loose with a schizophrenic rant, or sleeping on the tables, or urinating in their clothes. It's warm, there are newspapers to read, and the water fountains usually work and produce a quality product. But unless you are actually taking a book out, no one questions you or your right to be there. It was a long shot, but an educated one. If I didn't find him on the West Side, I'd do the East Side the next day.

I felt the man's eyes on me before I saw him. I walked in front of the reference librarian's desk, heading for the bank of carrels in the back, when I sensed a startled intense gaze. I was careful not to respond. I continued on my way, took a chair, and settled into the space, plugging in my laptop and signing in. Then I took a moment to gaze around the room, lazily, as though bored and waiting for my system to boot up.

He was a tall black man, mid- to late twenties, lanky but not thin—his height made him look thinner than he was—wearing army surplus khaki and boots, and a desert camo jacket. His eyes flicked away when I looked in his direction.

I wanted to bolt. I thought I was absurd. Paranoid. Resorting to racial profiling. Did I really think that my ghostly pursuers had found me in an uptown library? That they'd been waiting for me there? Or that this man, who had done the unthinkable and looked at me, was somehow a threat? I was breaking up, deep into the DMZ of paranoia. Drifting. I needed to take control, no matter what it cost me. The sane strategy would be to act the part of a lunatic—confront my fears and the man. I stared at him, glaring.

He hid behind a magazine. *Rolling Stone*. I kept glaring. He looked around the room, overacting his nonchalance, until our eyes met. I refused to blink. He stood up, dropped the magazine on the table, and walked out. Through the racks of new arrivals, I could see him pass the front desk and exit. He was gone.

I stayed for an hour, fueling my laptop, resting my feet, and attempting to reassure myself that what I was going through was nothing more than an episode. With a return to my life, these constant fears would dissipate, and I would be whole again. It was getting late.

The sun was dropping toward New Jersey as I headed up Saint Nicholas Avenue. I would have to start thinking of a place to spend the night very soon. There were parks up on the north end of Manhattan. It was going to be a cold night, but I had the long johns and the thermal socks—I was dressed for it and, in addition to my laptop and shoes, I had the sleeping bag tied to my backpack.

My street senses were all askew. I looked like someone that I would normally avoid. It kept me from looking too closely at the people I passed on the street. Another of McKenna's rules. *Avoid eye contact.* I kept my head down, the ball cap pulled low, and the sunglasses in place. What energy I could spare for observation was focused on keeping an eye out for a tall black man in desert camo. That's why I didn't see them until they were right on top of me.

Neither man was much over five foot four, but they were both broad-chested and powerful-looking. The first bumped me as I passed an alley between a Dominican chicken joint and an auto parts store. I stumbled slightly and the second one pushed hard from behind. I took three staggering steps into the alley, with both of them alternating jabs and shoves to keep me off-balance. I pulled away, broke clear, and put my back against a wall.

The two had me cornered. Both were wearing cheap sneakers, jeans, dark hoodie sweatshirts, and quilted polyester vests. One had a long, sharpened screwdriver with which he made jabbing motions in my direction, though he stayed back out of reach. The other had a knife, a heavy-bladed tool that would have been useful for chopping down small trees—or people. He advanced.

He said something in Spanish and pointed. My execrable foreign language skills were of no help, but I didn't really need them. He wanted my backpack. I almost laughed. These were not the men who had chased me and tried to trap me all across the country. These were not the hit men from a Central American drug cartel, there to take revenge. These were two pitiful muggers, no farther up or down the food chain than I was at that moment.

Then it hit me. In a single day on the street, my priorities had changed. The day before, I would have handed over the backpack and wished them well. A laptop, some warm clothes, a sleeping bag? Even the cash? These weren't things worth fighting or dying for. But it was a different day. I was terrified. My ability to survive without those clothes would be in jeopardy. My identity, what remained of it, as Jason Stafford was on those computer files. The path to reclaiming my life was there.

The cash. The cash was expendable. It was replaceable—somehow. It meant little to me, and might turn their weapons aside.

"Uno momento," I yelled, holding up a single hand in surrender, reaching into the bag with the other. It must have looked like a threatening move because the one with the knife took two quick steps closer and slashed the air in front of my face.

"No! No!" I screamed, unconcerned with letting my terror show. *"Dinero.* Much *dinero.* For you. Here. Here." I had stashed the money in various pockets in the backpack and my clothes. I found four fifties and threw them on the ground between us.

The guy with the screwdriver bent over and swept the ground. The fifties disappeared. I sensed a shift in hostilities. They were getting what they wanted without committing murder. There was a chance we would all be able to walk away from this. I found two more fifties and threw them to the ground. Wrong move. I had overplayed my hand. The knife-wielder, and the obvious brains of the team, saw the possibility of an even greater payoff. Just how many fifties were there in the bag?

He came forward and slashed at my face again. I leaned backward away from the knife and tripped over a black plastic bag of garbage. I fell.

"Take the goddamn bag," I yelled, trying to extricate myself from the garbage and the backpack straps. What a ridiculous cosmic joke, I thought, to outwit hit men and hackers, and to die in a garbage-strewn alley, done in by two muggers. I kicked ineffectually at the advancing man, his knife swinging in ever-narrowing arcs. I was mesmerized, like a mouse waiting for the snake to strike.

The little man was suddenly lifted into the air by someone from behind and tossed face-first into the wall.

"Hey! *Retaco! Basta ya!*" a deep voice ordered. The black man from the library grabbed the Latino's knife arm as he came off the wall. With one fluid motion, he pulled him forward and twisted the arm around and down. The mugger squawked like a throttled chicken and dropped the knife. His buddy ran. But not far. The black man kicked him in the leg as he passed and he dropped as though shot. With the first mugger dragging along, held by the overextended arm, the stranger walked over to the downed second man and kicked him again. This time in the ribs.

"Get that money out of your pocket," he said. "I want to see it. All of it, *conejo*." He let the man get up as far as his hands and knees and drew his leg back for another kick.

"No. No," the man cried, tossing the fifties back on the ground.

"Very good. Now get the fuck out of here. The both of yous." He swung the first man by the injured arm and let him fly back out onto the street. Both of them ran. Neither looked back.

I got up from the garbage and brushed myself off.

"Thank you. The money is yours. A reward."

He looked at me scornfully. "You're Jason Stafford."

I felt a major twinge of fear. "Who wants to know?"

"I heard you were smart. I don't think so. Pick up your things and let's go. I got someone wants to talk to you."

I didn't want to die in that alley, and from what I had just seen, this guy would have no problem making that happen. Nonetheless, I felt that some resistance was required.

"I'm not going anywhere with you. You've been following me. I saw you."

"I wasn't following you, numbnuts, I was waiting for you. My man said you'd be along and I could just wait you out. And there you were. And about time, too. Come on, it'll be dark soon and we got some walking to do."

I reviewed my chances of getting away. Slim and none. I picked up the bills and stuffed them back into my bag. "Ready," I said.

42

Halfway across the George Washington Bridge, the sun slid down behind the Palisades and the temperature, already cold, began to plummet.

"Come on, keep up," he called back. I was a good ten paces behind him, but there was no danger of my turning and running off. Where was I going to go? "I am freezing my ass off, and not liking it one bit."

I walked faster. It kept me warm. There hadn't been even a breeze walking through the city, but up on the south side of the bridge the unprotected walkway was open to a cold damp wind coming up the Hudson.

"Where are you taking me?" I asked again.

He didn't answer. He had not answered any of the other times I had asked.

"Move along, my man," he said. "And keep your head down. There's another camera coming up right along here."

I put my head down. "Can I take the damn glasses off?" The sunglasses were as good as a blindfold—I could barely see one step ahead of me.

"Soon." He led me to the end of the bridge and up the sidewalk toward Fort Lee. "This way." We jumped the chain-link fence, he was a lot more graceful than I, and took the next street along the top of the cliff. We kept walking. A neighborhood of shops and two-story homes gave way to a steeper section of the cliff. Luxury high-rises soared up above us, while down the cliff there were multilevel parking garages to service them. Below that there was nothing but rocks and trees and scrub brush cascading down toward the river.

"Keep smiling," he said. "We're almost there."

I tried to keep up, but my legs were starting to fail me. I'd covered too many miles on aching feet already that day. I was about to protest and plead for a break, when my guide—or captor, I still wasn't sure which—crossed the road and walked down the ramp into the darkness of one of the concrete garages.

The apartment building soared up an uncountable number of stories. Far above I could make out terraced balconies and floor-to-ceiling windows. The views from there of the Hudson and Manhattan must have been breathtaking. There was a curved driveway leading to a polished brass-and-glass entryway where two doormen stood guard. They were contentedly ignoring me, but I was sure that if I took more than a few steps toward the entrance, they would be all over me.

"You coming?" The man had returned to the bottom of the ramp and stood glaring at me. It wasn't really a question.

"I'm coming," I said, and crossed the street.

He led me to the far side of the lot and down two flights of stairs, our footsteps echoing coldly in the narrow stairwell. The only light came from a dim yellow bulb all the way at the top, yet I was still unprepared for the inky blackness of the lowest level of the garage when we arrived at the bottom.

"They got motion sensors that turn the lights on when you come down the ramp or use the elevator, but the stairs are on a different circuit. We don't like to advertise our comings and goings. This way."

Around the end of the last row of cars, there was a cutaway in the wall and we made a turn. The garage was open, with a chest-high concrete retaining wall running the length of the cutaway. Above the wall was a space six feet tall and thirty feet wide.

"How you holding up?" He sounded clinical, not concerned. He simply wanted information.

"My feet are killing me, and I could use a break. But if we're close, push on."

"We're here," he said, stopping at the half wall. "But this bit gets tricky. If you feel shaky, speak up."

Beyond the wall stretched treetops, partially screening the river and the city. Manhattan stretched out for ten miles downriver. Now lit from within, the buildings along the Hudson looked like glowing jewel cases. At that distance, the city was clean, and beautiful, and alluring. A place of incredible magic.

"Nice view, huh? The folks across the street have to pay big bucks for that view." He laughed, hitched his butt up onto the top of the wall, and swung around facing the city. "Last little bit. Come on."

I had decided that the murky, and all-powerful, forces that seemed to be able to track my every move across the country were not going to go through such an exercise to gull me into meeting them in the woods below Englewood, New Jersey. Though I wasn't sure what to expect, I had left all resistance behind.

On the far side of the concrete wall, someone had set up a long extension ladder that led down to darkness.

"I'll go first in case you need me to guide your feet. Just keep moving and don't look down," he said.

"What's to see? It's pitch-black down there."

"Let's go." There was nothing to do but follow.

I edged over the wall and started down the ladder. It creaked and groaned with our combined weight, but it held steady against the wall. Once down into the darkness under the garage, I realized that it was not quite so pitch-black. I could see the ground fifteen feet below. The ladder bowed a bit as I reached the halfway point but rebounded as I made my way down the last few steps.

"Welcome, Jason," a familiar voice said. "You're just in time for dinner."

43

Other than a swipe of black soot across his forehead, Dr. McKenna looked like life on the run agreed with him. He had shaved the beard and cut his hair, leaving a single conservative part. He was wearing a heavy winter-season blue suit, and a full-length apron over it proclaiming STUART SAYS, 'LICK MY RIBS,' CAN DO Q, CLARKSDALE, MISS, with a cartoon drawing of a smiling, round-faced man wearing a pig snout.

"Make yourself comfortable," he said, indicating the three canvas folding chairs near the mouth of the man-made cave. A single mammoth round concrete pillar supported the floor of the garage a good six feet over our heads. We were directly under the three-story structure. On both sides the rock curved upward, meeting the concrete and sealing off the area into a single high-ceilinged vault. A thin layer of soil on the floor softened the rough, jutting surface. McKenna, or his friend, had set up two small dome tents, a camp table, a kerosene heater, a small gas grill, and even shaded overhead lights. A heavy-duty orange extension cord ran up the side of the pillar to the garage. "Cozy, isn't it? Abraham has been living here since last spring, and when I heard about it, I thought it would be just perfect for my needs. We came to an agreement quite quickly. I provide the cash to maintain our lifestyle, and pay him to act as my assistant. We've spruced the place up quite a bit in the last few days. How do you like your steak?"

"Medium rare?" I looked around again. "Are you planning on spending the winter down here?"

"Well, for my part, I certainly hope not. I have a family I'd like to see again. But Abraham suffers from PTSD after two tours in 'Insanistan,' as he calls it. He doesn't do well inside four walls." McKenna gestured out at the woods in front of us. "This place is perfect for him."

"Nobody bothers you? No cops, or kids, or dogs, or . . ."

"Just the raccoons, so far. We have to keep both food and garbage under lock and key."

He opened the grill, flipped the steaks and sliced zucchini, and closed it again. "Another few minutes. Coffee or water? There's nothing stronger, I'm afraid. Abraham no longer touches alcohol—it interferes with his treatment—and I respect his quest."

Hot coffee sounded good. "I'll take a cup."

"Milk and sugar are in the big blue cooler."

Abraham, who seemed much less imposing once I knew that he had a name, had taken one of the chairs and was reading underneath a clip-on light attached to a broom handle stuck in the dirt. His feet were warming by the space heater.

"What are you reading?" I asked.

"A novel."

My reading list had shrunk to books about cars, which I read to the Kid, or books about kids with autism.

"Which one?"

He looked up. "Why do you care?"

"Sorry," I said. "I was just making conversation."

"Not necessary." He went back to the book.

The three of us ate around the camp table, Abraham continuing to read while McKenna and I spoke, only responding with a quick look when one or the other of us mentioned him. I caught sight of the book cover. Tom Young's *The Warriors*. The cover showed an armed soldier in silhouette against a blood-red background. A strange choice for a man with PTSD, but then again, maybe not.

"How did you find me?" I said when he looked up for a moment.

He went back to the book. McKenna answered. "I deduced that you would be looking for me in places with Wi-Fi—libraries being the most obvious choice. I told him to watch one for five days. If you hadn't shown up, we would have tried something else."

"He was inside. I thought you said he didn't do indoors."

"Even Abraham gets cold."

Abraham made a sound that could have been a grunt or it could have been a laugh.

"What's next?"

"I've been working on gaining access to Arinna's labs and security system. I've been assuming that was what you still wanted. Was I wrong?"

I had no trouble answering that one. "Not at all. It's the only way for me to clear this up. And don't worry, you're still on the payroll. I brought cash."

"I knew you were good for it. But if you want to get into their systems, we are still going to have to go out there—on-site. The way they've isolated their network, I'd have to be Homeland Security to see all the files."

"You're willing?" I said.

"All part of the service. I've been piggybacking on wireless connections from the high-rise across the street. Working at night, so I won't be noticed. I'm close. I could be ready as early as tomorrow night. Should we ask Abraham to join us?"

I thought of the way he had handled the two Latino muggers. "If we get to the point that we need his skills, we're in far too deep. What do you need me to do?"

"There are things that are known and things that are unknown, and in between there are doors. And I think that would be a very good thing for you to work on. Maps of the property, the offices. What security I will need to override. Then there's transportation. We need a vehicle."

"I've got that covered." The VW minibus, parked less than a mile away. "I'll go to work on the rest."

44

"You'll get better reception if you walk down along the top of the cliff for a bit. All this concrete blocks signals." McKenna was hunched over his laptop. Abraham had already taken down the ladder for the night and crawled into his tent. I was ready to crawl in the other and get some sleep, but I wanted to try Skeli first.

Ten feet away from the entrance to the cave the night closed around me like a hangman's hood. My other senses opened up, and I inhaled hydrocarbons from the space heater and the garage above. I stumbled over the tiny rocks and roots that had suddenly grown much larger. And I heard the rustlings of wind in the bare branches above. My imagination soared, too.

The call was routed through the house in Santa Fe, back to the VW nearby, then to the phone at Roger's apartment before connecting across a thousand miles of ocean. Pop picked up.

"Everybody's fine, but if you don't speak with Wanda immediately she's going to tear my arm off."

"Give her the phone, Pop." He was already gone.

"How are you?" Skeli cooed. I could hear her fear and concern, and I could hear her trying to hide it. Trying to make it easier for me.

"Well-fed. Well-exercised. No one has tried to kill me in hours. Couldn't be better. Soon I'll be climbing into a nice warm bed and thinking of you."

"Please don't kid. I'm not handling this very well as it is."

"You? You're the rock."

"I'm not. I'm frightened for you. I'm coping. Maintaining. But I'm not a rock."

I told her I loved her. I told her that I would take very good care of Jason Stafford because I loved her and the Kid and I knew they needed me as much as I needed them. I told her that I was close to being finished with this case, and that as soon as I was done I was catching the first plane to join them. That what I was doing was making them safe, too. And I told her that I would take no unnecessary or dangerous chances. And when I said it, I believed it.

"How's my boy?"

"Terrific. He's swimming. He calls it swimming, anyway. He's a water baby. Oh, and he opened up to me last night. You want to know why he was pissing in the cup?"

"He talked about it? You're incredible. How did you get him to even sit still for the conversation?"

"He saw Carolina cleaning the toilet, pouring some blue stuff in there. It got him upset."

I found myself laughing with a shaky relief. "She should try another color."

Skeli laughed back—also a bit shaky. "Does the stuff come in other colors? How do I know?"

"She can use the cheap vodka."

We both laughed again and let a moment's silence surround us.

I opened my mouth to say "I miss you" but Skeli spoke first.

"Will you be here for Christmas?"

It stopped me dead. I had no idea when Christmas was. I struggled to come up with the date. My mind worked backwards and forwards trying to find a moment that would define the present.

"What's today?" I finally said.

"That's a little scary, Jason. The twenty-third."

We were going to break into Arinna Labs on Christmas Eve. It might work in our favor. Who would be there? If all worked well, I could go public with whatever we found first thing Christmas morning. Once the story was out there, there'd be no reason for anyone to be trying to stop me. I'd be safe. So would my family.

"Maybe," I said. "I'll try for a late-afternoon flight."

"Be safe," she said.

Good advice.

45

One more time I made the drive out to Westwood. McKenna plugged his laptop into the charger, turned the heat up to max, and fell asleep.

I woke him an hour later. We were stopped on the side of the road by a stretch of woods, a few hundred yards before the turnoff.

"Magic time," I said.

"Where are we?"

"The Westwood property starts just up there, past the end of the stone wall."

"There's no fence?"

"You don't see it from the road. It's about twenty feet into the woods and it goes forever."

He fired up the laptop, and for the next few minutes there was nothing for me to do except fret. I was tired but pumped. The combination of fear, constant vigilance, and living on the run was starting to tell. I ached in almost every muscle. But I was ready.

"Pull up closer," he said. "I need a stronger signal before I do anything."

"You're in already?" I said.

"They've got a multimillion-dollar security system and a two-hundred-dollar firewall. I could teach a second grader how to do this."

I drove another hundred feet down the road and stopped again.

"Is here all right? I'm afraid of getting picked up by any cameras they might have along the road."

He didn't answer at first. He tapped at the keyboard. "I'm past the firewall. Okay. Remember what I said about beating a randomly generated code?"

I did, but I was feeling a bit impatient. "Just do it, okay?"

"There's a quicker way. Cheat."

"In this case, I'm in favor of cheating."

"Software engineers are as lazy as the rest of humanity," he said, still typing. "They don't want to have to struggle with passwords if they need to get into the system. So, they leave a back door at the admin level. Sometimes they hide it, but it's still there."

"And you've found it?"

"And cracked it. Let's go."

"Are you sure? Where am I going?"

"The front gate. I've disabled all of the cameras, so for the next ten minutes the guards will be watching frozen screens, which is fine . . ."

I put the car in gear and rolled forward. "As long as it's dark outside and nothing's moving."

"Go. Go."

I made the turn and rolled down the drive to the gate. The overhead spotlight came on and I froze, feeling like the world could see me attempting to break into the grounds of one of Long Island's wealthiest families.

"Quickly. Go."

"The goddamn gate is closed!" I hissed.

"Exactly. Sorry. Sorry." He tapped the keys again. "No one closed Selena's email account yet. And, there it is."

"You've got today's code?"

"Getting it. Keep going."

I stopped at the gate. No voice sounded out of the darkness. The front of the car was lit up like the top of the Empire State Building on the Fourth of July and no one seemed to notice us.

"Got it?" I was discovering that the ice-cold nerves of a foreign exchange trader did not serve quite as well for a break-in artist.

"Now listen, Jason. There's nothing I can do if the guards are listening, understand? I mean, if they're sucking down caffeine and watching reruns of squirrels skittering across the lawn, we're fine. But if they open the door and hear this jalopy drive by, well, there's not much I can do about it."

"I know. And we can't help it if those squirrels suddenly freeze and don't move. Put in the code, will you?"

McKenna's face was a pasty white in the glare from the overhead spotlight. He looked very young. It occurred to me for the first time that he was almost twenty years younger than I was. He probably looked up to me. He probably thought I knew what I was doing.

He typed in the code. There was a click, and a hum, and the gate rolled back.

I rolled through and continued down the driveway. No one screamed for us to stop. No shots rang out. To our right, the guardhouse was lit, shining through the trees like a strippers' bar in the Adirondacks.

"Turn off the lights if you're nervous."

"I'm not nervous," I said.

"Okay. And I'm not Irish-American from Buffalo, New York, with a wife and two daughters and a mother in a nursing home who calls me 'Everett' whenever I visit."

"Who is Everett?"

"How do I know? Early onset of dementia. The woman hasn't recognized me in years."

I turned off the van lights. It was dark—impossibly dark—but we could still see the pavement in front of us. We passed the turn-off for the guardhouse.

"The system resets automatically every ten minutes, so we need to be inside the building in another"—he looked at the screen again—"eight minutes."

"It's nice that one of us knows what he's doing."

We got to the lab parking lot with time to spare. I parked as far from the front door as possible, hoping that the van wouldn't be picked up by the cameras. McKenna jumped out and ran for the front door. I followed.

There was a plastic-and-metal plate in a small box next to the locked glass doors. McKenna took out a gadget that looked a lot like a garage door opener, held it against the plate, and pushed a button.

"What is that?" I said, trying to make myself appear inconspicuous.

"Electronic lock picker. I got the design for it off a YouTube video."

The door clicked. McKenna pulled open the door and we were in.

"Does that thing work on any door?"

"No. It's only programmed for the top three electronic lock companies."

"What would you have done if the lock was made by the fourth?"

"Picked up a rock and smashed the glass."

"Elegant," I said.

I led the way to the elevator, put my face in the retinal scanner, and waited. The elevator clicked and hummed, and a moment later the door opened. We both stepped in and I punched the button for the second floor. Nothing happened.

"I've got this," McKenna said. He held up the little black gadget and swiped it over the face of the panel. The lights flickered on and the elevator started up immediately. "Same code as the front door. It would have to be, or all your employees would have to carry two coded keys. You can only make security systems as careful as the people who will use them."

We stepped off the elevator into blackness, lit in spots by the glow from electronic indicator lights. Spots of red, green, and white were scattered about the offices, but the heavy drapes kept out any light that might have seeped in from outside.

"Find some lights," McKenna said. "We can't work like this."

"Great," I muttered, feeling along the wall for a switch.

"Here we go," McKenna said, and the room was flooded with light from above.

"Damn. Do we need that much light?"

"Are you worried? Who can see in?"

I turned on the gooseneck lamp over Haley's desk. "We don't need more than this. Turn those off."

He flicked the overhead lights back off and joined me at the desk. "Let's see what I can find."

I stepped aside and let him work. There was enough for me to do pacing, checking every sound in the empty building, and peering out into the darkness around the edge of the drapes, while being careful to let no stray ray of light escape. The *tap, tap, tap* of the keyboard and the occasional whirr of the hard drives on McKenna's and Haley's computers were a constant background to my anxiety. It felt like a very long time before McKenna called me over.

"It's just what you thought," he said. "The trade authorization for Phil Haley to short-sell shares of his own company and buy them back again after the stock tanked came from this computer. Clear as can be. *But*, this computer was being hacked at the time and the orders came from somewhere else."

"Selena."

He nodded. "I hacked her computer myself a week ago. I recognized the IP immediately. It's static because she was on the Arinna network."

"She didn't strike me as the hacker type."

"Yeah, well, we come in all sizes and colors, but I think you're right. Whoever did this was good. She had help," he said.

Penn would have been able to find her the help. Or maybe she just went to the DEFCON hackers convention and hired someone.

"Is this what you were hoping to find?" McKenna asked.

It cleared Haley of orchestrating the insider trading, but there was another question I wanted answered. I told McKenna about the license plate and what I had seen on the news.

"So you think someone doctored the file," he said.

"I'm positive. I saw the pictures the day after the murder. That plate was unreadable."

"Images. Digital images," he corrected.

"Fine. Images," I said, smiling around my clenched teeth.

"Here's why it's important. I can change the code so that your eye will be fooled, but I can't fool someone who looks at the code."

"What I want you to find out is if that change was made here—on this machine."

"And inserted into the security file?"

"Precisely," I said.

It didn't take him long. I stepped away and let him work.

"Aaaaahh . . . yup. Dead on. Here's what I've got." He opened a file. The Rolls-Royce appeared on the screen with the blurred license plate. "Now watch." He clicked again. Another license plate appeared, superimposed over the first. "That's one of his attempts. A little sloppy, right?" He clicked again and again. "He gets better with practice." The pictures fit together more exactly.

"Could he send them to the security files from here?" I said.

"He's got full admin access. But why would he risk it? I'm telling you, any competent technician could find the changes."

"He was betting it would never get that far. All he needed was to spread some doubt and get the cops looking for someone else as the murderer."

"So whose license plate is that?"

"I don't know, but I'll bet good money on Chuck Penn. I just don't know why Haley didn't wipe all this off his computer after he was done," I said.

"He thought he did. He deleted all this. But as we like to say, 'Nothing is ever lost, it's just misfiled.'"

"So what do we do? Can we copy all this to your laptop?"

"We can, but if you want hard evidence, you're going to have to take the computer. Who can say I didn't create all this myself?"

Once Penn was identified as the man behind the insider trading scam, and possibly as the murderer of his accomplice, I would be in the clear. He'd have no need to try and shut me up, and he'd be hip-deep in alligators fighting off the cops and the SEC. Much too busy saving his own skin to bother trying to take mine. Special Agent Brady would not appreciate a call from me on Christmas morning, but if I dumped the whole thing in his lap, I could still make an early-afternoon flight to Tortola.

"I'll take the computer. We're done here."

46

Here, hold this while I get my keys," I said, handing the computer to McKenna.

He put it under one arm and huddled up against the side of the van out of the breeze coming off the water. It was cold.

I fumbled through the pockets of the big overcoat before I found the missing keys in a pants pocket. "Got 'em. Let's go."

"Who's there?"

It was Haley's voice coming out of the darkness down the path between the rhododendron.

"Hurry up," I hissed at McKenna, opening the passenger door for him.

A bright beam of light skewered us at the moment of getting into the van.

"Hold it. Don't move. I've got a gun." He stepped closer. "Stafford? Is that Jason Stafford? What are you doing here? Who's that with you? And what the hell has he got?"

All I could see was the big bright light that engulfed us. If I'd been by myself I would have tried to run. Guns are dangerous, messy, but often inaccurate. I didn't imagine that Haley was a sharp-shooter, especially in the dark while holding a heavy searchlight in the other hand. But I couldn't leave McKenna. I decided to brazen it out.

"I'm still working to clear you, Haley. Let us go. We found the evidence on this computer. I can prove you're not guilty of insider trading. Your wife set it up. With help."

He kept coming until he was standing just a few feet away. The searchlight was giving off heat as well as light. It was very powerful.

"Is that right?" he said.

"We may even be able to find who killed her. It was probably her partner, right? Whoever helped her set you up. What do you think?"

McKenna dropped the computer and threw up. Some people handle stress less well than others.

"Who the hell is *he*?" Haley said.

"Muscle," I said. "He knows nothing. Let him go."

McKenna coughed and spat again. "Sorry."

"Is that my computer?" Haley said.

"Yes."

"Pick it up." His voice had gone from authoritative to pure cold.

I bent over but McKenna beat me to it.

"I came out here tonight to get that. I'm sorry that you two are here."

"Let us take it. It's your ticket to making this all go away." I took a step toward him.

"Don't fucking move, Stafford. I mean it." He briefly showed the gun in front of the light. It was an automatic of some kind. Big. It looked deadly. I stopped moving.

"I can help you," McKenna said.

"Yes, you can. Let's go. Follow the path." He indicated the way back toward the house on the cliff—the way he had just come. "And bring that."

I hesitated. McKenna started walking.

"Don't fuck with me, Stafford. You too."

I followed McKenna down the path. Haley shined the light ahead of us. There was not a moment when I was not aware of the gun in his hand. We walked through the forest.

McKenna's terror was a cloud of toxic gas around us. He reeked of fear. I didn't blame him. Haley was bent on destruction.

"To the right," he said, indicating with the light. Toward the top of the steps down to the beach. Where Selena had died.

"This won't work," I said. "Let us go. Take the computer. It'll be our word against yours. What's that worth?"

"Shut up." He jammed the barrel of the gun into my back. I kept moving.

"I'm gonna be sick," McKenna said with a moan. He stopped and turned to Haley. "I can't do this, dude. I'm nobody's goddamn hero. I just want to go home. Can I go home?"

POP! POP! POP! Three explosions sounded. I wanted to duck, to fall on the ground and whimper, but I was too afraid to move. *POP! POP! KA-BLAM!* A bright-red chrysanthemum lit up the eastern sky. Fireworks.

McKenna was crying. Tears ran down his cheeks. "Oh, man. Oh, man," he said over and over like a lifesaving mantra.

The fireworks continued. More. Bigger. Louder.

Haley laughed. It was a nasty laugh. He'd been as frightened as we were, but he was too afraid to admit it, so he laughed.

BAM! BAM! BAM! The explosions continued.

"Haley!" I shouted. "Let him go. Keep me. Keep the goddamn computer, but let him go."

"Shut up!" he cried in answer, his face still hidden behind the bright light.

Each explosion made McKenna jump. He was seconds, millimeters from exploding as well.

"Haley, let's talk. Put a number on it, man, and we're gone. Who do you think we are? Cops? Batman and Robin? We don't give a shit what you've done. What can we do to you?"

The fireworks were blossoming all over the bay. Christmas Eve fireworks. Who thought up that idea? New Year's. Fourth of July. But Christmas Eve? What demographic was some idiot politician hoping to suck up to with this light show?

I didn't know who was going to explode first. I could see the light in Haley's hand jerk with every explosion. McKenna whimpered each time. One or the other was going to break.

It was McKenna.

"Aaahhrrgh!" He threw the computer at Haley.

We had reached the landing at the top of the stairs to the beach. The eastern sky was lit with American flags dripping red and white sparks, blue hydrangeas blooming in fast-forward, and blasts of white like glimpses into a nuclear furnace.

The computer hit Haley in the center of the chest. The light flew up and away in an arc. I saw it spiral down over the cliff, exploding into darkness when it hit the ground. McKenna ran for the woods. He brushed by me, pushing me back and off-balance. My leg twisted behind me and my back hit the railing. I hit it hard. Too hard. The rail gave way behind me just as I heard the first explosion from Haley's gun. I saw McKenna stagger and run on. Haley fired twice more into the darkness and there was the sound of a brief, choked-off scream—then there was silence.

I had one arm wrapped around the rail post, feet dangling over the drop to the beach below. It was a long way down. If I pulled myself up, I would have to face Haley. If I let go, I might break a leg or two and still have to face him. Either way, the odds sucked. I got my other hand onto the top step and began pulling myself up.

I heard footsteps, and then Haley was standing over me. "He's dead," he said. My fingers slipped on the sand-covered stair and I felt myself losing my grip.

47

I was already falling when I heard the gun go off again. The sound and the pain in my temple were one, and I fell. Time stretched into a Möbius strip of never-ending descent, allowing me to review all of my regrets before I landed, ass-first, as limp as a piece of spaghetti. In the moment before new pains overtook me, I blacked out.

The pains were all still there when I awoke, shivering and nauseated, lying facedown in a puddle of blood and seawater on a hard plastic surface. The roar of a powerful outboard engine seemed to emanate inches away from my head, echoing and attacking from all directions at once. I spluttered and coughed up a thimbleful of water, the harsh sound lost in the din around me.

My head both throbbed and screamed, a searing line of fire seemed to be raging along my scalp. I made a full inventory of my pain. The middle of my back felt bruised and ached, but as I could also feel a cold cramp in my left leg, I determined that my spine was intact. One arm was pinned beneath me, and though it felt numb, I could wiggle my fingers.

My face slammed into the plastic surface three or four times as the boat—my brain finally registered that I was lying in the bilge of a fiberglass boat—skipped over a set of small waves before the engines roared even louder and the angle of the floor steepened as the boat went up into a plane.

My non-numb arm hurt, too, and seemed to have no strength, but I was still able to hold myself from sliding back farther into the puddle. I tasted gasoline and caught a faint aroma of long-dead fish bait. My stomach heaved, but I was too exhausted to puke. With a last regretful image of the Kid flickering in my mind, I surrendered and let warm unconsciousness spirit me away.

A fresh blast of pain brought me back to the land of the barely living as my wounded scalp banged against the deck. The boat had stopped and was rocking gently, the engines idling as we drifted slowly with the tide. A man—Haley—had just rolled my cold, wet, blood-soaked, unresisting body—indistinguishable from a corpse—away from the stern and he was now bending over and tying a rope around my ankle. I wanted to kick him, get up and beat him, to scream at him, but I didn't have the energy to even lodge a polite protest.

Deadlifting a one-hundred-and-eighty-pound barbell is a challenge, but it is also a misnomer. A barbell is rigid and balanced and totally different than a dead body. Lifting one hundred and eighty pounds of a nearly dead man is an ordeal.

Haley tried getting both arms around me and pulling. *You'll mess up your lower back that way,* I thought. *You've got to use your legs. Get under the weight.* My mental exhortations must have gotten through, or he figured it out on his own, because the next thing he did was to squat and wriggle both forearms under me. He rose up and I came up with him.

The boat rocked over a wave and Haley lost his footing. We both fell. I continued to roll, ending up where I had started—lying in a pool of bilgewater in the back of the boat. I could see Haley pull himself up and think twice about trying the same maneuver again immediately. He turned away, picked up a large square object, and tossed it over the side. The computer. It made a decent splash when it hit. He stood there, his back to me, his hands on the rail, looking down into the deep black water as though watching the evidence of his criminal cover-up sink to the bottom.

That was my chance. I was on a fishing boat. I had been on a fishing boat before. I knew that fishermen had knives and other weapons. I pulled myself to my knees and looked around. Clipped to the rail was a nasty-looking, big metal hook at the end of a short telescoping pole—a fish gaff. I pulled it free and rose up just as Haley turned around.

It was dark, but there was enough starlight for me to see the shock on his face as a dead body covered in blood rose up in front of him. He froze.

Before he could recover, I swung the pole as hard as I was able. If it hadn't been so sharp, it would have been a useless attempt. The hook drove through his coat and deep into the muscle of his upper right arm. I shook the pole, pulling it forward and back, while Haley strangled a scream and tried to grab it with his free hand. Suddenly, the lock on the telescoping handle freed itself and the pole extended. I stumbled at the sudden release of resistance and fell back onto the deck. The pole came with me, tearing out of Haley's arm and taking a chunk of flesh with it. This time his scream wasn't strangled—he let it flow. For a second, we were both stunned. Then he reached around with his left hand and began scrabbling at his right-hand pocket. I knew without seeing, that's where the gun was. I leaped at him.

His good arm was trapped between us, but he fought anyway. He flailed with his wounded arm, his punches harmless but distracting enough that he was able to headbutt me once. The wound across my scalp felt like someone had just dropped napalm on it. He tried again, and I ducked away—and felt his hand come out of his pocket. He had the gun.

I swung an uncoordinated roundhouse left into his bicep and he staggered, but immediately recovered. Retreat meant death. I attacked. I moved inside his reach. He swung the gun at me, but I was too close. I grabbed his wrist and pulled him to me. The gun fired.

The sound stunned us both and so did the bullet. It hit the deck at an angle and ricocheted off. It whistled by us, leaving huge starred cracks in the fiberglass, but no hole. The next few shots left holes.

I held Haley's arm down and probed with my index finger until we were both inside the trigger guard. He tried digging into my eye with the fingers on his injured hand, but there was no strength in the attack—the gaff must have cut through a tendon. I shook him off and squeezed the trigger. Over and over again, trying to empty the clip. The gun bucked in our hands sending bullets down into the deck—all over the deck. Holes appeared in four, five, six spots before the firing pin clicked down on an empty chamber.

Then I could fight. I let go of his arm, turned to face him, and began punching wildly. He staggered, but I had misjudged him. He was still dangerous. He swung the empty gun, using it as a short club. He missed my head—if he had connected at that point, I would have been done. He swung again and missed. I jumped back and looked for another weapon. The gaff was on the deck and out of reach. I grabbed a fishing pole and swung it as hard as I could into his wounded shoulder. It must have stung, but it didn't stop him. He came closer. I swung again and he dropped the gun, grabbed the fishing rod, and pulled it out of my grip.

At the same moment, I saw the knife. A long thin filleting knife in a plastic sheath secured to the side of the helm, below the wheel. Haley saw where I was looking, turned, and got to it first. He pulled it free and began the turn back toward me. I grabbed him from behind by his jacket and belt and, with a whoosh of expelled air, I swung him around hard, and released.

Haley sliced at me with the knife as he staggered backward toward the stern. He missed, and then he was too far away, too off-balance. The back of his legs hit the transom and he flew up and over and into the water.

I hung over the stern and looked for him, gasping for a breath, my brain spinning with exhaustion, pain, and the sudden letdown of lifesaving chemicals in my bloodstream. I wanted to collapse on the deck and sleep for a long time.

Haley surfaced five or six feet behind the boat, his face lit by the white navigation light on the stern.

"I'll die out here," he called. "The water's freezing. I won't last."

"Good," I said.

"You have to help me," he said.

"No. I don't."

He swam toward the boat, flailing one-handed.

"You try to get up here and I swear I will kill you," I said.

"Oh god. It's cold. How long do you think I can last in here? Minutes?" He was doing all right treading water—in no immediate danger of drowning.

"The water can't be much colder than the low forties. You're in good health. You might last forty-five minutes or more."

He swam toward the side of the boat, avoiding the still-idling outboards, and out of the range of the light. I looked around and found another extendable pole—a boat hook. I pulled it out as far as it would go and held it out over his head.

"I can as easily hold you off as pull you in," I said.

"Damn you."

"Yeah, and fuck you, too. You killed your wife." I was sure of it.

He didn't answer.

"And you altered the image on the file to put the blame on Penn," he said.

"He was trying to destroy me. They were in on it together."

"Did she tell you that?"

"She didn't have to," he said, his voice already getting shaky.

"I would have enjoyed hearing her confess to it," I said.

"Fuck you."

"So we're back to that."

"Damn, it's cold."

"Are you shivering yet? I understand you don't have to lose much of your core body heat before the organs start shutting down. After that, it's just like falling asleep."

He lunged for the pole. I lifted it out of reach.

"So here's the drill. You agree to confess to killing your wife and framing Penn, and I pull you back in the boat and save your worthless life. Deal?"

Water sloshed around my feet. I looked down in surprise. "Damn, Haley, make up your mind. This boat is sinking." Water was welling up from the bullet holes and was already an inch deep.

I looked around. Far ahead, I could make out the towers of Manhattan. It took a moment for my head to clear enough to recognize that New York was to the west. The boat was facing that way. West. The tide was taking us westward, toward New York City. I was quite proud of this bit of deduction. Therefore, the shore to my right must be north. It was better lit, but the southern shore, to my left, looked closer. A lighthouse blinked up ahead. I would need to come to some resolution soon, but I could still easily make landfall somewhere.

I lost Haley in the dark. It took a moment for my eyes to readjust after staring at the city lights. "Haley! What's it to be?" There was a splash from astern. I looked over. Haley had climbed halfway up onto the stabilizer and had gotten hold of a long piece of heavy nylon rope that was tied to a cleat. He was trying to pull himself out of the water. I smacked him across the back with the pole and he slid down again. "What's it going to be? You talk to the police, or you die out here?"

He was exhausted. He wasn't going to make another fifteen minutes, much less three-quarters of an hour. The wound in his shoulder must have been sapping his strength. A small wave lapped against the hull and splashed water over his face. He coughed and tried to vomit. You can drown by inhaling an ounce of water or less. The lungs sense the intrusion and the airways seize up. Your body suffocates you. It's called dry drowning. Haley lost his grip on the line. It fell in the water and he drifted back a few feet, still treading water, but looking a lot worse.

"Take the offer and live," I said.

He nodded his head. He was beyond speaking.

I held out the pole and he took the end with his good hand. I pulled him toward the rear of the boat until he was able to get some of his torso up onto the stabilizer fin. I reached down to offer my other hand to haul him up. That's when he moved.

Haley pulled down on the pole and for a split second I followed it, teetering on the rail before I let it go. I fell back into the boat. The pole splashed down into the water and Haley slipped back.

My own strength and balance were failing and I staggered, like a drunkard, backward into the steering wheel. I fell to the deck, catching the gear shifter under my armpit and throwing the big engines into reverse. They roared and the boat lurched backward, sending up a thick spray of seawater.

Haley didn't make a sound. He didn't have time to scream. The twin propellers grabbed his legs trailing in the water and pulled him under. There was a horrifying grinding noise and then the engines raced, but we stopped moving.

I pushed the throttle back to neutral and the engines quieted down to the *thrum, thrum, thrum* of idle speed. There was no sign of Haley over the stern. I couldn't see if there was blood in the water, the bright light turned everything into a stark black and white, with no colors or shades of gray.

The boat hook was floating a few yards away, much too far to reach with anything on board, so I took the gaff hook, extended it as far as it would go, and probed the water in back of the boat. Nothing. As I stood there at the rail, gasping, exhausted and horrified, I realized that the water in the boat was now up to my ankles. My clothes were all soaked through.

How much time did I have? Not much, if the water was already four inches deep or more. Would the speed accelerate as the boat settled deeper? It didn't matter. I had to move and quickly before the boat sank away beneath me.

I gently pushed the throttle forward. The engines revved, but nothing happened. The props were fouled. I looked over the stern again. The nylon rope was still tied to the cleat but the rest of it was as taut as steel, reaching down into the water behind the engines. I didn't know a lot about boats, but I knew that if that line was wrapped around the propellers, the boat was doomed to drift with the current until it ran aground or sank.

Radio? Next to the steering wheel—the helm—was a microphone on a short springy cord. I picked it up and clicked the receiver button. Nothing happened. Somewhere amid the dials and buttons in front of me there was one—or two—that controlled the radio. I tried one after another, and suddenly there was the loud crackle of static. I turned it down slightly and picked up the microphone again. I had no idea what I was doing. I held down the button and spoke.

"Mayday. Mayday." Or was that for airplanes? Was there a difference? "Anyone out there?" The static continued to crackle. "SOS. If anyone's listening, I am in a boat that is sinking. I'm in Long Island Sound." A body of water ninety miles long; I would have to be more specific. I tried to visualize a map of the area, but the only reference points I had were the city lights and the lighthouse ahead. "There's a lighthouse nearby. I can see the city to the west." I thought about what else I might add. "There's a man down. In the water. We need help." No answer.

A loud burst of static answered me. Then I realized that there was a voice in there somewhere, but I couldn't understand a word.

"SOS. Do you get that? I have no propulsion and the boat is taking on water." I looked around again for any landmark that might help. Everything was black. The aura of the city did little to illuminate the dark shores where I was.

The water was up to my knees.

I dropped the radio and began searching for anything I could use to possibly plug the holes. I opened one locker and found a pair of life vests. I pulled one out and strapped it on. Jammed down in the bottom of the locker was a foul, torn section of towel. It stank. I tore off a section, bent down, and felt along the deck until I found a spout of water coming up through a jagged hole. I stuffed the bit of towel into it and felt the rush of water there come to a halt. It was working.

I moved down the deck and filled another hole, but as I searched for a third, I saw the scrap from the first hole floating by beneath the surface.

Damn. I needed something to hold the towels in place. I got up and searched through the other two lockers. One had a large clear-plastic box. I pulled it out. In with a roll of duct tape and another of black electrician's tape, screwdrivers, a wire brush, O-rings, a tube of silicone goop, and miscellaneous screws, bolts, and nuts was a plastic bag with six or eight wooden plugs inside. I tore the bag open and the cork-shaped plugs scattered across the cockpit. I grabbed two and sank down again, searching for a hole. The first plug was far too large. I tossed it over the side and tried the other. It was tight. I pushed it down as hard as I could and searched for another hole.

A random thought floated through my mind—a half case of wine would come in very handy right then. The corks would be the perfect size. And I could drink myself stupid.

Another plug felt too tight. I placed the heel of my shoe over it and stood up, pressing down until I felt it sink and hold. Another plug fit with less persuading. I was winning. How many holes were there? I didn't know. Five? Six? Less? I couldn't remember. I hadn't been keeping a close count, I had been wrestling to save my life. I found another plug that looked almost right, felt along the floor until I found another underwater fountain, and jammed it in. The hole was too big. The plug bobbed out as soon as I took my hand away. The water was still rising.

I jammed the plug in again and did the trick with my foot, rising and pressing down hard. It seemed to work, but when I stood up I realized that the water was halfway up my thigh. I looked over the side of the boat. The rail was now less than a foot above the waterline. I wasn't winning, I was merely delaying the inevitable. The last plug popped out again and bobbed up in front of me. The deeper we sank, the more pressure on the plugs. I screamed in frustration.

"Shit! Shit!" I did not want to die that way. I reflected that I did not know how I wanted to die. Presumably at home in my bed, surrounded by loved ones, but not for many years to come. I wanted to have plenty of time—decades—to think it over.

The lights of Manhattan were noticeably closer. I had a good idea where I was. Somewhere in the blackness ahead were the two bridges connecting Queens to the Bronx. I had grown up there. It was difficult to judge how fast the current was pulling me to the west, but I knew that it would accelerate once I got past the first bridge. The East River started there, and I knew that it could rip through as fast as a grown man could jog. The river was narrower, but the sides were steeper and the water more dangerous. I needed to do something quickly.

I waded back to the controls and tried the radio again. Nothing, not even static. The rising water must have shorted something out. Then the navigation lights—the red and green on the bow and the white in the back—flickered out. The battery had been submerged for some time, but the water had just got through to it. The engines stopped. One moment their sound was the background to my nightmare, and the next it was silence that pressed in, as though a pillow had been pressed down over me, smothering my senses. I began to shiver.

My brain functions seemed to be slowing down. Concentration on my predicament, while still causing me great anxiety, also seemed to be a problem that I could deal with later—after I had rested a bit. I recognized it as the beginning of hypothermia and fought back.

I was on a boat. I had no power. No way of signaling for help. Drifting at a moderate pace in the general direction of a lighthouse. Was it manned? No one manned lighthouses anymore, did they? Everything was electronic. The light flashed at me again, and for a moment I lost my night vision. But it gave me a thought.

There must be some kind of signaling devices on board. Flares or a spotlight or a horn. Something. I went back to the lockers and began searching again. There was a big handheld spotlight—which had already been immersed too long. Nothing happened when I hit the switch. I found an air horn—a bit of plastic shaped like a trumpet on an aerosol container. I stuffed it into the pocket of my coat and kept looking.

A wave sloshed over the side. The boat was still six to eight inches over the water level, but it wasn't going to be much longer.

I found a blaze orange container—vaguely cylindrical, eight inches around and more than a foot long with a fabric loop connected to one end. There was a seam around the midway point but no obvious button or other way to open it. I forced myself to take my time and think clearly. I grabbed the two ends and twisted. It opened. Inside were flares, an orange smoke canister, and some other items—flags, possibly. There wasn't time to try any of them out. I closed the container, undid my belt, and ran it through the loop.

It was time to abandon ship. I climbed onto the raised area over the bow and reviewed the situation. The lighthouse was coming up on my right a quarter mile away—though it was almost impossible to judge distance accurately. Longer was okay, even twice that. The path that the boat was taking would pass the rocks around the little island by only fifty or sixty feet. I tried to judge the speed. One or two miles per hour. Definitely less than three. If I jumped in the water and swam, I would have seven or eight minutes to cover the fifty lateral feet to land on the near end of the island. How long was the island? I couldn't tell, but I had some grace to my calculations. If I didn't make the first landfall, there was still a very good chance of reaching some point on the island. Seven minutes was a long time to be in that cold water, but not deadly. I tightened the life vest, checked that the canister was secure, and jumped as far as I could to clear the boat.

After standing in the water for as long as I had been—it felt like hours—I blithely expected that I would have been immunized against the shock of total immersion. I wasn't.

I gasped and swallowed water. Rule number one for avoiding death by drowning: Keep mouth shut.

I spit out water, got my bearings, and started swimming. Bogged down by the long overcoat, heavy shoes, and life vest, I was not moving quickly, but I was moving and I had time. In the water, the pull of the tide was much more discernible. I hoped I had not misjudged the speed. I could be past the island completely before covering the lateral distance. I swam harder. I was tired, but if I arrived exhausted and spent, I would still be alive.

The first blow felt like a feeble punch in the middle of my back. It confused me more than anything. I had already taken another hard stroke toward shore before it occurred to me that I shouldn't be getting punched in the back—feebly or no—in the middle of Long Island Sound. Then it happened again, only this time it hurt. It stung. Something sharp had just penetrated my back.

"What the hell?" I yelled, now suddenly terrified. I whirled around in the water, seeking my attacker, only to find a long arm coming down at me, the sharp steel of the fishing knife reflecting in a flash of the beam from the lighthouse. I got my arm up in time, catching the man's forearm and pushing it away, receiving nothing more than a slice in the sleeve of my coat. I held tight and pulled him to me. It was Haley, but a Haley transformed. His handsome face was mangled and broken. One eye was sliced open, the cut running from his hairline to his jaw. His nose was half gone, and when he opened his mouth to scream at me, I saw that all of his front teeth were missing.

He threw his other, almost useless, arm over me, trying to pull me to him and down. I tried to kick myself away and missed, in the process losing my grip on his good arm. The knife swung up and tore my life vest open, narrowly missing my face. He swung again and the knife snagged on the jacket's heavy nylon strap. Haley tugged at it and it tore through and flew from his hand, sinking immediately. I threw a punch that landed on the side of his head, hurting me as much as him.

There was no elegance, thought, or expertise to our fight. It was sloppy and brutal, and would have been humorously ineffectual if we both were not so close to final collapse. But it was deadly.

The life vest, punctured in three places, had become an encumbrance, weighing me down, and I felt myself going under, Haley clambering on top of me. I struck out wildly, in a panic, and managed to land at least one blow, and for a moment I was free. I rose up to the surface and grabbed a breath—possibly my last.

Haley wasn't done. He punched hard between my legs, but the orange canister saved me, blocking the force of the blow. I thrashed backward, windmilling my arms through the water. He couldn't keep up, though he slashed at the water with that one good arm, as though hacking me to pieces.

I risked a look behind me. The current was taking us faster than I had expected. We had passed the first set of rocks and I was almost level with the lighthouse itself and still ten yards to go. I pushed harder.

Behind me, I could hear Haley trying to keep up—to catch up—but the sounds of his efforts became faint. He didn't have the strength. I didn't know where mine came from.

Then I realized that the closer I got to the rocky shore, the less effect the tide had on me. The rocks were moving by much slower. I was going to make it.

Another few strokes and my hand brushed against an underwater rock just a foot or so below me. It was smooth and slick with algae. I pushed on and then lunged forward to grab at the boulders along the shore. I slipped off the first, but by then I was drifting so slowly that I had time to prepare for the next. I grabbed again and this time I held on. Slowly, I pulled myself up. The rocks there had no watermarks or slime. It was close to high tide. I was cold, exhausted, in danger of succumbing to exposure, and marooned on a rocky outcrop in the middle of the Sound, with no idea if anyone would be looking for me. But at the moment, no one was trying to kill me, and unless I rolled over and fell back in the water, I was in no danger of drowning. Things were looking up.

48

I was awake and shivering. If I was shivering, I was still alive. I was very tired. If I could just sleep again—for another hour—then I'd be all right. Ready to start the day. So what was keeping me up? I was lying on a perfectly comfortable rock, still soaked to the skin, with a dull throbbing pain on one side of my head and a second in the middle of my back. I also thought I might have a cracked rib or two because it hurt when I breathed too deeply.

It was too early to get up. It was still very dark. I checked my watch. It was too dark to see it. Then I remembered. My watch was sitting on top of my dresser in my apartment. I wished that I was in my apartment. It would have been warmer. And drier.

Lights flashed by me. Searing white. Twirling blue and red. They came and went. Sometimes lights like that played across my ceiling, reflections from down on Broadway. Emergency vehicles. Ambulances heading to Roosevelt Hospital. Police cars or fire trucks.

I tried to roll over and almost fell off the rock. The water was a long way down. Three or more feet below me. It hadn't been that way before. Tides. Of course. Why was I feeling so stupid? Hypothermia. Brain function was beginning to fail. All organs not immediately involved in keeping the body warm were slowing down. I was dying. Slowly, it was true, but inevitably. I felt like HAL in the movie *2001*, trying to sing "Daisy."

"Hey . . . Help me . . ." The dark and the sea gobbled up my voice. It felt like I was yelling into an infinite expanse of marshmallows. I could barely hear myself.

I pulled myself higher onto the rock, muscle spasms overtaking the shivers. My arms cramped and froze. I had to tell them, one at a time, to release and let me reach for the container of flares.

The lights had passed by and were out in the blackness to the west. Not close, but close enough to register a flare. They'd have blankets.

I reached for the canister. It was much lighter than it should have been. It took me only a split second to realize what it was, and what must have happened. Only the screw-on top was still attached to my belt. The bottom half, with the flares, orange smoke, little emergency flags, and everything else, was gone. Haley must have hit it, aiming for me, and broken the seal, releasing the container and leaving me with nothing more than a plastic cap. My lifesaving flares were only twenty feet or so away—in forty feet of water.

I screamed. I tried to force myself to my feet, tripped and fell back onto the rock. I screamed again and again until my throat was as ravaged as the rest of me. No one heard me. Stupidity and lethargy took me back.

I heard voices. Some were weeping, some were angry. Occasionally one or another would scream wordlessly. I opened my eyes. It was as dark with my eyes open as closed. The few stars that had been out earlier were gone. I looked down over the edge of the rock. I still couldn't see the water, but I could tell it was there, writhing through the rocks, seeking me. But I was safe from the water. And

I was no longer shivering. Or even cold. Or rather, I did not feel cold, because I still understood that I was very cold. Deathly cold.

The voices murmured constantly, then rising in volume, they called angrily to me. It was like a chorus of drunken monks, one minute chanting indistinguishable words, the next laughing and shouting.

Then I began to see the faces below me. Luminescent faces beneath the waves, staring up, mouths open, calling and crying. I closed my eyes and still saw them. It was a relief. I was only hallucinating. They weren't real.

I ignored them and fell back onto my pillow of rock and into my cocoon of sleep.

The voices were back. They were still calling, but softer now. Not angry. I opened my eyes and looked down. I could see water now. Gray water lapping at black rocks, with occasional flashes of dull green or grayish white as foam formed and broke apart.

My very dull brain told me that this was important information, but it still took an eternity for me to form the facts into an idea. I could see. Therefore I was presumably not dead. That was important. But the fact that I could see also meant that it was morning. I had survived the night.

The voices were maddening. They were on the cusp of being understandable. If I could just silence the damn water and the mild wind, I might be able to hear what they were saying. They were speaking and calling to each other again. Male voices. Authoritative. With strong Long Island accents.

An outboard engine roared nearby and a yellow-and-black speedboat rocketed by me, those red and blue lights flashing. I saw two policemen in bright yellow slickers on the deck, their eyes fixed on the waters ahead. They were no more than thirty feet away.

"Help me . . ." It was useless. My throat was shot. I had no strength. They wouldn't have heard me if they were standing over me. I started to cry. I didn't want to, but it was so sad. I was going to die because Haley missed hitting me in the balls and broke the frigging canister instead. I rolled onto my back and stared up at the gray cloud-covered sky.

Far to the east there was a faint pink light behind the clouds. There was no horizon. Gray met gray. Then the pink began to spread and deepen. *Red sky in the morning. Sailors take warning.* I must have read that somewhere. Or heard it. Maybe on NPR. I started to cry again. I was going to die on a rock in a snowstorm while yards away and just beyond salvation, people searched for me.

There was a second boat. The other voice. The policemen had been calling to each other. Something about the search. This boat was slowly coming up the far side of the island. They would never see me. But they were looking, searching the shore. If I could just stand.

I tried again, got to my knees and collapsed. The muscles did not answer. The brain was making very specific demands and the nervous system was delivering orders but the muscles had given up. I fell. I fell and something hard in my coat pocket jabbed into my hip.

My coat was still wrapped around me. A good woolen coat once upon a time. Still a good coat. Wool warms. Cotton kills. Cotton holds the cold. Wool holds the heat. I was alive because of that coat. I twisted around until I could reach the pocket and find out what was jabbing me in the side. It was the horn. The horn that I had taken from the locker on Haley's boat when I found the flares. The horn that I had stuffed into my pocket and forgotten about.

BWAAANH. BWAANH. BWAANH. BWAANH. BWAANH.

I hit the switch over and over, lying there staring up at the sky, tears streaming down my face, until the policeman came and took the horn from my cold fingers and wrapped a silver-sided blanket about my shoulders.

49

Every time I closed my eyes, someone started yelling at me. I tried to tell the guy in the ambulance that I was just resting. I'd had a hard night. He thought I was drifting into a coma. I wasn't. I had no intention of dying ever again.

All the pain that I had put in reserve during my surrender to the cold returned as my body warmed. There was a brief period of apparent panic—the staff's, not mine—when my temperature dropped back into the low eighties, and the ER nurse became very stern with me, as though I had done it on purpose. But my vitals came back quickly and there were plenty of other cases to interest them on Christmas morning.

They moved me to a room upstairs—a private room, thanks to the insistence of the Nassau County police—where a new team of nurses gave me instructions, took my blood, hooked me up to machines, and otherwise fussed over me until I thought I might scream—if I thought my throat could handle it.

Eventually, someone with both a heart and a brain let me take a nap. I fell asleep to the beep of my vital signs monitor and woke up twelve hours later.

Special Agent Marcus Brady was sitting on the edge of the bed. Virgil Becker was asleep in the only chair.

"Welcome back," Brady said.

"What day is it?"

"It's still Tuesday." He checked his watch. "For another three hours. You missed a snowstorm and *A Charlie Brown Christmas*."

"We don't have a television."

"That's un-American."

"Maybe that's my problem. How bad is the snow?"

"Couple of inches out here. The city got less."

"I can get home, then?"

"How you feeling?"

I did an inventory. Head hurt. Back hurt. Ribs hurt. Fingers hurt. A lot. "Ready to go home."

"That's optimistic. I think they want you to stay a few days so that everybody gets a chance to take credit for saving your life."

"I'm outta here. As soon as my clothes are dry."

"Your buddy, Roger, just left. He's going by your place and he'll bring you some clothes in the morning. They were here for a couple of hours. Him and his . . ." He flipped his hand over and back to indicate that the relationship was unusual. It was.

"Assistant," I said.

"If you say so. She's very . . ." Brady arched his eyebrows.

"Yes. She is."

"Roger tried to talk her into giving you the cure."

"Oh?" I said.

"Which entailed her getting naked and hopping into bed with you to 'warm your core,' I think he said."

"Really? What did she say?"

"She instructed him to do something anatomically impossible, but she said it in such a way that you knew she came from a good family."

Virgil snorted in his sleep and his head came up briefly and flopped down again.

"He's been here all day," Brady said. "Anyway, you're not supposed to leave here until Nassau County gets your story."

"Am I under arrest?"

"No, but they left a uniform here to keep an eye on you. He's keeping busy flirting down at the nurses' station."

"What can you tell me?"

"You're something that washed up on the beach. No one knows what to do with you. But they've pegged you as a victim for the moment, rather than a perp, based on the knife wound in your back."

"What about McKenna?" I said.

"Who?"

"Haley shot a man. Back at the estate. I don't know his real name, but I called him McKenna."

"That's intriguing. But no, we've been all over the property. No dead bodies."

I thought it was more likely that McKenna had survived than that his body had somehow disappeared.

Brady was still talking. "But that might explain why the police in New Jersey found a VW van, registered to you, abandoned in Fort Lee. With fresh blood on the driver's seat, and a backpack under the seat with your wallet in it."

McKenna had made it. He was still free and on the run. I changed the subject.

"Did they find Haley?"

He nodded. "Some guy in a powerboat coming out of City Island almost ran into the boat."

"It didn't sink?!"

"It's a Steiger. You can't sink those boats. My brother-in-law's got one."

"What about Haley?" I said before I got to hear all about the brother-in-law's boat.

"Very bad, I hear. He was hanging off the back. All chopped up."

"He's alive?"

"What? No. He bled out. He was a mess. Cuts all over his face and chest. And he was missing half his right leg. They pulled chunks of bone and strips of those insulated overalls he was wearing out from around the props. He must have fallen over and got caught up somehow. It was ugly, from what I hear. Were you there? Did you see it happen?"

I had been there. "It was dark," I said.

Brady wasn't fooled. "Do you need a lawyer?"

I thought about it. There were no witnesses to any of what had gone down the night before. I could sanitize the story, or tell it all. I knew not to talk to the detectives without a lawyer, but Brady was different.

"Wake up Virgil. He'll want to hear this."

They both had questions when I was done. We kept going for the next two hours—well past when visiting hours were over. Brady had to badge the head nurse to get her to leave us alone. I described McKenna as "some homeless guy I paid fifty bucks to help me out." Brady knew there was more to the story, but he didn't push it.

"Haley killed his wife," I said. "He was going to kill me. You find that gun and I'm sure it will be a perfect match."

"And so what?" Brady answered. "Haley's dead. You can't try him for you or the wife. Penn's wanted for questioning, but that will go away as soon as his lawyers begin looking at those doctored pictures."

"Find the gun," I said.

"It's in a hundred feet of water, somewhere a mile or so east of the lighthouse."

"No, it's closer."

He laughed. "I admire your tenacity, but there is no way. If this was *CSI: Miami*, maybe, but not in the real world."

I knew he was right; it just felt wrong. "What about the insider trading? The setup. That's what put all this in motion and now there're dead bodies from here to Bermuda."

"What's your take?" Brady asked Virgil.

Virgil rubbed his temples before he spoke. "The insider trading setup? The proof is gone. Prosecutors will take the path of least resistance. We can't prove who was behind it, though we think it was Penn. No one is going to listen to your story. Haley is dead, therefore he was guilty. The SEC guys are upset that they're not going to get their day in court, but no one else cares. Case closed."

"What about the firm's stake in Arinna Labs. Aren't you going to take a bath on this?"

"Yes, but the best thing I can do for the firm is to let all this go away and be forgotten. Focus on our core businesses and make the money back."

Brady stood up, wrapped his arms around both shoulders, and cracked his back. It was loud enough to make Virgil wince. "He's spot-on, Jason. Whoever was working with the wife has covered his tracks too well. I think you're right. It's Penn behind it all. But so what? I can't sell that story to the U.S. Attorney's office."

Virgil cut in. "What makes you so sure it was Penn? I'm not disputing it—I agree with you—but I want to hear why you're so sure."

Brady answered. "It fits Penn's pattern. This is the way he works. He's done it before, more than once. And he's made enemies on six continents. What else? He has a private army of mercenaries he uses. Many have been with him since the beginning, killing

Peruvian peasants who got in the way of his mining operations and calling them terrorists."

"He tried to have me killed," I said to Virgil.

"An event that still does not officially exist," Brady said with an *I told you so* glare. "But I'd take comfort in the fact that it's over. With all the witnesses dead and all evidence gone or suspect, he's got no reason to go after you anymore. The story is old news already. You're no longer a threat to him."

He was right. I wasn't going to get justice and revenge doesn't pay bills. Or get me any closer to what I really wanted. I stared out the window. There was nothing to see.

"I would like to go home."

Virgil and Brady shared a smile. "We'll see if we can break you out tomorrow morning," Brady said.

"I'd like to go see my son."

50

The night nurse checked my vitals at four. I passed. Temperature normal. Blood pressure and pulse normal. I told her I was hungry. She said I could wait. They served breakfast early. I went back to sleep.

Breakfast *was* early. Pancakes and paper-thin slices of orange. Thin coffee. It all tasted extraordinary. Virgil called and said he would be there to pick me up in an hour. Then he said, "Check out the morning news."

"What am I looking for?"

"You won't be able to miss it," he said.

The television in my room didn't work. I was used to not watching and hadn't given it a thought. I tightened up my gown so a bit less of my butt showed, and hurried down to the nurses' station.

"Is there somewhere I can watch the morning news?"

"In your room. You should be in bed, sir."

"By the time I get some technician up to turn it on, I'll be checked out and on my way home. Cut me some slack, would you?"

She thought hard about giving me a hard time, but must have decided it was too much trouble.

"Try the waiting room outside radiology," she said, pointing farther down the hall.

The television was on, droning to an empty room. That always made me feel uncomfortable, as though I had stepped into some dystopian universe, with mankind mysteriously wiped out, but where the great idiot box continued to spew out reruns of sitcoms I never watched when they were on the first time around. I found the remote control and switched from *Mayberry R.F.D.* to CNN. Virgil was right. I didn't have to look very hard to find the day's big story.

Chuck Penn had been killed the night before while leaving a London restaurant. Two men had begun firing at him as he walked to his limo, killing both the billionaire and one of his bodyguards. A parade of thoughtful talking heads opined on whether the killers were terrorists or the remnants of some South American guerrilla group taking a belated revenge. They all made reference to the three prior attempts on Penn's life. Two other bodyguards were in the hospital and unavailable for comment.

Penn's oldest son bloodlessly assured investors that there would be no problems with the transition. An emergency board meeting was being called. The man was remarkably dry-eyed in front of the cameras.

Maybe there just wasn't any more he cared to say.

51

I checked my pockets—cash, keys, passport, sunglasses—and ran through my mental list again. One carry-on bag stuffed with presents for all, a few T-shirts, one bathing suit, a razor, a toothbrush. And a paperback copy of *Mother Warriors*—more to see why people got so angry with Jenny McCarthy than to discover the single great key to my son's condition or how to "cure" him by changing his diet.

Carolina was coming in next Monday. The apartment smelled dusty, unused, and a bit stale. I made another mental note to check with the office to see if there were any larger units for sale, and immediately forgot about it.

I took a look in the mirror. The hat I had picked up in Denver hid the bandages on my scalp—barely. There were still bags under my eyes—I would need another few days of sleep. I could get it lying on a beach.

The car service was due, so I locked up and took the elevator down to the lobby.

There was a new doorman on the downtown side of the building. He was talking on his cell phone as I approached. It struck me that I had never seen any employee of the building talking on a cell phone—but it didn't strike hard enough. He saw me looking and dropped the phone in his pocket.

"Where's Raoul today?" I said.

"Taking some vacay, Mr. Stafford."

"Is my car waiting?"

"Right outside." He opened the door and I stepped out into glaring sunlight. The realization that a new employee, whom I had never seen before, knew me on sight, despite the fact that I had not been there for the past week, came as I was already halfway across the sidewalk—much too late.

A black Rolls-Royce was sitting at the curb on Seventy-third Street, engine idling. The rear door was being held open by a man with the kind of Neanderthal forehead and deep, hooded eyes of a medieval torturer. Someone well-versed in the rack, the iron maiden, and the heated grating. I stopped and looked around for a path to escape. There was none. The doorman and three other men were already behind me, boxing me in, and one was the bruised-faced boxer from Newark Airport. The driver for the first attempt on my life. He wasn't smiling.

They didn't rush me. There was no need. I wasn't going to get by them and there were few people on the street who would pay attention—or be able to help—if I started screaming. I was caught. I turned back to the big car.

Harvey Deeter was sitting in the backseat on the far side. "Y'all better hop in before I catch a chill and sue your pitiful ass."

I held back. "I've got a car coming. Thanks anyway."

"No, you don't. I took the liberty of canceling your car, as I plan to take you out to the airport myself."

"Am I going to get there?"

He laughed. "You have my word. I'm not always what my wife, bless her memory, would have called a good Christian, but my word is still good. Come on now." He patted his hand on the leather seat as though coaxing a reluctant child.

I didn't have anything I wanted to say to Harvey Deeter. The investigation had cost me too much and I just wanted some peace and to see my family. The presence of the guy I had defeated with bottled soap a week before set off a series of changes in some of my assumptions. I had been wrong. Penn hadn't sent the bad guys after me. Deeter had.

"Mr. Deeter, thanks for the invite, but I would prefer to make my own way to the airport."

"I'm afraid that is not negotiable."

I could feel the heavies crowding in around me. There were no choices left. I pictured Skeli and the Kid under a tropical sky, smiling, expectant, and safe. Then I got in the car. The chauffeur closed the door behind me and the hired muscle dispersed. A moment later, we pulled away from the curb.

"Relax, Mr. Stafford. You have my personal guarantee—you are perfectly safe."

My mental tic on directions kicked in. "Would you tell him to go up through Harlem and take the Triborough? It's much faster than trying to get over to the Midtown Tunnel."

"No matter, it's the Van Wyck that's always a crapshoot, isn't it?" He pronounced it "Van Whike." Where I grew up—almost in the shadow of the highway—it was always "Van Wick." I didn't correct him. He pressed an intercom button. "Mr. Stafford suggests we take the Triborough Bridge, Hector. We will defer to his local knowledge."

"American Airlines," I said.

"Hector knows," he answered.

I sat back and waited. He had called the meeting, let him set the agenda. I didn't have to wait long.

"Hector, would you be so kind as to scan Mr. Stafford for any recording or transmitting devices? And if there're no issues, turn off the intercom and give us some privacy."

There was a slight hum—almost a high-pitched whistle—that went on for a few seconds and then quit.

"All clear, Mr. Deeter."

Deeter waited another half a minute before turning to me with an intense look and a forced smile.

"I don't get much practice at this, so I don't know if I'm any good at it, but I owe you an apology. I underestimated you, and that's a crime. You are a very resourceful human being."

This was a very different Harvey Deeter. The voice still came from the Deep South, but the cracker-barrel philosopher was gone, replaced by the Rhodes scholar. Yet beyond the veil of his quiet words were the eyes of a predator.

"You tried to have me killed," I said.

Directness did not faze him. "It was business. I was concerned that your meddling might upset my plan. I was wrong. You were good. And while I can't say that everything came down just the way I expected, it did turn out in my favor. And for that I thank you."

"Why are you telling me this? What is it you want?"

"We'll get to that. But for now it costs me nothing to answer your questions. Penn is dead. And the Haleys. There is no evidence, no trail leading back to me. Who would believe you? You served me well. I suppose I owe you something."

"I didn't do anything for you."

"Oh, I know that. Young Virgil just set you out and let you hunt 'em up. You flushed every bird. Nice work."

"Virgil? Was he part of this?" I said.

"No, not at all. This was my work, though it was Selena who came to me. We made an arrangement."

"She wanted revenge on her husband for cheating."

"Not quite. The cheating didn't bother her as much as the fact that he made that woman pregnant. She couldn't get pregnant, you know about that?" he said.

"I suspected."

"The grandfather. Nasty old piece of work. He raped her. Repeatedly. Then forced her to have an abortion, and that ended up ruining her chances of ever getting pregnant again. Pushing his drunken ass off that cliff was much too good for him. I would've given him to Hector for a day or two first. Hector worked with the contras in Nicaragua as a young man. He's slowed down some, but I doubt he's lost his touch."

"She pushed him?"

"Certainly. Not much later, the two Nassau County detectives who were in charge of the investigation both retired early. Now they both live in a gated, luxury community in Costa Rica, thanks to Selena's largesse."

"So why didn't she kill her husband, too?" I asked.

"I don't think she wanted him dead. She just wanted to take him down a few pegs. Break his spirit. She thought she could tame him."

"Why did she come to you?"

"Well, she needed help, the kind I can provide, and she knew I wanted to buy out the rest of the company. Only not at the going price." He snickered, quite proud of his plotting. "We agreed that I would buy her out in a private transaction at current levels. After Haley got into trouble, the stock would tank and I could pick up a lot more shares at a nice discount. I did warn her, you know."

"About Haley?"

"I told her she was shooting fireworks in a hand grenade factory. Eventually, there was going to be hell to pay."

"You were there that night. Is this the car I saw on the security tapes?" I asked.

"Oh yes. But she was alive when I left. But then, you know that, don't you? No one will believe it, of course. But you know Haley killed her."

"He set the cameras to fail before he left, drove to the marina, and came back in the boat. The same way as he did the other night. Then he killed her and tossed her over the rail." I couldn't prove it, but I knew it.

"And when he got out on bail, he doctored the pictures of the license plate to put the blame on Penn."

"You knew? That computer is sitting in one hundred feet of seawater. No one will ever be able to prove it wasn't Penn that night."

"Which suits me just fine. I've already made arrangements with the son to buy out Penn's stake in Arinna."

"What happened that night? When you went out to the house?"

He leaned back into the seat and closed his eyes for a moment. "Selena called me all in a lather. Told me to stay away. But I had my people hack into Haley's email and got his password. Then Hector drove me out there. She was sure you'd scoped out the whole game and we were going down. She was a mite agitated, but she convinced me." He opened his eyes and turned his head toward me. "There was nothing for it, then, but to take you out of the game. As I say, it wasn't personal, it was business. Just business."

"I hid my family."

"And you did a fine job of it, I'm sure of it. But I have to tell you, they were never in danger. I understand why you had to do it. I would have done the same."

"I watched my ex-wife get murdered while protecting our son, and all because of me."

"I don't think that's a healthy way of looking at it, if you don't mind me playing uncle for a bit."

"I had in my hands the very thing those men wanted. A few hours earlier, and there would have been no attack."

"You're not a religious man, are you?" he said, almost kindly. "I didn't think so. One subject the secular humanists always avoid is the question of evil. There is evil in this world. I don't mean original sin. That's just a way of forcing some humility and guilt on the flock. No, I mean Satan. Pure evil. Ted Bundy. Dahmer. That Mexican—the Zetas fella they finally caught up with. You didn't kill your ex-wife, and you did your best to prevent it. That's all any of us can do."

Letting go of my guilt was harder than living with it. I was comfortable there, being angry at myself.

"What about you?" I said.

"I doubt very much that I will see my late wife in the glorious hereafter, and I imagine she will take that disappointment in stride. I have looked into your history, and I believe that you are a man who can be bought. You frown. Am I wrong? Forgive me. I spoke with a man in Venezuela—an acquaintance of yours—who assured me that you are one of those rare men who can be bought and stay that way. Was I misinformed?"

The Kid's trust fund, which paid for his school, his doctors, therapist, and Heather, would not exist if I had not sold my silence. I had no qualms about that—it was worth all that and more. But there was another cache that I had squirreled away in Switzerland that sometimes gnawed away at my conscience.

"I'm well paid. I don't need more."

"I could use someone with your skills and I would pay better than Virgil—I know your arrangement. This is why I came to see you today. I am willing to answer any question you have—honestly—because I want you working with me. You could name your price."

He could afford honesty—he knew no one would easily believe me. Even Brady and Virgil would have a hard time after I had worked so hard to build a case against Penn. "Tell me why you wanted so badly to buy Arinna. It's all yours now, but without Haley to run that lab, there's no product. It's worthless."

"Maybe not. Haley solved all of the big problems. The rest is fine-tuning."

"So you're not going to close it down?"

"Oh, no. I will close it down. That's the point. I'm an oilman, Jason. Oil may be past its prime, but it's still got legs. When the time is right, I'll still own all the patents on Haley's product. I may yet bring Arinna back. But not yet."

"Suppose someone beats you to it?"

"No one has beaten me yet. I don't know if it's possible. But if it is, and somebody does it, well, God bless 'em. That's the American way."

"And in the meantime we keep pumping carbon into the atmosphere. Believe me, I never give it much thought, but when I do, I think it's pretty obvious we are seriously screwing with the environment. Someday soon we are going to have to pay the piper."

"Global warming? I spend a lot of money each year supporting research to prove that it's just a myth." He laughed. "It's just like all those studies that Big Tobacco used to do, proving that tobacco wasn't bad for you. They had to keep funding them just to muddy the waters. But I'm no idiot. The science is there. The earth is warming up, and it is only going to get worse, and it's all because of man's lust for fossil fuels."

"Then why perpetuate it? Even for a minute? Fix the bugs in Haley's system and you'll be the man who saved the planet."

"Don't think there aren't reasons. I'm no hero, that's true, and I don't think I could change if I tried. But there are reasons."

"Do I take that on faith?"

"No, I'll explain. First, you've got the Chinese."

"That was Haley's paranoid fantasy."

"They are the world's starlings. Starlings imitate better than mockingbirds. They imitate car alarms, women's screams, dogs barking. And they steal sparrows' nests to lay their eggs. Right now, the Chinese government is focused on solar cells and batteries. They're cornering the world's supplies of raw materials for both. But the minute they see that these algae are a real threat, they'll steal the code and make their own."

"So you bury it? That's the solution?"

"For the moment. Meanwhile, there're other considerations."

"Such as."

"Is global warming really all that awful? Man is adaptable. He is the most adaptable creature on the planet. Raise the average temperature five or ten degrees and man will find a way to produce cheaper air-conditioning. Hell, we survived how many ice ages? We keep coming back stronger. And if the sea level rises twenty feet and we lose some shorefront property, I will shed no tears. And those who can't adapt will not survive. I understand that. But you read the news. Tell me it's not time to thin the herd, son. We get all in a snit over racism in this country. Are we being PC enough? Too much? Look at northern Africa. They're enslaving, torturing, raping, and killing each other over shades of skin tone that we'd ascribe to a good tan. Or how about the Arab Spring? They take to the streets, overthrow the dictator, have an election, and elect a different dictator. That's the Russian model, I believe. I ask you, who do you want in charge at the end of the day? We're not perfect, I admit. But the fact that this country's Congress is incapable of passing one bit of legislation that has any effect on the world gives me great satisfaction. Do we really want to be another China, with the government telling us how many babies we can have? How many widgets we can produce? Where we can live and with whom? Freedom, Jason. That's what I'm talking about. It's what our forefathers fought and died for. The freedom to run our lives, our businesses, as we see fit."

"With you in the driver's seat."

He was amused. "I pay people to do my driving for me. That's why I want you, Jason. I can use you, and I will make you very wealthy. Your son will have unimaginable access to the best treatments in the world. You will have power over your fellow man and you will be using it for the betterment of the human race."

"Better as defined by you alone."

"And who better? I take good care of my own."

"What exactly would I be doing?"

His smile was exultant. He believed he was winning me over. "This and that," he answered.

I had no use for power, either for myself or my son. The best treatment in the world for him was my love and support. And Heather, and his school, and his doctors and therapists. Nevertheless, that was covered. He was already getting the best.

And for myself? Did I feel any flicker of desire? Great wealth? I had more than enough. Power? Of the kind that derives from executing the orders of the mighty? It was a form of exalted slavery.

"I'm going to disappoint you, Mr. Deeter. I sincerely thank you for the offer, but your racial paranoia is already out-of-date. It offends me aesthetically, but that's not my point. It's too late. The world is moving faster than any one man can control. Even you. I don't know who's going to win, but I know in the end you will lose."

"You can be blunt, I see."

"I'm not very good at being anything but. Not everyone takes it as well as you."

"We could argue the issue. I'm opinionated, I admit. But I'm not stupid. I could make some very good points."

"I'm sure. But you won't change my mind."

"What about your son?"

"My son is fine," I said. Even if he did occasionally put his urine in a plastic cup. "But even if he wasn't, I couldn't take your offer. I don't like your methods. I wouldn't fit in with your other lackeys. I made some mistakes, for which I served some time. Prison no longer frightens me. But if I ever go back, it will be for my mistakes and mine alone. I'm no saint. But I can live with my mistakes. I can't live with others'."

"I misjudged you again. I apologize. This may be a first for me. Two apologies in a single day."

"No need. I'm not offended by the offer, or even by your wealth and power. Only by your ideology and your means."

He nodded once and looked out the window. There was nothing to see but the traffic and the concrete walls of the highway. He cleared his throat thickly before he spoke. "Well, you have my marker, Mr. Stafford. I owe you a great favor. If you ever need a great favor in return, I would like to take the opportunity to balance the books. But I will also tell you that if I ever find you in my way again, I will not waste a moment and will have you taken out immediately. You are too dangerous a man to be working for the other side, whatever or whoever that may be."

It was my turn to be silent as we crossed over the Belt Parkway and entered the airport. Colored signs flickered by announcing airlines serving every corner of the globe, and for a moment I felt at one with all the thousands of travelers who came this way every day, harboring dreams of escape, conquest, romance, or success. By day's end, I would be with my son. Skeli. My father.

"I will keep that in mind, Mr. Deeter. Both the threat and the favor. But if there is ever a time when I can bring you down, without hurting myself or my son, I will take it."

Deeter smiled again, this time with real pleasure. "I will shake your hand on that." He did. The car came to a halt. We were at the terminal.

I began to get out and stopped. "By the way, whatever happened to that cowboy? In Santa Fe? The one who got attacked by the dog."

"Don't know. He lived, I'm sure, 'else somebody would have told me about it. The dog was put down. That I know. A shame."

I got out and stood on the curb as they pulled away. I took out my cell phone and quickly snapped a picture of the rear of the car and the license plate. You never know when some little shard of tile might be the key to revealing the whole mosaic.

52

I walked out of the airport into the late-afternoon sun with my jacket over my arm. My arm was already sweating.

"Can I help you, sir? Do you need a cab?" The speaker was a tall black man in creased black shorts and a crisp short-sleeved shirt with epaulets. He had a silver name tag over the pocket that read WINSTON.

"I think I do. I was told there was a ferry somewhere nearby that would get me over to the Aerie."

"No ferry. If you are a guest, they will send a boat to pick you up. That is the only way to get there. Are you expected?"

"Yes. My family is staying there."

"Ah. Very good then. The Aerie is very exclusive. Very private."

And costing me rock star kind of money. "Where do they pick me up?"

"The easiest for you is the dock at Aragorn's Studio."

"Will the cabbie know where that is?"

He smiled a big warm Caribbean grin. "You can walk there in three minutes." He pointed toward a footpath that led through a grove of tall palms. "It is just the other side of those trees."

"And how do I call for the boat?"

"You are from the States? Your cell phone will work here."

I offered Winston a ten, which he politely refused, and I started walking. Once I got away from the building, there was a breeze and the heat felt less oppressive. In fact, the warmth coming through the back of my shirt was making my muscles loosen almost immediately. I was entering vacation mode.

The woman who answered at the Aerie had the kind of accent that you hear on BBC News, as though she once attended the same school as the Royal Family. She assured me that a launch would be there in minutes.

The shade under the palms held back the direct heat of the sun, but inside the grove the breeze died. I was sweating heavily by the time I came through to the beach. My eyes took in the sparkling, pale green water, the snow-white sand, and the green hills surrounding the bay. I felt my New York winter defenses melting. I was no longer a fugitive. I was alive. My family was safe. And despite having been immersed in the frigid waters of Long Island Sound for hours, I was over my cold.

There were four small, makeshift docks sticking out into the bay, each with one or two inflatable dinghies or a scarred, ancient wooden skiff. I walked down the beach until I saw a sign for Aragorn's Studio, a shop that appeared to sell everything from local art to T-shirts to muffins. The dock out front reached out into slightly deeper water.

Before I reached the end of the dock, I heard the powerful motor of an open launch coming up the channel in the middle of the bay. The driver did a wide turn and expertly pulled up and gestured for me to board.

"Welcome to the Aerie, Mr. Stafford," said the young black man, dressed in a well-pressed khaki uniform. "May I see your passport?"

I handed it over. He checked that my face matched the scowling picture inside. "Ha! You see? You come to the islands and your smile improves very much right away." He handed it back.

A covered electric cart was waiting for us at the base of the pier across the bay. The lady with the BBC voice, or her auditory clone, was the driver.

"Mr. Stafford? We'll get you checked in and then find your family. Shall we?" The cart ran up a narrow paved path through two tight switchbacks to the top of the hill. The whole of the Sir Francis Drake Channel was laid out below us with Saint John rising highest at the far end. There were dozens of big white-sailed boats moving about over the dark blue water. It looked like a playground for millionaires.

Checking in meant giving my passport to a very large, very serious man who looked like he spent all of his spare time lifting very heavy objects and putting them back down again. He took it, scanned it, and sat reading something on his computer monitor. Evidently satisfied that I was not on any terrorist watch list, he returned the document to me and said, "Welcome to Aerie, Mr. Stafford. Enjoy your stay."

The BBC lady drove me along a series of paved paths down the back side of the hill, giving me a mini guided tour of the property. Three restaurants, a boathouse, tennis courts, and in the center the spa, the largest building in the community. We dropped down closer to the ocean beach and pulled up in front of a cluster of three huts with a small private soaking pool. We were steps above the beach and I could hear the sound of the gentle surf.

It was hard to believe that I was still on the same planet that I had woken up in the day before.

"Well, it appears they've all gone out for a bit," she said, after showing me in. "You may find them on the beach. Just through there and down the steps."

"Thank you," I said, fumbling in my pocket for a bill to give her.

"A kind thought," she said, shaking her hand to indicate a gentle negative. "The Aerie is a non-tipping resort. Your wife made dinner reservations for seven o'clock, but you may want to come up a bit earlier for cocktails and sunset." She hopped back in the cart and was gone.

My wife. It sounded good, possibly for the first time in my life.

I left my bag and jacket on one of the lounge chairs by the pool, noticing as I did the five toy cars lined up beneath it. Even with no one there, I knew I was in the right place. I stripped off my shoes and socks, rolled up my shirtsleeves and pant legs, and walked down to the beach. I kept the Outlaws hat on. There would be plenty of time later to explain why I had acquired a gunshot wound on my head.

The distance in height from the deck in front of the huts to the shoreline could not have been more than four or five feet. If Deeter and people like him won, all this would be gone in a generation or two, the ocean devouring most of the island. A blink of time in the history of man, but a very long time in my life. Perhaps I would never see it. But it is impossible to be a parent and not look at the world as you will leave it and wish that the beauty could be preserved.

There was another small island a quarter mile offshore and a flock of birds circled above it, wheeling and diving. The shadows of the hills to the west on Tortola were already beginning to throw sections of the beach in shadow. I put my feet in the water. The memory of a dream I used to have shuddered through me. I let it go and just let myself feel the pull and lift of the small waves.

"Jason!" It was Skeli, her voice full of exhilaration. Far down the beach a group of people began to form into shapes I recognized. A tall woman walking with a small child, whose hair shone like a beacon against the gathering dark. Skeli and the Kid. Behind them my father and Estrella. Skeli was waving madly. "Jason!"

I waved one arm, then two, my throat so tight with emotion I couldn't speak. Finally, "Helloooooo!"

Skeli and the Kid began running toward me. The Kid broke away and flew across the beach. I tried running to meet him and almost tripped head over heels as my feet sank into the soft sand at the water's edge. "Hellloooo!" I screamed.

The Kid slammed into me, wrapped his arms around my legs, and sank to the ground, laughing, gasping, and crying. I almost made the mistake of reaching down and hugging him back. Instead, I put the back of my hand in front of his face and he sniffed and laughed with real pleasure, then in a flash he became angry, his face contorting as he yelled at me, "Jason bad! Jason bad!"

"I'm sorry, bud. I was scared, too. Please don't be mad at me, my heart will just break."

He looked confused, but grabbed me tighter and turned his face away.

Skeli came up, laughing with pleasure. Neither of us said anything at first. We just wrapped arms around each other and stood there trying not to cry. I tried. Skeli didn't bother. "Oh, thank god," she said over and over.

Pop and Estrella came along slower, stopping a few feet away, hesitating to invade our tableau. I looked up and waved them over.

I stood on an idyllic beach, with a sunset just beginning that would rival any, anywhere, anytime, holding my family to me and wanting nothing more.

ACKNOWLEDGMENTS

My life is blessed in so many ways these days. The first blessing is and always will be my lovely wife, my Ruby—my greatest fan and severest critic. Then there are my agents, Judith Weber and Nat Sobel, and their fantastic team. Next, the people at Putnam who always give the impression that they are working solely on my behalf: Neil Nyren, Sara Minnich, Kate Stark, Ashley Hewlett, Chris Nelson, Michael Barson, Rob Sternitzky, and the copy editors who have saved me from embarrassment time and again. The community of writers, too many to name, who have extended their friendship or given me their support individually or through organizations like Private Eye Writers, Mystery Writers of America, International Thriller Writers, Sisters in Crime, and the International Crime Writers. The Muses and my readers who keep me honest and true to myself and my characters. The booksellers—the front line in the fight against the forces of darkness. And especial thanks to the various experts who have lit my way through the deep caverns of the judicial system: Larry Ruggiero, Melissa Mourges, Richard Fiske, and Tim O'Rourke. Whatever I got right is thanks to them, and whatever I still got wrong is entirely my fault.

And if by some chance, you recognize yourself in one of my characters, let me assure you that you are mistaken. You are much better-looking, much smarter, and you can even sing better. None of my characters are meant to mimic any person alive or dead, real or imagined by anyone other than me.